Kandy Shepherd ~~magazine editor~~ on a small farm Australia, with he of animal friends and real-life roma

Kandy loves to hear from her readers. Visit her website at: www.kandyshepherd.com.

Marion Lennox is a country girl, born on an Australian dairy farm. She moved on—mostly because the cows just weren't interested in her stories! Married to a 'very special doctor', Marion writes for the Mills & Boon Medical Romance and Mills & Boon True Love lines. (She used a different name for each category for a while—readers looking for her past romance titles should search for author Trisha David as well.) She's now had more than seventy-five romance novels accepted for publication.

In her non-writing life Marion cares for kids, cats, dogs, chooks and goldfish. She travels, she fights her rampant garden (she's losing) and her house dust (she's lost).

Cara Colter lives in British Columbia with her partner, Rob, and eleven horses. She has three grown children and a grandson. She is a recent recipient of an *RT Book Reviews* Career Achievement Award in the Love and Laughter category. Cara loves to hear from readers, and you can contact her or learn more about her through her website, www.cara-colter.com

One Winter's

COLLECTION

September 2018

November 2018

December 2018

One Winter's Day

KANDY SHEPHERD

MARION LENNOX

CARA COLTER

MILLS & BOON

Published in Great Britain 2018
by Mills & Boon, an imprint of HarperCollins*Publishers*
1 London Bridge Street, London, SE1 9GF

One Winter's Day © 2018 Harlequin Books S.A.

A Diamond in Her Stocking © 2014 Kandy Shepherd
Christmas Where They Belong © 2014 Marion Lennox
Snowed in at the Ranch © 2012 Cara Colter

ISBN: 978-0-263-26839-3

MIX
Paper from
responsible sources
FSC™ C007454

This book is produced from independently certified FSC™ paper to ensure responsible forest management.

For more information visit: www.harpercollins.co.uk/green

Printed and bound in Spain
by CPI, Barcelona

A DIAMOND IN HER STOCKING

KANDY SHEPHERD

To the A-team, Cathleen Ross, Elizabeth Lhuede
and Keziah Hill, with heartfelt thanks for the
friendship and support.

CHAPTER ONE

As Lizzie Dumont looked around at the soon-to-open Bay Bites café, her new place of employment, she vowed she would never reveal how she really felt about the way her high-flying career as a chef had crash-landed into a culinary backwater like Dolphin Bay. Not when people here had been so kind to her.

She would put behind her the adrenalin rush of working at star-rated restaurants in the gastronomic capitals of Paris and Lyon. Give up the buzz of being part of the thriving restaurant scene in Sydney. Embrace the comparatively lowly life of a café cook.

Her sigh echoed around the empty café. Who was she kidding? That heady time in France had been the pinnacle of her career. But she'd been sinking in Sydney. Working shift after shift until past midnight in restaurant kitchens— no matter how fashionable the venues— had hardly been compatible with being a good parent to her five-year-old daughter, Amy.

With no family in Sydney to fall back on, and few friends because she'd lived in France for so long before her divorce, she'd struggled to give Amy a reasonable life. Drowning in debt, swimming against the current of erratic babysitter schedules and unreasonable rosters, after less than a year she'd been going under.

By the time her sister Sandy had approached her to manage the new café adjacent to Sandy's bookshop, Lizzie had been on the edge of despair. She'd even been contemplating the unthinkable—letting Amy live permanently with her ex-husband Philippe in France.

Gratefully, she'd grabbed the lifeline Sandy had thrown her.

And here she was. Dolphin Bay was a rapidly growing resort town on the south coast of New South Wales, with a heritage-listed harbour and beautiful beaches. It was also, in her experience, a gastronomic wasteland—the only memorable meal she could ever remember eating was fish and chips straight from the vinegar-soaked wrapping.

But Sandy had offered her sanctuary and a new life with Amy. In return, Lizzie would throw herself wholeheartedly into making Bay Bites the best café on the south coast. Heck, why stop there? She would use her skills and expertise to make Bay Bites the best café in the country.

She let herself get the teeniest bit excited at the thought. After all, she would be in charge. No cranky head chef screaming insults at her. No gritting her teeth at an ill-chosen item on the menu she'd been forced to cook whether she'd liked it or not.

She continued her inspection, her spirits rising by the second. Sandy had done a wonderful job of the fit-out. The décor was sleek and contemporary but with welcome touches of whimsy. In particular, she loved the way the dolphin theme had been incorporated. Hand-painted tiles backed the service area. Carved wooden dolphins supported the wooden countertop and framed the large blackboard on the wall behind it where she would chalk up the daily specials.

There was still work to be done. Lots of it. Boxes were stacked around the perimeter of the café waiting for her to unpack. Large flat packages, wrapped in brown paper, were propped against the walls. She itched to get started.

But someone had started the unpacking. Outsized glass jars were already lined up at the other end of the counter to the cash register, their polished chrome lids glinting in the late afternoon sun that filtered through the plate glass windows that faced the view of the harbour.

She could envisage the jars already filled with her secret recipe cookies. Nearby was the old-fashioned glass-fronted rotating cabinet for cakes and pies she'd asked Sandy to order. The equipment in the kitchen was brand new. It was perfect. *She would make this work.*

Lizzie ran her hand along the wooden countertop, marvelling at the intricacy of the carved dolphins, breathing in the smell of fresh varnish and new beginnings.

'Those dolphins are kinda cool, aren't they?' The deep masculine voice from behind her made her spin around. She recognised it immediately.

But the shock of seeing Jesse Morgan stride through the connecting doorway from Bay Books next door expelled all the breath from her lungs. Her heart started to hammer so hard she had to clutch her hands to her chest to still it.

Jesse Morgan. All six foot three of him: black-haired, blue-eyed, movie-star handsome. Jesse Morgan of the broad shoulders and lean hips; of honed muscles accentuated by white T-shirt and denim jeans. Jesse Morgan, who was meant to be somewhere far, far away from Dolphin Bay.

Why hadn't someone warned her he was in town?

Lizzie's sister was married to Jesse's brother Ben. Six months ago, Jesse had been the best man and she the chief bridesmaid at Ben and Sandy's wedding. Lizzie hoped against hope Jesse might have forgotten what had happened between them at the wedding reception.

One look at the expression in his deep blue eyes told her he had not.

She cringed all the way down to her sneaker-clad feet.

'What are you doing here?' she managed to choke out once she had regained use of her voice. She was aiming for nonchalance but it came out as a wobbly attempt at bravado.

'Hello to you, too, Lizzie,' he said with a Jesse-brand charming smile, standing there in her café as confident and sure of himself as ever. A confidence surely bred from an awareness that since he'd been a teenager he would always be the best-looking man in the room. But she noticed the smile didn't quite warm his eyes.

She tried to backtrack to a more polite greeting. But she didn't know what to say. Not when the last time they'd met she'd been passionately kissing him, wanting him so badly she'd been tempted to throw away all caution and common sense and go much further than kissing.

'You gave me a fright coming in behind me like that,' she said with a rising note of defensiveness to her voice. Darn it. That was a dumb thing to say. She didn't want him to think he had any effect on her at all.

Which, in spite of everything, would be a total lie. Jesse Morgan exuded raw masculine appeal. It triggered a sudden rush of awareness that tingled right through her. Any red-blooded woman would feel it. *Lots* of red-blooded women had felt it, by all accounts, she thought, her lips thinning.

'I didn't mean to scare you,' he said. 'But Sandy told me you were in here. She sent me to give you a hand with the unpacking. I've made a start, as you can see.'

He took a step towards her. She scuttled backwards, right up against the countertop, cursing herself for her total lack of cool. She was so anxious to keep a distance between them she didn't register the discomfort of the dorsal fin of the wooden dolphin pressing into her back.

It wasn't fair a man could be so outrageously handsome. The Black Irish looks he'd inherited from his mother's side gave him the currency he could have chosen to trade for a career as an actor or model. But he'd laughed that off in a self-deprecating way when she'd teased him with it.

Which had only made him seem even more appealing.

How very wrong could she have been about a man?

'I only just got here from Sydney, after a four-hour drive,' she said. 'I…I haven't really thought where to start.'

'Can I get you a drink—some water, a coffee?' he asked.

He sounded so sincere. *All part of the act.*

'No, thank you,' she said, regaining some of her manners now the shock of seeing him had passed. After all, he was her sister's brother-in-law. She couldn't just ask him to leave, the way she'd like to. 'I stopped for a bite to eat on the way down.'

Despite herself she couldn't help scanning his face to see what change six months had brought him. Heaven knew what change he saw in her. She felt all the stress of the last months had aged her way more than her twenty-nine years.

He, about the same age, looked as though a care had never caused his brow to furrow. His tan was deeper than when she'd last seen him, making his eyes seem even bluer. A day away from a shave, dark growth shadowed his jaw. His black hair was longer and curled around his ears. She remembered the way she had fisted her hand in his hair to pull him closer as she'd kissed him.

How could she have been so taken in by him?

She squirmed with regret. She'd known of his reputation. But one champagne had led to one champagne too many and all the tightly held resolutions she'd made after her divorce about having nothing to do with too-handsome, too-charming men had dissolved in the laughter and fun she'd shared with Jesse.

Was he remembering that night? How they'd found the same exhilarating rhythm dancing with each other? How, when the band had taken a break, they'd gone outside on the balcony?

She'd been warned that Jesse was a heartbreaker, a womaniser. But he'd been fun and there hadn't been much fun in her life for a long time. It had seemed the most natural thing in the world to slip into his arms when he had kissed her in a private corner of the balcony lit only by the faintest beams of moonlight. His kiss had been magical—slow, sensuous, thrilling. It had evoked needs and desires long buried and she had given herself to the moment, not caring about consequences.

Then a group of other guests had pushed through the doors to the balcony with a burst of loud chatter, and broken the spell.

It had been the classic wedding cliché—the chief

bridesmaid and the best man getting caught in a passionate clinch.

Lizzie cringed at the memory of those moments. The hoots and catcalls of the other guests as they'd discovered them kissing. 'Jesse's at it again,' someone had called, laughing.

She'd never felt more humiliated. Not because of being caught kissing. They were both single adults who could kiss whomever they darn well pleased. She'd laughed that off. No. The humiliation was caused by the painful awareness she'd been seen as just another in a long line of Jesse's girls. Girls he had kissed and discarded when the next pretty face had come along.

But, despite knowing that, it hadn't stopped her from going back for more with Jesse that night. Why had she imagined he'd be any different with her?

What an idiot she'd been.

Now she cleared her throat, determined to make normal—if stilted—conversation; not to let Jesse know how shaken she was at seeing him again. How compellingly attractive she still found him.

'Aren't you meant to be gallivanting around the world doing good works? I thought you were in India,' she asked. Jesse worked for an international aid organisation that built housing for the victims of natural disasters.

Jesse shook his head. 'The Philippines this time. Rebuilding villages in the aftermath of a gigantic mudslide. Thousands of houses were destroyed.'

'That must have been dangerous,' she said. Jesse was a party guy personified, and yet his job took him to developing countries where he used his skills as an engineer to help strangers in need. She'd found that contradiction fascinating.

Just another way she'd been sucked into his game.

'Dangerous and dirty,' he said simply. 'But that's what we do.'

She shouldn't feel a surge of relief that he had escaped that danger without harm. But she did. Though she told herself that was just because he was part of the extended family now. The black sheep, as far as she was concerned.

'So you're back here because…?'

'The "good works" led to an injured shoulder,' he said. He raised his broad right shoulder to demonstrate and in doing so winced. His so-handsome face contorted in pain and the blood drained, leaving him pale under his tan.

Her first reaction was to rush over and comfort him. To stroke his shoulder to help ease the pain. Or offer to kiss it better…

No! She forced her thoughts away from Crazyville. Gripped her hands tightly together so she wouldn't be tempted. She was furious with herself. Wasn't she meant to now be immune to his appeal?

Getting together with Jesse Morgan at the wedding had been like nibbling on just one square of a bar of fine Belgian dark chocolate and denying herself the rest even though she knew it would be utterly delicious. Quite possibly the best chocolate she had ever tasted.

But she prided herself on her willpower when it came to chocolate. And men who offered her nothing more than a fleeting physical thrill.

Her aim was to build a new life for her and Amy. She didn't want a man around to complicate things. Not now. Maybe not ever. And if she did decide to date again it wouldn't be with someone like Jesse Morgan. She'd been there, done that, with her good-looking charmer of an ex-husband who had let her down so badly.

The next man for her—if she decided to go there—would be steady, reliable, living in the same country as her and average-looking. She wanted a man who only had eyes for her.

Jesse was a player and Lizzie didn't want to play. Her party-girl days were far behind her. It would be work, work, work for her in Dolphin Bay. And being the best mother she could possibly be to her precious daughter.

Not that Jesse was giving her any indication that he had a real interest in her. Not now. Not then. It still stung. *How could she have believed in him?*

After they'd been interrupted on the balcony, she'd rushed away to look in on Amy. When she'd returned, out of breath from her hurry to get back to Jesse, she had found him dancing with a beautiful dark-haired woman, his head too close to hers, his laughter ringing out over the noise of the band. Had he taken her out onto the balcony and kissed her too? Lizzie hadn't hung around to find out. She'd avoided him for the rest of the evening.

'I'm sorry to hear you've been hurt,' she said stiffly. *Boy, had she wanted to hurt him back then.*

'All in the line of duty,' he said. 'My own fault for grappling with a too-large concrete beam without help.'

'So you've come home to recuperate?' she asked. She became aware of the carving pressing into her back and moved from the countertop, being careful not to take a step closer to him. Her reaction to him had unnerved her. She didn't know that she could trust herself not to reach out to him if she got too near.

'That's right,' he said. 'But I'm bored with all the physiotherapy and "taking it easy". I've been helping Ben and Sandy finish off the café.' He looked around him with a proprietorial air that she found disconcerting. 'Impressive, isn't it?'

'Very,' she said. 'I love the dolphin carvings. Every business in this town has to display some kind of dolphin motif, if I remember correctly. These are works of art.'

She kept her tone neutral but inside she was seething. In all their phone calls and Skype discussions about the progress of the café, Sandy had never once mentioned that Jesse was back in town. Her sister, along with everyone else in this gossip-ridden small town, knew she and Jesse had been caught making out on the balcony.

It wouldn't have been a huge deal anywhere else but here it was big news. Jesse was the kind of guy the locals kept odds on. The big bets were on that he would never settle down with one woman.

She found herself nervously glancing out of the plate glass windows that led to the street for fear people walking by might notice her and Jesse alone together.

She didn't want to become part of the Jesse mythology. Be a butt of local jokes. But her indiscretion on the night of the wedding meant, most likely, she'd been added to the list of his conquests. Why hadn't Sandy warned her Jesse had made an unscheduled visit home? That he'd be working on the café? It would be almost impossible to avoid him.

As Jesse reached out to touch the dolphin carvings, she jerked away from him to avoid any possible contact. He raised a dark eyebrow but didn't say anything. Which made her feel even more ill at ease.

'They're by the same Balinese carvers as the fittings next door in Bay Books,' he said, stroking the dolphin. She couldn't look, couldn't let herself remember how good his hands had felt on the bare skin of her back in her strapless bridesmaid dress. 'Sandy had the countertop custom-made and then imported it. I only finished installing it yesterday.'

'So you've completed work on the fit-out now?' She spoke through gritted teeth. *Please, please, please let him be on his way back to his job in the Philippines.*

'Just about.'

She sighed with too-obvious relief. 'So you won't be around much longer.'

Only a tightening of his beautifully chiselled lips betrayed he'd noticed her tone.

'There's the unpacking to do. And I still have to finish off some tiling upstairs in your apartment,' he said.

'You've been working up there?' She regretted the squawk of alarm as soon as it had escaped from her mouth. Jesse in her bathroom; maybe in her bedroom? The thought was disconcerting, to say the least.

But she couldn't let him know she was worried he would invade her private thoughts when she was alone in those rooms. *She mustn't let that happen.*

'Sandy wanted the bathroom remodelled to be as comfortable as possible for you and your little girl,' he said.

'Thank you for your help,' she managed politely. 'It was a big order to get it ready in time for us to move in.'

Her real gratitude was to Sandy. How many other down-on-their-luck chefs had a sister who had offered not only a job but also a place to live, rent-free?

But having Jesse Morgan around hadn't been part of the deal. She didn't want to be reminded of her lack of judgement on the night of the wedding. Of the folly of being in his arms. She should have known better than to fall for that kind of guy again.

Because, no matter how many times over the last six months she'd told herself that Jesse was bad news, seeing him again made her aware she'd be lying if she thought she was immune to him. He was still out-and-out the most attractive man she'd ever met. She would have to fight that attraction every moment she found herself in his company. Dear heaven, let there not be too many of those moments.

She looked purposefully around her again. 'I'd hate for the building work here to delay your recuperation.'

Jesse's deep blue eyes narrowed. 'So I can get the hell out of Dolphin Bay, you mean?'

She struggled to meet his gaze. 'I…I didn't mean it like that,' she lied.

His face set in grim lines. 'You might not like it but you'd better get used to me being around. I'm going to be here for at least another month while my shoulder heals.'

She couldn't help her little gasp of horror. 'What?'

Only the twist of his mouth indicated he'd heard. 'Sandy needs help to get this venture up and running and I intend to give it to her. The Morgan family is grateful to Sandy. Heaven knows where Ben would be if she hadn't come back into his life after all those years.'

'Of course,' she said, suddenly feeling shamefaced that all she was thinking about was herself.

Lizzie and Sandy had first visited Dolphin Bay on a family vacation as teenagers. They'd stayed in the Morgan family's character-filled old guest house. Lizzie remembered Jesse from that time as an arrogant show-off, flexing his well-developed teenage muscles at any opportunity. But Sandy had fallen in love with Ben. They hadn't met again until twelve years later, after Ben had lost his first wife and baby son in the fire that had destroyed the guest house. Together they'd taken a second chance on love.

'I want to make this café a success for Sandy as well,' Lizzie continued. 'And for Ben, too—he's a marvellous brother-in-law. They've both been very good to me.'

Sandy was the only person she felt she could really trust. They'd been allies in the battleground that had been their family, led by their bully of a father. Her older sister had always watched out for her. Just like she was watching out for her and Amy now. Lizzie owed her.

'Then we're on the same page,' Jesse said.

'Right,' she said, unable to keep the anxiety from her voice.

'Bay Bites opens in a week's time. We don't have time to waste bickering,' Jesse said.

He took a few steps towards her until she was back up against that dolphin fin again and she couldn't back away from him any further. She felt breathless at his proximity, the memories of how good it had felt to be in his arms treacherously near the surface.

But this wasn't the fun, charming Jesse she'd known at the wedding bearing down on her. This Jesse looked tough, implacable and she didn't think it was her imagination that he seemed suddenly contemptuous of her.

'So better grit your teeth and bear being in my company for as long as it takes,' he said.

She'd had no idea his voice could sound so harsh.

CHAPTER TWO

JESSE NEARLY LAUGHED out loud at the expression of dismay on Lizzie's face. She so obviously didn't want to work with him any more than he wanted to work with her. Not after her behaviour at Ben and Sandy's wedding.

He could brush off his reputation as a player—but that wasn't to say he liked it. And he hadn't liked being made a fool of by Lizzie in the public arena of his brother's wedding reception. He hadn't appreciated having to make so many gritted teeth responses to his Dolphin Bay friends as they'd asked why Lizzie had left him high and dry when they'd so publicly been having a good time together. That had been difficult when he'd had no idea himself. There had been only so many jokes about whether he needed to change his deodorant that he could take. His banter had run dry long before he'd realised Lizzie wasn't coming back.

He indicated the packages propped up against the wall. 'Right now I'm here to help you get those artworks up on the walls.'

'I'm not sure I need help,' she said, folding her arms in front of her. 'I'm quite capable of placing the artwork myself.'

Lizzie's looks were deceptive. Tall and slender with

a mass of white blonde, finely curled hair, she gave the initial impression of being frail. But he knew there was steel under that fragile appearance. Her arms might be slim but they were firm with lean muscle. At the wedding she'd explained that hauling heavy cooking pans around a restaurant kitchen was a daily weight training regime.

'No,' he said curtly. 'That's my job and I'm here to do it.'

'What about your shoulder? Surely you shouldn't be lifting stuff.'

'Canvas artworks? Not a problem. This phase of my rehab calls for some light lifting.'

'But I need time to sort through them, to decide which paintings I like best.'

Her bottom lip stuck out stubbornly. She was putting up a fight. *Tough.* He'd promised Sandy he'd help out. For the years Ben had been immersed in grief, Jesse felt he had lost his adored older brother. Sandy's love had restored Ben to him. He could never thank her enough. If that meant having to spend too much time with her sister, he'd endure it. Lizzie could put up with it too.

He thought into the future and saw a long procession of family occasions where he and Lizzie would be forced into each other's company, whether they liked it or not. He had to learn to deal with it. So would she. And he would have to forever ignore how attractive he found her.

'That's where we read from the same page,' he said patiently, as if he were talking to a child. 'You choose. I hammer a nail in the wall and hang the picture. Then the artists want the rejects back ASAP.'

She looked startled. 'Rejects? I wouldn't want to offend any artists. Art appreciation is such a personal thing.'

'The artists have supplied these paintings to be sold on consignment,' he explained. 'You sell them through the café and get a commission on each sale. If they don't get hung this time, maybe they'll survive your cull next time.'

Lizzie nodded. It was the first time she'd agreed with him, though he sensed it took an effort. 'True. So I should probably compile an A-list for immediate hanging and a B-list for reserves. The Bs can then be ready to slip into place when the As are sold.'

'In theory a good idea. But keep the grading system to yourself. This is a small community.'

'Point taken,' she said, meeting his gaze square on. 'I'll defer to your small-town wisdom. We city people don't understand such things.'

He didn't miss the subtle edge of sarcasm to her words and again he had to fight a smile. He'd liked that tough core to her.

In fact when he'd met Lizzie at the pre-wedding party in Sydney for Ben and Sandy, he'd been immediately drawn to her. And not just for her good looks.

With her slender body, light blonde hair and cool grey eyes set in the pale oval of her face, she'd seemed ethereally lovely. But when she'd smiled, her eyes had lit up with a warmth and vivacity that had surprised him.

'Let's celebrate these long-lost lovers getting together in style,' she'd said with a big earthy laugh that had been a wholehearted invitation to fun. From then on, the evening had turned out a whole lot better than he'd expected.

Lizzie had made him laugh with her tales of life in

the stressful, volatile world of commercial kitchens. That night had been memorable. So had the wedding reception a few days later. She'd kept him entertained with a game where she made amusing whispered predictions about the favourite foods of the other guests. All based on years of personal research into restaurant guests' tastes, she'd assured him with a straight face.

He hadn't been sure whether she was serious or not. Thing was, she'd been right more often than she'd been wrong. She'd had him watching the wedding guests as they made their choices at the buffet. He'd whooped with her when she'd got it right—his father heading straight for the fillet of beef—and commiserated with her when she'd got it wrong—an ultra-thin friend of the bride loading her plate with desserts. The game was silly, childish even, but he had thoroughly enjoyed every moment of her company. Those moments out on the balcony where she'd come so willingly into his arms had been a bonus.

At that time, he'd been in dire need of some levity and laughter, having just unexpectedly encountered the woman who had broken his heart years before. He'd first met the older, more worldly-wise Camilla when he'd been twenty-five; she'd been a photojournalist documenting his team's rebuilding of a flood-damaged community in Sri Lanka. He'd thought he'd never see her again after their disastrous break-up that had left him shattered and cynical about love, loyalty and trust.

At the wedding, lovely, spirited Lizzie had been both a distraction and a reminder that there could be life after treacherous Camilla.

Until Lizzie had walked out on him at the wedding without warning.

And now he was facing a completely different Lizzie.

A Lizzie where it seemed as if the spark had fizzled right out of her. She was chilly. Standoffish. Hostile, even.

It made him wonder why he had found her appealing. He'd been so wrong about Camilla; seemed as if he'd misjudged Lizzie too.

He hadn't been on top of his game at that time; that was for sure.

And now, by the mere fact her sister was married to his brother, he was stuck with her. Trouble was, he still found her every bit as beautiful as when he'd first met her.

The sooner they got the paintings hung and the boxes unpacked, the sooner he could get out of here and away from her prickly presence. He'd endured some difficult situations in his time. But it looked as if putting up with Lizzie was going to be one of the most difficult of all. Even twenty minutes with her was stretching his patience. But there was work to be done and he'd made a commitment to Sandy.

He'd break his time working with Lizzie into manageable blocks. He reckoned he could endure two hours of forced politeness in her company; manage to ignore how lovely she was. He'd make a strict schedule and stick to it. He looked at his watch. One hour and forty minutes to go. 'Let's get cracking on sorting those paintings. There's an amazing one of dolphins surfing I think you might want to look at first.'

Under her breath, Lizzie let off a string of curse words. She swore fluently in both English and French—it was difficult not to pick up some very colourful language working in the pressure cooker atmosphere of commercial kitchens.

But these days she kept a guard on her tongue. No way did she want Amy picking up any undesirable phrases. So she kept the curse words rolling only in her mind. This particular stream was directed—non-verbally of course—towards her sister. What had Sandy been thinking to trap her in such close confines with Jesse Morgan?

He was insufferable. Talking to her as if she was an idiot. Well, she had been an idiot to have fancied him so much at the wedding. To have let physical attraction overrule good sense. But that was then and this was now.

Like many chefs, during the years she had worked in other peoples' restaurants, she had entertained the idea of running a restaurant of her own. In fact she and Philippe had been working towards just that until she'd unexpectedly fallen pregnant and everything had changed.

For sure, her dream of running her own show hadn't centred on a café in a place like Dolphin Bay but she could make the most of her downgraded dream. She knew what it took to make customers want to come to a restaurant—and to keep them coming. She didn't need Mr Know-It-All Jesse Morgan telling her how to choose the art for the walls. For heaven's sake, was he going to tell her what dishes to put on the menu?

She made a point of looking at her watch too. Two could play at this game. 'Okay, let's unwrap the paintings one at a time and then I'll compare them and decide which ones I like best. Without being so insensitive as to grade them, of course.'

For a moment she thought she saw a smile lurk around the corners of his grimly set mouth. It passed so quickly she could have imagined it. But for a sec-

ond—just that second—she'd seen again that Jesse from
the wedding who had appealed to her so much. Boy,
had she got him wrong.

She walked across to the stacks of paintings. 'Shall
we start with the largest one first?' she said.

Jesse nodded as he followed her over. 'That's the
surfing dolphins one.'

She immediately wished she'd decided to open the
smallest ones first. But she couldn't backtrack now.

The painting was bracketed with sheets of cardboard
and then wrapped with thick brown paper. She started
to open it but the paper was too tough to tear. Silently,
Jesse reached into his pocket and pulled out a retract-
able-blade utility knife. Again without saying a word,
he clicked it free of its safety cover and handed it to her.

'Thanks,' she muttered, biting down on the urge to
tell him not to keep such a dangerous tool in his pocket.
She knew she was being unreasonable, but Jesse seemed
to have that effect on her. As much as she hated to admit
it, she'd been hurt by his behaviour at the wedding, and
she would do whatever it took to protect herself from
feeling that way again.

She crouched down and carefully slit the paper
across the top of the wrapping. As she went to cut down
the side, Jesse reached out a hand to stop her.

She flinched. *Don't touch me*, she wanted to snarl.
But that would sound irrational. She gritted her teeth.

'Leave that,' he said. 'If you don't cut the sides the
painting will be easier to get back in the wrapping.'

She stilled for the long moment his hand stayed on
her wrist. Of course he had beautiful hands, just like
the rest of him—she couldn't fail to register that. His
fingers were warm and immediately familiar on her
bare skin. She closed her eyes tight. *She couldn't deal*

with this. But she was just about to shake off his hand
when he removed it. She realised she was holding her
breath and she let it out in a controlled sigh that she
prayed he didn't register.

'Good idea,' she managed to choke out. *Why did he
have to stand so close beside her?*

'I'll give you a hand to slide the painting out. It's too
heavy for one person.'

She had to acknowledge the truth in that. It would
seem churlish not to. 'Thanks,' she said.

She stood at one end of the painting and he at the
other and they lifted it free of its wrappings. As the
image emerged, she could not help a gasp. The artist
had perfectly captured in acrylic, on the underside of a
breaking aquamarine wave, a pod of dolphins joyfully
surfing towards the beach. 'It's wonderful. No. More
than wonderful. Breathtaking.'

Jesse would have been justified in an I-told-you-so
smirk. Instead he nodded. 'I thought so too,' he said.

Lizzie reached out a hand to touch the painting then
drew it back. 'This artist is so talented. It looks like Big
Ray beach, is it?' Big Ray was the local surf beach. It
had a different name on the maps. The locals called it
Big Ray because of the two enormous dark manta rays
that periodically glided their way from one headland to
the other. As a kid, visiting Dolphin Bay, she had been
both fascinated by and frightened of them.

'Yep. One of the smaller paintings is of the rays.'

'Let's open that one next.' She couldn't keep the excitement from her voice.

'So the big one passes muster?'

'Oh, yes,' she said. 'It gets a triple A. You were absolutely right. It's perfect.' She indicated a central spot
on the wall. 'It would look fabulous right there.'

'I agree,' he said. 'The artist will be delighted. She was really hoping you'd choose one of her paintings.'

'*She?*' The word slipped out of her mouth.

Jesse's eyes darkened to the colour of the sea on a stormy day. 'Yes. She. Is that a problem?'

'Of course not. It's just—'

'It's just that you've jumped to the immediate wrong conclusion. The artist is a friend of my mother. A retired art teacher. I know her because she taught me at high school. Not because she's one of the infamous "Jesse's girls".'

'I…I didn't think that for one moment. Of course I didn't.' *Of course she had.*

At the wedding, she had wanted to be with Jesse so much, she had refused to acknowledge his reputation. Until he himself had shown her the truth of it.

She took a step away from him. His physical presence was so powerful she was uncomfortably aware of him. His muscular arms, tan against the white of his T-shirt. The strength of his chest. His flawless face. Stand too close and she could sense his body heat, breathe the spice of his scent that immediately evoked memories she was desperately trying to suppress.

She thought quickly. 'I…I just thought the artist might have been a man because of the sheer size and scale of the painting.'

'Fair enough,' he conceded, though to her eye he didn't look convinced. In fact she had the impression he was struggling to contain a retort. 'If you're sure you want this painting as the hero, let's get it up first so we can then balance the others around it.'

'That could work,' she said. He was right, of course he was right. And she could not let her memories of how he had hurt her hinder her from giving him the courtesy she owed him for his help.

He stood in front of the wall and narrowed his eyes. After a long pause he pointed. 'If we centre it there, I reckon we'll be able to achieve a balanced display.'

'Okay,' she said.

It wasn't a good idea to stand behind him. His rear view was even more appealing than she had remembered. Those broad shoulders, the butt that could sell a million pairs of jeans. She stepped forward so she was beside him. Darn, her shoulders were practically nudging his. Stand in front of him and she'd remember too well how he'd slid his arms around her and nuzzled her neck out on that balcony. *How she'd ached for so much more.* She settled for taking a few steps sidewards, so quickly she nearly tripped.

As it happened, she needn't have bothered with evasive tactics. He headed for a toolbox she hadn't noticed tucked away behind the counter and took out an electric drill, a hammer, a spirit level, a handful of plastic wall plugs and a jar of nails. 'It's a double brick wall with no electrics in the way so we can hang the picture exactly where we want it.'

'I can't wait to see it up,' she said.

She found his continual use of the word 'we' disconcerting. No way did she want to be thought as part of a team with Jesse Morgan. But, she had to admit, she was totally lacking in drilling skills. Sandy knew that. And why pay a handyman when Jesse was volunteering his time?

He pulled a pencil from out of his pocket, marked a spot on the wall and proceeded to drill. It seemed an awkward angle for someone with a shoulder injury but who was she to question him? But he easily drilled a neat hole, with only the finest spray of masonry dust to mar the freshly painted wall. 'Done,' he said in a satisfied tone.

He put down the drill, picked up the hammer and the wall plug. He positioned the wall plug with his left hand and took aim with the hammer in his right. His sudden curse curdled the air and the hammer thudded to the floor.

'Jesse! Are you okay?'

'Just my shoulder,' he groaned, gripping it and doubling over. 'Not a good angle for it.'

'How can I help?' She felt useless in the face of his pain. Disconcerted by her immediate urge to touch him, to comfort him.

He straightened up, wincing. 'You hold the nail and I'll wield the hammer using both hands, it'll take the strain off the shoulder.'

'Or you could let me use the hammer.'

'No,' he said. 'I'll do it.'

Was it masculine pride? Or did he honestly think she couldn't use a hammer? Whatever, she had no intention of getting into an argument over it. 'Okay,' she said.

He handed her the nail and, using her left hand, she positioned it against the wall plug. She was tall, but Jesse was taller. To reach the nail he had to manoeuvre himself around her. Her shoulders were pressed against the solid wall of his chest. *He was too close.* Her heart started to thud so fast she felt giddy; her knees went wobbly. She dropped the nail, twisted to get away from him and found herself staring directly up into his face. For a long, long moment their eyes connected.

'I...I can't do this, Jesse,' she finally stuttered as she pushed away from him.

Three of his large strides took him well away from

her before he turned to face her again. He cleared his throat. 'You're right,' he said. 'We can't just continue to ignore what happened between us at the wedding. Or why you ran away the next day without saying good-bye.'

CHAPTER THREE

THE LIZZIE JESSE had known six months ago hadn't been short of a quick retort or a comment that bordered on the acerbic. Now she struggled to make a response. But he didn't prompt her. He'd waited six months for her excuse. He could wait minutes more.

Instead he tilted back on the heels of his boots, stuck his thumbs into the belt of his jeans and watched her, schooling his face to be free of expression.

She opened her mouth to speak then shut it again. She twisted a flyaway piece of her pale blonde hair that had worked itself free from the plait that fell between her shoulder blades.

'Not ignore. *Forget,*' she said at last.

'Forget us getting together ever happened?'

'Yes,' she said. 'It was a lapse of judgement on my part.'

He snorted. 'I've been insulted before but to be called a "lapse of judgement" is a first.'

She clapped her hand over her mouth. 'I didn't mean it to come out quite like that.'

'I'm tough; I can take it,' he said. He went to shrug his shoulders but it hurt. In spite of his bravado, so had her words.

'But I meant it,' she said. 'It should never have hap-

pened. The…the episode on the balcony was a mistake.'
She had a soft, sweet mouth but her words twisted it
into something bordering on bitter.

'I remember it as being a whole lot of fun,' he said
slowly.

She tilted her chin in a movement that was surprisingly combative. 'Seems like our memories of that night
are very different.'

'I remember lots of laughter and a warm, beautiful
woman by my side,' he said.

By now she had braced herself against the back of
the counter as if she wanted to push herself away from
him as far as she possibly could. 'You mean you've forgotten the way a rowdy group of your friends came out
and…and caught us—'

'Caught us kissing. Yeah. I remember. I've known
those people all my life. They were teasing. You didn't
seem to be bothered by it at the time.'

'It was embarrassing.'

'You were laughing.'

That piece of hair was getting a workout now between her slender fingers. 'To hide how I really felt.'

He paused. 'Do you often do that?'

She stilled. 'Laugh, you mean?'

He searched her face. 'Hide how you really feel.'

She met his gaze full on with a challenging tilt to
her head. 'Doesn't everyone?'

'You laughed it off. Said you had to go check on
Amy.'

Her gaze slid away so it didn't meet his. 'Yes.'

'You never came back.'

'I did but…but you were otherwise engaged.'

'Huh? I don't get it. I was waiting for you.' He'd
checked his watch time and time again, but she still

hadn't shown up. Finally he'd asked someone if they'd seen Lizzie. They'd pointed her out on the other side of the room in conversation with a group of the most gossipy girls in Dolphin Bay. She hadn't come near him again.

Now she met his eyes again, hers direct and shadowed with accusation. 'You were dancing with another woman. When you'd told me all dances for the evening were reserved for me.'

He remembered the running joke they had shared— Jesse with a 'Reserved for Lizzie' sign on his back, Lizzie with a 'Reserved for Jesse' sign. The possessiveness had been in jest but he had meant it.

He frowned. 'After the duty dances for the wedding—including with your delightful little daughter— the only woman I danced with that evening was you. Refresh my memory about the other one?'

She turned her head to the side. Her body language told him loud and clear she'd rather be anywhere else than here with him. In spite of the café and Sandy and family obligations.

'It was nothing,' she said, tight-lipped. 'You had every right to dance with another woman.'

He reached out and cupped her chin to pull her back to face him. 'Let's get this straight. I only wanted to dance with you that night.'

For a long moment he looked deep into her eyes until she tried to wiggle away from him and he released her. 'So describe this mystery woman to me,' he said.

'Black hair, tall, beautiful, wearing a red dress.' It sounded as if the words were being dragged out of her.

He frowned.

'You seemed *very* happy to be with her,' she prompted.

Realisation dawned. 'Red dress? It was my cousin. I

was with my cousin Marie. She'd just told me she was pregnant. She and her husband had been trying for years to start a family. I was talking with her while I waited for you to come back.'

'Oh,' Lizzie said in a very small voice, her head bowed.

'I wasn't dancing with her. More like whirling her around in a dance of joy. A baby is everything she's always wanted.'

'I...I'm glad for her,' Lizzie said in an even more diminished voice.

He couldn't keep the edge of anger from his voice. 'You thought I'd moved on to someone else? That I'd kissed you out on the balcony—in front of an audience—and then found another woman while you were out of the room for ten minutes?'

She looked up at him. 'That's what it seemed like from where I was standing. I've never felt so foolish.'

'So why didn't you come over and slap me on the face or whack me with your purse or do whatever jealous women do in such circumstances?'

'I wasn't jealous. Just...disappointed.' Her gaze slid away again.

'I was disappointed when you didn't come back. When you took off to Sydney the next day without saying goodbye. When you didn't return my phone calls.'

'I...I...misunderstood. I'm sorry.'

She turned her back on him and walked around the countertop so it formed a physical barrier between them. When she got to the glass jars she picked one up and put it down. He noticed her hands weren't quite steady.

Even with the counter between them, it would be easy to lean over and touch her again. Even kiss her.

He fought the impulse. She so obviously didn't want to be touched. And he didn't want to start anything he had no intention of continuing. He wanted to clear up a misunderstanding that had festered for six months. That was all. He took a step back to further increase the distance between them.

'I get what happened. You believed my bad publicity,' he said.

'Publicity? I don't know what you mean.' But the flickering of her eyelashes told him she probably had a fair idea of what he meant.

'My reputation. Don't tell me you weren't warned about me. That I'm a player. A ladies' man. That you'd be one of "Jesse's girls" until I tired of you.'

How he'd grown to hate that old song from the nineteen-eighties where the singer wailed over and over that he wanted 'Jessie's girl'. Apparently his parents had played it at his christening party and it had followed him ever since; had become his signature song.

She flushed high on her cheeks. 'No. Of course not.'

'You should know—reports of my love life are greatly exaggerated.'

He used to get a kick out of his reputation for being a guaranteed girl magnet—what free-wheeling guy in his teens and early twenties wouldn't?—though he'd never taken it seriously. But now, as thirty loomed, he was well and truly over living up to the Jesse legend. A legend that had always been more urban myth than fact.

But he'd done nothing to dispel it. In fact it had been a convenient shield against ever having to explain why he'd closed his heart off against a committed relationship. Why he dated fun-for-now, unchallenging girls and always stayed in control of where the relationship went.

Camilla's words haunted him. *'You won't miss me for a minute; a guy as good-looking as you can get any woman you want just by snapping your fingers—there'll always be another one waiting in line.'* It wasn't true, as she herself had proven. He had wanted her. Badly. And she had gutted and filleted his heart as surely as his father did the fish he caught. He would never expose himself to that kind of pain again.

'I didn't need to be warned,' Lizzie said. 'I figured it out for myself. You and Kate Parker, Sandy's other bridesmaid, were the talk of the wedding. How you'd come back from your travels and hooked up with her. How Kate wouldn't have more luck with getting you to commit than any other of the long line of girlfriends before her.'

As he'd suspected, the Dolphin Bay gossips had struck again. Didn't the women in this town have anything better to do with their time? Though for all their poking their noses into other people's business, they'd never come close to ferreting out the reasons why he'd stayed so resolutely single.

Kate had been his childhood friend. There'd been a long-standing joke between their families that if they hadn't met anyone else by the time they were aged thirty they'd settle down with each other.

'Not true. We kissed. Once. To see if there was anything more than friendship between us. There wasn't. We were just friends. Still are friends.'

Lizzie shrugged. 'I realised that. I soon sussed out she only had eyes for the other groomsman, your friend Sam Lancaster.'

'True. It seemed like one minute Kate was organising Ben and Sandy's wedding, the next minute she was planning her own.'

'I heard they eloped and got married at some fabulous Indian palace hotel.'

'You heard right. I was Sam's best man. It turned out great for them,' he said.

He was really happy for his old friends. But if he was honest with himself, there had been an awkward moment when Kate had made it very clear the kiss had been a disaster for her. Coming on top of what had happened with Camilla it had struck a serious blow to his male pride. By the time of the wedding he'd been in a real funk, questioning things about himself he'd never before had cause to question.

Meeting Lizzie had done a lot to help soothe his bruised ego—until she'd walked away without a word of explanation.

But that had been six months ago. He'd moved on. Now his circumstances were very different. He'd come to a real turning point in his career and the path he chose was crucial to his future. The recent encounter with Camilla had made him realise it could be time to move on from his work with the charity. He'd told his boss there was a good chance he wouldn't return after his shoulder healed. He would not turn his back on it completely but would remain involved as a volunteer and as a fund-raiser.

A new direction had opened with the offer of a fast-track job with a multinational construction company based in Houston, Texas. It would be a challenging, demanding role in a ruthlessly competitive commercial environment. But living in the United States would mean he'd rarely make it home to Dolphin Bay.

As far as Lizzie went, he just wanted to clear up a misunderstanding that had left her resentful of him and him disappointed in her. They'd missed their chance to be any kind of couple, even the most casual. Once the misunderstanding was sorted, they could work together without awkwardness. After all, she was part of the family now and would always be around. They had to come to some sort of mutual good terms.

'Weddings have a lot to answer for,' she said. 'All that romance and emotion floating around makes people do things they really shouldn't. Fool around when they shouldn't. Behave in ways they later regret.'

'Just for the record, I wasn't just fooling around with you at the wedding,' he said.

She flushed redder. 'Maybe I was just fooling around with you.'

'Maybe you were.'

'Maybe *I'm* the player,' she said. There was a return of that teasing spirit he'd liked so much, a spark that warmed her cool grey eyes. He found himself wanting her to smile.

Jesse only vaguely remembered Lizzie from her first visit to Dolphin Bay. She'd been sixteen, beanpole-thin and flat-chested. He'd been sixteen, too. But testosterone had well and truly kicked in and he'd considered himself a man.

He wasn't ashamed to admit he hadn't found her attractive then. He'd been a typical teenage boy who'd looked to the more obvious.

That summer, his brother Ben had been busy falling in love with Sandy. Jesse had been busy trying to decide between three curvaceous older girls who'd made their interest in him more than clear. He hadn't chosen any of them. Even then he hadn't valued what came to him too easily.

When he'd met Lizzie again, more than twelve years later, he'd been knocked over at the woman she'd become. Elegant; sensual without being blatantly sexy; classy. Now she wore simple narrow-legged jeans and a plain white shirt with the sleeves rolled up. Her hair was tied back off her face in a plait. She looked sensational without even trying.

'Are you a player?' he asked. 'I somehow doubt that.'

Her eyes dimmed and it was as if that hint of party-girl Lizzie had been extinguished again. 'No. I'm a divorced single mum with a social life on hold indefinitely. I'm here to work hard at making this café a success and to devote myself to Amy.'

'I get that,' he said. 'Being a lone parent must be one of the toughest gigs around.'

'Tougher than I could have imagined,' she said. 'But it's worth it. Amy is the best thing that ever happened to me.'

'You were young when you had her.'

'Becoming a mother at age twenty-three wasn't part of my game plan, I can assure you. But I don't regret it even for a second.'

He frowned. 'Where is Amy? Didn't she drive down with you from Sydney?'

Lizzie's daughter was a cute kid; she'd been the flower girl at the wedding and charmed everyone. He'd been sorry he hadn't had the chance to say goodbye to her too.

'She's spending the school vacation in France with her father and his parents. They love her and want her to grow up French. That's another reason I have to make a success of this café. Philippe would like sole custody and is just waiting for me to fail.'

Sandy had told Jesse a bit of Lizzie's background. The domineering father. The early marriage. The break-up with the French husband. She hadn't had it easy. Just as well nothing more had happened with them at the wedding. He wouldn't want to have added to her burden of hurt. He knew what that felt like.

'You'll have a lot of support here,' he said. 'Sandy's a Morgan now and the Morgans look after their own.'

'I know that. And I'm grateful. But I'll still have to work, work, work.' She took a deep breath, looked directly up at him. 'I'm truly sorry I misread the situation with your cousin. But what happened between us at the wedding can't happen again; you know that, don't you?'

Relief flooded through him that she had no expectations of him. She was lovely, quite possibly the loveliest woman he knew. But right now he didn't want to date anyone either. Not seriously. And Lizzie was the type of person who would expect serious.

'Lizzie, I—' he started, but she spoke over him.

'I told you my social life is on hold. That means no dating. Not you. Not anyone.'

'I get that,' he said.

His life was so far removed from Lizzie's. His job took him to all the points of the earth for extended periods of time. If he ever committed to a woman it would have to be someone without ties. Camilla would have been ideal—a freelance photojournalist with no kids, feisty, independent. But what had happened with Camilla had soured him against getting close to her type of woman.

'Good,' Lizzie said, rather more vehemently than his ego would have liked.

'I hope you can remember what we had at the wedding as no-strings fun that I certainly don't regret,' he said.

She nodded. He didn't know whether he should be insulted, the way she was so eager to agree.

'But it—' he started to say.

'Can't happen again,' she joined in so they chorused the words.

He extended his hand to her over the counter. 'Friends?'

She hesitated and didn't take his hand. 'I'm not sure about "friends"—we hardly know each other. I don't call someone a friend lightly.'

He resisted the urge to roll his eyes. 'Yep.'

Her eyes widened at his abrupt reply. 'I don't mean to be rude,' she said. 'Just honest about what I feel.'

Yeah. She was. But her honesty had a sharp edge. All in all, it made him wonder why he'd want to be friends with her anyway. Especially when he knew she was off-limits to anything more than friendship. It would be difficult to be 'just friends' with someone he found so attractive. That two-hour limit he'd set himself on the time he spent with her might just be two hours too much.

'So "just acquaintances" or "just strangers stuck with each other's company" might be more to the point?' he said.

She gasped. 'That sounds dreadful, doesn't it?' Then she disarmed him with a smile—the kind of open, appealing smile that had drawn him to her in the first place. 'Too honest, even for me. After all, we can *try* to be friends, can't we?'

'We can try to be friends,' he agreed. *Two hours at a time.* Any more time than that with her each day and he might find himself wanting more than either of them was prepared to give. And that was dangerous.

'Okay,' she said, this time taking his hand in hers in a firm grip, shaking it and letting it go after the minimum contact required to seal the deal.

CHAPTER FOUR

LIZZIE LEANED BACK from the last of the artworks they'd rewrapped to send back to the artist, kneading with fisted hands the small of her back where it ached. 'That's it,' she said. 'All done, thank goodness. That was harder work than I'd thought it would be.'

'But worth it,' said Jesse from beside her.

'Absolutely worth it. The paintings add to the atmosphere of the café like nothing else could. I hope the artists come in so I can thank them with a coffee.'

But Lizzie felt exhausted. Not just from the effort of unpacking, holding the paintings up against the wall and then repacking the unwanted pictures. But from the strain of working alongside Jesse.

In theory, learning to be 'just friends' with him should have been easy. He was personable, smart, and seemed determined to put their history behind them. Gentlemanly, too—in spite of his shoulder injury he insisted on doing any heavy lifting.

Trouble was, she found it impossible to relax around him. She had to consider every word before she uttered it, which made her sound stilted and awkward. The odd uncharacteristic nervous giggle kept bubbling into her conversation.

Could you ever be just friends with a man you'd

kissed, wanted, cried over? Especially when that man was so heart-stoppingly attractive. *Could you pretend that time together had never happened?*

She would have to try.

If it were up to her, she would choose never to see Jesse Morgan again. Even though they'd cleared up the misunderstanding about his cousin, it was hard to be around someone she'd fancied, kissed, liked…when nothing would—or could—ever happen between them. But with the family situation being the way it was, she had to make a real effort to nurture a friendship with him—be pals, buddies, good mates. Future family occasions could be incredibly awkward if she didn't.

Right now, Jesse stood beside her as they both surveyed the arrangement of paintings on the wall. He was not so close that their shoulders were in danger of nudging but close enough so she was aware of his scent, an intoxicating blend of spicy sandalwood and fresh male sweat. It was *too* close. Being anywhere within touching distance of Jesse Morgan was too close. Memories of how wonderful it had felt to be in his arms were resurfacing.

She leaned forward to straighten the small painting of the manta rays and used the movement to edge away, hoping he didn't notice.

'They look good,' Jesse said. 'You chose well.'

She thought about a friend-type thing to say. 'To be fair, we both made the final selection.'

'You exercised your power of veto more often than not.'

'Is that another way of saying I'm a control freak?' she said without thinking at all.

'I didn't say that,' he said, a smile lurking at the corners of his mouth. 'But…'

If he was a real friend, she would have punched him lightly on the arm for that and laughed. She wished it could be that way. But there would be no casual jesting and certainly no touching with Jesse. It was too much of a risk.

Instead she made a show of sighing. 'The success or failure of Bay Bites rests on my shoulders and I'm only too aware of that.'

'That's not true,' he said. 'You do have help. Sandy. Ben. The staff she's hired for you. Me.'

She turned to face him. 'You?'

'I can work with you for two hours a day.'

'Two hours?' That seemed an arbitrary amount of time to allocate. Maybe it was all he could manage with his shoulder. But she couldn't help wondering what other commitments Jesse had in Dolphin Bay. And if they were of the female kind.

He nodded. 'Whatever help you need, I'm there for two hours every day.'

That was the trouble with denying attraction when that attraction was an ever-present tension, underlying every word, every glance. The air seemed thick with words better left unspoken. At a different time, in a different life, she could think of some exciting ways to spend two hours alone with Jesse Morgan in her bedroom. *But not now.*

She cleared her throat. *Think neutral, friend-type chat.* 'I appreciate the help with the paintings. Though I'm the one who will be looking at them all day and—call me a control freak—but I really couldn't say yes to the one of the bronze whaler sharks, no matter how skilfully it was done.'

He'd argued hard for the sharks and he continued to argue. 'Sharks are part of the ocean. As a surfer I learned to respect them. They're magnificent creatures. That painting captured them perfectly.'

She shuddered. 'They're predators. And I don't like predators. Also, remember people will be eating in this place. They don't want to look up and see pictures of creatures that might eat *them*.'

Jesse grinned, his perfect teeth white against his tan, those blue, blue eyes glinting with good humour. *A woman could forget all caution and common sense to win a smile like that.*

Again she found herself wishing things could be different, that they could take up from where they'd left off out on that balcony. She had to suppress a sigh at the memory of how exciting his kisses had been.

'Good point,' he said. 'But I still think there are too many wussy pictures of flowers.'

'So we agree to disagree,' she said with an upward tilt of her chin.

'Wussy versus brave?' he challenged, still with that grin hovering on his so-sexy mouth.

'If by brave you mean you want to swim with the sharks, then go for it. I'll stick with dolphins, thanks.'

'I've always liked a challenge,' he said.

The challenge of the chase? Was that what he meant? Lizzie really didn't want to know. Or to think too much about how it would feel to be caught up again in Jesse's arms. She'd just steer clear of him as much as she could. It wasn't that she didn't trust him not to overstep the boundaries of a new friendship—it was herself she didn't trust.

'I do love the painting of the dolphins surfing,' she said. 'If I could afford the price tag, I'd buy it myself.'

He sobered. 'You'll have to make sure you don't get too attached to any of the paintings. You want to sell as many as you can. It's an added revenue stream for the café.'

'You're right. I'll just get heartbroken when that particular one goes.'

'Just think of the commission on the sale,' he said. 'The quicker the café gets in the black, the better it will be for all concerned.'

She was surprised at how hard-headed and business-like he sounded. But of course Jesse would be used to not getting attached to pretty things. And that was when she had to bite down on any smart remarks. Not if they were going to try to be friends.

'Thanks again for your help,' she said. 'I'd offer you some lunch but, as you can see, I'm not set up for food just yet.'

'I hear you're still finalising the menu. I'm looking forward to being an official food taster on Saturday.'

Lizzie stared. 'You're coming to the taste test?'

'Sandy rounded up all the family to help you try out the recipes.'

'Oh,' she said, disconcerted. If she'd thought she'd only be seeing Jesse occasionally during his time back home in Dolphin Bay, she was obviously mistaken. Talking herself out of her attraction to him was going to get even more difficult.

'When it comes to taste-testing good food, I'm your man,' he said.

She remembered the game they'd had such fun playing together at the wedding, predicting the favourite foods of the guests. He'd been such good company she'd forgotten all the worries that plagued her that night. *Good company and something more that had had her aching for him to kiss her out on that balcony.*

'Let me guess,' she said, resting her chin on her hand,

making a play of thinking hard. 'The other volunteers will have to fight you for the slow-roasted lamb with beetroot relish. And maybe the caramelised apple pie with vanilla bean ice cream?'

He folded his arms in front of his chest. 'I'm not going to tell you if you're right or wrong about what I like. You'll have to wait for the taste night to see.'

'Tease,' she said.

'You don't like being made to wait, do you?' he said, that slow smile still playing at the corners of his mouth.

'There are some things that are worth waiting for,' she said, unable to resist a slow smile of her own in return.

For a long moment her eyes met his until she dropped her gaze. *She had to stop this.* It would be only too easy to flirt with Jesse, to fall back into his arms and that way could lead to disaster. She had to keep their conversations purely on a business level.

She glanced through the connecting doorway and into the bookshop. Sandy was due to see her at any time and there was only a small moment of opportunity left with Jesse.

She lowered her voice. 'Can I ask you something in confidence?'

His dark brows rose. 'Sure. Ask away.'

'I'm concerned about the food I've got to work with.'

'Concerned?'

'It…it might not be up to scratch.'

He frowned. 'I'm not sure what you mean. Aren't the food supplies being ordered through the Hotel Harbourside restaurant? Ben's hotel is one of the best places to eat in town.'

Ben had built the modern hotel on the site of the old guest house. Alongside, he'd built a row of shops, including Bay Books and Bay Bites.

She winced at Jesse's understandably defensive tone. But who else could she ask? 'That's the problem. I have to tread carefully. But I have to be blunt. The Harbourside is good pub grub. Nothing more. Nothing less. And it's not up to the standard I want. Not for Bay Bites.'

Lizzie did tend to be blunt. Jesse had noticed that six months ago. Personally, he appreciated her straightforward manner. But not everyone in Dolphin Bay would. No way could the café succeed if Lizzie was going to look down her straight, narrow little nose at the locals. Could she really fit in here?

'But isn't it just a café?' he said.

'*Just* a café? How can you say that?' Her voice rose with indignation. 'Because it's a café doesn't mean it can't serve the best food I can possibly offer. Whether I'm cooking in a high-end restaurant or a café, my food will be the best.' She gave a proud toss to her head that he doubted she even realised she'd made.

There was a passion and an energy to her that he couldn't help but admire. But he also feared for her. Small country towns could be brutal on newcomers they thought were too big for their boots.

'You're not in France now, Lizzie.'

'More small town wisdom for me?' Her half-smile took the snarkiness out of the comment.

'Some advice —you don't want to make things too fancy. Not a good idea around here to give the impression you think everything is better in France. Or in Sydney.'

Her response was somewhere between a laugh and a snort. 'You seriously think I'm going to transplant fancy French dining to a south coast café and expect it to work? I might have lived in France for years, but

I'm still an Aussie girl and I think I've got a good idea of what my customers will like.'

He knew she had a reputation as a talented chef who had established her credentials at a very young age—he wasn't sure she had the business sense to go with them.

'And that would be?' he asked.

'The very best ingredients served simply.' She gave another toss of her head that sent her blonde plait swishing across her back. 'That's what I learned in France. Not necessarily at the fine-dining establishments in Paris but in the cafés and markets of Lyon and from the home cooking of Amy's French grandparents. You know they say the heart of France is Paris, but its stomach is Lyon?'

'I didn't know that.' He'd raced through a see-Europe-in-two-weeks type backpacker tour when he was a student that had included Paris and Versailles but that was as far as his knowledge of the country went. 'My journeys have mainly been of the have-disaster-will-travel type. And the food…well, you wouldn't want to know about the food.'

'Of course,' she said, nodding. 'I remember now you told me about some of the out-of-the-way places you've been sent to.'

She'd seemed so genuinely interested in the work he was doing to rebuild communities. Not once had she voiced concern that he had veered off the career track to big bucks and business success. Other girls had been more vocal. He hadn't seen the need to explain to them that he'd been fortunate in the land he'd inherited from his grandparents and the investments he'd made. He could afford to work for a charity for as long as it suited him and not have to justify it to anyone.

Though that might be about to change. The Houston company wanted his expertise and their offer came with a salary that had stunned him with the amount of zeroes.

'So what's your problem with ordering through the hotel?' he asked.

'Their suppliers will be fine for the basics and the hotel gives us better buying power. It's the organic and artisan produce I worked with in Sydney I need to source. Farm to plate stuff. I don't know where to get it here.'

'Farm to plate? That sounds expensive. Do you really want expensive for the café?' He looked around at the fresh white décor, the round tables and bentwood chairs, the way the layout had been designed for customers to wander in from the bookshop. It said casual and relaxed to him.

'Actually, farm to plate can be less expensive because you cut out the middle man.'

'That's a point,' he said.

'I know ridiculously high prices would be the kiss of death to a café serving breakfast and lunch,' she said with that combative tilt to her chin that was starting to get familiar in an endearing kind of way.

'It's good we agree on that one,' he said.

'But if Bay Bites is to succeed it has to be so much better than the existing cafés around here. What would you prefer—a cheap burger made with a mass-produced beef patty or pay a dollar or two extra for free-range, hand-ground beef? Frozen fries or hand cut fries with home-made mayo?'

'That's a no-brainer,' he said, his stomach becoming aware it was lunchtime and rumbling at the thought of the burger. Though the slow-roasted lamb might give it some competition. 'So you are talking café food, not fancy-schmantzy stuff?'

'Of course I am,' she said, not hiding her exasperation. 'I know people will expect the basics.'

'Egg and bacon roll?' he said hopefully.

'The best you've ever tasted. But there will be some more creative options too, depending on seasonal ingredients. And wonderful desserts every day, of course. We'll do morning and afternoon tea as well as breakfast and lunch.'

'You mentioned apple pie?' The longing crept into his voice, in spite of himself.

She nodded with a knowing smile. He'd given himself away. There was no dessert he liked better than apple pie. She'd guessed right again.

'What I'm asking you is how I source that produce without offending Sandy and Ben,' she said.

'How long is it since you've spent any time in Dolphin Bay?'

'There was the wedding. And I drove down to see the building when Sandy first approached me about the café.'

'So basically your memories of the food here are based on when you were sixteen?' Back when there'd been a fish and chip shop, a short-lived pizza place and the best food in town had been from his mother's kitchen.

'Well, yes.'

'Better get yourself up to date. This area has become somewhat of a foodie haven.'

'Dolphin Bay?' Disbelief underscored her words.

'Maybe not the actual town,' he conceded. 'But certainly the areas surrounding it. Didn't you look into that when you did your business plan?'

She pulled a face that made him want to smile but she was so serious he kept his expression neutral.

'Sandy and Ben did the business plan,' she said. 'And they're dead certain there's a market for a bookshop café with a harbour view. But I had to finish a work contract in Sydney and didn't have time to do as much research into the local area as I would have liked.'

'If you had, you would have found one of the well-known television chefs opened a restaurant in the next town and others have followed. Every time I come home on leave, there seem to be more restaurants.'

Her fine eyebrows rose in surprise. 'That's good. Hopefully the rising tide will float all our boats. But where are they sourcing the artisan produce? And how do I get it without offending my sister?'

Did he want to get this involved with this woman, helping her beyond what he'd agreed to with Sandy when he'd volunteered to give a hand while he was on leave? He knew the answer before he'd even finished asking himself the question.

He'd promised Sandy to do his best to make the café succeed. If that meant getting Lizzie what she wanted, he didn't have a choice. And it had nothing to do with how lovely she was, he told himself. Or how intriguing he found her.

'Ben and I grew up with people who have established organic farms and orchards in the area, if that's what you're looking for. And the seafood comes fresh from our own father's boats.'

'Really?' Her cool grey eyes lit up. 'Sandy told me about the seafood. But I didn't know about the organic farms.'

He tilted back on his boot heels again and stuck his

thumbs in his belt. 'I suspect all you need is here if you know where to look for it.'

'Trouble is, I don't.' She tilted her head to the side as she looked at him and smiled very sweetly.

Jesse suppressed a groan. He knew what was coming. 'You're going to ask me to introduce you to those places, aren't you?'

'Of course I am.' Again he was struck by how a smile brought such light to her face. She'd been so warm and vivacious at the wedding that he'd found it hard to leave her side for even a minute.

'Okaaay…' He drew out the word in mock reluctance. 'I guess I can do that for you.'

It wouldn't be a hardship to show her around, if he kept his distance from anything too personal. *Trying to be friends—that was all*. It would also be a chance to catch up with people he hadn't seen for ages. His job meant he'd lost touch with more friends from the area than he'd like.

'Does that count in your daily two hours of rationed help?' she asked.

His immediate impulse was to say *of course not*. But then he thought twice.

On meeting Lizzie again, he'd thought he'd only be able to endure two hours of her chilly, stand-offish company. Now the Lizzie he'd first fallen for was starting to reveal herself. Warm. Funny. With a touch of snark that challenged him. He didn't want his initial attraction to her to be reignited. That meant seeing as little of her as possible. Now that two-hour limit would be not because he didn't like her—rather because he didn't want to get to like her too much.

Lizzie could never be a casual encounter. An *it's been nice but I don't want to get serious* type of thing.

No. Anything with Lizzie would be serious with a capital S. She was a mother with a child, making the relationship equation two-plus-one, rather than the one-plus-one he was used to. She was also his brother's sister-in-law. If they started something and it broke up, the repercussions would be endless.

There were many reasons to steer clear—not least that he saw in her the same kind of spirited, challenging personality that had drawn him to Camilla with such disastrous results. His life was on track with the prospect of a new start in America. He didn't want any awkward emotional confrontations to derail him if he again fell for the wrong woman.

Six months ago he'd been very taken with Lizzie, had seen the possibility of something more than a casual hook-up at a wedding. Looking back, he could see he'd been raw from his recent encounter with Camilla. Lovely Lizzie's laughter and passionate kisses had been affirmation of his appeal as a man, balm to his shattered heart and bruised ego. But her inexplicable cold treatment of him had plunged him back into his resolve to stay clear of women with the power to wound him.

Now this job offer had further strengthened his resolve to avoid anything remotely connected to commitment to a woman. He needed to remain unencumbered if he were to move up to this new stage in his career. The CEO of the Houston company had pretty much spelled out it was a job for a single man—travelling, lots of overtime and weekend work.

That two-hour restriction on time with Lizzie would stay—he couldn't let himself get to like her too much. He genuinely wanted to try and become friends, though. After all, she'd be part of his life for as long as her sister was married to his brother and that looked likely to be for ever. Two hours a day was more than enough to develop the kind of superficial friendship that didn't make any demands on him—or, in fact, on her. He couldn't deny his attraction to Lizzie—but he could stop himself from acting on it.

'Yes, two hours is all I can spare,' he said. 'None of the farms we'll be going to is far from here.'

He could tell she was perplexed by the time restriction but he had no intention of explaining it to her.

'Okay,' she said. Starting tomorrow, please. I don't have time to waste.'

Lizzie was grateful that Jesse was able to help her with her dilemma. She was about to tell him so when Sandy swept into the shop, all exclamations of delight at how the café was shaping up.

Lizzie silently implored Jesse with her eyes to please not say anything of their conversation about the supplies. Thankfully, he indicated with a slight incline of his head that he would keep her confidence. Not in a million years would she want to cause offence to Sandy or Ben. At the same time, she had to have the best for the café.

Brown-haired, hazel-eyed Sandy swept her into a big hug and she squeezed her sister back hard. The wonderful thing about being in Dolphin Bay was it meant more time with her.

'I am *so* glad you got here okay,' Sandy said. She then looked to Jesse. 'I'm still pinching myself that I got a chef of my sister's calibre to run Bay Bites for us. Aren't we fortunate?'

'We're very lucky,' he agreed.

Sandy hugged Jesse, too, and it gave Lizzie pleasure to see the depth of affection between her sister and her brother-in-law.

She and Sandy had both been so emotionally damaged by their controlling cheater of a father that for a while it had looked as if neither of them would find happiness with a man. But Sandy was now blissfully married to Ben and had been lovingly welcomed into the close-knit Morgan family.

One out of two sisters sorted with a happy-ever-after wasn't bad, Lizzie thought. Philippe had done such a good job of destroying any trust she'd had left in men she doubted there'd ever be a second chance of happiness for her. And certainly not if she kept getting attracted to gorgeous love-'em-and-leave-'em guys like Jesse. She didn't regret kissing him at the wedding. Could never forget how wonderful her time with him had been. But it would never happen again.

'I'm so glad to be here,' she said to Sandy. 'It's the new start I need.'

'I see you two have reacquainted yourselves,' Sandy said, waving to Jesse.

With an emphasis on *acquaintance* Lizzie wanted to say, but knew it would come out sounding ill-mannered.

'Yes,' she murmured, avoiding Jesse's gaze. He just nodded.

Lizzie did not fail to detect the speculation in her sister's eyes as Sandy looked from her to Jesse and back again.

Guess she'd better get used to seeing that look in other people's eyes, too, when they saw her and Jesse together—until it became obvious the incident at the wedding was all there ever was going to be between them.

Sandy spun around to the wall behind her. 'The paintings look amazing the way you've hung them.'

'I have to give credit where credit is due,' said Lizzie,

indicating Jesse with a sweep of her hand. 'He put them all up.'

'The boss is the one who chose them,' said Jesse.

'The boss?' asked Lizzie.

'That's you,' he said. 'I jump to your command.' His words were light-hearted but his already deep voice dropped an octave or two as he spoke.

She had to disguise her gasp of awareness with a cough. Oh, she could think of lots of commands she could give to beautiful Jesse, alone and behind closed doors. But not when they were 'just friends'. Not when he was her sister's brother-in-law. Not when he was a man who had a reputation for toying with women's hearts.

She was spared making any kind of smart reply by Jesse himself. He glanced at his watch. 'I didn't realise it was that late. Gotta go.'

'Your two hours are up?' she said, still intrigued by the limit he had given her on his time.

'What two hours?' asked Sandy.

'Something to do with his shoulder,' said Lizzie.

'Yeah, my shoulder, that's it,' said Jesse gruffly. 'I'll pick you up at ten tomorrow,' he said to Lizzie. 'Bye, Sandy.'

Lizzie watched in silent admiration as Jesse strode out of Bay Bites with a masculine loping grace. His back view really was something to see. Broad shoulders tapered to a tight behind. Worn denim jeans hugged muscular legs. And those tanned brown arms rippled with muscle. If he were any other gorgeous guy than Jesse Morgan she'd want to give him a wolf whistle.

'No!' said her sister, once Jesse was out of earshot.

'What do you mean "no"?'

'I saw the way you were looking at Jesse.'

'And you weren't too?'

'Of course I wasn't,' Sandy said primly. 'He's my brother-in-law.'

'And that doesn't stop you appreciating what a finely crafted specimen of masculinity he is?'

'Of course it does,' Sandy said. 'I'm a married woman.' But then the giggles she was suppressing pealed out. 'I wouldn't be female if I didn't appreciate how hot Jesse is. And he's a nice guy too. But he's a commitment-phobe of the first order.'

'I know, I know. If you told me once you told me a million times.'

'And at the wedding you totally ignored my warnings.'

'That was different. Cut me a break, Sandy. I was lonely. Starved for male company. Heck, starved for adult company outside of a commercial kitchen. And Jesse was…was irresistible.'

Lizzie swallowed hard against a hitch in her voice when she remembered the magic of those hours with Jesse. It hadn't been just physical—for her, anyway. At the wedding she'd seen a spark of 'what might have been' if circumstances had been different.

'I love Jesse to pieces. But I don't want to see you hurt.' Sandy paused. 'Or, for that matter, see Jesse hurt.'

'What do you mean, "see Jesse hurt"?'

'Were you serious about him at the wedding? Or was he just a fling before you got back to the reality of being a single mum?'

'Of course I wasn't serious—how could I be with all those warnings echoing in my head?' *Though there had been moments when she'd been guilty of daydreaming of something more.* 'Jesse was fun. A diversion. He made me laugh at a time when I didn't have a whole lot to laugh about.'

'That's what I mean. We'd be angry if a guy toyed with a pretty woman just for a diversion. Why would it be different for a woman with a handsome guy?'

'You can't be serious. I wasn't *toying* with Jesse. It's not the same thing at all.'

'Isn't it? Seems to me there's a lot more to Jesse than he lets on. Sometimes I think it might be a disadvantage to be as good-looking as he is. Does he ever wonder if women flock to him because of how he looks or because of who he is?'

'It's not something I've thought about,' Lizzie said.

'People think women are throwing themselves at him all the time and he wouldn't care if someone dumped him like you did. He was gutted when you went home without another word to him, though he tried to hide it.'

'R-really?' was all Lizzie could manage to stutter. Could that be true? She'd only thought of her own hurt feelings. 'There…there was a misunderstanding. But we've sorted that out. It's been six months. I…I'm sure there've been other women for him in the meantime.'

It was ridiculous, but her heart twisted painfully at the thought of Jesse with someone else. Even now, when she'd put him strictly off-limits.

She'd been stabbed by a sharp and unexpected shard of jealousy when she'd rushed back to the wedding reception to find Jesse with the woman she now knew was his cousin. Her jealousy had been disproportionate to the incident, she knew; after all, she'd had no claim on him. Seeing him laughing with the lovely woman had brought its own brand of pain but had also ripped the scab off buried memories of Philippe's behaviour. *Never, never could she allow herself to fall for a man like that again.*

'Jesse hasn't mentioned any girls,' said Sandy slowly.

'Would he tell you?'

Sandy shook her head. 'I guess not. He seems to live by the code "a gentleman doesn't kiss and tell".'

'That's a good point in his favour. But there's no need for you to worry about me and Jesse. We've agreed we're going to try and be friends as we're connected by family, but that's all.' *No-strings fun.* That was how he'd described it and it wouldn't happen again.

'Good,' said Sandy with rather too much emphasis. 'Please keep it that way.'

'What do you mean?'

'Jesse is so not for you.'

Lizzie felt stung by Sandy's assumption. 'I know that. I've figured it out all by myself. I don't need my big sister to tell me,' she said through gritted teeth. 'I am not interested in Jesse as anything other than…than an acquaintance. Someone I have to try to be friends with because you're married to his brother.' *She would keep telling herself that.*

'I'm glad to hear it,' said Sandy with an air of relief that Lizzie found more than a tad insulting.

'By the way,' she said, 'thanks for not telling me Jesse would be here when I arrived in Dolphin Bay.'

Sandy looked shamefaced. 'Yeah. That. I didn't know he was going to injure his shoulder and land home here, did I? He's staying in the converted boathouse where we lived before we built the big house.'

'You could have warned me.'

'I was worried you'd get yourself wound up at the thought of seeing him. I didn't want you worrying about it. You've got enough on your plate.'

They'd always looked after each other and her sister's advice was well meant. 'Oh, Sandy, you don't have to worry about me. I've no intention of letting any guy get to me again.'

'After all you went through with Philippe, you know I can't help but worry about you. When I think of how you were in Sydney all by yourself having the baby while he—'

Lizzie put up her hand to stop her sister's flow of words. She didn't want to even think about that time, let alone talk about it. 'I'm older and wiser now. And much, much tougher.'

'Maybe I was wrong not to warn you about Jesse being home in Dolphin Bay.'

'No. You were right. It did give me a shock to see him here. Then to find out I'll be working with him every day…' *Maybe if she'd known, she'd have found a way to put off the opening of the café until Jesse had gone.*

'Don't knock back any offers of help—even if you don't particularly want to spend time with Jesse,' said Sandy. 'It's a big ask to get this café open for business in seven days. Besides, he's only here for a few weeks.'

'Four, to be precise,' Lizzie said. 'But don't worry, Sandy. I've got very good at resisting temptation. Jesse Morgan is no danger to my heart, I can assure you. I promise I'll make an effort to get along with him for your sake.'

CHAPTER FIVE

JESSE HADN'T LIVED in Dolphin Bay for any length of time for years. If he took the new job he'd been offered in Houston, Texas, he'd rarely be back to his home town. Yet he took pride in showing Lizzie more of the area where he, his father and his grandfather had grown up.

He had seen so many parts of the world devastated by floods, tornadoes, earthquakes and other disasters he never took its beauty for granted. No matter the growth of the town itself, the heritage-listed harbour, the beaches and the national park bushland stayed reassuringly the same. Whatever the ups and downs of his life, he took comfort from that.

'All I've seen of this part of the world is the town, the beach and the road in and out,' Lizzie said when she settled into the SUV he'd borrowed from his father. She was wearing white jeans and a simple knit top that gave her a look of cool elegance, of discreet sexiness he found very appealing. 'I'm looking forward to seeing more.'

'Then we'll drive the long way around to the places we're going to visit,' he said.

Spring was his favourite time here, the quiet months before the place became overrun with summer tourists. The bush was lush with new growth, a haze of fresh green splashed with the yellow of spring-flowering wattle. The ocean dazzled in its hues of turquoise reflecting cloudless skies; the sand almost white under the sun.

After they'd left the town centre behind, he drove along the road that ran parallel to the sea and stopped at the rocky rise that gave the best view right down the length of Silver Gull, the beach south of Big Ray. He was gratified when Lizzie caught her breath at her first sight of the rollers crashing on the stretch of pristine sand, the stands of young eucalypt that grew down to the edge of it. He owned a block of land on the headland that looked right out to the ocean. One day he'd build a house there.

'I don't know if you've been away long enough to be impressed that in the evening kangaroos sometimes come down to splash in the shallows,' he said.

Her smile was completely without reticence. 'I would never not be impressed by that. If I saw kangaroos there now, I'd go crazy with my phone camera. My French friends would go crazy too when I sent them the photos.'

'You might want to bring your daughter down one evening,' he said, smiling at her enthusiasm, as he put the car into gear and pulled away.

'Amy would love that, and so would I,' she said. 'Our Aussie beaches were one of the things I really missed when I was living in France.'

'France must have had its advantages,' he said, tongue-in-cheek.

'Of course it did. Not just the food but also the fashion, the architecture—I loved it. Thought I would always live there.' He didn't miss the edge of sadness to her voice.

'I'm sorry it didn't work out,' he said.

'Thank you,' she murmured and turned her head to

look out of the window, but not before he saw the bleakness in her eyes.

He'd like to know what had gone wrong with her marriage. What kind of a jerk would let go a woman like Lizzie and her cute little daughter? But it wasn't his business. And he didn't want to talk on an intimate level with her. Not when he was determined to deny any attraction he still felt for her.

'If I remember right you used to surf when you were a teenager,' she said after a pause that was starting to feel uncomfortable.

'Correct,' he said. 'I was a crazy kid, always looking for bigger waves, greater challenges. My first year of university, a group of us went down to Tasmania to surf Australia's wildest waves. It was a wonder none of us was killed.'

'Would you do that now?'

'Go surfing?' he said, deliberately misunderstanding her question. 'Not without a wetsuit. The water's still too cold.'

'I meant surf those extreme waves. I couldn't imagine anything more terrifying.'

Should he share his worst ever surfing story with her? The experience that had completely changed his life? He wanted to keep the time he spent with her on an impersonal level. But now that she'd dropped her chilly persona, he found her dangerously easy to talk to. 'I lost my taste for extreme surfing when I had to outrun a tsunami.'

She laughed in disbelief. 'You were surfing a tsunami? C'mon, pull the other leg.'

'Not surfing. Running. Literally running away from the beach as a monster wave thundered in.'

'You're serious!'

'You bet I am.' Even now his gut clenched with terror and he gripped hard on the steering wheel at the memory of it. 'I took a gap year when I finished my engineering degree. Thought I'd surf my way around all the great breaks of the world. This particular beach was on the south coast of Sri Lanka. That morning I came out very early to surf. The boy who manned the amenities hut screamed at me to get off the beach and to run to the high ground with him.'

She gasped. 'That must have been terrifying.'

'His village was wiped out. But he saved my life. I stuck around to help in any way I could. The organisation I work for now came to rebuild and there was lots of work for a volunteer engineer. When we were done, they offered me a paying job.'

'That's quite a story,' she said. 'I wondered how you'd got into your line of work.' He felt her eyes on him but he kept his straight ahead on the road. 'The thing is, you don't look like a do-gooder type.'

Her comment so surprised him, he took his hands off the wheel for a second and had to quickly correct the swerve of the car. 'And what does a do-gooder look like?'

'Not like he could be an actor or a model. Not like... like you.'

He laughed. 'It doesn't matter what you look like when people need help.'

He knew he hadn't been hit with the ugly stick so didn't demur with false modesty when people commented on the fortunate combination of genes he'd been blessed with. Your looks you were born with. He'd learned it was the personality you developed that counted. Lizzie, for example, was turn-heads lovely but it was her energy and warmth that had drawn him to her. Camilla had been older than him, eye-catching rather than beautiful, but her smarts and confidence had drawn him to her.

'Is that why you do it? To help people? When a guy like you could do anything he wanted?'

'What else?' He went to shrug but winced at the resulting pain in his shoulder. 'That first project—the camaraderie, seeing people rehoused so quickly, it was a high. I wanted more.'

The tsunami had cured him of his adrenalin-junkie taste for extreme sports. The surfing on five-metre waves, the heli-skiing on avalanches, the mountain biking off the sides of mountains. After seeing real disaster he no longer wanted to court it in the name of sport.

But recently he'd been wondering if he had replaced one sort of thrill for another. The thrill of being called to dangerous sites of recent catastrophes, the still present danger, the high of being needed. It was a rewarding life. But he gave up a lot to do it. Regular hours, a permanent home. Of course that made for a convenient excuse to stay single. But Lizzie was the last person he wanted to discuss that with.

'It must be dangerous and uncomfortable at times,' she said. 'I admire you. I don't think I could do it. The world is lucky to have people like you.'

He liked that she got it. Seemed that Lizzie took people for what they were.

'When it all boils down to it, it's a job the same as any other,' he said. 'Not, perhaps, one I'd want to do for the rest of my life. But one I've been glad to do while I can.'

'I don't believe that for a moment. It's like a calling.'

'Maybe,' he said, not wanting to be drawn further

into a conversation that might have him facing awkward truths about his motivations.

He distracted Lizzie by pointing to a flock of multi-coloured rainbow lorikeets hanging upside down off the branches of an indigenous grevillea bush. They were intoxicated by a surfeit of spring nectar from its spiky orange blossoms. When he and Ben had been kids, they'd found the sight of drunken parrots hilarious. He was gratified when Lizzie found it funny too. And tried not to be entranced at the sight and sound of her laughter.

Lizzie carefully stacked her finds into the back of Jesse's SUV, feeling more excited about the café than she had since she'd arrived in Dolphin Bay. Jesse had driven her through unsealed roads that twisted through acres of bushland to a property where the parents of one of Jesse's old school friends had a beekeeping business.

On the spot she'd bought honey harvested from bees that had feasted on blossoms of the eucalypts growing in the adjoining national park and named for the trees: Spotted Gum, Iron Bark, River Gum.

Jesse seemed bemused she'd bought so many jars. 'This is liquid gold,' she explained as he slammed shut the door of the boot. 'Each honey has a particular flavour and they're not always available. I'm thrilled to bits. It's also considerably cheaper buying it direct from the farmer.'

'Your head is buzzing with ideas on what to cook with all this?' he asked.

She smiled at his joke and he met her smile with one of his own. When she'd first climbed into his car this morning she'd felt tense and on edge in his company but had gradually relaxed to the point she felt she could have a normal conversation without being choked by self-consciousness. 'You could say that. I love to cook with honey but I also like to drizzle it over, say, baked ricotta for breakfast.'

'Ricotta cheese for breakfast! A hungry man coming into the café won't think much of that.'

'How about served with a stack of buttermilk pancakes?'

'With a side of bacon?'

'With a side order of bacon,' she said.

'Much better,' he said. 'I like a big breakfast to start the day. I might become a regular customer while I'm in town.'

There was something very appealing about a big man with a hearty appetite. She remembered—

No! She would not even *think* about Jesse in relation to other appetites. Not for the first time she thanked heaven that her time with him at the wedding had been interrupted. She might have been very, very tempted to go much further than kisses and that would have been a big mistake of the irredeemable kind. Mere kisses were easy to put behind her. *Though not without a degree of regret that they could never take up where they'd left off.*

'Why not?' she said lightly. 'I guarantee we'll have the best breakfasts and lunches in town. If you're still hungry after one of my breakfasts I'll give you your money back.'

'Is that a challenge?'

'An all-you-can-eat challenge? You'll just have to wait and see the food, won't you?'

'What about the coffee? A café will live or die on its coffee.'

'The beans they're ordering for me through the Harbourside are single origin beans from El Salvador and Guatemala. Fair trade, of course. I have no quibble with

them.' Her voice trailed away at the end. She'd decided
not to complain too much about anything to Jesse in
case it found its way back to Ben and Sandy.

He turned to her. 'You don't sound as confident about
the coffee as you do about the food.'

'How did you know that?'

'Just an edge to the tone of your voice.'

It was scary how quickly he'd learned to read her.
Was that the Jesse way with women? Or a genuine
friendship building between them? Still, she decided
to confide in him—this was just business. 'You're right.
We've got a state-of-the-art Italian coffee machine. But
I'm not sure how good the girl is we've employed to
use it.'

'If she's no good, employ someone else,' he said,
again displaying the ruthless business streak that surprised her.

'Easier said than done in a place like Dolphin Bay.
There's not a lot of need for highly skilled baristas; as
a result there aren't many to call upon.'

'I'm sure you'll sort it out,' he said. 'You're likely to
have a few teething problems to overcome.'

'But I don't want teething problems,' she said stubbornly. 'I want the café to run perfectly from the get-go.'

'You really are a perfectionist, aren't you?'

'Yes,' she admitted. 'Which isn't always a good
thing. It means I'm often disappointed.'

She knew there was a bitter edge to her words but
she couldn't help it. *No man is perfect,*' Philippe had
shouted at her when she'd refused to take him back
that final time. Was it so unreasonable to want a man
who wouldn't cheat and lie? Who could manage to stay
faithful?

Another reason to keep Jesse strictly hands-off. He

was a player like Philippe. With all the potential for heartbreak that came with that kind of guy.

She forced herself away from old hurts and back to the café.

'Tell me if you think this is a good idea—I want to ask your mother if she could share some of her favourite recipes from the old guest house. It would be nice to have that link to the Morgans in the café menu.'

Morgan's Guest House had been such a wonderful place, especially for a girl interested in cooking. Maura was an exceptional home-style cook.

Jesse paused for a long moment before he replied. She wondered if it had been a bad idea. She let out her breath when he answered, not realising she had been holding it. 'It's a great idea,' he said slowly. 'I'm sure Mum would be flattered. I'd certainly like it.'

'I'm so glad you think so,' she said with a rush of relief. 'I have such happy memories of helping Maura cook in the kitchen. She taught me to make perfect scrambled eggs. I've never found a better technique than hers.'

'When my mother heard you'd become a chef she was tickled pink that she might have had an influence on you.'

'I'm glad to hear that, because she was a big influence. My own mother encouraged me too.'

'And your father?'

She looked away from the car so she didn't have to face him. 'You've probably heard something from Sandy about what my father was like,' she said stiffly.

'Ben said Dr Randall Adam was an officious, domineering snob who—'

Lizzie put up her hand to halt him. 'Don't say it. After all he's done, he's still my father.'

'Sure,' he said, and she felt embarrassed at the sympathy in his voice. She didn't want him to feel sorry for her.

She scuffed at the ground near the back tyres of the car with the toe of her sneaker. 'Shall we say, he was less than encouraging when I didn't want to follow the academic path he'd mapped out for me. I wasn't the honours student Sandy was but he didn't get that. He wanted me to go to university. When I landed an apprenticeship at one of the most highly regarded restaurants in Sydney he didn't appreciate what a coup that was. He…well, he pretty much disowned me.'

Under threat of being kicked out of home without a cent to support her if she didn't complete her schooling, she'd finished high school. But the kitchen jobs she'd worked during her vacations had only reinforced her desire to become a chef. When she'd got the apprenticeship at the age of seventeen her father had carried out his threat and booted her out of home. It had backfired on him, though. Her mother had finally had enough of his bullying and infidelities. He went. Lizzie stayed. It was a triumph for her but one she hadn't relished—she'd adored her father and had been heartbroken.

Jesse shook his head in obvious disbelief. 'Isn't he proud of what you've achieved now?'

It was an effort to keep her voice steady. 'He sees being a chef as a trade rather than a profession. I…I think he's ashamed of me.' She shrugged. 'That's his problem, isn't it?'

'And not one you want to talk about, right?' Jesse said, his blue eyes shrewd in their assessment of her mood.

She had to fight an urge to throw herself into his arms and feel them around her in a big comforting hug.

At Sandy's wedding ceremony she'd sobbed, not just with joy for her sister but for the loss of her own marriage and her own dreams of happiness. Jesse had silently held her and let her tears wet his linen shirt. She could never forget how it had felt to rest against his broad, powerful chest and feel his warmth and strength for just the few moments she had allowed herself the luxury. *It had meant nothing.*

'That's right,' she said. Then gave a big sigh. 'I won't say it doesn't still hurt. But I'm a big girl now with a child of my own to raise.'

'And you're sure as heck not going to raise her like you were raised,' he said.

'You're sure right on that,' she said with a shaky laugh.

'I was so lucky with my parents,' said Jesse. 'They're really good people who love Ben and me unconditionally. I didn't know what a gift that was until I grew up.'

'Looking back, I realise how kind Maura was,' Lizzie said. 'She must have found me a terrible nuisance, always underfoot. But there was so much tension between my parents, I wanted to avoid them. And Sandy was always off with Ben.'

'Of course she wouldn't have found you a nuisance,' said Jesse. 'Out of all the guests she had over the years, Mum always remembered you and Sandy. I think she'd love to share her recipes with you. Maybe…maybe it's time to revive some happy memories of the guest house.'

They both fell silent. Ben's first wife and baby son had died when the old guest house had burned down. That meant Jesse had lost his sister-in-law and nephew. She wondered how the tragedy had affected him. But it wasn't the kind of thing she felt she could ask. Not now. Maybe never.

'Can you ask about the recipes for me?' she said.

'Sure. Though I'm sure Mum would love it if you called her and asked her yourself.'

'I just might do that.'

Jesse glanced at his watch.

'I know, the two hours,' she said, resisting the urge to ask him just what catastrophe would befall him if he spent longer than that in her company. 'We'd better hurry up and get back in the car.' She walked around to the passenger side, settled into her seat and clicked in her seat belt. 'We're heading for a dairy next, right?'

'Correct,' said Jesse from the driver's seat. 'The farmer and his wife are old schoolfriends of mine. I hear they've won swags of awards for their cheeses and yogurts. I thought that might interest you.'

She turned to look at him, teasing. 'How do you know exactly what I need, Jesse Morgan?'

He held her gaze with a quizzical look of his own. 'Do I?' he said in that deep voice that sent a shiver of awareness down her spine.

Shocked at her reaction, she rapidly back-pedalled. 'In terms of supplies for the café, I meant.'

His dark brows drew together. 'Of course you did,' he said. 'What else would you have meant?'

She kept her gaze straight ahead and didn't answer.

CHAPTER SIX

THE SATURDAY TASTE-TESTING brunch at the café was in full swing. Bay Bites was packed with people, most of whom Lizzie didn't recognise, all of whom she wanted to impress. She'd spent all of Friday prepping food and working with the staff Sandy had hand-picked for her. They'd bonded well as a team, united by enthusiasm for the new venture. Now it was actually happening and it was exhilarating and scary at the same time.

She took a moment out from supervising her new kitchen staff to stand back behind the dolphin-carved countertop and watch what had turned into a party of sorts.

So far, so good. Her menu choices were getting rave reviews. She'd decided to serve small portions from the basic menu, handed around from trays, so people could try as many options as possible. She'd gone as far as printing feedback sheets to be filled in but the Dolphin Bay taste-testers were proving more informal than that. They simply told her or the wait staff what they thought. She took their suggestions on board with a smile.

'I'd go easy on the chilli in that warm chicken salad, love,' Jesse's seventy-five-year-old great-aunt Ida said. 'Some of us oldies aren't keen on too much of the hot stuff.'

'The only problem with those little burgers was there weren't enough of them,' said the bank manager, a friend of Ben. 'Your other greedy guests emptied the tray.'

'The triple chocolate brownies? Bliss,' said one well-dressed thirty-plus woman. 'I'll be coming here for my book club meetings—it's ideal with the bookshop next door.'

Lizzie soon sensed an immense goodwill towards the new venture. Not, she realised, because of any reputation of hers. Because of Ben and Sandy, she was accepted as a member of the well-loved Morgan clan.

And then there was the Jesse effect. A number of these people were the wedding guests who had discovered her and Jesse kissing on the balcony. She was, and always would be in their eyes, one of 'Jesse's girls' and included in their general affection towards him. Who would have thought it?

From her corner behind the counter, she watched Jesse as he worked the room, towering head and shoulders above most of the guests. Was he aware of how many female eyes followed him? Her eyes were among them. No matter where he was in the café she was conscious of him. It was as if he had some built-in magnet that drew female attention. She was no more immune than the rest of them. She just had to continue to fight it if she was going to be able to work with him.

He'd insisted on wearing the same blue jeans, white T-shirt and butcher-striped full apron in sea tones of blue and aqua as the wait staff. How could a guy look so hot in such pedestrian work-wear? But then a guy as handsome and well-built as Jesse would look good in anything. *Or nothing.* She shook her head to rid both her brain and her libido of such subversive thoughts. Jesse was off-limits—even to her imagination.

He'd arrived this morning before anyone else. 'I'm here to help,' he'd said. 'If I wear the uniform, people will know it.'

'I thought you were here to taste the food,' she'd protested as he'd tied on the apron, succeeding in looking utterly masculine as he did so. The colours of the stripes made his impossibly blue eyes look even bluer.

'I can do both,' he'd said in a tone that brooked no argument.

She'd let it go at that, in truth grateful for the extra help. And he had excelled himself. It appeared he knew most of the guests—and if he didn't he very soon did. Through the hum of conversation, the clatter of cutlery, the noise of chairs scraping on the tiled floor, she could hear the deep tones of his voice as he made people welcome to Bay Bites and talked up the food while he was at it.

If she had hired an expensive public relations consultant they wouldn't have done better than Jesse in promoting the new business.

She froze as she saw him bend his dark head to chat with Evie, the pretty blonde wife of the dairy farmer Jesse had introduced her to on Thursday. Straight away Lizzie had sensed that the girl was more than a mere acquaintance. Sure enough, it turned out she had dated Jesse in high school.

How many other women in this room had Jesse been involved with? *Was involved with right now?*

Was he really a player in the worst sense of the word, moving on once he'd made a conquest? Or was he just a natural-born charmer? She suspected the latter. The nurses in the hospital where he'd been born had prob-

ably gone gaga over him as he'd lain kicking and gurgling in his crib. And she'd bet he'd been a teacher's
pet all the way through school—with the female teach-
ers, anyway.

Evie had come to the taste-testing without her husband; rather she was accompanied by a curvy auburn-
haired girl who was a friend visiting from Sydney.
Lizzie gripped tight onto the edge of the counter as
Evie's companion laughed up at Jesse. She schooled
her face to show no reaction. He could talk and laugh
with whatever woman he pleased. *It was nothing to her.*

That uncomfortable twinge of jealousy she felt as
she watched them was further reason to keep Jesse at
a distance.

Jealousy. She had battled hard with herself to overcome what she saw as a serious character flaw. As a
child she'd been jealous of Sandy, not just for her toys
or pretty dresses, but also because she'd been convinced
her father loved Sandy more than he'd loved her. Thankfully, her mother had identified what was going on and
made sure no rift ever developed between the sisters.
She'd helped the young Lizzie learn to handle jealousy
of other kids at school and later jealousy when she'd
thought people at work had been favoured over her. As
an adult, Lizzie had thought the demon had been well
and truly vanquished. Until she'd met Philippe.

She'd been just twenty-one and working at an up-
market resort in Port Douglas in tropical far northern
Queensland. She had worked hard and played hard with
talented young chefs from around the world on working holidays. Good-looking, charming Philippe had
been way out of her league. But he'd made a play for
her and she'd fallen hard for his French accent and his
live-for-the-moment ways. It hadn't mattered that other

girls never stopped flirting with him because he had
assured her he loved only her. She'd followed him to
France without a moment's hesitation.

But the jealousy demon had reared back into full
flaming life after she'd given birth to Amy. For the
first six months she'd been stuck at home living with
his parents while he'd continued the work-hard-play-
hard lifestyle they'd formerly enjoyed together. And
Philippe had not been the type of man to do without
feminine attention.

Just like Jesse, she thought now as he smiled at the
auburn-haired girl who was hanging onto his every
word. Who could blame the girl for being dazzled by
his movie-star looks and genuine charm? *She couldn't
let it get to her.* Women of all ages gravitated to Jesse
and he gravitated to them. That was the way he was
and it wasn't likely to change. It was the reason above
all others that she could never be more than passing
friendly with him.

If Jesse had been more than a friend, she would by
now be racked with jealousy. It wasn't a feeling she enjoyed. She had hated the jealous, suspicious person she
had become towards the end of her marriage; she never
wanted to go there again.

Jesse must have felt her gaze on him because he
said something to the two women, turned and headed
towards her. He indicated his near-empty tray where
a lone piece of chicken sat in a pile of baby spinach
leaves. 'Want some?'

She shook her head. 'Can't eat. Too concerned with
feeding all of this lot.'

'You're sure? You need to keep your energy up. It's
delicious. Made with free-range chicken breast stuffed

with organic caramelised tomato and locally produced goat's cheese and wrapped in Italian prosciutto.'

She smiled. 'You're doing a good job of selling it to me, but no thanks all the same.'

'Can't let it go to waste,' he said, popping it into his mouth.

'Glad you approve,' she said as he ate the chicken with evident relish. A similar dish had been one of the most popular items in the Sydney restaurant she'd worked in when she'd first come back from France. Served with a salad for lunch, she hoped it would be popular here too.

'The slow-cooked lamb was a huge success,' he said. 'Although some people said they'd prefer an onion relish to the beetroot relish.'

'*Some* people,' she said, arching her brow. 'How many people? One person in particular, perhaps?'

'One in particular has never much liked beetroot. He'd like the onion.'

'So maybe the chef was correct in her guess that that particular person would like the slow-cooked lamb?'

'Maybe.'

'You refuse to admit I was right about what you'd like best?'

'I haven't finished tasting everything yet. I'll let you know at the end. By the way, the asparagus and feta frittata was a big hit with the ladies. I told them it was low calorie, though I don't know whether that's actually true.'

Was he born with an innate knowledge of what appealed to women? Or was it some masculine dark art he practised to enchant and ensnare them? *She could not let herself fall under his spell—it would be only too easy.*

'Make sure you don't miss out on the apple pie, I'm

sure you'll love it,' she said. 'But don't even think of telling anyone it's low calorie. I might get sued when my customers start stacking on the weight.'

He put down the tray, leaned across the counter towards her and spoke in a low voice, his eyes warm with what seemed like genuine concern. 'Seriously, are you pleased how it's going?'

She nodded. 'Really pleased. I don't want to jinx myself but people are booking already for our opening day on Thursday.'

'The buzz is good. I was on door duty a while ago and had to turn passers-by away. Lucky we put the "Closed for Private Function" sign on the door or I reckon we'd have been invaded.'

'I've handed out a lot of leaflets letting people know about the opening hours and menu.'

'So everything is going as planned?'

'I'm happy but—'

'You're not happy with the staff.'

Again, she was surprised at how easily he read her. Especially when he scarcely knew her. 'No. Yes. I mean I'm really happy with the sous chef. He's excellent. In fact he's too good for a café and I doubt we'll keep him.' She glanced back at the kitchen. But with the noise level of the café there was no way the chef could hear her.

'You'll keep him. He's already got one kid and another on the way. He can't afford to leave Dolphin Bay.'

'I don't know whether to be glad for us or sad for him.'

'Try glad for him. He's happy to have a job in his home town. What about the others?'

'The kitchen hand is great with both prep and clearing up and the waitresses are enthusiastic and friendly, which is just what I want.'

'I can hear a "but" coming.'

'The waitress who is also the barista—Nikki. She's a nice girl but not nearly as experienced with making coffee as she said and I'm worried how she'll work under pressure.'

'You know what I said. With a small staff and a reputation to establish you can't afford any weak links.'

'I know. And…thanks for the advice.'

He picked up the tray again, swivelling it on one hand. 'The kitchen is calling.'

She'd noticed how adeptly he'd carried the tray, served the food. 'You know, if you weren't an engineer and helping the world, you'd have a great future in hospitality,' she teased.

'Been there. Done that. I worked as a waiter for an agency while I was at university. I'm only doing it again to help make Bay Bites a success.'

She bet she knew which agency. It employed only the handsomest of handsome men. It figured they'd want Jesse on their books even if only in university vacations.

Jesse took off again, stopping for a quick word with his mother on his way to the kitchen.

Lizzie waved to Maura, and Maura smiled and blew her a kiss. Jesse's mother was a tall, imposing woman with Jesse's blue eyes and black hair, though hers was now threaded with grey. Lizzie had taken up with her again as if it had been yesterday that she'd been a teenager helping her in the kitchen and soaking up the older woman's cooking lore.

Thankfully, Maura had been delighted at the idea of sharing some of the guest house favourites based on the cooking of her Irish youth. They'd made a date for Monday to go through the recipes. *Just to go through the recipes, not to talk about Jesse*, Lizzie reminded herself. Or to do anything as ridiculous as to ask Maura to show her his baby photos. Her thoughts of him being doted over as a baby had sparked a totally unwarranted curiosity to see what he'd looked like as a little boy.

As Jesse picked up a tray of mini muffins, he wondered what the heck he was doing playing at being a waiter in a café. He hadn't enjoyed the time he'd spent in the service industry during university, had only done it to fund his surfing and skiing trips. Being polite to ill-mannered clients of catering companies hadn't been at all to his liking. In fact he'd lost his job when he'd tipped a pitcher of cold water over an obnoxious drunken guest who wouldn't stop harassing one of the young wait-resses. The agency had never hired him again and he hadn't given a damn.

He'd promised to help Sandy with the café but the building work he'd already done was more than his sister-in-law would ever have expected. No. He had to be honest with himself. This café gig was all about Lizzie. Seeing her every day. Being part of her life. And that was a bad, bad idea. Even for two hours a day.

Because he couldn't stop thinking about her. How beautiful she was. Her grace and elegance. Her warmth and humour. Remembering how she'd felt in his arms and how he'd like to have her there again. Her passion-ate response to his kisses and how he'd like—

In short, he was failing dismally in thinking of Lizzie Dumont as a family acquaintance trying to be friends. *Could it ever really be platonic between them?* There would always be an undercurrent of sexual attraction, of possibilities. Even in that white chef's jacket and baggy black pants she looked beautiful. He even found it al-luring the way she tasted food in the kitchen—how she closed her eyes, the way she used her tongue, her murmurs of pleasure when the food tasted the way it should.

Lizzie wasn't sexy in a hip-swinging, cleavage-baring way. But there was something about the way she carried herself, the way she smiled that hinted at the passionate woman he knew existed under her contained exterior.

However, his reasons for not wanting to date her were still there and stopped him from flirting with her, from suggesting they see each other while he was in town. There could be no 'fun while it lasts' scenarios with Lizzie. And the alternative—something more serious—was not on for him. The last time he'd tried serious it had taken him years to recover from the emotional battering.

He had fallen so hard and fast for Camilla he hadn't seen sense. Hadn't realised when he'd talked to her about his feelings she had answered him with weasel words that had had him completely stymied, fooled into thinking she cared for him. He cringed when he thought about how naïve and idealistic he'd been. When he'd proposed to her she had virtually laughed in his face.

No way would he risk going there again with Lizzie. He had to stop looking at her, noticing her, admiring her.

There was also the sobering truth that Lizzie didn't seem to want anything to do with him other than as a family friend. In fact he suspected she disapproved of him.

He'd noticed the way she'd watched him as he'd worked the room, offering samples of food, talking up the café, Lizzie's skills as a chef, the bookshop next door, how it would all work when Bay Bites opened. He'd talked to guys too, but it was the women who'd wanted to linger and chat. As it always had been. And Lizzie was clocking that female attention.

Ever since he'd turned fourteen women had made it obvious they found him attractive. *'You don't even have to try, you lucky dog,'* Ben had often said when they were younger.

When his mates had been trying to talk girls into their beds he'd been trying to get them out of his. Literally. More than once he'd come home and found a girl he scarcely knew had climbed through his bedroom window and was waiting for him, naked in his bed.

He'd found that a turn-off rather than a turn-on. He'd had to ask them to leave in the nicest possible way without hurting their feelings. When Jesse made love to a woman it was always going to be memorable— and his choice.

His brother Ben stopped him to snag first one muffin then another from his tray. 'Sure I can't convince you to stay in Dolphin Bay and work here? With your way with the ladies, I reckon we'll double the numbers of female customers. Look at them, flocking to your side like they've always done.'

'Ha ha,' he said, ignoring the bait, conscious that Lizzie might overhear the conversation with his brother.

As he'd said to Lizzie, his prowess with the opposite sex was greatly exaggerated. And he hadn't taken advantage of his gift with women. He had always been honest about his feelings. Dated one girl at a time. Made it clear when he wasn't looking for anything serious. Bailed before anyone got hurt. Let her tell everyone *she* had dumped *him*. Had stayed friends with his ex-girlfriends—as far as their boyfriends or husbands would allow.

But today, seeing himself through Lizzie's eyes, he

wasn't so sure he was comfortable with all that any more. Most of his Dolphin Bay friends were married now. Though the guys moaned and complained about being tied down, he didn't actually believe them when they said they envied him his life. They seemed too content.

Now he sometimes wondered what they really thought about him being single as he faced turning thirty. He knew the townsfolk had laid bets on him always staying a bachelor. It was beginning to bug him. But he had never treated their interest in his ladies' man reputation as anything other than a laugh; never talked about the reasons he'd stayed on his own.

He hadn't told anyone in Dolphin Bay—even his family—about what had happened with Camilla. Had never confided how the deaths of his sister-in-law Jodi and little nephew Liam had affected him. How terrified he'd been at seeing Ben suffer the life-destroying pain caused by the loss of love. On the cusp of manhood, Jesse had resolved he would never endure what Ben had endured. He'd put the brakes on any relationship that threatened to get serious.

Gradually, however, he'd realised Ben's pain should not be his pain. That he had to love his own way, take his own risks. He'd let down his guard by the time he'd met Camilla and hurtled into a relationship with her. Only for her callous rejection of his love to send him right back behind his barricades.

Was that enough now?

He looked over to Lizzie but she had disappeared into the kitchen again. He'd seen yet another side of her today. Calm. Competent. Ruthlessly efficient under pressure. He liked it.

He admired her for her commitment. Surely a café

serving toasted ham and cheese sandwiches—even if she called them *croque monsieur*—was a huge comedown for someone with Lizzie's career credentials. Dolphin Bay must be just a pit stop for Lizzie. She had a half-French daughter. How long before she got fed up with flipping fried eggs and turned her sights back to Europe?

Or did he have that wrong? It was logical for him to base future plans purely on his career. Maybe it wasn't so for Lizzie. She was a mother—perhaps that was why she could settle for Bay Bites? Maybe because it was in the best interests of her daughter.

He couldn't imagine how it would be to put someone else first. Wife. Child. Suiting himself had seemed just fine up to now. *A charming Peter Pan*. That was what Camilla had called him at their most recent encounter. She'd said it with a laugh. Hadn't meant it to sound like an insult. But it had stung just the same. And made him think.

He headed back into the fray. 'Be quick before these muffins are all snatched off the tray,' he said to the nice redhead friend of Evie's. 'They're made with organically grown rhubarb, locally produced sour cream—in fact from Evie's farm—and—'

The girl picked one up from the tray, sniffed it, broke off a piece, tasted it. 'And pure maple syrup from the forests of Quebec, if I'm not wrong—together with Queensland pecans,' she pronounced.

He stared at her, taken aback. 'Sounds good to me. I'll check with the chef.' He must ask Lizzie. He really wasn't cut out to be a waiter.

Lizzie slumped in one of the bentwood chairs, exhausted. The guests had gone. The clearing up was done. The staff dismissed. Only Sandy, Ben and Jesse remained.

Sandy was incandescent with joy. 'Ever since I first set foot in the bookshop, I dreamed of there being a café next door. If today was an indication of how it's going to turn out, I think my dream is on its way to coming true. Thanks to my sister.'

She grabbed both Lizzie's hands and pulled her to her feet. 'Hug,' she commanded. Lizzie smiled and did as she was told. If she could repay Sandy's kindness with a successful café she'd be happy.

'C'mon, Ben too,' said Sandy. 'And you, too, Jesse. Group hug. Family hug.'

Alarmed, Lizzie stiffened. 'I don't think—'

But, before she knew it, both she and Sandy were enveloped in a bear hug from tall, blond Ben whom she already loved as a brother. Then Jesse joined in and it was a different feeling altogether. Every nerve went on alert as she felt Jesse's strong arms around her, was pulled against the solid wall of his chest, breathed in his maleness and warmth. Could he feel her heart pounding at his nearness?

She could never, ever think of Jesse as a brother.

And right at this moment it was darn near impossible to think of him only as a friend.

CHAPTER SEVEN

THE NEXT DAY, mid-morning, Jesse drove from the boat-house where he was staying towards Silver Gull beach. He knew the surf would be flat with just the occasional swell; he'd checked it while he was on his early morning run just after dawn. But that didn't bother him. Surfing wasn't possible right now, with his shoulder injury. He couldn't paddle out to where the waves would usually be breaking and he couldn't use his shoulders to get him into a wave. That right shoulder was aching today. Carrying all those food-laden trays yesterday probably hadn't been the wisest thing he could have done in terms of shoulder rehabilitation.

But he could swim. Cautiously. No freestyle. But some breaststroke. Maybe some back-kick that left his shoulders right out of it. Heck, just to float around would be better than nothing.

The beach should be near-deserted at this time of morning. It wasn't as popular as Big Ray, which was one of the reasons he liked it. All the early morning run-ners and dog walkers would have gone home by now and October wasn't yet peak swimming season. Al-though it was gloriously sunny, with very little breeze, the water was still too cold for all but the intrepid to swim without a wetsuit.

The first thing he saw as he approached the beach access was Lizzie's small blue hatchback parked carefully off the road. He didn't know whether to be glad or annoyed she was here. The more he saw of her, the more he was perturbed by his attraction to her. That group hug the night before had tested his endurance. Having Lizzie back in his arms—well, half of Lizzie considering the nature of a group hug—had brought desire for her rushing back in a major way. He hadn't stopped thinking about her since.

For a long moment he left the engine idling. Go or stay?

No contest, he thought as he killed the engine. It wasn't a good idea for Lizzie to be swimming by herself. Not at Silver Gull with its dangerous rip undertow that could pull an unwary swimmer out to sea. He needed to keep an eye on her, keep her safe. He zipped himself into his wetsuit, grabbed a towel and headed towards the sand dunes that bordered the southern end of the beach.

As he'd thought, there wasn't another soul there. Almost straight away he saw Lizzie on the sand halfway between where the gum trees grew down to the edge of the beach and where the small breaking waves swirled up onto the sand in lacy white foam. She was lying on her back on a bright pink towel, her lovely body covered only by a turquoise and white checked bikini. Her long slender limbs were stretched out in total relaxation, her pale hair loose and glinting like silver in the sunlight, an expression of bliss on her face.

Jesse clenched his fists by his sides and a cold sweat broke out on his forehead. It would have been better if he'd kept on driving and gone to a different beach.

He could not deny there had been times since he'd

met Lizzie that he had wondered how she looked under her clothes. But the reality of her in the skimpy bikini far surpassed any fantasy—her breasts high and round, her hips flaring gently, her body slender not skinny. She was perfect in every way. He couldn't help but observe that she had certainly filled out since her teenage years.

He coughed to alert her to his presence, not wanting to be seen to stare at her for so long it could be perceived as untoward. Startled, she sat up quickly, looked up at him. She took off her sunglasses and then used her hand to shade her eyes, blinking to focus on him. 'Jesse. You…you surprised me.'

He wasn't sure whether it was shock or pleasure he saw in her eyes. 'Catching some rays?' he asked, trying to sound casual when all he could think about was how sexy she looked in that bikini. Of how, in fact, the design of a bikini didn't so much cover up but draw attention.

'I desperately need to get some colour,' she said, stretching out her arms with unconscious grace. 'Feeling the sun on my skin is heaven. There won't be much beach time once the café opens.'

Already the smooth skin of her shoulders was tinged with gold. 'Are you planning to swim?' he asked.

She turned to look towards the water, calm, translucent, sparkling in the sunlight as far as the eye could see. 'Just thinking about it now. The water looks so inviting.'

'It will be very cold in.'

She indicated the beach bag to the left side of the towel. 'I borrowed Sandy's wetsuit.'

He gritted his teeth. 'Might be an idea to put it on.'

'I will soon. I'm enjoying—'

'Put it on now, will you.' His voice came out harsher than he had intended.

She frowned. 'But—'

'I can't talk to you while you're wearing that bikini.' He spoke somewhere over her head, not trusting himself to look at her.

'But it's a modest bikini—'

'It does nothing to hide what a beautiful body you have. That's more than a guy who's trying to be just friends can take.'

'Oh,' she said and blushed so the colour on her cheeks rivalled that of her towel.

He tossed her his navy striped towel. 'Here. Cover up, will you.'

She caught the towel. 'Sure. I didn't think…' She pulled his towel around her, twisting to tuck it into her bikini top between her breasts. *Lucky towel.* Then she went to get up from the sand.

Automatically, he offered her his hand to help her. For a long moment she just stared at it with an expression he couldn't read. Then she put her narrow hand in his much larger one. He pulled her to her feet, unable to keep his eyes from how lovely she was.

She faced him, standing very still. She was tall, but he was taller and she had to look up to him, exposing her slender neck, her delicate throat where he could see a pulse throbbing. Their gazes locked. Her grey eyes seemed brighter, perhaps reflecting the blue of the sky and the sea. 'Thank you,' she murmured.

Jesse still held her hand and when she made no effort to free it he tightened his grip—now he had her so close he couldn't bear to let her go. He noticed a few grains of sand sprinkled on her cheek, maybe from where she'd pushed her hair away from her face. Reluctant to let go of her hand, he used his other hand to gently wipe off the tiny grains from where they adhered to her smooth skin.

She closed her eyes with a flutter of long fair lashes and he could feel her tremble beneath his touch as his fingers then traced down her cheek towards her mouth. He traced the outline of her soft, lovely mouth with his fingers and now it was he who trembled with awareness and a stunned disbelief she wasn't pushing him away.

Her lips parted just enough for her to breathe out a slow sigh and open her eyes. Jesse saw in them both wariness and desire. 'Jesse, I...' Whatever she might have been about to say faltered to nothing. She swayed towards him.

He dropped his hand and used it to take her other hand and pull her closer to him, so close he could feel the heat from her sun-warmed body. He pressed his mouth to hers in a soft questioning kiss—she gave him the answer he wanted with the pressure of her lips back on his. As he deepened the kiss he felt the same fierce surge of possessive hunger he'd felt the first time he'd kissed her. Had kissed her, then been parted from her through a stupid misunderstanding before he'd had the chance to think about what that flare of attraction between them could mean.

Six months between kisses and she tasted the same. Felt the same. And he wanted her just as much—more. She kissed him back with a fierce intensity that sent a surge of excitement pulsing through him. He dropped his hands so he could lock his arms around her. With a little murmur she wound her arms around his neck and pulled him close. The towel slid to the sand between them. 'Leave it,' he growled against her mouth then slanted and deepened the angle of his kiss.

The longing for her he'd been holding back overwhelmed him. All this platonic friendship stuff was bulldust as far as he was concerned. He'd wanted her from the time she'd first swept him up with her warmth and laughter, set him the challenge of that cool exterior and the promise of passion beneath. He slid his hands up her slender waist, skimmed her small, firm breasts as her heart thudded under his hand and she gasped under his mouth.

There were master chefs, master sommeliers, master chocolatiers—but Jesse was truly a master kisser, Lizzie mused, her thoughts barely coherent through a fizz of excitement. Delicious shivers of pleasure tingled across her skin as Jesse worked seductive magic with his lips and tongue. The scrape of the stubble on his chin was an exciting contrast to the softness of his mouth; the hard strength of his body to the tenderness of his hands on her bare skin. The last man to kiss her had been Jesse six months ago. The way he kissed her now was everything she'd remembered, everything that had excited her that night on the balcony and awoken needs she'd tried to deny.

She'd been daydreaming about him when she'd been lying on the beach—and then suddenly he'd been there, as if conjured up from her fantasies. She was so dazed that before she knew it she was in his arms, with no time to worry about whether it was right, wrong or ill-advised. Another public kiss with Jesse? Her craving to be close to him was so strong the possibility of being caught again, being teased again, had scarcely registered.

Jesse looked so hot in that wetsuit, the tight black

fabric moulding his broad chest, flat belly, muscular limbs. Unshaven, his black hair carelessly tousled as if he'd just run his hand through it in his hurry to get to the beach, he'd never looked more should-be-on-billboards handsome. When he'd taken her hand to help her up from the sand, she'd known where it would lead. Known and felt dizzy with anticipation.

Now she kissed him back, lost in the overwhelming pleasure of being with Jesse again. She'd found it impossible to clamp down on her attraction to him—no matter how many times she'd told herself Jesse wasn't right for her. She might be able to deny herself that Belgian chocolate—but not this.

Desire bloomed in the tightening of her nipples, the ache to be closer, and she tightened her arms around his neck, breathing in the intoxicating scent of his skin. Wanting him. Craving more than kisses. She had never been kissed the way Jesse kissed. Jesse the master kisser would be Jesse the master lover and she shivered in sensual anticipation of the discovery.

What was she thinking? She stilled in his embrace.

She could not let herself want Jesse this much. Too many other women wanted Jesse. It would only lead to heartbreak, to agony. *He couldn't give her what she needed.*

She broke the kiss and drew away, pushing against his chest, her breath ragged. He murmured a protest and gathered her back into his arms but he let her go when she continued to maintain her resistance. His expression, passion fading to bewilderment and—yes— hurt wrenched at her heart. She hated that she was the cause of that.

What had just happened was purely physical, she reminded herself. Oh, she wanted Jesse all right. And the more she'd got to like him, the more she'd wanted him. But she needed to be cherished, loved for herself, not be the latest in a line of conquests. She wanted to love and be loved—but she also wanted to trust.

How hard would it be to trust a player again?

'Jesse, I can't do this. I won't do this.' Her voice came out wobblier than she would have liked. But Jesse got the message.

He choked out just the one word. 'Why?'

Jesse gulped in deep breaths of salt-tangy air to try and get back his equilibrium. He was convinced that Lizzie had enjoyed being with him as much as he'd enjoyed being with her. He could see her aroused nipples through the fabric of her bikini top. She was flushed, her eyes dilated, her mouth swollen from his kisses. She had never looked lovelier.

But she turned away from him. Bent down and picked up his towel where it lay rumpled on the sand at her feet. With hands that weren't steady she draped it around her shoulders but it covered less than it revealed. *He wanted her so much it hurt*.

She twisted the corner of the towel until it was scrunched into a knot, untwisted it and twisted it again before she looked back up at him. 'Because all those reasons that make it a bad idea for us to get together are still there,' she said.

Somewhere in the realm of good sense he knew that. Hell, he had his reasons too. Desire this strong could lead to pain as wrenching as Camilla had inflicted on him. But his body didn't want to listen to his brain. He wanted Lizzie and he wanted her now. If not now this afternoon, this evening, tonight—and hang the consequences.

'It was…a mistake. We have to forget it happened. This…this shouldn't ch-change anything between us,' she stammered.

He cleared his throat. 'How can it *not* change things between us?'

She looked up at him, her eyes huge in the oval of her face. 'Jesse, I want you so much I'm aching for you.' Her voice caught and she took in a deep breath but it did nothing to steady it. 'If…if things were different there's nothing more I'd want than to make love with you right now.'

He made a disbelieving grunt in response.

'Oh, not on the beach. But back in my apartment. In a hotel room. At your place. Somewhere private where we could explore each other, please each other, satisfy our curiosity about each other. Even…even if that was all we ever had.'

He groaned and when he spoke his voice was edged with anger. 'Do you realise what you're doing talking to me like that? Don't be a—'

'A tease? Believe me, I'm not teasing.' She swallowed hard. 'In the six months since I last saw you, even though I thought you'd gone off with another woman, I dreamed of you. I kept waking up from dreams of you. Wanting you. Aching for you. Reaching for you, to find only an empty bed.'

'Then why—?'

'Because desire isn't enough.' She took in another of those deep breaths that made her breasts swell over her bikini top in such a tantalising way. 'I'm sometimes accused of being blunt but I have to be honest with you,' she said.

He swallowed a curse word. Whenever anyone used that 'honest' phrase he knew he was about to hear something he didn't want to hear. Lizzie's expression didn't give him cause to think otherwise.

'Fire away,' he said through gritted teeth.

'I've told you, right now there's no room in my life for a man.' She was having trouble meeting his eyes. Not a good sign. 'But if I do start to date again, I want it to be someone…someone serious, dependable, reliable. Not—'

'Not someone like me,' he finished for her, his voice brusque.

She bit her lip. 'That didn't come out well, did it?' she said with a quiver to her voice. 'It's not that you're not gorgeous. You are. In fact you're too gorgeous.'

'I don't know how being told I'm gorgeous sounds like an insult, but I get the gist of it.'

Her eyes widened. 'I didn't want that to sound like an insult. I wouldn't want to hurt you for the world.'

I wouldn't want to hurt you for the world. Jesse felt uncomfortably aware that he had used something like that phrase more than once when kindly breaking up with a woman. But those words directed at him did not feel good. They made him feel scorned like he'd felt when Camilla had rejected him—though she hadn't been as kind about it as Lizzie was being.

'No offence taken,' he said gruffly.

'I…I'm not very good at this,' she said, looking down at the ground, scuffing the sand with her bare foot.

Amazing that while she was thrusting the knife deep into his gut and then twisting it, he felt sorry for her having to deliver the message. In the interests of being *honest.*

'No one is good at it,' he said.

'I do want to try to explain. Because…because I've come to really like you.'

Like. It was a runner-up word. A consolation prize word. A loser word. How could he have exposed himself again to this?

'Continue,' he said gruffly.

'My ex was a good-looking guy with the charisma to go with it. I was always having to look over my shoulder to see what woman was pursuing him, what woman he was encouraging.'

'He was a *player*, right?' He practically spat out that word he was getting sick of hearing applied to him.

She nodded. 'I never want to endure a relationship with someone like that again. I can't live with that feeling that I'm not the only woman in my man's life. To be always suspicious of girls he works with, girls he encounters anywhere. I want to come first, last and in between with a man. Not...not always feeling humiliated and rejected.'

Jesse clenched his fists by his sides. He wasn't that guy. How could she be so wrong about him? A nagging inner voice gave him the answer. *Because that's the way you appear.* He'd done such a good job of acting the player to cover up his fears and pain that he'd given Lizzie the wrong impression of him.

It was true, over the years he'd been flattered by all that female attention. *But he didn't want it now.* He didn't want people taking bets on his marital status. Most of all he didn't want Lizzie so unfairly lumping him in a category of cheats and heartbreakers.

'What makes you think I'm like your ex-husband? You're implying that he cheated on you—I've never cheated or been unfaithful to a girlfriend. *Never.*'

'I...I believe you,' she said but her eyes told a different story. She'd stuck him in the same category as her ex and nothing he'd done—or the reputation he had acquired—had changed her mind.

He was not the guy she thought he was. He had to prove that to her.

'What happened at the wedding to cause you to think I'd gone off with another woman was a misunderstanding,' he said. 'So what makes you think I live up to my reputation?'

Her smile was shaky. 'Women adore you. Not just young attractive women who want to date you. Older women dote on you. Ex-girlfriends like Evie want you still in their life. Even children are fans. Amy was beside herself with excitement when I told her on the phone last night that Uncle Jesse would be here when she got back from France. You were such a hit with her at the wedding when you danced her right around the room.'

He frowned. 'And that's a bad thing? Would you prefer I was the kind of guy women loathed? Feared even?'

'Of course not.' She shook her head as if to clear her thoughts. 'I'm not getting this across at all well, am I? Fact is, it's not all about you; it's—'

He put up his hand. 'Whoa. If you're going to say "it's not you; it's me" forget it, I don't want to hear that old cliché.'

'What I'm trying to tell you is that I...I'm a jealous person.' She looked down at her feet for a moment as if she was ashamed of her words before she faced him again. 'A jealous woman and a chick-magnet guy are not a good combination, as I found out in my marriage. It wasn't just his infidelity that ended it; my jealousy and suspicion made it impossible for us to live with each other.'

'In my book, infidelity is unforgivable.' He clenched his jaw.

She looked across him and out to sea as if gathering her words before she faced him again. 'There…there can be shades of grey…'

He shook his head. 'Fidelity is non-negotiable. No cheating, end of story. If either party cheats—the relationship is over. For good.'

Did she believe him? Or had she heard too many lies from that ex-husband to believe an honest guy?

Her brow furrowed. 'That stance is not…not what I would have expected of you.'

'You've been listening to gossips.' He snorted in disgust. 'What would they know about my private life? You think I don't know about betrayal? You think I haven't been hurt?'

'I…I only know what I've heard.' She bit down on her lower lip, her face a picture of misery.

'I thought I'd found the woman I wanted to be with for the rest of my life. Turned out she was a cheat and a liar. But I don't lie or cheat. Never have. Never will.'

'I'm sorry, Jesse, if I got it wrong. But I can't take risks when it comes to men. For my sake and for my daughter's.' Only then came that familiar tilt to her chin. 'No matter how much I might want that man.'

He glanced down at the small scars on her hands and forearms. Scars she'd got in the kitchen, she'd told him, from burning oil and scalding steam and knives that had slipped. Now he realised she had scars on the inside too. Her ex-husband—and maybe before that her father—had chipped away at her trust, at her belief that she could inspire lasting love and fidelity. *That she deserved to be cherished and honoured.*

Whoa. He wasn't thinking the L word here. Just the

crazy attraction. Then the friendship. And the other L word. He realised how much in these last few days he had grown to like and admire Lizzie. In this context, 'like' was not a loser word. It was a feeling that built on that instant physical attraction to something that packed a powerful punch.

Lizzie was right—the reasons they both had for keeping the other at friend status were still there. He didn't want to put his heart on the line again and he didn't want to risk wounding her with further scars.

He ached to take her in his arms again but had no intention of doing so. It wasn't what she wanted. She didn't need a man like him in her life.

'I'd like to give you a big hug but...but I don't think it's a good idea,' he said, trying to sound offhand but failing dismally, betrayed by the hitch in his voice.

Warm colour flushed her cheeks. 'I agree. And... and no more kissing. I can't deal with how it makes me feel.'

He realised how vulnerable she was under that blunt-speaking front.

'No more kissing,' he agreed though he hated the idea of never being able to kiss her again.

She looked up at him, eyes huge, hair a silver cloud around her face. 'Jesse, I...I wasn't lying when I said how much I liked you. I do count you as a friend now.'

He nodded. 'Yeah. I like you too. We're friends.' But he didn't offer his hand to shake on it. No touching. No kissing. No physical contact of any kind. That was how it would have to be. No matter how difficult that stance would be to maintain when he had to see her every day.

He looked towards the water. It was still a low swell. Still good for swimming. And he needed to get in there.

Physical activity was always his way of dealing with stress and difficult situations. 'Are you going to swim?' he asked her.

She shook her head. 'I should be getting back to the café.'

Good. He didn't want her to join him in that water. Splashing around with her in a wetsuit moulded close to her curves would be more than he could endure.

'I'm going in,' he said. 'This is my favourite beach and I want to spend as much time as I can here while I'm home.'

She walked back to where her towel and bag were on the sand. She picked up her pink towel and turned her back to him as she swapped his towel for hers. Her back view was beautiful, with her hair tumbling around her shoulders, her narrow waist and shapely behind. *He wanted her but he couldn't have her.* He turned his head away. 'Just leave my towel there,' he said gruffly.

'Will you…will you be coming to the café today?' she asked, facing him again.

He hadn't given her two hours of help today but he needed distance from her. 'No. I'm driving to Sydney tonight.'

'Oh,' she said.

'I've got an appointment tomorrow with the orthopaedic specialist for my shoulder,' he said. And he had a video interview with the executives of the company in Houston. 'I'll see you when I get back.'

He was going to find it difficult working those two hours a day with her for the rest of his time back home in Dolphin Bay. But he had a commitment to Sandy that he would honour. He also wanted to be a friend to Lizzie now that they'd got this far.

But if she was to respect him as something other than a good-looking player—even in the context of a family connection friendship—he had to prove that the Jesse of his reputation and the real Jesse were not one and the same.

CHAPTER EIGHT

IT WAS SEVEN o'clock on the morning of the official opening of Bay Bites and the café doors were due to open
in half an hour for their very first breakfast service.
Lizzie had been working in the kitchen since five. She
was confident she and her team had done all they could
to prepare but still she was so nervous she had to keep
wiping her hands down the side of her apron.

She'd worked at a start-up before. But not as the
person in charge. It was a very different matter taking orders in the kitchen from someone else compared
to being the one responsible for the success or failure
of the venture. She twirled that piece of her hair that
always escaped when she tied back her hair so hard it
tugged at her scalp and made her wince. *What if no
one showed up?*

That line of thought was crazy; she knew that—
they had confirmed bookings for breakfast, brunch and
lunch. Okay, so some of them were Morgan family and
friends who had promised to be there to show support.
But they would only be there the first few days; after
that it would be up to word-of-mouth and reputation for
the business to work.

Sandy, whose background was in advertising and
marketing, had told her not to worry about all that—it

was up to her to promote the new business. It was up to Lizzie to make the food—and the coffee—good enough for people to return again and again. It was all about the food, Sandy had said several times.

Lizzie took a deep steadying breath. She was confident the food was good, that she could hold up her end of the deal. Service had to be good too. Fingers crossed that Nikki, the young barista, could deal with the pressure.

She kept looking up to see if any early customers had arrived yet. The best marketing for a café was a line of people waiting to get in—though the line couldn't be so long that it put people off.

She was packing one of the big glass jars with freshly baked salted caramel and pecan cookies. She looked up again. And then again. But in the end she had to admit to herself she wasn't looking for early customers peering through the plate-glass windows. She was looking for Jesse.

Jesse, who had taken off to Sydney on Sunday, telling her he wouldn't be back until Wednesday evening.

One part of her was upset he would go to Sydney just days before the café was due to open. Another part of her knew she had no right to expect him to be there to help her with all those last-minute things. Especially when she had told him in no uncertain terms she would never want to date him. Both Sandy and Ben had been there after hours to help instead.

Of course the kisses on the beach had changed things between them. How could they not? The kisses at the wedding had been with a hot guy she scarcely knew. But the beach kisses had been with her friend Jesse, a man she'd got to like and in whose company she felt at ease. His kisses had been sensuous, exciting, arousing—but, more than that, it had felt somehow *right* to be sharing such pleasure with Jesse. In spite of all the strikes against him.

She missed him. She missed him more than she could have imagined. She missed his laugh, she missed his manly way of getting things done, most of all she missed that wonderful feeling of being in his arms. Had she been mistaken about him?

She thought about what she'd said to him on the beach, when she'd tried to be honest, but had succeeded only in wounding him—she'd seen the hurt in his eyes. Was she wrong in filing him under P for Player, with a sub-category of H for Heartbreaker? Had she misjudged him? After all, she still didn't know him that well. But what she'd got to know she liked. Liked a lot.

Her caution stemmed from his reputation. But surely her own sister wouldn't have warned her against him if there hadn't been something to be cautious about?

She'd met Philippe when she was twenty-one and had only had one serious boyfriend before him and none after him. Truth was, she didn't have a lot of man mileage on the clock and not a lot of experience on which to make judgements.

Delicious smells wafted into the café, reminding her she needed to be back in that kitchen. Tension was mounting. There had been raised voices, tears, the odd thrown utensil but now all was calm efficiency again.

By seven-twenty a.m. there was a line-up outside the door. By seven forty-five she was so run off her feet she didn't have time to worry about missing Jesse. By eight-thirty young Nikki was in such a fluster managing the constant orders for coffee, Lizzie could see customers tapping impatiently on table tops waiting for their cappuccino, skinny lattes, flat whites and so on. Nightmare!

As she plated an order for French toast with car-amelised bananas and blueberries she tried to think what to do. Ask Sandy if she could borrow another waitress from the Hotel Harbourside? Make coffees herself? She'd run through the machine a few times to familiarise herself with it and could probably churn out a halfway acceptable beverage.

Whatever she did, she had to keep calm—if she didn't the whole place would fall apart. She'd have to expect teething problems, Jesse had said. But paying customers were harsh critics. A café would live or die on the reputation of its coffee—if she didn't fix the coffee problem Bay Bites would be going backwards on its first day.

Then, at eight thirty-five, Jesse was there. In the kitchen beside her, tying on his blue-striped apron, joking to the staff that he'd be in trouble with the boss for being tardy.

Her breath caught in her throat and her heart started to hammer so fast she felt giddy. *Jesse.* She ached to throw her arms around him and tell him how glad she was to see him. How she'd felt as though part of her was missing when he wasn't here. But that couldn't happen. They were friends. And he was talking to her as if she were the boss and he was the volunteer helper who was late for work. As it should be, of course. She swallowed down hard on a wave of irrational disap-pointment.

'I got caught up so couldn't get here until now,' he explained with nothing more than courtesy.

She didn't care where he'd been, just so long as he was with her now. She forced her voice to sound pro-fessional and boss-like. 'I'm so glad you're here. Nikki isn't coping with the coffee. If I can ask—'

'I'll take over the coffee machine.'

'What do you mean? How can you do that?'

'I worked a coffee machine when I was a student. Got quite good at it.'

'You didn't tell me.'

'Thought I'd be too rusty to be of any use to you. While I was in Sydney I did a barista course to get me up to speed.'

'You *what?*'

He pulled out a folded up sheet of paper from one pocket then a glasses case from the other. He put on black-framed glasses and unfolded the paper. 'It's a certificate proving I'm officially accredited as a barista. Turns out since I last did this, I first had to do a course in kitchen hygiene so I've got that qualification there too.' He added the last sentence in his mock modest, self-deprecating way she liked so much.

Lizzie didn't know what shocked her most—the fact Jesse had gone to Sydney to train as a barista or how hot he looked in glasses. It added a whole extra layer of hotness to his appeal—not that he actually needed any extra layers.

She lowered her voice so the chef and the kitchen hand who were working nearby couldn't overhear her. 'Why did you do it?'

'I knew you were worried about Nikki. I wanted to help. But I wanted to make sure I wouldn't be more hindrance than help if I'd forgotten how to froth the milk. Turns out I hadn't. And I got a good score for my coffee art, too.'

She stared at him. 'You can do coffee art?'

'Rosettes, hearts. I need some more practice to do a dolphin but I'll get there,' he said, deadpan.

'I'm seriously impressed,' she said. *He'd done it for her and her heart skipped a beat at the thought.*

'It's just steamed milk on espresso, not difficult really.'

As a chef, she knew presentation was a big part of customer appreciation. These days, people had very high expectations of their coffee; they wanted it to look good as well as taste good.

'There's more than that to it; I didn't know you were an artist.' Then she remembered he'd studied art in high school. She was beginning to realise she still had a lot to learn about Jesse. What other surprises were waiting to be discovered?

He shrugged and then winced. 'Your shoulder? What did the doctor say?' she asked.

'It's healing much better than expected,' he said. 'I can probably go back to work soon.'

Her heart plummeted to the level of her clogs.

'That's good,' she said, forcing her voice to be level.

At the back of her mind she'd thought she'd at least have a few more weeks with him around. But there was no time to ask what he intended to do. It would have to wait. Even in the few minutes she'd been speaking to him the orders were piling up.

Jesse got down to business. 'Give Nikki a break from the coffee machine. I'll take over. Let her wait tables. Later I'll spend some time training her and we'll see if she's good enough to stay.'

Lizzie was too darn grateful that Jesse was back to ask him if he was only going to be there for the two hours he'd defined as his time with her.

The last thing Jesse had thought he'd ever be doing again was making coffee for customers. He was a highly regarded engineer, considered an expert in the quick construction of mass pre-fabricated housing, who had a major corporation jockeying for his skills. He'd had a teleconference with the CEO of the company while he was in Sydney and again they had expressed their keenness in having him on board. They were, in fact, pressuring him to make a decision.

But he also wanted to prove to Lizzie he was not the shallow womaniser she seemed to believe he was. The player label she'd been only too ready to tag him with was really beginning to irk him.

The gratitude and relief on Lizzie's face when he'd told her about the barista course was enough to justify his decision. He'd sensed there'd be trouble with Nikki and had taken the steps that would enable him to help Lizzie achieve her aim of a wrinkle-free launch.

But he'd missed her while he'd been in Sydney. Missed her so much his future—be it in Texas or Asia or wherever he might end up—had seemed somehow bleak without her in it in some way. Never had a hotel room seemed so lonely. The way he'd felt raised questions he wasn't sure of the answers to. He forced himself not to think about it and focused his attention on making coffee.

Flat white, cappuccino, espresso, soy latte, decaf—the orders kept on coming and he kept on filling them. He knew half the customers and had to put up with a lot of good-natured banter.

His answer to the inevitable, 'Hey, Jesse, why the new career path?' was always, 'To help out Sandy and Ben while I'm on leave.'

No way would he admit to anyone that he was doing it with the aim of proving to Lizzie that he was not the guy she thought he was.

But there were customers he didn't know too, total strangers who'd found their way to Bay Bites. People with no connection to the family would be the lifeblood of the new business. Those and the tourists who would eat here a few times, recommend it to their friends, come back next time. He'd noticed lots of empty plates and contented faces. He'd also seen customers photographing their meals with their phones. Free Wi-Fi in the café would pretty much guarantee there would be online reviews up by evening.

He looked up to see Evie's redhead friend he'd met at the taste-test had settled herself at a table and was perusing a menu. She caught his eye and waved. What was her name? Dell, that was right, Dell.

She came up to the counter to say hello. 'Nothing like a handsome barista to bring in business,' she said with her easy, friendly manner.

He smiled. 'I'm also on the front line if they don't like the coffee. But I haven't had any thrown back at me yet.'

Dell smiled back. 'So far, so good, huh? The menu is impressive.'

'All Lizzie's work; I'm just the help.'

'Evie told me Lizzie is a chef who worked in some top restaurants in France and then in Sydney too.'

'That's true,' he said. 'She's highly regarded and has won all sorts of awards.' He felt a swell of unexpected pride in recounting Lizzie's achievements.

'So what brings her to Dolphin Bay?'

'Family,' he said firmly. He was protective of Lizzie's personal life when it came to discussing it with strangers. No one needed to know about her broken marriage, her ongoing custody issues. *The Morgans looked after their own.*

Dell nodded. 'I hope it all goes well for her.'

Just then Lizzie came out of the kitchen. Immediately Jesse felt her gaze go from him to Dell and back to him. Was that jealousy he saw glinting in her narrowed grey eyes? If so, there wasn't much he could do about it but reassure her she had nothing to worry about. Women liked him. He liked women. But he was not flirting with this girl. And Dell was certainly not sending off any flirty vibes. How could he let Lizzie know that?

He beckoned Lizzie over and introduced her to Dell. 'Dell's been saying some very nice things about the menu.'

'Yes,' said Dell with a friendly smile 'I was at your taste-test party on Saturday. Everything I tried was superb. Kudos to you.'

'Thank you,' said Lizzie.

'And I was saying to your boyfriend that every café needs a handsome barista.'

Lizzie flushed. 'Jesse's not my—'

'We're friends,' Jesse was quick to say. 'Just friends.'

'My mistake,' said Dell. 'I thought… Anyway, I'd better get back to my table and stop holding you guys up. It looks busy.'

'Nothing the kitchen can't handle,' said Lizzie a little stiffly.

Dell rewarded her with a big smile. 'I'm looking forward to my lunch. Congratulations, the café is awesome. I'll bring my guy with me next time; I know he'll love it too.'

Now, at last, Lizzie smiled back. Jesse was puzzled by her sudden change of attitude. Was this some kind of girl talk he wasn't privy too? Had Dell given her a secret semaphore message to make her thaw?

Whatever, he didn't have time to worry about it as the lunchtime coffee orders stepped up. He had worked way more than his allocated two hours but who was counting?

CHAPTER NINE

LIZZIE DIDN'T KNOW how she could thank Jesse enough for what he'd done. To train as a barista just to help her out wasn't something she'd ever imagined Jesse would do. It had caused a radical shift in her opinion of him.

'You saved the day,' she said as they shut up shop at four p.m. Everyone else had gone home and they were the last two remaining in the café, empty now but somehow still echoing with the energy of all the meals cooked, eaten and enjoyed. Bay Bites had been well and truly launched. They'd even sold two paintings. She looked up at Jesse. 'Did I tell you how much I appreciate what you did?'

'Only about a gazillion times, but you can say it again if you like,' he said with the laid-back smile that had appealed to her from the get-go.

'So here's my "thank you number gazillion and one",' she said. 'No matter how good a job we did with the food, our opening day would have been a fail if we hadn't had good coffee.'

'It was far from a fail, Lizzie,' Jesse said. 'I think you can chalk up your first day as a success.'

'Don't say that,' she said quickly. 'We don't want to jinx ourselves.'

He quirked a dark eyebrow. 'I didn't put you down as superstitious.'

'You know how theatre people are full of superstitions? So are restaurant people. No one would be surprised if I had the building blessed, maybe brought in a feng-shui expert. Or burned sage to get rid of any bad karma from the previous business on this site. Maybe even hung crystals in strategic places. And don't even think about whistling in the kitchen. Especially a French kitchen.'

'You're kidding me?'

She shook her head. 'A lot happens in restaurants. First dates. Break-ups. Celebrations. Illicit liaisons. They leave energy. We want good energy. Opening day of a new restaurant is rather like the opening night of a new play. The cast. The audience. The need to have butts on seats. So let's just say I'm cautiously optimistic about how today went and leave it at that.'

He laughed. 'Okay, I'll grant you that. But I still say—'

Lizzie swiped her thumb and first finger across her lips to zip it. 'Don't say it or I'll blame you if anything goes wrong.'

Jesse pretended to cower. Lizzie laughed and ushered him through the back door to the car park. She punched in the alarm code, followed him out and locked the door behind them.

For the first time an awkward silence fell between them. The door that led upstairs to her apartment was only a few metres to the left. Did she invite him upstairs? Be alone with him again? She hadn't been able to stop thinking about how exciting his kisses had been. How much she'd missed him. How maybe she had misjudged him. Would it be wise?

She gestured to the door. 'I can offer you a coffee

but I suspect that might be the last thing you want to face right now.'

'I wouldn't say no to a beer,' he said.

'I've got some in the fridge upstairs. I could do with one too.' She gave a sigh that was halfway to a moan of exhaustion. 'There's nothing I want to do more than take off these clogs and kick back.'

The apartment over the café was compact but Sandy had done a wonderful job of refurbishing it for her and Amy. With polished wooden floors throughout, it had been painted in muted neutral tones with white shutters at the windows. Furniture comprised simple, comfortable pieces in whitewashed timber and a plump sofa and easy chairs upholstered in natural linen. The living room window framed a magnificent view of the harbour. The effect was contemporary but cosy and Lizzie's heart lifted every time she came through the door.

'You've settled in,' Jesse said as he followed her through to the small but well-equipped kitchen.

'I just need to get a few more personal touches in place before Amy gets here. Is it "thank you number gazillion and two" if I say how much I appreciate the work you did here?' she said. 'Sandy told me how much of this place is due to your efforts.'

'Enough with the grovelling,' he said with a grin. 'Just get me that beer.'

Lizzie grabbed two beers from the fridge and cut lime quarters to press into the bottle necks. She handed one to Jesse and carried her own through into the living room. 'No food to offer you, I'm afraid,' she said. 'It's all downstairs.'

'I've been snacking on stuff all day,' Jesse said. 'I don't need any more. How do you stay so slim working with all that delicious food?' He cast an appreciative eye over her figure.

'I learned early on to only have very small servings—just tastes really. Then there's the fact that cooking is hard physical work. I'm standing all day every day.'

She flopped down onto the sofa and kicked off her clogs. 'My feet are killing me. They're always killing me. My feet, my knees, my back. It's so good to sit down.'

She wiggled her toes, rotated her ankles, but it didn't do much to ease the deep, throbbing ache in her feet. Damaged feet were an occupational hazard of being a chef.

Jesse sat down on the sofa next to her. 'Let me rub your feet for you.'

Lizzie's gaze met his and there was a question in his eyes that asked so much more than she knew how to answer.

She knew saying yes to his suggestion would be going beyond the bounds of their tentative friendship. But she longed to have his strong, capable hands on her feet, stroking and massaging to ease the pain. Stop kidding herself: she longed to have his hands on her body, full stop. She had gone beyond denying her attraction to him. But was this foot massage a good idea?

'There's some peppermint lotion in the fridge,' she said. 'It's more soothing when it's chilled.'

Jesse returned from the kitchen with the peppermint lotion. He sat down on the sofa again, put the container on the coffee table. 'Swivel around on the sofa and put your feet across my legs.'

It seemed an intimate way to start a foot massage but she didn't protest. The alternative was to have him kneeling at her feet and that wouldn't do.

Her feet were so sore that Jesse's first firm, sure strokes were painful and she yelped. 'Just getting the knots out,' he explained. He then settled into an easier rhythm, probing, stroking, squeezing with his strong fingers and thumbs, smoothing in the cool, sharply scented lotion.

She moaned her pleasure and relief. 'This is heaven, absolute heaven. Where did you learn to massage like this?'

'Nowhere,' he said. 'I'm just giving you what you seem to need.'

'Oh,' she said, not meeting his gaze.

She didn't know what to say to that. What she did know was she had to keep thoughts of other needs, and the way Jesse might meet them, on a very tight rein.

Her whole body thrummed with the pleasure of what his hands were doing to her heels, toes, soles. She'd never thought of feet as sensual zones but what Jesse was doing was nothing short of bliss.

'I'm just going to lie back and enjoy every minute,' she said, settling further back into the cushions, shifting her feet to fit more comfortably on his thighs.

'You do that,' he said in that deep, resonant voice that had become so familiar. Everything was beautiful about Jesse. His face. His voice. His hands— especially his hands. She moaned again as he massaged the pain away so that now his touch brought only pleasure.

She closed her eyes, zoned out into another world that focused on the rhythmical stroking of Jesse's hands on her feet; the scent of peppermint mingled with the faint aroma of coffee that clung to him; the sound of their breathing, his strong and steady, hers becoming slower, calmer. She could hear the tick, tick, tick of the kitchen clock in the silence of the apartment. *Please don't stop—don't ever stop.*

Eventually, when her feet felt utterly boneless, he finished by stretching out her toes one by one, squeezing her feet one final time, then stroking right up to her shins. 'Done,' he said.

'Mmm…' she murmured as she drowsily sat up, swinging her feet away so she sat near him on the sofa. He might have been massaging her feet but her entire body felt relaxed. 'You're a man of many talents, Jesse Morgan. I guess that's "thank you number gazillion and three". I…'

Her voice got lost in her throat at the intensity of Jesse's expression. She gazed into his face for a long moment, those incredible blue eyes fringed with black lashes, the dark eyebrows, his chiselled mouth. She knew she shouldn't use the word 'beautiful' to describe a man but there wasn't another word that worked as well. Handsome. Good-looking. Striking. He was more than all of those combined. A wave of intense longing for him surged through her.

Now was her chance to move away. To get off the sofa and make an excuse to go into another room. Even to yawn in an exaggerated manner and tell him she needed her beauty sleep and it was time for him to go home.

But she didn't. Instead she reached out her hand and explored his face with her fingers, stroking the tousled hair from his forehead, tracing the line of his thick brows, the ridge of his sculptured cheekbones, the roughness of the dark shadow of his beard, until she reached his mouth. His lips were smooth and warm, the top one slightly narrower than the bottom. His eyes stayed locked on hers. He caught her fingers with his strong white teeth, nipped them gently and she gasped at the unexpected pleasure-pain.

She leaned forward and caressed his mouth with hers. His lips parted under hers and she gave herself over to the sensation of lips, tongue, taste in a slow, easy tender kiss. When he pulled her to him she sank into the embrace of his strong arms around her.

But what had started as gentle rapidly deepened into something more passionate, more demanding that had her winding her fingers through his hair to bring him closer, pressing her body to his hard strength, her heart hammering.

She had been so long without the touch of a man, of skin on skin, the heady delight of breathing in a man's scent. And this was Jesse, who she liked so much, who she was growing to trust, who had appealed to her from the get-go. She wanted so badly to be close to him.

They were alone in the apartment. Anything could happen. But it shouldn't. Not now. Not yet. Sex too soon with Jesse was not a good idea.

She harnessed all the willpower she could muster and pulled away from him. 'That…that wasn't a friend kiss,' she said when she got her breath back.

'No. No, it wasn't,' he said, his voice husky, his breath ragged. 'I like you as much more than a friend, Lizzie. I'd be lying if I said otherwise.'

She shifted a little further away from him on the sofa. With their thighs touching she found it difficult to keep her thoughts straight. 'Me too. I mean…there was a spark between us at the wedding. Now it…it's grown.'

'We got off onto a bad start with each other. You thought I was a guy who picked up and then discarded women just because I could.'

'And you thought I was a…I don't know what you

thought I was. Someone too quick to jump to the wrong conclusion?'

'Someone who's trying so hard to protect herself she might not see what could be there,' he said.

She paused to let the implication of his words sink in. 'Perhaps,' she said.

'You seem to have a distorted idea of who I am based on gossip and innuendo. I want to prove to you I'm a decent guy.'

Again she realised that some of her reactions to him might have hurt him. She hastened to reassure him. 'You've shown me that in so many ways. The fact you went off and trained to be a barista just to help me is the latest example.' She looked away and then back. 'It's just…just the other women thing.'

Jesse sighed. She didn't like the sound of it. 'I saw the way you watched me as I talked to Evie's friend.'

'Dell.'

'Were you jealous?'

'A…a little. She's very attractive.'

'Is she? I didn't notice. She's friendly, pleasant.'

'How could you not see how cute she is?'

'Contrary to that bad old reputation of mine, I don't look with lust at every female I meet because I want to bed her and run.'

She managed a weak smile. 'I never thought that for a minute.' Though she'd certainly been told that was what Jesse was capable of. She was beginning to realise the gossips had got him wrong.

Jesse shifted on the sofa, a movement that brought him closer to her. 'I haven't spent much time in Dolphin Bay in recent years. I don't like people knowing my business. It's suited me to let them think Jesse the player has waltzed through life unscathed. If I'd brought

Camilla home to marry her it would have been a triumph. But when it turned out such a disaster I was glad I'd never mentioned her. I didn't want anyone to know I'd been brought down so low.'

Lizzie was shocked at the slight edge to his voice. 'Camilla?' she asked.

'She was a photojournalist who came to do a feature story on our team. We were rebuilding tsunami-ravaged villages in Sri Lanka a few years back. I wasn't attracted to her at first but she singled me out for a lot of one-on-one photography.'

'I bet she did,' Lizzie murmured under her breath.

'What was that?' asked Jesse.

'Nothing,' she said and decided to keep her comments to herself. She couldn't be jealous of someone in Jesse's past and it sounded petty to criticise the unknown woman.

'I spent a lot of time with her being interviewed, being photographed.'

'And you fell for her.'

'Hard and fast.'

Lizzie jumped down hard on an unwarranted twinge of jealousy. Her imagination was running crazy wondering what kind of photos Camilla had taken of Jesse and whether he'd been wearing any clothes. But she couldn't ask.

'Her time with us was limited,' Jesse continued. 'It was a pressure cooker environment. I managed to get hold of a sapphire ring. I proposed. She laughed. Then turned me down.'

'She *laughed*?' Indignation for Jesse swept through Lizzie.

'Seemed what I'd thought was a serious relationship was a casual fling to her. She already had a fiancé at home in London. That was the first I'd heard of him. She had never told me she was anything other than single.' The delivery of his words was matter-of-fact, emotionless, as if he didn't care. But the rigid line of his mouth told Lizzie otherwise.

'You must have been devastated.'

He shrugged. 'You could say that.'

'So what happened?'

'She went home to London to marry the poor sucker.'

'And you never saw her again?'

He paused. 'Not from choice.'

'What…what do you mean?'

'She showed up in India at the start of this year to do a follow-up feature.'

'On you?'

'On the organisation I worked for. I wanted nothing to do with her.'

Something about the tone of his voice made her ask, 'But she wanted you?'

'To take up where we left off. Another fling. She was married by then and prepared to betray her husband.'

Under her breath, Lizzie uttered some choice swear words in French.

'I don't dare ask what that meant,' Jesse said with a shadow of his grin.

'Don't,' said Lizzie.

'Probably nothing I wouldn't have said myself,' he said. 'I told her what I thought of her and got transferred to another site.'

Lizzie put her hand on his arm. 'I hate her on your behalf,' she said vehemently. 'How dare she do that to you? And what an idiot to…to have let you go. I would have…' Her voice tapered off as she realised what she had said. What she had revealed. 'I…I mean—'

Jesse cradled her face in his hands, dropped a kiss on her mouth. 'That's sweet of you,' he said.

She managed a weak smile. 'I…I think you're kinda wonderful. I can't imagine every other woman wouldn't think so too.'

'I'm glad you think I'm wonderful.' He rolled his eyes in self-mockery.

'You…you must know I do. I don't mean that as a joke.'

Her breath hitched with awareness of how attractive she found him but it was so much more than the way he looked. 'I missed you terribly while you were away in Sydney. It…it scared me. The thought of what it would be like when you leave for your job.'

'I missed you too. I thought about you every minute of that four-hour trip to Sydney and all the way back.'

He took her hand in his, twined his fingers through hers. 'So what are we going to do about it?'

Jesse tightened his grip on Lizzie's hand. 'What's to stop us being more than friends? From seeing what else we could be to each other if we gave it a chance. What are the real issues—issues that can't easily be resolved? Can we discuss that?' They could beat about the bush for weeks over this—and he didn't have weeks.

She answered the pressure of his hand with hers. 'There's the fact we don't live in the same country for a start. You seem to be in a different place every few months.'

'That's the nature of my current job.'

'Current? There's something else in the offing?'

'A job that would still involve travel. But I'd be based in Houston, Texas. That is *if* I choose to take the job.'

She released her hand from his, smoothed her hair

away from her forehead in a nervous gesture that was becoming familiar. 'Texas is a long way from here. Even further than the Asian countries you seem to work in now. That's a real issue.'

'In the short-term. Long-term, Houston is a good city to live in. With plenty of good restaurants.'

She found her favourite errant lock of hair and twisted it around her finger. 'But there's not just me to consider. There's Amy. She needs stability in her life. She's already been uprooted from France, then from Sydney. And her father still wants her with him every long school vacation. I don't want to disrupt her again.'

'Does it make a huge difference where she lives when she's only five years old?'

Lizzie threw up her hands in an exaggerated shrug. 'I don't know. Maybe. Maybe not. I'm still learning to be Amy's mum. Trying to do my best for her when at times it's been quite difficult. I can't tell you how much I miss her when she's away, like now. But, for her sake, I do everything I can to keep up the relationship with her papa. She loves him and she loves her French grandparents.'

'I can understand that,' he said. That didn't mean he had to like the guy.

Lizzie shifted on the sofa; the movement took her further from him. 'I guess we've already segued into the next issue that might stop us being together—my daughter. Bringing a man into our lives would have ramifications I haven't really thought through. All I know is Amy has to come first.'

'It's not an issue for me,' Jesse said. 'You and Amy come as a package deal and I'm okay with that. We'd have to play it by ear what my role would be with Amy.'

'You know I'm not looking for a father for Amy?'

'I get that.'

'She has a father. Philippe has his faults but he loves his daughter.'

'You said he wants custody?'

'He and his parents want her brought up French. His parents love her too. And she loves her *grand-maman* and *grand-père*. They're wealthy. They think they can give her a good life.'

'Not as good as with her mother.' He felt a fierce surge of protectiveness towards both Lizzie and Amy.

'That's another point I have to consider. Amy is the reason I'm in Dolphin Bay. Thanks to Sandy I've got a job and a home and family nearby. Your mother has said she'll help me with Amy. The local school seems good. I wouldn't give all that up easily.'

'You'd have to weigh up the pros and the cons of another possible change.'

'Yes. That's exactly what I'd have to do.'

He spoke slowly. 'And I have to think about what a possible commitment would mean for me.'

Her quick intake of air told him he'd hit the mark with that one. He knew about the wagers laid on his ongoing bachelor ways. He knew even Sandy called him a 'commitment-phobe'. He wouldn't be surprised if she'd warned her sister off him.

'Did what happened with Camilla make you…make you back away from relationships?' Lizzie asked.

'Yeah. It did. Just when I'd…I'd got over the fire.' Lizzie was the first person he had confided in about Camilla and now this. If he wanted to take their attraction further he owed it to her to be honest.

'The fire that burned down the guest house? When… when you lost Ben's first wife and little boy.'

'It affected us all. We probably should have had

trauma counselling. But Morgans don't go in for that. You know what happened to Ben. He was so deep in despair no one could reach him. Until Sandy came back.'

'Thank heaven,' she said.

'Mum doted on her little grandson. Dad as well. She went extra dotty over dogs after we lost Liam and Jodi.'

'And you?' Lizzie's eyes were warm with compassion.

'I was gutted.'

'But everyone was probably so concerned for Ben they didn't think about the effect on you.'

'And rightly so. But seeing what happened to him made me decide it was never going to happen to me.'

'If you didn't love, you couldn't lose.'

'Something like that. By the time I met Camilla my defences were cracking. I'd realised I had to take my own risks. Make my own way.'

'And then you got hit with Camilla's betrayal.'

'And went backwards.'

Lizzie's smile was shaky at the edges. 'We're quite a pair, aren't we? Both scared of what happened to us in the past happening to us again. Me with Philippe. You with Camilla.'

'I don't know that I'd use the word "scared",' he said.

Jesse thought of the defences he'd thrown up around the idea of a committed relationship with a woman. The job. The travel. His ongoing career.

Mentally, he pulled himself up. *Stop kidding yourself, mate.*

Work was the wimp excuse. *The wussy versus the brave.* From somewhere deep inside him he had to drag out the truth. At the wedding, he'd felt a real connection to Lizzie that he had never felt before—a connection that had been severed with a painful cut by the way she'd behaved. Now he realised that link could easily fuse together again. *Go further with her and he could get hurt.*

And there was nothing wimpy about avoiding the kind of hurt that could destroy a man. Like the pain he'd felt when Camilla had ended it with him so brutally. Like when Ben had lost his family.

But Ben had found new happiness with Sandy. All around him were people in settled, fulfilling relationships. And he was headed for thirty, older and wiser, he hoped. He realised just telling Lizzie about Camilla's behaviour and hearing Lizzie's outrage on his behalf had done him good.

It had also made him realise how very different the two women were. He doubted that blunt, straightforward Lizzie had it in her to be as devious as Camilla. What good reason—what real, valid reason—was there left for him not to be brave when it came to Lizzie?

'What are we waiting for to happen?' he asked her. 'If we don't take this chance while we're actually both in the same country, will we live to regret it?'

She got up from the sofa, walked across the room, stood with her back to him for a terrifyingly long moment. Then she turned to face him again, took the steps to bring her closer to him again. He got up from the sofa to meet her.

'I've had a horrible thought,' she said, still keeping a distance between them.

'Tell me,' he said, bracing himself for her words.

She tilted her head to one side. 'What if we walked away from this and kept up the pretence we were just friends, then the next time we met was at one of our weddings to someone else?'

A shudder racked him at the thought. 'That is a horrible thought.'

'Too horrible to contemplate,' she said. 'I don't know that I could bear it.'

'Me neither. I say we forget the pretence of friendship. If there's something real between us then we can address my job, your jealousy and any other barriers we've put between us.'

She covered the distance between them in a few steps, opened her arms and put them around him. 'Yes,' she said. 'I say yes. We give it a go.'

He drew her tightly to him. This. This was what he wanted.

Lizzie stood close to Jesse in the circle of his arms. She couldn't remember when she'd last felt this mix of happiness and anticipation. Facing the future—even if they were only talking the immediate future—felt so much less scary when she was facing it with Jesse. She could almost feel those barricades she'd put up against him falling down one by one with a noisy clatter.

Her voice was muffled against his shoulder. 'One more thing. There might be a puppy to throw into the mix of things we have to consider.'

He groaned. 'You've been talking to my mother.'

Lizzie pulled away from him so she could look up at his face but stayed in the protective circle of his arms. 'How did you guess?'

'Her house is full of foster dogs and she's always on the lookout for homes for them.'

'Amy would love a puppy. So would I. My father would never allow us to have pets. I always wanted one.'

'Needless to say, we always had dogs when I was

growing up. How could I not love them? I admire Mum for her commitment to rescues.'

'I hear a "however" there,' she said. These days, she picked up on the slightest nuances in his voice.

'Some of the parts of the world I've worked in, children live worse lives than our pampered pooches. It's charities for kids I support.'

Was Jesse saying the things he knew she wanted to hear? She shook her head to rid herself of the thought. She had decided to trust him.

'Are you too good to be true, Jesse Morgan?' she asked.

He shook his head. 'I'm just me, Lizzie—take me as you find me. I didn't tell you that looking for praise,' he said. 'But it's a good way to segue into the fund-raising dinner the dog shelter my mother supports is having on Saturday night.'

'Maura did mention it, so did Sandy. But I said no. I can't afford a late night when I'll have such an early start next day. I'm expecting Sunday to be one of our busiest days at the café.'

'What if you made it an early night?' he coaxed. 'Just come for the dinner and then I take you straight home?'

Her smile was teasing, mischievous. 'Are you asking me on a date, Jesse?'

'I guess I am. Surely it can't be all work and no play for you.'

'No, but—'

'Where's the "but", Lizzie? You can't use the "just friends" argument any more.'

'I...I don't want everyone in Dolphin Bay knowing our business.' She would never forget that dreadful moment at the wedding when that raucous crowd had discovered her and Jesse kissing on the balcony.

'I understand. And feel the same way. So we keep it private,' he said.

'Even from my sister and your brother?' Sandy was the last person she'd want to know about the change in status of her relationship with Jesse. She didn't want any more warnings or disapproval. Not when she'd decided to switch off her own inner warning system when it came to Jesse.

'If that's what you want,' he said. 'I've never confided in Ben about my relationships.'

'And Amy too, when she gets here on Wednesday. Until…until we know for sure where we're going.' If Jesse were to be a part of her life, they would have to introduce the idea to her daughter with great care.

'Fine by me,' he said.

He cradled her face in his hands. Kissed her briefly, tenderly. Even on that level of kiss, he was a master.

'I'll come to the fund-raiser with you,' she said. 'To everyone there we'll just be friends, but to us—'

'We'll be finding out if we can be so much more.'

'Yes,' she said.

CHAPTER TEN

SATURDAY MORNING WAS so busy at Bay Bites that Lizzie had to call in a casual waitress for extra help. It wasn't just for help with table service; the phone was also ringing off the hook with advance bookings. She was elated and also somewhat surprised that the word had spread so quickly. Don't jinx it, she reminded herself.

She was in the kitchen checking a new batch of the rhubarb and strawberry muffins that had just come out of the oven when Sandy burst in the back door, fizzing with excitement. She grabbed Lizzie by the arm. 'Forget those—they look perfect, smell divine and will probably be gone in ten minutes. Come outside, will you.'

Bemused, Lizzie let herself be dragged outside by her sister. Sandy waved the Saturday edition of Sydney's major newspaper in her face. 'Check this out in the Lifestyle section. Bay Bites has been included in an article about the foodie scene on the south coast.'

Lizzie felt her stomach plummet to below the level of her clogs. There had already been positive reviews from customers on the internet review sites. But to be reviewed by this newspaper was something different altogether. The review would go on its website too and find its way into prominent positions on search engines.

A bad review could seriously damage them at this baby steps stage of the business.

She took hold of the newspaper with shaking hands and focused on the page with some difficulty. The headline was bold and black: *Take the South Coast Gourmet Food Trail*.

She scanned the first paragraphs. They talked about 'the ever-growing food and wine scene', mentioning the lush soil, mild climate, and singling out for praise some of her newly sourced suppliers.

Then there was a list of 'Six Foodie Hotspots' on the south coast. The television chef's restaurant was included. But high on the list was also, to her heart-pounding excitement, Bay Bites.

'Read it out—I've read it ten times already but I want to hear it again,' urged Sandy.

'I…I don't think my voice will work,' Lizzie said.

'Sure it will; come on—read.'

Lizzie cleared her throat and started to read in a voice that started off shaky but gained in strength and confidence as she read:

'"France's loss is the south coast's gain. Talented Aussie chef Lizzie Dumont has returned home to Oz from stints in top restaurants in Lyon and Paris to bring her particular flair to must-visit café Bay Bites in the charming coastal town of Dolphin Bay. The menu is a clever blend of perfectly executed café favourites and more innovative specials that showcase locally sourced ingredients. Don't miss: sublime scrambled eggs; rhubarb and strawberry muffins; slow-cooked lamb with beetroot relish. Then there's the excellent coffee served by the most swoon-worthy barista you'll see this side of Hollywood."'

The review was accompanied by a photograph of

the café interior looking bright and fashionable and another close-up of a muffin broken open with crumbs scattered artfully alongside. Jesse was there beside the coffee machine but his image was blurred, as if in motion, so you couldn't readily identify him.

Lizzie sagged with relief. She looked at the by-line of the journalist who had written such a gratifying review. Adele Hudson. She peered closer at the small photo that accompanied it. She blinked then looked again to make sure she hadn't got it wrong. 'I don't believe it. It's Dell. Adele Hudson is Dell.'

'Who is Dell and how do you know her?' said Sandy.

'She's a friend of Evie from the dairy farm. She was here for the taste-test and then again on our opening day.'

'The redhead flirting with Jesse?'

'Turns out she was interviewing him, in a subtle way,' Lizzie said slowly. She'd thought Dell had been flirting with Jesse too. She felt sick at the memory of the jealousy that had speared her. The review could have gone completely the other way if she'd acted on it.

'Wait. There's more,' she said. 'Adele Hudson is also a well-known food blogger with tens of thousands of followers.'

'Not so well known to us,' said Sandy. She pulled out her e-tablet from her handbag, scrolled through. 'Her blog is called "Dell Dishes". Look, she's written about Bay Bites here, too.'

Lizzie read it out.

'"Good food and good books—two of my greatest loves. I got a taste of both with the newly opened Bay Bites café that's an extension of my favourite south coast bookshop Bay Books."'

She looked up, her excitement rising. 'And there's so

much more about how good the food is. She's picked up on the link between the café and the Hotel Harbourside too and called the hotel restaurant "pub grub at its best".'

'We're on the map now,' said Sandy with a great sigh of satisfaction. 'Along with those five-star ratings on the user review websites, I think we're on our way.' Lizzie laughed as her sister danced her around in a little jig of joy.

'I wondered how word of mouth spread so quickly; we've got a truckload of advance bookings,' said Lizzie. The glowing review certainly took some of the sting out of her demotion in status from fine dining to café cook.

Just then the door from the café opened and the man who had been taking up so much of her thoughts emerged. 'I'm on the hunt for our missing boss,' said Jesse with great exaggeration. He looked from Lizzie to Sandy and back again. His expression grew serious. 'Is something wrong?'

'It's very, very right,' said Lizzie exultantly. She wanted to throw herself into his arms and share with him her excitement and relief.

Sandy rolled her eyes heavenward. 'Better show the review to the "most swoon-worthy barista you'll see this side of Hollywood".'

'What are you talking about?' said Jesse as he grabbed the newspaper. He scanned the pages then groaned loudly and theatrically. 'This will do wonders for my reputation. Please let's hope my mates don't see it.'

'Your handsome face is doing wonders for butts on seats in our café,' said Sandy. 'Would you consider a full-time career change?'

Jesse laughed. 'It's nothing to do with the barista

and everything to do with this one.' He swept Lizzie up
in his arms and twirled her around. 'Congratulations,
boss. You deserve this.'

Now Lizzie felt really elated but as Jesse swung her
to a halt she noticed her sister's narrowed, appraising
eyes. Sandy's words came back: 'Jesse is so not for you.'

She caught Jesse's eye and, in one of those silent moments of communication they were having more often,
he got the message. *Keep Sandy in the dark about us.*

Jesse immediately swung Sandy up and twirled her
around too. 'The incredible Adam sisters triumph.'

'I'm a Morgan,' corrected Sandy.

'Dumont for me,' added Lizzie.

Both she and Sandy had been glad to kiss goodbye to
their father's name when they'd married. She'd thought
of reverting to her maiden name when she'd divorced
Philippe but had decided against it for Amy's sake. It
had been disruptive enough for her without Mummy
having a different name. *Morgan was a nice name.*

She refused to let the thought go further. Anyway,
that would be weird. Two sisters marrying a pair of
brothers? *Never going to happen.*

CHAPTER ELEVEN

THE STAR OF the fund-raiser for Dolphin Bay Dogs, the shelter Jesse's mother Maura was involved with, was the cast of dogs, ranging from cute puppies to venerable senior citizens with grey around their muzzles.

They sat in a row along the raised platform that acted as a stage for the ballroom of the Hotel Harbourside. The volunteer carers who kept the dogs in check were busy either soothing the nervous ones or calming the excitable ones who just wanted to be part of the action.

It was clever marketing on his mother's part, Jesse thought. He was sure people would be more inclined to open their wallets when they saw those pleading canine eyes.

But, appealing as the puppies were, Jesse's eyes were only for Lizzie. They'd agreed she'd arrive with Sandy and Ben so as not to draw attention to the way their 'friendship' had escalated into something so much more.

And now she was here. As she made her way across the room to him he was literally lost for words. His heart thudded into overdrive and his mouth went dry.

Last time he'd seen her she'd been wearing her chef's jacket and black pants, her hair pulled tightly back from her face and her cheeks all flushed from the heat of the kitchen. He'd thought she'd looked lovely then. But the transformation from chef to seductress was nothing short of sensational.

Her dress clung to her slender shape and left her shoulders bare, with a tantalising suggestion of cleavage, and its colour was a tint of aqua that glistened like the underside of a wave on Silver Gull beach. Her hair puzzled him for a moment until he realised it looked so different because her wild curls had been tamed into a style that was straight and sleek and falling around her face. She looked sophisticated. Elegant. And sexy as all get-out.

'Lizzie,' he said in the most casual just-friends voice he could muster, 'you're looking very lovely.'

'Thank you,' she said in the tone she used to accept a compliment about the food from a customer, but lit by a mischievous sparkle in her eyes. 'So glad you approve.'

'I approve, all right,' he said, his voice more the hoarse whisper of a lover than the light tone of a pal, no matter how he tried to keep it casual.

The silver high heeled shoes that strapped around her ankles brought her to easy kissing height. She kissed him lightly, first on one cheek and then the other. 'Just friends, remember,' she murmured into his ear.

It was an effort not to clamp her possessively to his side. To beat away anyone who came near her. She aroused caveman instincts he hadn't known he possessed.

'You look so beautiful,' he murmured back. 'No man would want to stop at just being friends.'

She laughed as she pulled away from him to normal conversation level. He had better try and mask the hunger in his eyes.

'I bought this dress in Paris years ago. It's so long

since I dressed up I could hardly remember how. I thought it was going to be a big fail.'

'Count it as a first class honours pass,' he said.

She wore make-up too, dark stuff around her eyes that brought out a purple ring around her iris. And deep pink lipstick on her sweet, seductive mouth. It only made him want to kiss it off.

'This is the same room where Sandy and Ben's wedding reception was held, isn't it?' Lizzie asked in a low murmur. 'Do you get a feeling of déjà vu?'

'In a way,' he said. 'You're the loveliest woman in the room again.'

'I bet you say that to all the girls,' she said in mock flirtation, but he saw a touch of wariness in her eyes.

'No, I don't, and that's the truth,' he said. He bent to whisper in her ear. 'You have to learn to trust me, Lizzie.' *As he had to trust her.*

She nodded. 'I know.'

He wanted to kiss her to reassure her, but of course he couldn't. Not with the eyes of a sizable number of his family and friends upon them.

'One thing is for sure,' she said, as if she'd read his mind. 'Nothing could take me out onto that balcony again.'

He didn't want to share her. Wanted her all to himself somewhere very private. But she was right—that place wasn't the balcony. No matter how beautiful the view of the full moon over the bay.

He was about to tell her that when Ben came up beside them. He slapped his brother on the shoulder in greeting. 'It's not you I've come to talk to,' Ben said. 'It's Lizzie.'

'Okay,' said Lizzie. Did she feel as annoyed as he did at being interrupted?

'Mum wants to show you something special,' Ben said to Lizzie. 'She's over there near the stage. Please don't be surprised if it's a dog.'

Lizzie laughed. 'I don't mind at all if it's a dog. Isn't that what we're here for?'

She casually brushed her hand against Jesse's arm as she left—he got the message she would rather stay with him and it pleased him.

'I actually do want to talk to you,' said Ben. He went from smiling to serious, as he did when money and investment was concerned.

Jesse's interest was sparked. When he was younger, he'd trusted Ben with financial advice that had paid off very handsomely. A generous inheritance plus business savvy and wise investment meant that at his age he was well off. Well off enough to be able to take the weight right off Lizzie's feet if that was what she wanted; maybe into a job that wasn't so physically demanding. It concerned him to see her so exhausted and in pain at the end of a long day in the kitchen.

'I want to talk to you about a business proposition,' Ben said.

'If you want to hire me as a full-time barista, forget it,' Jesse said with a grin.

'Sandy would sign you up in a moment,' Ben said. 'But that's not the money-making proposal I have for you.'

As Lizzie walked away from Jesse, she was surprised to realise how much she was enjoying herself. She couldn't help but contrast the last time she'd been in this room for Sandy's wedding.

Then she'd been the bride's sister who didn't know anyone. Now, even after only a few weeks in Dolphin

Bay, she recognised lots of faces and they were all very complimentary about Bay Bites. Several people told her they'd put in bids for the prize of lunch for two she'd donated to the silent auction.

Maura came bustling up and swept her up into a hug. 'Gorgeous, gorgeous dress,' she said. 'So glad to see you having a night out.'

'We had another busy day in the café today,' Lizzie told her. 'The fish pie I made from your recipe was a sell-out. And we've already got customers asking us to put your strawberry sponge cake on the regular menu.'

'Only serve that cake when strawberries are at their finest,' Maura advised. 'It's at its best with the freshest, sweetest strawberries. Anything else is a compromise and the flavour will suffer.'

Lizzie smiled. Maura truly was a woman after her own heart when it came to food. 'I'll keep that advice in mind,' she said.

'I'm pleased about that, dear. But we're not here to talk about cooking. There's someone I want you to meet.'

Lizzie followed Maura up onto the platform where the dogs were waiting to play their roles for the evening with varying degrees of good behaviour.

'If we can appeal to people's hearts for adoptions tonight that will be grand,' said Maura. 'If we can get them to open their wallets, too, that's all the better.'

Lizzie suppressed a smile. It appeared the Morgan family were born businesspeople. That augured well for the future of Bay Bites—and her own security in Dolphin Bay.

Maura led Lizzie to where a puppy snuggled with a teenage girl. 'He's sad, Mrs Morgan,' she said. 'He misses his brother and sister who got adopted.'

'Sad? Maybe a little lonely,' said Maura. 'But he's quiet because he's exhausted from being run around the yard all afternoon.' She turned to Lizzie. 'Meet Alfie.'

At the sound of his name, the puppy sat up. He was black with a few irregular white patches, soulful dark eyes and long floppy ears that made Lizzie think he had some spaniel in him. He gave a sweet little whine and lifted up a furry paw to be shaken.

Lizzie was smitten. 'Oh, he's adorable.' She shook the puppy's warm little paw.

'Mother, are you up to your "get the puppy to shake paws" tricks again?' Jesse spoke from behind her and Lizzie turned. Her heart missed a beat at the sight of how devastating he looked in a tuxedo. She hadn't thought he could look more handsome than he did in his jeans and T-shirt but he did. Oh, yes, he did.

'And if a few tricks help a homeless animal find his way into someone's heart, who am I to miss the opportunity?' said Maura with the charming smile that was so like her son's.

'He's won my heart already—can I pick him up?' Lizzie asked.

As soon as he was in her arms the puppy tried to enthusiastically lick her face. Lizzie laughed. 'Jesse, isn't he cute?'

'He is that,' said Jesse with a smile she could only describe as indulgent.

'Amy would adore him.'

'Yes, she would,' said Maura. 'A dog can be a great friend to a little girl.'

'Her *grand-maman* in France has a little dog that Amy loves. She's heartbroken every time she says goodbye to her. It might help her to settle here if she had a dog of her own.'

'But is it practical for you to have a puppy?' Jesse asked.

'Not right now,' Lizzie said reluctantly, kissing the puppy's little forehead. 'Who knows what the future might bring for us? But he's utterly enchanting.'

She turned to Maura. 'Amy will be here on Wednesday. If Alfie hasn't found a home by then I'll bring her to see him.' She gave the puppy one more pat, to which he responded with enthusiastic wagging of his tiny tail, and reluctantly handed him back to his carer.

Maura put her hand on Lizzie's arm. 'You have to do what's best for you and your daughter. But a dog brings such rewards.'

If Lizzie stayed in Dolphin Bay a dog would be possible. For one thing, she'd be happier if Amy had the comfort of a puppy while she settled into her new home and made new friends. But it was still early days yet.

It wasn't just the possibility of something serious with Jesse that made her hesitate. She only had a job here if the café was a success. Otherwise she'd be back in Sydney flat-hunting in a difficult rental market with the added hindrance of a dog in tow.

And then there was Jesse's career. If they had a future together, where might it be?

'Don't you have to give your speech soon, Mum?' Jesse said.

'Yes, of course I do,' said Maura. 'You just keep little Alfie in mind, Lizzie.'

Jesse put his arm casually around Lizzie's shoulder as he led her down from the platform. 'Don't let her talk you into something you're not ready for. A dog's a big commitment.'

'Don't I know it,' she said.

She was silent for a long moment. Holding the squirming little bundle in her arms had brought back memories of Amy as a baby. Amy often asked if she could have a little brother or sister, but another baby had never been on the agenda. Why was she thinking about it now?

As the evening progressed Lizzie couldn't help being overwhelmed by that déjà vu. They were in the same room as the wedding reception. She was enjoying the opportunity to wear a beautiful dress, do something special with her hair—she loved the effect of having it straight—and wearing more make-up than usual.

With the Parisian dress she felt she had donned some of her old Lizzie party-girl spirit. That Lizzie had been pretty much smothered by maternal responsibilities and anxieties. She loved Amy more than she could ever have imagined loving another person. But there were times she wanted to be Lizzie, not just Mummy or Chef. This was one of them. She was determined to enjoy every second of the evening.

She even enjoyed the speeches. She wasn't the only one near tears when Maura spoke about the homeless dogs and cats in the area and the maltreatment some of them received before they got to the shelter. Someone else spoke convincingly about spaying and neutering to help bring down the number of unwanted kittens and puppies.

When Maura returned to the table after the speeches, she saw the pride in Jesse's father's eyes as he helped his wife of heaven knew how many years back into her chair. She realised Jesse had been brought up in a family where love and kindness ruled.

How very different from her family, where her father, a specialist anaesthetist, believed in excessive discipline, rigorous academic achievement and ruthless competition. No wonder both she and Sandy had rebelled. No wonder her mother had eventually divorced him and moved to another state.

Her father hadn't been a part of her life for a long time but he had asked to see her when she'd brought Amy back to Australia. She'd hoped he'd regretted the way he'd treated her, maybe wanted to make up for it by developing a relationship with his granddaughter. But no. He wanted to pay to send Amy to an exclusive girls' boarding school where she could develop her academic potential, away from her mother's influence. Needless to say, Lizzie had declined the offer.

The food at Maura's function was good, but not as good as she'd expected from the Hotel Harbourside catering. 'Should I mention it to Sandy?' she whispered to Jesse. They were seated together at the Morgan family table, surreptitiously holding hands under cover of the tablecloth.

'When the moment is right,' Jesse said, keeping his voice very low, pretending not to be too interested in what she was saying. 'You'll need to be diplomatic.'

'Aren't I always diplomatic?' she started to say in a huff.

He smiled. 'You can't pride yourself on being both blunt and diplomatic at the same time.' He squeezed her hand to emphasise he didn't mean it as an insult.

'Point taken,' she said.

Again she marvelled at how quickly Jesse had got to know her. She didn't feel she knew him as well but was enjoying each revelation of what lay beneath the heartbreakingly handsome exterior. So far she'd discovered he was a thoughtful, highly intelligent man with a good heart, a good head for business and a whole lot of common sense. That was on top of being a master kisser.

'Do you know what I'm missing?' she said. 'The music. I wish I could get up and dance with you. Do you remember how we danced together at the wedding?'

'How could I forget?'

'I think dancing with you was when I—' She swallowed the words that bubbled to the surface. *When I thought I might have found someone special.*

'When you…?' Jesse prompted.

'When I…when I realised you were so much more than the best man who I, as the chief bridesmaid, was obligated to spend time with.'

And now? *Now she was falling in love with him.* She'd fought it so hard she hadn't let herself recognise it. *Could you fall in love this quickly?*

'You okay?' asked Jesse. 'You seem flustered.'

'Yes. Yes. Of course I'm okay.' *How did she deal with this?*

'I want to dance with you too,' said Jesse in a husky undertone. 'The evening is winding up. In half an hour we leave separately, then—'

'Yes?' she asked, her heart thudding.

'Then we have our own private dance on the beach.'

CHAPTER TWELVE

JESSE WAITED UNTIL a moment when his mother had got back up onstage and was introducing the audience to the dogs. She held up a particularly cute puppy with one ear that flopped all the way over. All attention was on the puppy as the other guests oohed and aahed at its cuteness. He didn't think anyone would notice him slip away and make his way out of the hotel.

Ten minutes later he saw Lizzie creep out of the Hotel Harbourside exit and cross the road to where he waited. For a moment she didn't see him and her wary look made his heart leap.

He couldn't have anticipated how fast things were moving with her. But he was a man used to making quick life-or-death decisions. He had decided he wanted to take a chance on Lizzie Dumont—and no obstacle was going to be allowed to stand in the way of them becoming a couple. That included his own doubts.

She caught sight of him and smiled—a joyous smile tinged with mischief, just like the smile he had fallen for when he had first met her at the pre-wedding outing. She ran over the road to meet him under the palm tree that edged the beach. 'I feel like a naughty school-girl sneaking out like this,' she said with a delightful giggle.

Funny, he hadn't been attracted to her when she was a schoolgirl. It was the woman she'd become who'd caught his attention.

'So where's the dance floor?' she asked.

'Down there.' He indicated the beach with an expansive wave of his hand. 'If we dance down there and to the left we'll be out of sight of the hotel.'

Her gasp of pleasure was the biggest reward he could have asked for. 'So we twirl and whirl on the sand,' she said.

She balanced on his shoulder as she leaned down to unbuckle the straps on her silver shoes and slip them off. She tucked them alongside his own shoes, socks and bow tie where he'd discarded them at the base of the palm tree.

'The wet sand near the edge of the water will be firmer,' he said with his engineer's brain.

The full moon was high in the sky and its reflection lit a shimmering path of palest gold from the horizon, over the water to where the tiny waves of the bay sighed onto the sand.

'Magic by moonlight,' she breathed.

It was so light he could clearly see Lizzie's eyes, her face pale, uplifted to the moon, her hair glinting like silver. She looked ethereal, like some kind of fairy princess in her shimmering dress.

Jesse could hardly believe he was thinking such thoughts. He was an engineer. Practical. Mathematical. *Madness* by moonlight, more like it.

She wound her arms around his neck. 'I feel like I'm in some kind of enchanted world,' she whispered. 'And you're the handsome prince spiriting me away to dance on moonbeams. Have I found my way onto the pages of one of Amy's fairy tale books?'

He kissed her, lightly, possessively. 'If that's the case, you're the fairy princess.' *Had he actually said that?*

'I had no idea you were so romantic, Jesse,' she murmured.

'I'm not usually,' he said. 'It…it's you.'

This was the Lizzie who had captivated him at the wedding. During the last ten days he'd got to see the other sides of Lizzie. And the more he got to know her, the more he wanted her in his life.

She laughed and the slightly bawdy edge to her laughter reminded him how utterly real and womanly she was. 'Where's the music, Prince Charming? Can you conjure it up from the moonlight?'

'The prosaic engineer in me would tell you I can play music through my smartphone.'

'Whereas Prince Charming might say we can dance to the music of the stars,' she suggested.

'And the rhythm of the waves,' he said.

'With those chirping crickets adding some bass.'

He laughed. 'If you say so.'

'It's perfect,' she whispered.

She went into his arms and together they danced barefoot on the cool, wet sand with the occasional tiny cold wave swishing over their feet and making her squeal. They danced not with the expertise of ballroom dancers—he'd never mastered that art—but in their own rhythm, making up their steps as they went along, her glittering skirt twirling around them.

'I don't know that the music of the moon and stars is enough; it hasn't quite got a beat,' she murmured. 'Shall I hum? I can't sing, so humming will have to do.'

'Go ahead and hum,' he said, falling more under her spell each minute, totally enchanted by her.

He stood quite still as she started to hum the tune of

the old song about Jesse's girl that had tormented him for so many years. But in her slightly tuneless hum, it was the most melodious music he'd ever heard. And her particular version of the words echoed in his heart as she murmured them.

He smoothed her hair back from her face, cupped her face in his hands. 'Do you really want to be Jesse's girl?'

Her eyes were luminous in the moonlight. 'Oh, yes,' she said.

Lizzie pulled Jesse back for another kiss. She couldn't bear to spend a minute out of his arms on this magical evening where her own Prince Charming was dancing her along an enchanted beach. Only too soon her prince might have to go across those waters to the badlands to fight his own battles and maybe never come back to her.

She'd not been one for fairy tales. As a mother, she'd tried to steer Amy in the direction of feminist tales of hard-working women who met men on an equal footing, who had no room for Prince Charmings riding to their rescue on white chargers when they could rescue themselves perfectly well, thank you very much.

But tonight with Jesse she felt differently. Whether it was indeed the magic of the full moon or because she was falling in love with him, she wanted Jesse to be her prince, sweep her up into his arms and carry her away to make her his.

Even if it was only for tonight she wanted this, wanted him. She lost herself in his kisses, yielding to his lips, to his tongue as his mouth claimed hers, trembled with pleasure at the sensation of his hands on her bare shoulders.

'It's about at this stage Prince Charming sweeps

the princess off to his fairy tale castle,' she murmured against his mouth.

Jesse lifted his head to meet her gaze. 'To make her his?'

He had never looked more handsome than at this moment. His hair raven's wing black in the moonlight, his eyes reflecting the indigo of the deep night sea.

'Yes,' she breathed. 'To make her his in every sense of the word.'

'Are you sure?' His voice was deep, husky with a slight hitch that betrayed his fear she might say no.

There was no risk of that. She nodded. 'My Cinderella garret above the café is all mine right now. On Wednesday the junior princess will be in residence. You might find I turn back into a pumpkin then.'

Jesse laughed, his perfect white teeth gleaming in the moonlight. 'I think you're getting your analogies mixed. Even I know it was the carriage that got turned back into a pumpkin. You've left your shoes on the beach. It will be the prince doing the rounds of every house in the magical town of Dolphin Bay trying to find whose foot fits the silver stiletto.'

She smiled. 'So, not a pumpkin. But it's true that at five a.m. I'll turn back into a servant wearing rags and clogs as I stoke the fires of the café kitchen. Well, maybe not rags but—'

He dropped a kiss on her nose. 'The clock is ticking.'

'My castle or yours?' she said.

'As I'm staying in the boathouse, your garret might be more private.'

'My garret it is,' she said.

Laughing, kissing, Jesse danced her over the sand and back up to where they had stashed their shoes. He knelt in the sand and helped her wipe off the sand from her feet. Then he kissed the arch of each foot before he slipped on her silver stilettos.

'I had to stop myself from doing that the night I massaged your feet,' he said.

Delicious ripples of pleasure shimmered through her. 'No need to stop now,' she whispered.

Totally engrossed in the magic of being with Jesse, Lizzie didn't care who might see them make their way hand in hand towards her apartment. There, in true fairy tale prince fashion, he gathered her into his arms and carried her up the stairs and into the magical kingdom of her bedroom.

CHAPTER THIRTEEN

JESSE HAD AGREED with Lizzie to keep secret the new turn their relationship had taken. In the three days since their dance on the beach they'd managed not to arouse suspicion. Neither of them wanted to be subject to the inevitable teasing the revelation they were dating would bring. To him, Lizzie was not just one in a stream of 'Jesse's girls'. As far as he was concerned, she was the one and only Jesse's girl.

This wasn't something short-term. He was convinced of that. Lizzie wasn't underhand and dishonest like Camilla had been. He trusted her.

He intended to talk to her today about the proposition he had discussed in depth with Ben. His brother had suggested they pool some of the land they each owned around Dolphin Bay and form a property development company.

Jesse had been involved in the building of the Hotel Harbourside and was a part-owner of the new spa resort Ben was building. At the back of his mind he'd always wanted to go into business for himself; he came from a long line of entrepreneurs. It was a logical—and exciting—next step.

Relocating back to Dolphin Bay would also knock down the major barrier that remained between him and

Lizzie—that they lived in different countries. It was a move that checked all the boxes. Importantly, it would give them time to really get to know each other.

He'd arranged to meet Lizzie after the café closed for the day. The young waitress Nikki had responded so well to his training and confidence-boosting, he'd done himself out of his job as a barista. His role at Bay Bites now comprised helping out for a few hours over lunch-time—and that was only an excuse to be with Lizzie. His two-hour time limit? Twenty hours of Lizzie's company a day wouldn't be enough.

She was already there when he got to the lookout, a block away from the café, with the best view in Dolphin Bay of the harbour. It was a perfect afternoon, the water sparkling aquamarine under a cloudless sky. Fishing boats and pleasure craft of all shapes and sizes bobbed on the water and the melodic chime of rigging against masts carried across to where he stood.

Lizzie wore a pink sundress that bared her shoulders and arms. Fine tendrils of her pale blonde hair had escaped from the band that held it back from her face and wafted in the slight breeze. There was no reason for her to be anything but happy and relaxed. But he could see straight away that something was bothering her—he'd learned to read the way anxiety tightened her face and dimmed the light in her eyes.

They greeted each other with a discreet kiss on the cheek—as friends, colleagues and family connections would. After a night of lovemaking, he'd left her warm and satisfied in her bed when he'd exited before dawn. It had been difficult to leave her but they both wanted to keep their new intimacy a secret.

'What's up?' he asked.

'How do you always know?' she asked with the shadow of a smile.

'Just observant,' he said.

But it was more than that. The connection between them grew stronger with each minute they spent together. It was a bond he'd never had before. But it also brought fear of the inevitable pain if that connection was ever severed. *Wussy versus brave,* he reminded himself. He'd chosen to take the brave path, to let feeling grow rather than stifle it with fear. So, it seemed, had she.

Lizzie took his hand and gave it a surreptitious squeeze. He knew without further words being spoken that she valued the depth of their connection too.

She looked up at him 'You know Amy is due back tomorrow?'

'I know how much you're looking forward to seeing her. Why the glum face?'

'Philippe is escorting her on her flight from Lyon. I was going to drive up to Sydney to meet her plane. Now he'll hire a car to bring her here.'

'Your ex? Here in Dolphin Bay?' He was hit by a blow of dismay. Lizzie's ex-husband played an active role in Amy's life. But having him here on home turf was not a move he welcomed.

'It's as much a surprise to me as it is to you,' she said.

For her sake, he suppressed the stab of jealousy that knifed him. 'That's good for Amy.'

'Yes. The airline does a wonderful job of escorting her. In fact she enjoys the fuss the attendants make of her so much she's probably protesting having her papa with her. But I worry every second she's on the plane by herself so in that way I'm glad he'll be there.'

'Of course you are.'

He admired Lizzie's dedication to her daughter. Amy

was a fantastic little kid, smart, funny, outgoing. If—
and it was still a big if—he got to be a permanent part of
Lizzie's life he would welcome a role in Amy's life too.

'I'm worried about why Philippe wants to see me
so much he's flying all the way to Australia.' That favourite stray piece of hair was getting another workout
between her fingers.

'Maybe because he's missing you.' Jesse spoke
lightly but his gut roiled.

'Nothing like that,' she said, shaking her head with
a vehemence Jesse should have found reassuring but
didn't. If he'd had Lizzie for his own, he would never
have let her get away. Her ex-husband must have regretted it a million times. Maybe that was what he wanted
to tell her. Perhaps he had a good story to spin about
how he'd changed.

'He says there's something important that has to be
said face to face,' Lizzie continued.

The ex wanted her back. Jesse just knew it. 'So what
do you think your ex wants?'

'I'm terrified he's going for full custody of Amy. He's
used it as a threat before to try and keep me in France.
I can't think what else he would need to see me about.'

Jesse thought he knew only too well what her ex
would want: Lizzie and Amy back with him. But he
didn't share his thoughts. Instead he reassured her.
'You're a wonderful mother. You can provide a secure
home for Amy. No way would he have grounds to say
you're unfit for custody. Don't the courts usually rule
in favour of the mother?'

Lizzie snatched her hand to her mouth. 'The courts?
Please don't let it get that far.'

'You'll know tomorrow what he wants. There's nothing you can do in the meantime. Try to stop worrying.'

He didn't want her to be preoccupied with her ex on the last night they had together alone before Amy came home. The dynamic between them would be changed when they had to fit their private time around the needs of a five-year-old.

'If their flight is on time and all goes well, he and Amy should be here by midmorning.'

She banged the railing of the seafront wall with such force it surely must have hurt her hand. 'Why is he doing this to me? After all he put me through before? I've done everything I can to be civilised about the divorce, to make it easier for Amy. Letting her go to France half of every school holidays. Video calls every week. Why?' She muttered under her breath in what Jesse could only assume was a string of fluent French swear words.

It was the closest to anger he had seen her, though he'd heard a few explosions coming from the kitchen at Bay Bites. 'You really don't want to see him, do you?'

'Of course I don't. Why would I?'

Jesse's spirits lifted at the thought. Sounded as if any possible reunion could be wishful thinking on the ex-husband's part.

'Do you want me to be there when you meet with him?'

'No.'

Her answer came with such swiftness that Jesse felt as if he'd been hit with an unexpected punch between the eyes. 'Whatever,' he said.

Her face filled with contrition. She reached out and touched him fleetingly on the cheek with slender, cool fingers. 'I didn't mean to sound hurtful. Of course I would like you by my side when I confront Philippe. But if he's after sole custody, I wouldn't want him to know I was in a relationship with a man.'

'I don't want to jeopardise anything,' Jesse said. 'But I'll be at hand. Just in case.'

'No need for that,' she said. 'Philippe hasn't got a violent bone in his body. I wouldn't let Amy spend so much time with him if he had any tendencies that way. No. I can handle this by myself—like I did with the issues that ended the marriage.'

Jesse muttered assent. But no way would he let Lizzie go into this by herself. When she met with her ex he would be nearby.

But, to help her, he needed to know what had happened to end the marriage in such a drastic way she'd come back to Australia to raise her child on her own.

'Lizzie, we've skirted around this. But what actually happened to end your marriage? To make you so wary of men like your ex.'

Lizzie hated reliving the past. She and her sister had handled what had happened with their father by having a 'water under the bridge' policy that had so far served her well.

But Jesse deserved to know.

'I don't really like to talk about this, so I won't linger on the details,' she said.

'Fine by me,' he said. He leaned back against the lookout wall with his back to the view. Lizzie couldn't help thinking she'd rather look at Jesse than any number of rustic stone breakwaters and charming boats in the harbour, no matter how picturesque.

'I met Philippe when we were both working at a hotel up in Port Douglas. When he left to go back home to France I went with him. It was an adventure—and good for my career. Living in Paris was a ball, working all hours then partying hard.'

'I hear a "but" coming on.'

She nodded. 'I fell pregnant. It was unplanned. But we got married, made the best of it. When there were some complications in the pregnancy, I wanted to go home to have the baby. My French had improved out of sight by then but I didn't feel I really understood the doctors and the hospitals. Philippe didn't much like it—and his family were horrified—but I came home to stay with Sandy.'

'Why didn't your husband go with you?'

'He had a really good job; I didn't want him to give it up. Not when we were about to have a child to support. Neither of us wanted to accept money from his parents with the strings that went with it.'

'I wouldn't have let you go by yourself. Under any circumstances.'

'You're you. Philippe was Philippe.' She looked up at Jesse. 'I really, really hate talking about this.'

'I wish I could hug you but, in case you hadn't noticed, a couple of my mother's friends are walking on the other side of the road. If I touch you, the whole town will soon know.'

Lizzie turned around. Sure enough, two older ladies who had become regulars at the café and drank more cups of tea in the space of an hour than she had imagined anyone could possibly drink, had drawn level to them. She forced a smile and waved to them.

She turned back to Jesse. 'I see what you mean. I want to hug you too. More than you could know. But I'll get on with the story so I can be done with it.' She gritted her teeth. 'I got back to France and knew immediately something was different.'

'To cut a long story even shorter, he'd met someone else,' said Jesse with a scowl.

'How did you know that?'

'Lucky guess,' he said.

He must dislike hearing this as much as she disliked saying it. She appreciated how difficult it must have been for him to tell her about that dreadful Camilla.

'She was a *commis,* a junior chef, in the restaurant where Philippe worked. He said it meant nothing.'

'He was lonely; she threw herself at him,' Jesse drawled, contempt edging his voice.

'All that. He confessed and begged my forgiveness.'

Jesse's mouth tightened to a thin line. 'You know my opinion. No cheating under any circumstances.'

Was Jesse judging her? She wished she hadn't started this conversation.

'What choice did I have? I was twenty-three, had a brand new baby. We moved to Lyon to make a fresh start. I went back to work when Amy was six months old. But things were very different. No more party girl Lizzie.'

'I think I can predict the rest.' Jesse's hands were curled into fists.

'He swore he was faithful but I couldn't believe him. I was so jealous and suspicious I became a horrible person no one would want to live with. I stuck it until Amy was four. You know the rest.'

'Did you love him?' Jesse's question came from left field.

'I thought I did.'

'What do you feel about him now?' Jesse's voice was tight, his eyes guarded.

She frowned. 'That's a strange question to ask after what I've been telling you. Philippe is done and dusted as far as I'm concerned. Not only do I not love him, I don't actually like him.'

Jesse's face darkened. 'Best I don't meet the guy tomorrow. You might not be able to hold me back.'

'I've probably said too much. But now you know why I resisted getting involved with someone I thought might hurt me in the same way.'

CHAPTER FOURTEEN

THE NEXT DAY Lizzie was so nervous about the upcoming confrontation with Philippe she felt nauseous. She had organised extra help in the kitchen so she could spend the day with Amy. That also allowed her time for a private meeting with her ex-husband. Dread that he might try to take Amy away from her put her so on edge she wasn't fit to work anyway.

In the fairy tale her life in Dolphin Bay with Jesse had become, she cast Philippe in the role of the ogre who could take her happiness away. She was ready with sword and shield to fight him. She had given up her career and moved to Dolphin Bay for Amy's sake. She could give her daughter a good life here. She would never, ever let her go.

The reunion with Amy had been ecstatic, as it always was when they'd been apart for any length of time. She'd held her darling girl tightly to her, breathed in the apple shampoo freshness of her, laughed and pretended to squirm at Amy's exuberant hugs and kisses.

As usual after Amy had been with her father and his family it had taken her a few minutes to adjust to speaking English, to being a little Australian girl again. But after Lizzie had shown her the café—where the staff had made a huge fuss of her—and her new home upstairs, Amy had happily gone off with Maura. No doubt she would be introduced to little Alfie and then the begging and pleading to keep him would start. Lizzie decided to keep an open mind on that one.

Maura had so much grandmotherly love to give— and Amy was the only child in their family she had to lavish it on. Lizzie was aware of the thread of sadness underlying Maura's warmth, stemming from the tragic loss of Ben's little son.

With Amy settled with Maura, now it would be just her and Philippe, squaring up against each other as adversaries with their child the spoils of battle. She hadn't seen her ex-husband for more than a year. Sometimes she liked to imagine he didn't exist. But he was here in Dolphin Bay. She took a deep steadying breath to centre herself and headed to the Hotel Harbourside. *Let the battle begin.*

She'd chosen neutral territory, a quiet corner of the guest lounge. At this time of day, during the week, there should be no one to disturb them. She regretted the hurt that had flashed across Jesse's face when she had declined his offer to accompany her. But this was something she had to do by herself.

She cast a quick eye around the room. Jesse had said he would be nearby in case he needed to rush in to her defence—like a true Prince Charming would. She couldn't see him anywhere, but she trusted he was there. Jesse was true to his word. Although she knew the confrontation with Philippe wouldn't get physical— unless he'd changed out of sight—it was reassuring to know that Jesse was close.

Then Philippe was there, greeting her with his accented English that had charmed her years ago. She braced herself and looked up at her ex, his handsome

face with his prominent nose and Amy's eyes, his dark
blond hair. He had once been so dear to her; they had
started off with such high hopes, now he meant nothing.
There was an element of sadness—of failure—to her
thoughts but no regret. If it wasn't for Amy, she would
be happy never to have to see him again.

Jesse knew the layout of the Hotel Harbourside very
well. It had not been difficult to find a spot where, with
the help of a large wall mirror, he could sit in a large,
high-backed lounge chair and keep an eye on Lizzie
without her—or her ex-husband—seeing him. He held
an open newspaper in front of him and flicked through
its pages without seeing a word. It was like a stake-out.
Cloak and dagger stuff. Only this was a game where
the stakes were very high.

Lizzie had come into the guest lounge by herself. She
was dressed more formally than he had seen her, wearing narrow black trousers and a tight cropped jacket
with the sleeves pushed up. Her hair was pulled back
in a thick plait that hung in pale contrast down the back
of the black jacket. She looked elegant, stylish and so
unfamiliar it disconcerted him.

He could tell by the way Lizzie squared her shoulders
and measured her stride that she was nervous. Was that
why she had dressed like that? As armour? The ugly
thought intruded. Or to look good for her ex?

She only had seconds to pace the floor by herself
before she was joined by a tall guy wearing grey trousers and a lightweight sweater. Lizzie had always said
her cheater of an ex was a good-looking guy. Yeah.
He could see that. The Frenchman was big with broad
shoulders and a powerful body.

The first thing they did was kiss each other. Twice.

Once on each cheek. Jesse knew that was the European way, but still he gripped tight onto the arms of the chair at the sight of Lizzie in an embrace with another guy. Not just another guy. The man she'd married, had intended to spend her life with, the father of her child. *Someone she'd loved.*

Ex-husband and ex-wife started to talk. Jesse hadn't hidden close enough to hear their actual words, just the sound of their voices. The conversation seemed to be more intense than angry with Philippe doing a lot of the talking. They were switching between English and French.

It was a shock to see Lizzie speaking French. She looked different—her mouth, her face—and she gesticulated with her hands in a Gallic way. This was a Lizzie who seemed to slip right back into a different persona altogether. It made him wonder how well he actually knew her.

He wished he'd sat closer so he could hear but he would have risked exposure. Was Philippe laying down terms for custody of Amy? Or was he putting his argument for his family to return to him in France? If the dude got angry with Lizzie, Jesse would be up there like a shot to protect her.

But, far from being an angry confrontation with her ex, Lizzie's meeting seemed amicable. Very amicable. *Too* amicable.

Lizzie smiled. She laughed. She *hugged* the guy who she'd told Jesse had made her life hell. The ex smiled too. He seemed too damn happy for a man who was being told his ex-wife would not give him custody of their daughter. Any sense of fun Jesse had felt in staking out Lizzie and her ex was quickly replaced by bitter disbelief.

There was too much laughter and goodwill going on. Lizzie had said she dreaded the meeting but it looked to Jesse as if she was enjoying every minute of it.

Lizzie had problems with jealousy? Jesse had never before been bothered by it, had never understood the emotion. He sure as hell understood it now. Violent jealousy flamed through him at the sight of Lizzie with her ex-husband.

He felt excluded and it wasn't a feeling he liked. All the foundations he'd been building around Lizzie felt threatened.

They hugged *again*. Then they walked out to the lobby and towards the exit, chatting as they went.

Jesse got up from his lounge chair, slammed the newspaper on the table and headed towards the side door that led to the terrace. From there he would actually be able to hear their farewells unless Lizzie walked her ex to his rental car.

But no. They stayed put and did the one-kiss, two-kiss thing again. Then Lizzie looked up into her handsome ex-husband's face and said very clearly in English. 'I will see you in Lyon. For the start of a new life.'

Then she watched him get into the car and waved as he pulled out of the hotel driveway and headed north to Sydney.

Those final words reverberated through Jesse's mind. *I will see you in Lyon. For the start of a new life.*

What the hell had that meant? It was difficult not to draw the obvious conclusion.

He'd been played for a fool again.

He wouldn't make the same mistake he'd made with Camilla. He was in deep with Lizzie, but he had an out. The job in Houston.

But first he'd give her a chance to explain herself.

If she didn't come clean then he'd know he had been lied to again. That Lizzie intended to have her fun with him until it was time to go back to her other man. Like Camilla had.

His hands fisted by his sides, he stepped out from the terrace so Lizzie could see him as she approached.

Her face lit up when she saw him and she hastened her steps to get to him quicker. It made his gut churn at how much he had come to care for her.

'So there you are,' she said. 'I've been looking for you. I've got good news.'

'Fire away,' he said gruffly.

'Philippe has dropped his plans to sue for sole custody. He flew all the way here to apologise about the way he behaved during our time together and to tell me—and to tell me…' She spluttered to a halt.

'To tell you what?' He felt choked by a grim foreboding.

'To…uh…to tell me how much he cared for Amy and how she would always be his first priority.'

She was lying. He couldn't fail to notice how she'd pulled herself up. No way would her ex come to the other side of the world just to tell her he was sorry for his behaviour of years ago. He believed the guy had apologised. But what had come next? Reconciliation? There'd been a lot of smiling and hugging. What the hell had that been about?

'That's good,' he muttered.

'You were a big hit with Amy, by the way, Uncle Jesse.' Lizzie chattered on, seemingly oblivious to his dark change of mood.

'Yeah, she's a great kid.' He'd been working at the café, educating Nikki in the finer aspects of pulling espresso shots, when Lizzie had brought Amy in to show her the café. Her little face had lit up when she'd seen him and she'd come tearing up to him to hurtle herself at him with a squeal of delight. 'Uncle Jesse!'

Laughing, he'd swept her up into his arms. It had taken him a long time after the fire to be comfortable around kids. He'd loved Ben's little boy Liam. It had seemed disloyal to pay attention to other children when his nephew had gone. He had taken his role as uncle very seriously. What role in his life might Amy play?

'Be flattered,' Lizzie had said. 'She doesn't take to everyone.'

'I wanted to introduce you to Philippe,' Lizzie said now.

He frowned. 'Why would you do that?'

So he'd be friendly to him when they got back together?

He thought back to one of the reasons he'd resisted pursuing Lizzie—if things went wrong he'd still have to see her at every family gathering. Her and her current man—perhaps her reconciled husband.

Not if he was in Houston, he wouldn't.

'Because, well, because he was here and because he's Amy's father I—'

'You told me how this guy cheated on you and made your life hell. Why would I want to shake his hand?' He paused. 'Unless things have changed between you.'

She looked confused. 'Well, yes, they have changed.'

Here it came—the confession.

'What I meant is, *he's* changed. Grown up at last. Admitted his mistakes.'

'And?'

She frowned. 'What do you mean "and"? I don't know what you're talking about.'

'Haven't you got something to tell me?'

She flushed. 'Well, yes. I do.' She looked around her. 'But this isn't the time or the place to talk to you about it. What it means for us.'

He cursed inwardly. *So he hadn't misunderstood those overheard words.*

'There's something *I* need to tell *you*,' he said, unable to meet her eyes. 'The company in Houston contacted me this morning. They want a decision by close of business today and a start date of Monday if I accept. I'd have to leave Dolphin Bay tomorrow.'

The blood drained from her face. 'Oh,' she said. 'Wh-what will you do?'

'I'm going to take it.'

'Wh-what about your shoulder?'

'It's healed enough for desk duties.'

He hadn't meant to be so harsh about it. Hadn't wanted to wound her. But hell, she had dealt him a body blow. Just like Camilla had.

'You'll be gone tomorrow?' Her voice was so faint he had to strain to hear it.

He nodded, unable to find the words that would take that stricken look off her face. Yet she still wouldn't admit she was going back to her husband. Or give him an explanation of why she'd lied. Why she had no explanation for those words he'd overheard.

He wanted to tell her he loved her. That he wanted to make decisions based on *their* future, not just his.

But she wasn't giving anything away. Not a word about her plans for going back to France to take up a new life with her old husband. Or why she was going to Lyon if it wasn't for that.

'So,' she said, with that familiar tilting of her chin. 'You'll be leaving Dolphin Bay?'

'Looks like it,' he said.

'Wh-what does that mean for us?' She turned her face away.

'You still don't have anything you want to tell me?' Anger and frustration and disbelief that he'd been caught again raged through him.

'It's not anything you'd want to hear,' she said in a very small voice.

That sealed it.

Then she met his gaze straight on. 'You'd better go make that phone call.'

She turned and he let her go.

CHAPTER FIFTEEN

LIZZIE WALKED AWAY from Jesse, expecting him to come after her. To tell her it was all a mistake. Reeling in shocked disbelief, she got halfway back to her apartment before she realised it wasn't going to happen. *Jesse had dumped her.* After all the emotional ups and downs she'd been through today, she was finding it impossible to stay steady on her feet. She had to stop and lean against one of the famous dolphin rubbish bins. Its smiling mouth seemed to mock her.

In a daze, she dragged her feet one step after another until she reached the door to her apartment and then hauled herself up the stairs.

The empty rooms derided her. Jesse was everywhere. His handprint all over the place—the tiles he'd laid, the walls he'd painted, the room he'd prepared for Amy. He was on the sofa where the aroma of peppermint still lingered. Most of all, he was in her bedroom. How could he have made love to her with such tenderness and passion, only to dump her when her daughter came home?

Her heart contracted with the agony of the realisation of what it felt to be one of Jesse's disposable girls.

She'd cleared the bedroom of every trace of him so Amy wouldn't be aware Uncle Jesse had been sleeping over in Mummy's bed. She and Jesse had agreed it was too soon for her to know. She laid her head on the pillow where only this morning his beautiful dark head had rested. Where they had slept entwined in each other's arms. She lay where he had lain, breathed in deeply, hoping for a lingering trace of his scent but she'd stripped the bed and washed all the linen. There wasn't a trace of him left.

What had gone wrong?

He'd given her no clue. His change of heart had come completely out of the blue. Was it something to do with her meeting with Philippe? The meeting that had released her from the chains of resentment that had held her back from fully trusting Jesse.

The first thing Philippe had done was to apologise for the way he'd behaved during their marriage. Then he'd told her he was getting married again. To a French-Canadian girl named Thérèse who was also a chef.

Lizzie's first thought had been for Amy. But Philippe had reiterated his love for his daughter and said Thérèse wanted to be a good stepmother. In fact she wanted to meet Lizzie so she could discuss Amy's shared care when her little girl spent time in France. There was no longer any question that Philippe would seek sole custody.

For Amy's sake she had accepted the hand of reconciliation that Philippe had extended. 'We learn from our mistakes, yes?' Philippe had said.

She had agreed and, in doing so, had realised how unfair it had been of her to judge Jesse on the mistakes she had made with her ex-husband. *The men were nothing alike.*

Her relationship with Philippe had been founded on youthful passion fired by rebellion. She and her ex-husband had never been friends like Jesse and she had become. Jesse was both friend and lover—it was a formidable combination. She doubted her ex had understood her after several years together the way Jesse already understood her.

As she'd spoken with Philippe, something in her heart that had been frozen with bitterness and resentment had thawed. She'd felt freed from heavy chains she hadn't realised had been tethering her so tightly.

The revelation had had nothing to do with Philippe and everything to do with Jesse. Her feelings for him had changed everything. Had made her ready to forgive and move on with no lingering fears from the past to poison the present with jealousy and suspicion.

Jesse was the real deal. The happily ever after. The till death us do part.

Then she'd sought out Jesse, anxious to tell him what had happened—and to explain how the burden of Philippe's past behaviour had lifted so she was free to love again without the hindrance of bad old energy from the marriage gone wrong.

But Jesse had blocked her every way. Grim Jesse with the charming good looks gone dark and glowering. *Black Irish.* Jesse with the harsh voice, the eyes with the shutters suddenly down against her.

Jesse who, to all intents, had done exactly what she'd feared he'd do. *Made a conquest of her and then dumped her.* And boy had she been an easy conquest. She'd barely put up a struggle before she'd fallen so joyously into bed.

Just another of Jesse's girls after all. She'd believed she'd been so much more. How could she have been so naïve, so stubborn, not to listen to her own sister's advice? She'd listened to her heart instead and it had led her wrong.

And yet.

She'd grown to believe in Jesse so strongly it was hard to let that trust go. She had truly thought he wouldn't do this to her. But there was no escaping that he had.

If she looked at it brutally, dispassionately, the timing was right for him to get rid of her. Amy had come home. With a five-year-old in residence, they would have to snatch time together, might go days without intimacy. He needed to free himself for new conquests. Those Texan girls didn't know what they were in for. Jesse the Player. Jesse the Heartbreaker.

She thought back, puzzling, seeking clues. *Philippe.* It all came back to his visit. Maybe Jesse was concerned about the ongoing contact with her ex-husband. There wasn't anything she could do about that. Amy deserved to have a loving relationship with her father and she was determined to facilitate that in any way she could.

What had Jesse meant? He'd asked her if she had something to tell him three times.

Did he want to know he had a place in her and Amy's life when there was a father still so actively involved with his daughter—even though said father lived on the other side of the world?

Maybe Jesse wanted assurance.

Maybe Jesse wanted her to tell him how she felt.

Maybe she needed to tell Jesse she loved him, wanted him, would go to Houston with him. Would go anywhere with him—the Philippines, India, any old where. Because she realised with a huge whoosh of pain that made her double over with the agony of it that life without Jesse would be intolerable.

She got up from the bed. She had to find him. Tell him she loved him. And if it all blew up in her face, if she was after all the latest in a long line of discarded Jesse's girls, at least she would have tried.

She clattered down the stairs of her apartment, waved to one of the waitresses who stood outside the door of the café talking on her phone. She kept her demeanour calm, her face controlled. As far as anyone else in Dolphin Bay knew, she and Jesse were just friends. It wouldn't look right for her to be stressed and tearful and hunting around town for him.

But where could she find him?

She didn't want to call him on his mobile phone to alert him she was coming after him. She went to the boathouse. No Jesse. His car was gone too.

If Jesse was indeed taking off for Texas tomorrow, surely he'd want a farewell swim at his favourite beach. She'd take a punt he'd gone to Silver Gull. If he hadn't gone there she'd keep on looking until she found him. Even if she had to drive to Sydney and confront him at the airport.

No way was she going to let Jesse go until she'd made absolutely sure there was no hope left for them.

Jesse swam up and down the length of the beach, churning through the freezing water until his shoulder ached too much to go on. He'd had to fight a strong swell to get out beyond the breaking waves. That was nothing to the fight he'd had against himself. But the salt water and the vigorous exercise had cleared his head.

He'd been an idiot. The worst of the wussies. He'd let all the pain and fear from his early decision to avoid love make him act like an irrational, bad-tempered fool. He'd let the pain of Camilla's old betrayal blind him to the fact that Lizzie was not Camilla. Lizzie had not set out to hurt him. *He had hurt her.*

While he'd raged against the idea that Lizzie was going back to her ex-husband, she had never actually said she was. Remembering the bewildered look on her lovely face made him realise his anger had stopped him thinking straight.

Now he understood what Lizzie had struggled with—jealousy could turn a person crazy.

He should have asked Lizzie outright about what he'd overheard. Instead he'd set her a test of honesty she hadn't even known she had to pass. He'd been totally out of order. Cruel. Cowardly. Worse, he had betrayed the trust she'd worked so hard to build up from a baseline of emotional abuse.

He strode out of the water. Slung a towel around him and headed towards his car. He had to find her. Grovel. Apologise. Grovel some more. *Tell her how much he cared for her.*

Only to see Lizzie walking across the sand towards him. Her face was a mass of contradictions. Fear. Determination. And something else shining from her eyes that made his heart leap inside his chest.

He ran to meet her. But as he got closer she put up her hand to stop him. 'Before you come any further, Jesse Morgan, I want to answer that question you kept asking me before—have I got anything to tell you?'

He groaned. 'That was a mistake. I—' But she spoke right over him in that blunt, determined Lizzie way.

'I *have* got something to tell you. I don't know if it's what you wanted to hear but you're going to hear it anyway. I love you, Jesse. I fancied you the moment I met you. Then I fell in love with you when you danced me around a deserted beach in the moonlight to the sound of the stars. Or maybe when you massaged my feet. It could even have been when you pulled coffees all day just to help me out. Whatever. I nearly lost you the first time through a silly misunderstanding and I don't want to lose you again through another one. Is that what you wanted me to tell you?'

Her eyes were huge and her mouth quivered as she waited for his answer.

She loved him.

How could he have been such an idiot as to risk losing her?

He wanted to pull her into his arms and tell her he loved her too and that she was the most amazing woman he'd ever met. That she had become his favourite person in the whole world. That it would be like wrenching out his soul if he couldn't have her in his life. But that was beyond his limited skills as an orator. And he feared she wouldn't welcome his touch. Especially as he was dripping salt water.

'No, it wasn't,' he said. 'You gave me a better answer.'

'What do you mean?' she said, hope struggling to life amid the woeful expression on her face. 'You're talking in riddles, Jesse, and I'm in no mood to try to solve them.'

He took a deep breath. 'I overheard you talking to your ex. You hugged him, kissed him and said: "I will see you in Lyon. For the start of a new life."'

Why the hell hadn't he asked her that directly?

She frowned. 'You were there? Listening?'

'I heard every word of your farewell. Then, when we met up afterwards, I wanted you to tell me what you had meant by that promise to see him in Lyon. Did it mean you were going back to him? That's the conclusion I jumped to. But if you say you love me, I guess you won't be boarding a plane to France any time soon.'

She crossed her arms in front of her. 'I certainly

won't be going back to Philippe. That was never, ever on the cards. Why didn't you just ask me?'

'Because I was a stupid, insecure idiot, too blinded by fear of losing you to think straight. So I'll ask you now. Why *are* you going to France to see your ex-husband?'

'You might be going too,' she said.

'Now you're the one talking in riddles.'

'Let me explain,' she said, uncrossing her arms.

'Please do,' he said. *Man, had he made a mess of this.*

'Philippe asked me to keep this secret for Amy's sake. But you're more important than keeping his confidence. He's getting married and his fiancée wants me and Amy to be there at the wedding next April in Lyon. You're invited too. Actually, I invited you. But Philippe didn't want Amy to know until closer to the time and he asked me not to tell anyone in case she overheard.'

'Your ex is getting married?' That was the last thing he had expected to hear.

'Is it so surprising? People do get remarried, you know. And I'm happy for him.'

'I thought he wanted you back.'

Now her eyes were accusing. 'How could you possibly think I'd go back to him after what you and I have shared together? The…the fairy tale magic. What kind of a woman do you think I am?'

'Obviously one I'm not worthy of,' he said slowly. He tasted regret, bitter and stinging.

All her indignation and anger fled from her face and her eyes softened. She reached up and laid her fingers across his mouth. 'Oh, Jesse, don't say that. After all we've been through to get here.'

He took her fingers in his hand. 'Can you forgive me?'

'If you'll forgive me for keeping secrets from you. I

should have told you straight away about the wedding in Lyon. I love you, Jesse. I couldn't bear to lose you.'

Relief swelled through him. 'That's twice you've told me you love me. Can you give a man a chance to catch up?'

He couldn't wait another second to gather her close to him. She squealed. 'You're wet and cold but I don't care.'

He claimed her mouth in a kiss. 'I love you, Lizzie,' he said, revelling in the sound of the words and how it made him feel to say them. 'I love you, Lizzie,' he repeated. 'That's twice I've said it. We're even.'

She locked her arms around his neck. 'I'm going to tell you how much I love you a lot more times than that. I'm coming to Texas with you. Amy too.'

'You'd leave the café?'

'Funnily enough, though it didn't seem the best job in the world when I came down to Dolphin Bay, I've got attached to it. But not as attached as I am to you. So yes, I'll leave it after training someone else to take over so I don't let Sandy down.'

'You don't have to leave. I'm staying right here in Dolphin Bay.'

'What do you mean?'

'I'm going into business with Ben.'

She frowned. 'Is it what you really want? You're not compromising for my sake? Because if—'

'It's what I really want. I want you too. No more pretending to be "just friends" either. No more being jealous because we're not certain of each other.'

'Jealous? You?'

'You turned me into a jealous guy when I saw you hugging and kissing Philippe.'

She shrugged in that Gallic way. 'It's just a French thing. The kissing. Nothing to be concerned about.'

'I didn't like it.'

'So we're both jealous. Do two people being jealous cancel out the jealousy?'

She was making light of it. But he knew how concerned she was about her jealousy causing problems.

'I have a better idea,' he said. 'Love. Security. Commitment. Knowing the other person is always in your court. That could go a long way to cancelling out the jealousy.'

She went very still. He was aware of the sound of the waves. The thudding of his own heart. 'I…I'm not sure what you're getting at,' she said.

He'd thought about this when he'd been swimming up and down in the surf. How he couldn't bear to be without Lizzie in his life. How he could think of nothing better than making her and Amy his family. How what she needed had become what he needed. 'A wedding ring firmly circling your finger is my idea of a jealousy buster,' he said.

'And a matching one circling yours is mine,' she said. Her wonderful warm laugh rang out across the beach. 'Did you just propose to me, Jesse Morgan?'

'Did you just accept my proposal, Lizzie Morgan to-be?'

'I did,' she said, planting a kiss on his mouth. 'And… and I couldn't be happier.'

'Me too,' he said and kissed her back. His heart actually ached with joy.

She broke away from the kiss. 'You realise there will be a lot of upset people in town when this news leaks out?'

'Who? My family will be delighted.'

'The punters who laid bets you'd never marry.'

'Serves them right for giving you the wrong impression of me and making it so tough for me to win you.'

She smiled. 'I'm glad you changed my mind about that. I love you, Jesse.'

'I love you too,' he said. 'That makes three times we've said it.'

'Shall we try for thirty times before the day is over?'

'Why not?' he said. 'I'll never tire of hearing those words from you.'

EPILOGUE

Two months later

AS A CHILD, Christmas had not been Lizzie's favourite time of year—her family Christmas Days had always seen the sad cliché of every bitterness and conflict getting a good airing over the roast turkey and plum pudding.

As an adult, she had embraced Christmas as a joyous celebration, growing to love festive traditions whether celebrated in the winter of Europe or the Australian summer.

But this year's Christmas was going to be the most magical and memorable of all—because this year Lizzie was celebrating Christmas as a bride.

On Christmas Eve—a perfect sunny south coast morning—Lizzie let Sandy fuss around fixing her hair, which had been braided into a thick plait interwoven with white ribbons and creamy frangipani flowers. In her ears were the exquisite diamond studs Jesse had given her as an early Christmas present.

The sisters were getting ready in a location van parked on the approach to Silver Gull beach. As the most significant moments of their courtship had taken place on beaches, she and Jesse had decided Silver

Gull would be the perfect venue for their exchange of vows.

The location van had been Sandy's idea; she was familiar with such luxuries from her days working on advertising shoots. Lizzie marvelled at the set-up—the interior was like a dressing room complete with mirrors and even a small bathroom. It was the ideal place to prepare for a wedding at a beach.

'Now, let me check the dress,' said Sandy, who was taking her duties as Lizzie's bridesmaid very seriously.

Lizzie was so happy to be getting married to Jesse she hadn't imagined she'd be plagued by any wedding day nerves. Not so. She wasn't worried about the details of the ceremony; they had all been organised by Kate Lancaster, who had done such a marvellous job as wedding planner for Sandy and Ben's wedding. Or about the reception—a small informal affair which was to be held back at Bay Bites. Lizzie's team had all that under control.

No. Lizzie's concern was that she wanted to look beautiful for Jesse.

She did a twirl as best she could in the confines of the van. 'Do you think Jesse will like it?' she asked Sandy, unable to suppress the tremor in her voice. She loved the ankle-length dress for its elegant simplicity: a V-neck tunic in soft off-white tulle lace layered over a silk under-dress and caught in with a flat bow in the small of her back.

'Jesse won't be able to keep his eyes off you,' said Sandy. 'I've never seen a lovelier bride, and I'm not saying that because you're my baby sister. That dress is divine—simple, elegant, discreetly sexy. Just like you.'

Lizzie hugged her. 'You're okay about me marrying Jesse, aren't you?' she asked. 'You warned me off him so many times. But he isn't what people said, you know. He makes me happier than I ever could have imagined.'

She was taken aback by Sandy's burst of laughter. 'Ben and I couldn't be more delighted you two are getting married. You and Jesse are perfect for each other. But you're so stubborn you would have run the other way if I'd told you that. You had to find each other in your own way.'

Lizzie's first reaction was to huff indignantly. But instead she smiled. 'You did me a favour and I'm grateful.' She paused. 'Sisters married to brothers. It's worked out so well for us, hasn't it? Our guys from Dolphin Bay.'

'Yes,' said Sandy. Her hand went protectively to the slight swell of her belly. She and Ben were expecting a baby in six months' time—an event anticipated with much joy by the Morgan clan. 'We're both getting our happily-ever-after endings.'

Then Sandy bustled Lizzie towards the door of the van. 'Come on, bride, your gorgeous groom is waiting for you.'

Lizzie waited at the start of the 'aisle' formed by double rows of seashells that led to a white wooden wedding arch adorned with filmy white fabric and sprays of the small red flowers of the New South Wales Christmas bush. The aquamarine waters of the ocean with the white waves rolling in formed the most glorious backdrop for her wedding ceremony. When she drew in some deep calming breaths, the salt smell of the sea mingled with the sweet scent of the frangipani in her hair.

Both Sandy and Amy, her only attendants, had preceded her down the aisle. They both wore pretty knee-length dresses in a shade of palest coffee. Barista coffee, Lizzie had joked. They were all barefoot, with their toenails painted Christmas red in honour of the festive season.

There was one more thing to do before Lizzie took her journey down the aisle. She laid aside her bouquet of Christmas bush. Then slipped off her diamond engagement ring from the third finger of her left hand and transferred it to her right hand. Jesse had surprised her with the superb solitaire in a starkly simple platinum setting just days after he had proposed to her on this very beach.

She watched as Sandy reached the wedding arch and took her place beside Ben, Jesse's best man. On her other side, Amy held her aunt's hand. Then it was Lizzie's turn to walk down the aisle to get married to Jesse.

The sand either side of the aisle was lined with well-wishers but they were just a blur to Lizzie. She recognised Maura standing by with Amy's adored Alfie and Ben's golden retriever Hobo firmly secured by leashes. But the only face she wanted to see was Jesse's.

And then she was beside him; he was clean-shaven, his black hair tamed, heart-achingly handsome in a stone-coloured linen suit and an open-neck white silk shirt. Any doubts she might have had about him finding her beautiful on her wedding day were dispersed by the look of adoration in his deep blue eyes as he took her hand in his and drew her to his side.

'I love you,' he murmured.

'I love you too,' she whispered.

'That's three thousand and sixty-three times we've said it,' he said.

'And we have a lifetime ahead of us to keep on saying it,' she said, tightening her clasp on his hand.

The celebrant called the guests to order. Before she knew it, they'd exchanged vows and Jesse was slipping the platinum wedding ring on her finger and then her diamond ring on top. 'I declare you man and wife,' said the celebrant.

'Now I can kiss my bride,' said Jesse, gathering her into his arms. 'Mrs Lizzie Morgan.'

Their kiss should have been the cue for classical wedding music to play through the speakers placed strategically near the wedding arch.

But, as Jesse claimed his first kiss as her husband, Lizzie was stunned to hear instead the distinctive notes of Jesse's signature tune rearranged for violin and piano.

'Where did that music come from?' she asked Jesse.

Jesse laughed. 'No idea. But I like it. Now you truly are Jesse's girl.' He kissed her again to the accompaniment of clapping and cheering from their friends and family. 'My wife—the best Christmas present ever.'

* * * * *

CHRISTMAS WHERE
THEY BELONG

MARION LENNOX

This book is dedicated to Lorna May Dickins.
Her kindness, her humour and her love are an
inspiration for always.

CHAPTER ONE

'DIDN'T YOU ONCE own a house in the Blue Mountains?'

'Um…yes.'

'Crikey, Jules, you wouldn't want to be there now. The whole range looks about to burn.'

It was two days before Christmas. The Australian world of finance shut down between Christmas and New Year, but the deal Julie McDowell was working on was international. The legal issues were urgent.

But the Blue Mountains… Fire.

She dumped her armload of contracts and headed for Chris's desk. At thirty-two, Chris was the same age as Julie, but her colleague's work ethic was as different from hers as it was possible to be. Chris worked from nine to five and not a moment more before he was off home to his wife and kids in the suburbs. Sometimes he even surfed the Web during business hours.

Sure enough, his computer was open at the Web browser now. She came up behind him and saw a fire map. The Blue Mountains. A line of red asterisks.

Her focus went straight to Mount Bundoon, a tiny hamlet right in the centre of the asterisks. The hamlet she'd once lived in.

'Is it on fire?' she gasped. She'd been so busy she hadn't been near a news broadcast for hours. Days?

'Not yet.' Chris zoomed in on a few of the asterisks. 'These are alerts, not evacuation orders. A storm came through last night, with lighting strikes but not much rain. The bush is tinder dry after the drought, and most of these asterisks show spot fires in inaccessible bushland. But strong winds and high temperatures are forecast for to-morrow. They're already closing roads, saying she could be a killer.'

A killer.

The Blue Mountains.

You wouldn't want to be there now.

She went back to her desk and pulled up the next con-tract. This was important. She needed to concentrate, but the words blurred before her eyes. All she could see was a house—long, low, every detail architecturally designed, built to withstand the fiercest bush fires.

In her mind she walked through the empty house to a bedroom with two small beds in the shape of racing cars. Teddies sitting against the pillows. Toys. A wall-hanging of a steam train her mother had made.

She hadn't been there for four years. It should have been sold. Why hadn't it?

She fought to keep her mind on her work. This had to be dealt with before Christmas.

Teddies. A wardrobe full of small boys' clothes.

She closed her eyes and she was there again, tucking two little boys into bed, watching Rob read them their bedtime story.

It was history, long past, but she couldn't open her eyes. She couldn't.

'Julie? Are you okay?' Her boss was standing over her, sounding concerned. Bob Marsh was a financial wizard but he looked after his staff, especially those who brought as much business to the firm as Julie.

She forced herself to open her eyes and tried for a smile. It didn't work.

'What's up?'

'The fire.' She took a deep breath, knowing what she was facing. Knowing she had no choice.

'I *do* have a house in the Blue Mountains,' she managed. 'If it's going to burn there are things I need to save.' She gathered her pile of contracts and did what she'd never done in all her years working for Opal, Harbison and Marsh. She handed the pile to Bob. 'You'll need to deal with this,' she told him. 'I'm sorry, but...'

She couldn't finish the sentence. She grabbed her purse and went.

Rob McDowell was watching the fire's progress on his phone. He'd downloaded an app to track it by, and he'd been checking it on and off for hours.

He was in Adelaide, working. His clients had wanted to be in the house by Christmas and he'd bent over backwards to make it happen. Their house was brilliant and there were only a few decorative touches left to be made. Rob was no longer needed, but Sir Cliff and Lady Claudia had requested their architect to stay on until tomorrow.

He should. They were having a housewarming on Christmas Eve, and socialising at the end of a job was important. The *Who's Who* of Adelaide, maybe even the *Who's Who* of the entire country would be here. There weren't many people who could beckon the cream of society on Christmas Eve but Sir Cliff and Lady Claudia had that power. As the architect of their stunning home, Rob could expect scores of professional approaches afterwards.

But it wasn't just professional need that was driving him. For the last few years he'd flown overseas to the ski fields for Christmas but somehow this year they'd lost their appeal. Christmas had been a nightmare for years but finally he was beginning to accept that running away didn't help. He might as well stay for the party, he'd decided, but now he checked the phone app again and felt worse. The house he and Julie had built was right in the line of fire.

The house would be safe, he told himself. He'd designed it himself and it had been built with fires like this one in mind.

But no house could withstand the worst of Australia's bush fires. He knew that. To make its occupants safe he'd built a bunker into the hill behind the house, but the house itself could go up in flames.

It was insured. No one was living there. It shouldn't matter.

But the contents...

The contents.

He should have cleared it out by now, he thought savagely. He shouldn't have left everything there. The tricycles. The two red fire engines he'd chosen himself that last Christmas.

Julie might have taken them.

She hadn't. She would have told him.

Both of them had walked away from their house four years ago. It should have been on the market, but...but...

But he'd paid a housekeeping service to clean it once a month, and to clear the grounds. He was learning to move on, but selling the house, taking this last step, still seemed...too hard.

So what state was it in now? he wondered. Had the bushland encroached again? If there was bushland growing against the house...

It didn't matter. The house was insured, he told himself again. What did it matter if it burned? Wouldn't that just be the final step in moving on with his life?

But two fire engines…

This was ridiculous. He was thinking of forgoing the social event of the season, a career-building triumph, steps to the future, to save two toy fire engines?

But…

'Sarah…' He didn't know what he intended to say until the words were in his mouth, but the moment he said it he knew his decision was right.

'Yeah?' The interior decorator was balancing on a ladder, her arms full of crimson tulle. The enormous drawing room was going to look stunning. 'Could you hand me those ribbons?'

'I can't, Sarah,' he said, in a voice he scarcely recognised. 'I own a house in the Blue Mountains and they're saying the fire threat's getting worse. Could you make my excuses? I need to go…home.'

At the headquarters of the Blue Mountains Fire Service, things looked grim and were about to get worse. Every time a report came in, more asterisks appeared on the map. The fire chief had been staring at it for most of the day, watching spot fires erupt, while the weather forecast grew more and more forbidding.

'We won't be able to contain this,' he eventually said, heavily. 'It's going to break out.'

'Evacuate?' His second-in-command was looking even more worried than he was.

'If we get one worse report from the weather guys, yes. We'll put out a pre-evacuation warning tonight. Anyone not prepared to stay and firefight should leave now.' He looked again at the map and raked his thinning hair. 'Okay, people, let's put the next step of fire warnings into place. Like it or not, we're about to mess with a whole lot of people's Christmases.'

CHAPTER TWO

THE HOUSE LOOKED just as she'd left it. The garden had grown, of course. A couple of trees had grown up close to the house. Rob wouldn't be pleased. He'd say it was a fire risk.

It was a fire risk.

She was sitting in the driveway in her little red coupé, staring at the front door. Searching for the courage to go inside.

It was three years, eleven months, ten days since she'd been here.

Rob had brought her home from hospital. She'd wandered into the empty house; she'd looked around and it was almost as if the walls were taunting her.

You're here and they're not. What sort of parents are you? What sort of parents were you?

She hadn't even stayed the night. She couldn't. She'd thrown what she most needed into a suitcase and told Rob to take her to a hotel.

'Julie, we can do this.' She still heard Rob's voice; she still saw his face. 'We can face this together.'

'It wasn't you who slept while they died.' She'd thrown that at him, he hadn't answered and she'd known right then that the final link had snapped.

She hadn't been back since.

Go in, she told herself now. *Get this over.*

She opened the car door and the heat hit her with such force that she gasped.

It was dusk. It shouldn't be this hot, this late.

The tiny hamlet of Mount Bundoon had looked almost deserted as she'd driven through. Low-lying smoke and the lack of wind was giving it a weird, eerie feeling. She'd stopped at the general store and bought milk and bread and butter, and the lady had been surprised to see her.

'We're about to close, love,' she said. 'Most people are packing to get out or have already left. You're not evacuating?'

'The latest warning is watch and wait.'

'They've upgraded it. Unless you plan on defending your home, they're advising you get out, if not now, then at least by nine in the morning. That's when the wind's due to rise, but most residents have chosen to leave straight away.'

Julie had hesitated at that. The road up here had been packed with laden cars, trailers, horse floats, all the accoutrements people treasured. That was why she was here. To take things she treasured.

But now she thought: *it wasn't*. She sat in the driveway and stared at the house where she'd once lived, and she thought, even though the house was full of the boys' belongings, it wasn't possessions she wanted.

Was it just to be here? One last time?

It wasn't going to burn, she told herself. It'd still be here…for ever. But that was a dumb thought. They'd have to sell eventually.

That'd mean contacting Rob.

Don't go there.

Go in, she told herself. *Hunker down. This house is fire-safe. In the morning you can walk away but just for tonight… Just for tonight you can let yourself remember.*

Even if it hurt so much it nearly killed her.

* * *

Eleven o'clock. The plane had been delayed, because of smoke haze surrounding Sydney. 'There's quite a fire down there, ladies and gentlemen,' the pilot had said as they skirted the Blue Mountains. 'Just be thankful you're up here and not down there.'

But he'd wanted to be down there. By the time he'd landed the fire warnings for Mount Bundoon had been upgraded. *Leave if safe to do so.* Still, the weather forecast was saying the winds weren't likely to pick up until early morning. Right now there was little wind. The house would be safe.

So he'd hired a car and driven into the mountains, along roads where most of the traffic was going in the other direction. When he'd reached the outskirts of Mount Bundoon he'd hit a road block.

'Your business, sir?' he was asked.

'I live here.' How true was that? He didn't live anywhere, he conceded, but maybe here was still…home. 'I just need to check all my fire prevention measures are in place and operational.'

'You're aware of the warnings?'

'I am, but my house is pretty much fire-safe and I'll be out first thing in the morning.'

'You're not planning on defending?'

'Not my style.'

'Not mine either,' the cop said. 'They're saying the wind'll be up by nine, turning to the north-west, bringing the fire straight down here. The smoke's already making the road hazardous. We're about to close it now, allowing no one else in. I shouldn't let you pass.'

'I'll be safe. I'm on my own and I'll be in and out in no time.'

MARION LENNOX 15

'Be out by the time the wind changes, if not before,' he said grudgingly.

'I will be.'

'Goodnight, then, sir,' the cop said. 'Stay safe.'

'Same to you, in spades.'

He drove on. The smoke wasn't thick, just a haze like a winter fog. The house was on the other side of town, tucked into a valley overlooking the Bundoon Creek. The ridges would be the most dangerous places, Rob thought, not the valley. He and Julie had thought about bush fire when they'd built. If you were planning to build in the Australian bush, you were stupid if you didn't.

Maybe they'd been stupid anyway. Building so far out of town. Maybe that was why...

No. Don't think why. That was the way of madness.

Nearly home. That was a dumb thing to think, too, but he turned the last bend and thought of all the times he'd come home, with kids, noise, chaos, all the stuff associated with twins. Sometimes he and Julie would manage the trip back together and that was the best. *'Mummy, Daddy—you're both here...'*

Cut it out, he told himself fiercely. *You were dumb to come. Don't make it any worse by thinking of the past.*

But the past was all around him, even if it was shrouded in smoke.

'I'll take their toys and get out of here,' he told himself, and then he pulled into the driveway... and the lights were on.

She'd turned on all the lights to scare the ghosts.

No. If there were any ghosts here she'd welcome them with open arms—it wasn't ghosts she was scared of. It was the dark. It was trying to sleep in this house, and remembering.

She lay on the king-sized bed she and Rob had bought the week before their wedding and she knew sleep was out of the question. She should leave.

But leaving seemed wrong, too. Not when the kids were here.

The kids weren't here. Only memories of them.

This was crazy. She was a legal financier, a good one, specialising in international monetary negotiations. No one messed with her. No one questioned her sanity.

So why was she lying in bed hoping for ghosts?

She lay completely still, listening to the small sounds of the night. The scratching of a possum in the tree outside the window. A night owl calling.

This house had never been quiet. She found herself aching for noise, for voices, for…something.

She got something. She heard a car pull into the driveway. She saw the glimmer of headlights through the window.

The front door opened, and she knew part of her past had just returned. The ghost she was most afraid of.

'Julie?' He'd guessed it must be her before he even opened the door. Firstly the car. It was a single woman's car, expensive, a display of status.

Rob normally drove a Land Rover. Okay, maybe that was a status thing as well, he conceded. He liked the idea that he might spend a lot of time on rural properties but in truth most of his clients were city based. But still, he couldn't drive a car like the one in the driveway. No one here could. No one who commuted from here to the city. No one who taxied kids.

Every light was on in the house. Warning off ghosts?

It had to be Julie.

If she was here the last thing he wanted was to scare

her, so the moment he opened the door he called, 'Julie, are you here? It's Rob.'

And she emerged from their bedroom.

Julie.

The sight of her made him feel… No. He couldn't begin to define how he felt seeing her.

It had been nearly four years. She'd refused to see him since.

'I slept while they died and I can't forgive myself. Ever. I can't even think about what I've lost. If I hadn't slept...'

She'd thrown it at him the day he'd brought her home from hospital. He'd spent weeks sick with self-blame, sick with emptiness, not knowing how to cope with his own grief, much less hers. The thought that she blamed herself hadn't even occurred to him. It should have, but in those crucial seconds after she'd said it he hadn't had a response. He'd stared at her, numb with shock and grief, as she'd limped into the bedroom on her crutches, thrown things into a suitcase and demanded he take her to a hotel.

And that had pretty much been that. One marriage, one family, finished.

He'd written to her. Of course he had, and he'd tried to phone. *'Jules, it was no one's fault. That you were asleep didn't make any difference. I was awake and alert. The landslip came from nowhere. There's nothing anyone can do when the road gives way.'* Did he believe it himself? He tried to. Sometimes he had flashes when he almost did.

And apparently, Julie had shared his doubts. She'd written back, brief and harsh.

I was asleep when my babies died. I wasn't there for them, or for you. I can barely live with myself,

much less face you every day for the rest of my life.
I'm sorry, Rob, but however we manage to face the
future, we need to do it alone.

And he couldn't help her to forgive herself. He was
too busy living with his *own* guilt. The mountain road to
the house had been eroded by heavy spring rains and the
collapse was catastrophic. They'd spent the weeks before
Christmas in the city apartment because there'd been so
much on it had just been too hard to commute. They were
exhausted but Julie had been desperate to get up to the
mountains for the weekend before Christmas, to make everything perfect for the next week. To let the twins set up
their Christmas tree. So Santa wouldn't find one speck of
dust, one thing out of place.

He'd gone along with it. Maybe he'd also agreed. Perfection was in both their blood; they were driven personali-
ties. They'd given their nanny the weekend off and they'd
driven up here late.

But if they'd just relaxed… If they'd simply said there
wasn't time, they could have spent that last weekend playing with the boys in the city, just stopping. But stopping
wasn't in their vocabulary and the boys were dead because of it.

Enough. The past needed to be put aside. Julie was
standing in their bedroom door.

She looked…beautiful.

He'd thought this woman was gorgeous the moment
he'd met her. Tall, willow-slim, blonde hair with just a
touch of curl, brown eyes a man could drown in, lips a
man wanted to taste…

It was four years since he'd last seen her, and she
was just the same but…tighter. It was like her skin was
stretched to fit. She was thinner. Paler. She was wearing

a simple cotton nightgown, her hair was tousled and her eyes were wide with…wariness.

Why should she be wary of him?

'Julie.' He repeated her name and she stopped dead.

She might have known he'd come.

Dear heaven, he was beautiful. He was tall—she'd forgotten how tall—and still boyish, even though he must be—what, thirty-six?—by now.

He had the same blond-brown hair that looked perpetually like he spent too much time in the sun. He had the same flop of cowlick that hung a bit too long—no hairdresser believed it wouldn't stay where it was put. He was wearing his casual clothes, clothes he might have worn four years ago: moleskins with a soft linen shirt, rolled up at the sleeves and open at the throat.

He was wearing the same smile, a smile which reached the caramel-brown eyes she remembered. He was smiling at her now. A bit hesitant. Not sure of his reception.

She hadn't seen him for four years and he was wary. What did he think she'd do, throw him out?

But she didn't know where to start. Where to begin after all this time.

Why not say it like it was?

'I don't think I am Julie,' she said slowly, feeling lost. 'At least, I'm not sure I'm the Julie you know.'

There was a moment's pause. He'd figure it out, or she hoped he would. She couldn't go straight back to the point where they'd left off. *How are you, Rob? How have you coped with the last four years?*

The void of four long years made her feel ill.

But he got it. There was a moment's silence and then his smile changed a little. She knew that smile. It reflected his intelligence, his appreciation of a problem. If there was a puzzle, Rob dived straight in. Somehow she'd set him one and he had it sorted.

'Then I'm probably not the guy you know, either,' he told her. 'So can we start from the beginning? Allow me to introduce myself. I'm Rob McDowell, architect, based in Adelaide. I have an interest in this house, ma'am, and the contents. I'm here to put the most…put a few things of special value in a secure place. And you?'

She could do this. She felt herself relax, just a little, and she even managed to smile back.

'Julie McDowell. Legal financier from Sydney. I, too, have an interest in this house.'

'McDowell?' He was caught. 'You still use…'

'It was too much trouble to change it back,' she said and he knew she was having trouble keeping her voice light.

'You're staying despite the fire warnings?'

'The wind's not due to get up until tomorrow morning. I'll be gone at dawn.'

'You've just arrived?'

'Yes.'

'You don't want to take what you want and go?'

'I don't know what I want.' She hesitated. 'I think… there's a wall-hanging… But it seems wrong to just…leave.'

'I had two fire engines in mind,' he admitted. 'But I feel the same.'

'So you'll stay until ordered out?'

'If it doesn't get any worse, maybe I can clear any debris, check the pumps and sprinkler system, fill the spouts, keep any stray spark from catching. At first light I'll go right round the house and eliminate every fire risk I can. I can't do it now. It's too dark. For the sake of a few hours, I'll stay. I don't want this place to burn.'

Why? she wanted to say. *What does this house mean to you?*

What did it mean to her? A time capsule? Maybe it was. This house was what it was like when…

But *when* was unthinkable. And if Rob was here, then surely she could go.

But she couldn't. The threat was still here, even if she wasn't quite sure what was being threatened.

'If you need to stay,' she ventured, 'there's a guest room.'

'Excellent.' They were like two wary dogs, circling each other, she thought. But they'd started this sort of game. She could do this.

'Would you like supper?'

'I don't want to keep you up.'

'I wasn't sleeping. The pantry's stocked and the freezer's full. Things may well be slightly out of date…'

'Slightly!'

'But I'm not dictated to by use-by dates,' she continued. 'I have fresh milk and bread. For anything else, I'm game if you are.'

His brown eyes creased a little, amused. 'A risk-taker, Jules?'

'No!'

'Sorry.' Jules was a nickname and that was against the rules. He realised it and backtracked. 'I meant: have you tried any of the food?'

'I haven't tried,' she conceded.

'You came and went straight to bed?'

'I…yes.'

'Then maybe we both need supper.' He checked his watch. 'It's almost too late for a midnight feast but I could eat two horses. Maybe we could get to know each other over a meal? If you dare, that is?'

And she gazed at him for a long moment and came to a decision.

'I dare,' she said. 'Why not?'

* * *

He put the cars in the garage and then they checked the fire situation. 'We'd be fools not to,' Rob said as they headed out to the back veranda to see what they could see.

They could see nothing. The whole valley seemed to be shrouded in smoke. It blocked the moon and the stars. It seemed ominous but there was no glow from any fire. 'And the smoke would be thicker if it was closer,' Rob decreed. 'We're safe enough for now.'

'There are branches overhanging the house.'

'I saw them as I came in but there's no way I'm using a chainsaw in the dark.'

'There's no way you're using a chainsaw,' she snapped and he grinned.

'Don't you trust me?'

'Do I trust any man with a chainsaw? No.'

He grinned, that same smile... *Dear heaven, that smile...*

Play the game. For tonight, she did *not* know this man.

'We have neighbours,' Rob said, motioning to a light in the house next door.

'I saw a child in the window earlier, just as it was getting dark.'

'A child... They should have evacuated.'

'Maybe they still think there's time. There should still be time.'

'Let me check again.' He flicked to the fire app on his phone. 'Same warnings. Evacuate by nine if you haven't already done so. Unless you're planning on staying to defend.'

'Would you?' she asked diffidently. 'Stay and defend?'

'I'd have to be trustworthy with a chainsaw to do that.'

'And are you?' The Rob she knew couldn't be trusted within twenty paces of a power tool.

'No,' he admitted and she was forced to smile back. Same Rob, then. Same, but different? The Rob of *after*.

This was weird. She should be dressed, she decided, as she padded barefoot back to the kitchen behind him. If he really was a stranger…

He really is a stranger, she told herself. Power tool knowledge or not, four years was a lifetime.

'Right.' In the kitchen, he was all efficiency. 'Food.' He pushed his sleeves high over his elbows and looked as if he meant business. 'I'd kill for a steak. What do you suppose the freezer holds?'

'Who knows what's buried in there?'

'Want to help me find out?'

'Men do the hunting.'

'And women do the cooking?' He had the chest freezer open and was delving among the labelled packages. 'Julie, Julie, Julie. How out of the ark is that?'

'I can microwave a mean TV dinner.'

'Ugh.'

But Rob did cook. She remembered him enjoying cooking. Not often because they'd been far too busy for almost everything domestic but when she'd first met him he'd cooked her some awesome meals.

She'd tried to return the favour, but had only cooked disasters.

'What sort of people occupied this planet?' Rob was demanding answers from the depths of the freezer. 'Packets, packets and packets. Someone here likes Diet Cuisine. Liked,' he amended. 'Use-by dates of three years ago.'

She used to eat them when Rob was away. She'd cooked for the boys, or their nanny had, but Diet Cuisine was her go-to.

'There must be something more…' He was hauling out

packet after packet, tossing them onto the floor behind him. She was starting to feel mortified. Her fault again?

'You'll need to put that stuff back or it'll turn into stinking sog,' she warned.

'Of course.' His voice was muffled. 'So in a thousand years an archaeological dig can find Diet Cuisine and think we were all nuts. And stinking sog? For a stink it'd have to contain substance. Two servings of veggies and four freezer-burned cubes of diced meat do not substance make. But hey, here's a whole beef fillet.' He emerged, waving his find in triumph. 'This is seriously thick. I'm hoping freezer burn might only go halfway in or less. I can thaw it in the microwave, chop off the burn and produce steak fit for a king. I hope. Hang on a minute.'

Fascinated, she watched as he grabbed a torch from the pantry and headed for the back door. That was a flaw in this mock play; he shouldn't have known where a torch was. But in two minutes he was back, brandishing a handful of greens.

'Chives,' he said triumphantly and then glanced dubiously at the enormous green fronds. 'Or they might have been chives some time ago. These guys are mutant onions.'

Clarissa had planted vegetables, she remembered. Their last nanny...

But Rob was taking all her attention. The Rob of now. She'd expected...

Actually, she hadn't expected. She'd thought she'd never see this man again. She'd vaguely thought she'd be served with divorce papers at some stage, but she hadn't had the courage or the impetus to organise it herself. To have him here now, slicing steak, washing dirt from mutant chives, took a bit of getting used to.

'You do want some?' he asked and she thought *no*. And then she thought: *when did I last eat?*

If he had been a stranger she'd eat with him.

'Yes, please,' she said and was inordinately pleased with herself for getting the words out.

So they ate. The condiments in the pantry still seemed fine, though Rob dared to tackle the bottled horseradish and she wasn't game. He'd fried hunks of bread in the pan juices. They ate steak and chives and fried bread, washed down by mugs of milky tea. All were accompanied by Rob's small talk. He really did act as if they were strangers, thrust together by chance.

Wasn't that the truth?

'So, Julie,' he said finally, as he washed and she wiped. There was a dishwasher but, as neither intended sticking round past breakfast, it wasn't worth the effort. 'If you're planning on leaving at dawn, what would you like to do now? You were sleeping when I got here?'

'Trying to sleep.'

'It doesn't come on demand,' he said, and she caught an edge to his voice that said he lay awake, as she did. 'But you can try. I'll keep watch.'

'What—stand sentry in case the fire comes?'

'Something like that.'

'It won't come until morning.'

'I don't trust forecasts. I'll stay on the veranda with the radio. Snooze a little.'

'I won't sleep.'

'So…you want to join me on fire watch?'

'I…okay.'

'You might want to put something on besides your nightie.'

'What's wrong with the nightie? It's sensible.'

'It's not sensible.'

'It's light.'

'Jules,' he said, and suddenly there was strain in his voice. 'Julie. I know we don't know each other very well.

I know we're practically strangers, but there is only a set-
tee on the veranda, and if you sit there looking like that…'

She caught her breath and the play-acting stopped, just
like that. She stared at him in disbelief.

'You can't…want me.'

'I've never stopped wanting you,' he said simply. 'I've
tried every way I know, but it's not working. Just because
we destroyed ourselves… Just because we gave away the
idea of family for the rest of our lives, it doesn't stop the
wanting. Not everything ended the night our boys died,
Julie, though sometimes…often…I wish it had.'

'You still feel…'

'I have no idea what I feel,' he told her. 'I've been trying my best to move on. My shrink says I need to put it all
in the background, like a book I can open at leisure and
close again when it gets too hard to read. But, for now, all
I know is that your nightie is way too skimpy and your
eyes are too big and your hair is too tousled and our bed is
too close. So I suggest you either head to the bedroom and
close the door or go get some clothes on. Because what I
want has nothing to do with reality, and everything to do
with ghosts. Shrink's advice or not, I can't close the book.
Go and get dressed, Julie. Please.'

She stared at him for a long moment. Rob. Her husband.

Her ex-husband. Her ex-life.

She'd closed the door on him four years ago. If she was
to survive, that door had to stay firmly closed. Behind that
door were emotions she couldn't handle.

She turned away and headed inside. Away from him.
Away from the way he tugged her heart.

He sat out on the veranda, thinking he might have scared
her right off. She didn't emerge.

Well, what was new? He'd watched the way she'd closed

down after the boys' deaths. He was struggling to get free of those emotions but it seemed Julie was holding them close. Behind locked doors.

That was her right.

He sat for an hour and watched the night close in around him. The heat seemed to be getting more oppressive. The smoke hung low over everything, black and thick and stinking of burned forest, threatening enough all by itself, even without flames.

It's because there's no wind, he told himself. Without wind, smoke could hang around for weeks. There was no telling how close the fire was. There was no telling what the risks were if the wind got up.

He should leave. He should make Julie leave, but then… But then…

Her decision to come had been hers alone. She had the right to stay. He wasn't sure what he was protecting, but sitting out on the veranda, with Julie in the house behind him, felt okay. He wasn't sure why, but he did know that, at some level, the decision to come had been the right one.

Maybe it was stupid, he conceded, but maybe they both needed this night. Maybe they both needed to stand sentinel over a piece of their past that needed to be put aside.

And it really did need to be put aside. He'd watched Julie's face when he'd confessed that he wanted her and he'd seen the absolute denial. Even if she was ever to want him again, he'd known then that she wouldn't admit it.

Families were for the past.

He sat on. A light was still on next door. Once he saw a woman walk past the lighted window. Pregnant? Was she keeping the same vigil he was keeping?

If he had kids, he'd have them out of here by now. Hopefully, his neighbour had her car packed and would be gone at dawn, taking her family with her.

Just as he and Julie would be gone at dawn, too.

The moments ticked on. He checked the fire app again. No change.

There were sounds coming from indoors. Suddenly he was conscious of Christmas music. Carols, tinkling out on…a music box?

He remembered that box. It had belonged to one of his aunts. It was a box full of Santa and his elves. You wound the key, opened the box and they all danced.

That box…

Memories were all around him. Childhood Christmases. The day his aunt had given it to them—the Christmas Julie was pregnant. 'It needs a family,' his aunt had said. 'I'd love you to have it.'

His aunt was still going strong. He should give the box back to her, he thought, but meanwhile… Meanwhile, he headed in and Julie was sitting in the middle of the living room floor, attaching baubles to a Christmas tree. She was still dressed in the nightgown. She was totally intent on what she was doing.

What…?

'It's Christmas Eve tomorrow,' she said simply, as if this was a no-brainer. 'This should be up. And don't look at the nightgown, Rob McDowell. Get over it. It's hot, my nightie's cool and I'm working.'

She'd hauled the artificial tree from the storeroom. He stared at it, remembering the Christmas when they'd conceded getting a real tree was too much hassle. It'd take hours to buy it and set it up, and one thing neither of them had was hours.

That last Christmas, that last weekend, the tree was one of the reasons they'd come up here.

'We can decorate the tree for Christmas,' Julie had said. 'When we go up next week we can walk straight in and it'll be Santa-ready.'

Now Julie was sitting under the tree, sorting decorations as if she had all the time in the world. As if nothing had happened. As if time had simply skipped a few years.

'Remember this one?' She held up a very tubby angel with floppy, sparkly wings and a cute little halo. 'I bought this the year I was trying to diet. Every time I looked at a mince pie I was supposed to march in here and discuss it with my angel. It didn't work. She'd look straight back at me and say: "Look at me—I might be tubby but not only am I cute, I grew wings. Go ahead and eat."'

He grinned, recognising the cute little angel with affection.

'And these.' Smiling fondly, he knelt among the ornaments and produced three reindeer, one slightly chewed. 'We had six of these. Boris ate the other three.'

'And threw them up when your partners came for Christmas drinks.'

'Not a good moment. I miss Boris.' He'd had Boris the Bloodhound well before they were married. He'd died of old age just before the twins were born. Before memories had to be put aside.

They'd never had time for another dog. Maybe now they never would?

Forget it. Bauble therapy. Julie had obviously immersed herself in it and maybe he could, too. He started looping tinsel around the tree and found it oddly soothing.

They worked in silence but the silence wasn't strained. It was strangely okay. Come dawn they'd walk away from this house. Maybe it would burn, but somehow, however strange, the idea that it'd burn looking lived in was comforting.

'How long do Christmas puddings last?' Julie asked at last, as she hung odd little angels made of spray-painted macaroni. Carefully not mentioning who'd made them. The twins with their nanny. The twins...

Concentrate on pudding, he told himself. Concentrate on the practical. *How long do Christmas puddings last?* 'I have no idea,' he conceded. 'I know fruitcakes are supposed to last for ever. My great-grandma cooked them for her brothers during the War. Great-Uncle Henry once told me he used to chop 'em up and lob 'em over to the enemy side. Grandma Ethel's cakes were never great at the best of times but after a few months on the Western Front they could have been lethal.'

'Death by fruitcake...'

'Do you remember the Temperance song?' he asked, grinning at another memory. His great-aunt's singing. He raised his voice and tried it out. *'We never eat fruitcake because it has rum. And one little bite turns a man to a...'*

'Yeah, right.' She smiled back at him and he felt strangely triumphant.

Why did it feel so important to make this woman smile?

Because he'd lost her smile along with everything else? Because he'd loved her smile?

'Clarissa made one that's still in the fridge,' she told him. Nanny Clarissa had been so domestic she'd made up for both of them. Or almost. 'And it does contain rum. Half a bottle of over-proof, if I remember. She demanded I put it on the shopping list that last... Anyway, I'm thinking of frying slices for breakfast.'

'Breakfast is what...' he checked his watch '...three hours away? Four-year-old Christmas pudding. That'll be living on the edge.'

'A risk worth taking?' she said tightly and went back to bauble-hanging. 'What's to lose?'

'Pudding at dawn. Bring it on.'

They worked on. There were so many tensions zooming round the room. So many things unsaid. All they could do was concentrate on the tree.

Finished, it looked magnificent. They stood back, Rob flicked the light switch and the tree flooded into colour. He opened the curtains and the light streamed out into the darkness. Almost every house in the valley was in darkness. Apart from a solitary light in the house next door they were alone. Either everyone had evacuated or they were all sleeping. Preparing for the danger which lay ahead.

Sleep. Bed.

It seemed a good idea. In theory.

Julie was standing beside him. She had her arms folded in front of her, instinctive defence. She was still in that dratted nightgown. Hadn't he asked her to take it off? Hadn't he warned her?

But she never had been a woman who followed orders, he thought. She'd always been self-contained, sure, confident of her place in the world. He'd fallen in love with that containment, with her fierce intelligence, with the humour that matched his, a biting wit that made him break into laughter at the most inappropriate moments. He'd loved her drive to be the best at her job. He'd understood and admired it because he was like that, too. It was only when the twins arrived that they'd realised two parents with driving ambition was a recipe for disaster.

Still they'd managed it. They'd juggled it. They'd loved...

Loved. He looked at her now, shivering despite the oppressive heat. She looked younger, he thought suddenly.

Vulnerable.

She'd never been vulnerable and neither had he.

But they'd loved.

'Julie?'

'Yes?' She looked at him and she looked scared. And he knew it was nothing to do with the fires.

'Mmm.'

'Let's go to bed,' he said, but she hugged her arms even tighter.

'I don't…know.'

'There's no one else?'

'No.'

'Nor for me,' he said gently. He was treading on egg-shells here. He should back off, go and sleep in the spare room, but there was something about this woman… This woman who was still his wife.

'We can't…at least…I can't move forward,' he told her, struggling to think things through as he spoke. 'Relation-ships are for other people now, not for me. But tonight… For me, tonight is all about goodbye and I suspect it's goodbye for you as well.'

'The house won't burn.'

'No,' he said, even more gently. 'It probably won't. At dawn I'll go out and cut down the overhanging branches—and even with my limited skill with power tools, I should get them cleared before the wind changes. Then we'll turn on every piece of fire-safe technology we built into this house. And after that, no matter what the outcome, we'll walk away. We must. It's time it was over, Jules, but for tonight…' He hesitated but he had to say it. It was a gut-deep need and it couldn't be put aside. 'Tonight, we need each other.'

'So much for being strangers,' she whispered. She was still hugging herself, still contained. Sort of.

'I guess we are,' he conceded. 'I guess the people we've turned into don't know each other. But for now…for this night I'd like to take to bed the woman who's still my wife.'

'In name only.' She was shivering.

'So you don't want me? Not tonight? Never again?'

And she looked up at him with those eyes he remembered so well, but with every bit of the confidence, humour, wit and courage blasted right out of them.

'I *do* want you,' she whispered. 'That's what terrifies me.'

'Same here.'

'Rob...'

'Mmm.'

'Do you have condoms? I mean, the last thing...'

'I have condoms.'

'So when you said relationships are for other people...'

'Hey, I'm a guy.' He was trying again to make her smile. 'I live in hope. Hope that one morning I'll wake up and find the old hormones rushing back. Hope that one evening I'll look across a crowded room and see a woman laughing at the same dumb thing I'm laughing at.'

That had been what happened that night, the first time they'd met. It had been a boring evening: a company she worked for announcing a major interest in a new dockland precinct; a bright young architect on the fringes; Julie with her arms full of contracts ready to be signed by investors. A boring speech, a stupid pun missed by everyone, including the guy making the speech, and then eyes meeting...

Contracts handed to a junior. Excuses made fast. Dinner. Then...

'So I'm prepared,' Rob said gently and tilted her chin. Gently, though. Forcing her gaze to meet his. 'One last time, my Jules?'

'I'm not...your Jules.'

'Can you pretend...for tonight?'

And, amazingly, she nodded. 'I think...maybe,' she managed, and at last her arms uncrossed. At last she abandoned the defensive. 'Maybe because I need to drive the ghosts away. And maybe because I want to.'

'I need more than *maybe*, Jules,' he said gently. 'I need you to want me as much as I want you.'

And there was the heart of what she was up against. She wanted him.

She always had.

Once upon a time she'd stood before an altar, the perfect bride. She remembered walking down the aisle on her father's arm, seeing Rob waiting for her, knowing it was right. She'd felt like the luckiest woman in the world. He'd held her heart in his hand, and she'd known that he'd treat it with care and love and honour.

She'd said I do, and she'd meant it.

Until death do us part…

Death had parted them, she thought and it would go on keeping them apart. There was no way they could pick up the pieces that had been their lives before the boys.

But somehow they'd been given tonight.

One night. A weird window of space and time. Tomorrow the echoes of their past could well disappear, and maybe it was right that they should.

But tonight he was here.

Tonight he was gazing at her with a tenderness that told her he needed this night as well. He wanted that sliver of the past as much as she did.

For tonight he wanted her and she ached for him back. But he wasn't pushing. It had to be her decision.

Maybe I can do this, she thought. *Maybe, just for tonight, I can put my armour aside…*

Her everyday life was now orchestrated, rigidly contained. It held no room for emotional attachment. Even coming here was an aberration. Once the fire was over, she'd return to her job, return to her life, return to her containment.

But for now…that ache… The way Rob talked to her… That he asked her to his bed…

It was like a siren call, she thought helplessly. She'd loved this man; she'd loved everything about him. Love had almost destroyed her and she couldn't go there again, but for tonight… Tonight was an anomaly—time out of frame.

For tonight, she was in her home with her husband. He wasn't pushing. He never had. He was simply waiting for her to make her decision.

Lie with her husband…or not?

Have one night as the Julie of old…or not?

'Because once we loved,' he said lightly, as if this wasn't a major leap, and maybe it wasn't. Maybe she could love again—just for the night. One night of Rob and then she'd get on with her life. One night…

'But not if you see it as scary.'

His gaze was locked on hers. 'It's for pleasure only, my Jules,' he said softly. 'No threats. No promises. No future. Just for this night. Just for us. Just for now. Maybe or yes? I need a yes, Jules. You have to be sure.'

And suddenly she was. 'Yes,' she said, because there was nothing else to say. 'Yes, please, Rob. For tonight, there's no maybe about it. Crazy or not, scary or not, I want you.'

'Hey, what's scary about me?' And he was laughing down at her, his lovely eyes dancing. Teasing. Just as he once had.

'That's just the problem,' she whispered. 'There's nothing crazy about the way I feel about you. *That's* what makes it so scary. But, scary or not, for tonight, Rob, for the last time, I want to be your wife.'

For those tense few minutes when they'd first seen each other, when they'd come together in the house for the first time in years, they'd made believe it was the first time. They were strangers. They'd relived that first connection.

Now…it was as if they'd pressed the fast forward on the replay button, Rob thought, and suddenly it was the first time he was to take her to bed.

But this was no make-believe, and it wasn't the first time. He knew everything there was to know about this woman. His wife.

But maybe that was wrong. Yes, he knew everything there was to know about the Julie of years ago, the Julie who'd married him, but there was a gaping hole of years. How had she filled it? He didn't know. He hardly knew how he'd filled it himself.

But for now, by mutual and unspoken consent, those four years didn't exist. Only the fierce magnetic attraction existed—the attraction that had him wanting her the moment he'd set eyes on her.

They hadn't ended up in bed on their first date, but it had nearly killed them not to. They'd lasted half an hour into their second date. He'd gone to her apartment to pick her up…they hadn't even reached the bedroom.

And now, here, the desire was the same. He'd seen her in her flimsy nightgown and he wanted her with every fibre of his being. And even if it was with caveats—*for the last time*—he tugged her into his arms and she melted.

Fused.

'You're sure?' he asked and she nodded and the sound she made was almost a purr. Memories had been set aside—the hurtful ones had, anyway.

'I'm sure,' she whispered and tugged his face close and her whisper was a breath on his mouth.

He lifted her and she curled against him. She looped her arms around his neck and twisted, so she could kiss him.

Somehow he made it to the bedroom door. The bed lay,

invitingly, not ten feet away, but he had to stop and let himself be kissed. And kiss back.

Their mouths fused. It was like electricity, a fierce jolt on touching, then a force so great that neither could pull away. Neither could think of pulling away.

He had his wife in his arms. He couldn't think past that. He had his Julie and his mind blocked out everything else.

His wife. His love.

She'd forgotten how her body melted. She'd forgotten how her body merged into his. How the outside world disappeared. How every sense centred on him. Or on *them*, for that was how it was. Years ago, the moment he'd first touched her, she'd known what marriage was. She'd felt married the first time they'd kissed.

She'd abandoned herself to him then, as simple as that. She'd surrendered and he'd done the same. His lovely strong body, virile, heavy with the scent of aroused male, wanting her, taking her, demanding everything, but in such a way that she knew that if she pulled away he'd let her go.

Only she knew she'd never pull away. She couldn't and neither could he.

Their bodies were made for each other.

And now…now her mouth was plundering his, and his hers, and the sensations of years ago were flooding back. Oh, the taste of him. The feel… Her body was on fire with wanting, with the knowledge that somehow he was hers again, for however long…

Until morning?

No. She wasn't thinking that. It didn't matter how long. All that mattered was now.

Somehow, some way, they reached the bed, but even before they were on top of it she was fighting with the buttons of his shirt. She wanted this man's body. She wanted to feel the strength of him, the hardness of his ribs, the tightness of his chest. She wanted to taste the salt of him.

Oh, his body… It was hers; it still felt like hers.

Four years ago…

No. Forget four years. Just think about now.

His kiss deepened. Her nightgown was slipping away and suddenly it was easy. Memories were gone. All she could think of was him. All she wanted was him.

Oh, the feel of him. The taste of him.

Rob.

The years had gone. Everything had gone. There was only this man, this body, this moment.

'Welcome home, my love,' he whispered as their clothes disappeared, as skin met skin, as the night disappeared in a haze of heat and desire.

Home… There was so much unsaid in that word. It was a word of longing, a word of hope, a word of peace.

It meant nothing, she thought. It couldn't.

But her arms held him. Her mouth held him. Her whole body held him.

For this moment he was hers.

For this moment he was right. She was home.

He'd forgotten a woman could feel this good.

He'd forgotten…Julie?

But of course he hadn't. He'd simply put her in a place in his mind that was inaccessible. But now she was here, his, welcoming him, loving him.

She tasted fabulous. She still smelled like…like… He didn't know what she smelled like.

Had he ever asked her what perfume she wore? Maybe it was only soap. Fresh, citrus, it was in her hair.

He'd forgotten how erotic it was, to lie with his face in her tumbled hair, to feel the wisps around his face, to fin-

ger and twist and feel her body shudder as she responded
to his touch.

The room was in darkness and that was good. If he
could see her…her eyes might get that dead look, the look
that said there was nothing left, for her or for him.

It was a look that had almost killed him.

But he wouldn't think of that. He couldn't, for her fingers were curved around his thighs, tugging him closer,
closer…

His wife. His Julie. His own.

They loved and loved again. They melted into each other
as if they'd never parted.

They loved.

He loved.

She was *his*.

The possessive word resonated in his mind, primeval
as time itself. She was crying. He felt her tears, slipping
from her face to his shoulder.

He gathered her to him and held, simply held, and he
thought that at this moment if any man tried to take her
his response would be primitive.

His.

Tomorrow he'd walk away. He'd accepted by now that
their marriage was over, that Julie could never emerge
from the thick armour she'd shielded herself with. In order
to survive he needed to move on. He knew it. His shrink
had said it. He knew it for the truth.

So he would walk away. But first…here was a gift he'd
long stopped hoping for. Here was a crack in that appalling armour. For tonight she'd shed it.

'For tonight I'm loving you,' he whispered and she
kissed him, fiercely, possessively, as if those vows they'd
made so long ago still held.

And they did hold—for tonight—and that was all he was focusing on. There was no tomorrow. There was nothing but now.

He kissed her back. He loved her back.

'For tonight I'm loving you, too,' she whispered and she held him closer, and there was nothing in the world but his wife.

CHAPTER THREE

NOTE: IF A bush fire's heading your way, maybe you should set the alarm.

He woke and filtered sunlight was streaming through the east windows. Filtered? That'd be smoke. It registered but only just, for Julie was in his arms, spooned against his body, naked, beautiful and sated with loving. It was hard to get his mind past that.

Past her.

But the world was edging in. The wind had risen. He could hear the sound of the gums outside creaking under the weight of it.

Wind. Smoke. Morning.

'Jules?'

'Mmm.' She stirred, stretched like a kitten and the sensation of her naked skin against his had him wanting her all over again. He could...

He couldn't. Wind. Smoke. Morning.

Somehow he hauled his watch from under his woman.

Eight-thirty.

Eight-thirty!

Get out by nine at the latest, the authorities had warned. Keep listening to emergency radio in case of updates.

Eight-thirty.

Somehow he managed to roll away and flick on the

bedside radio. But even now, even realising what was at stake, he didn't want to leave her.

The radio sounded into life. Nothing had changed in this house. He'd paid to have a housekeeper come in weekly. The clock was still set to the right time.

There was a book beside the radio. He'd been halfway through it when…when…

Maybe this house should burn, he thought, memories surging back. Maybe he wanted it to.

'We should sell this house.' She still sounded sleepy. The implication of sleeping in hadn't sunk in yet, he thought, flicking through the channels to find the one devoted to emergency transmissions.

'So why did you come back?' he asked, abandoning the radio and turning back to her. The fire was important, but somehow…somehow he knew that words might be said now that could be said at no other time. Certainly not four years ago. Maybe not in the future either, when this house was sold or burned.

Maybe now…

'The teddies,' she told him, still sleepy. 'The wall-hanging my mum made. I…wanted them.'

'I was thinking of the fire engines.'

'That's appropriate.' Amazingly, she was smiling.

He'd never thought he'd see this woman smile again.

And then he thought of those last words. The words that had hung between them for years.

'Julie, it wasn't our fault,' he said and he watched her smile die.

'I…'

'I know. You said *you* killed them, but I believed it was me. That day I brought you home from hospital. You stood here and you said it was because you were sleeping and I said no, it wasn't anyone's fault, but there was such a big part of me that was blaming myself that I couldn't go any further. It was like…I was dead. I couldn't even speak. I've thought about it for four years. I've tried to write it down.'

'I got your letters.'

'You didn't reply.'

'I thought…the sooner you stopped writing the sooner you'd forget me. Get on with your life.'

'You know the road collapsed,' he said. 'You know the lawyers told us we could sue. You know it was the storm the week before that eroded the bitumen.'

'But that I was asleep…'

'We should have stayed in the city that night. We shouldn't have tried to bring the boys home. That's the source of our greatest regret, but it shouldn't be guilt. It put us in the wrong place at the wrong time. I've been back to the site. It was a blind curve. I rounded it and the road just wasn't there.'

'If we'd come up in broad daylight, when we were both alert…'

How often had he thought about this? How often had he screamed it to himself in the middle of troubled sleep?

He had to say it. He had to believe it.

'Jules, I manoeuvred a blind bend first. A tight curve. I wasn't speeding. I hit the brakes the moment I rounded the bend but the road was gone. If you'd been awake it wouldn't have made one whit of difference. Julie, it's not only me who's saying this. It was the police, the paramedics, the guys from the accident assessment scene.'

'But I can't remember.' It was a wail, and he tugged her back into his arms and thought it nearly killed him.

He was reassuring her but regardless of reason, the guilt was still there. *What if…? What if, what if, what if?*

Guilt had killed them both. Was killing them still.

He held her but her body had stiffened. The events of four years ago were right there. One night of passion couldn't wash them away.

He couldn't fix it. How could it be fixed, when two small beds lay empty in the room next door?

He kissed her on the lips, searching for an echo of the night before. She kissed him back but he could feel that she'd withdrawn.

Same dead Julie…

He turned again and went back to searching the radio channels. Finally he found the station he was looking for— the emergency channel.

'...*evacuation orders are in place now for Rowbethon, Carnarvon, Dewey's Creek… Leave now. Forecast is for forty-six degrees, with winds up to seventy kilometres an hour, gusting to over a hundred. The fire fronts are merging...*'

And all his attention was suddenly on the fire. It had to be. Rowbethon, Carnarvon, Dewey's Creek… They were all south of Mount Bundoon.

The wind was coming from the north.

'*Fire is expected to impact on the Mount Bundoon area within the hour,*' the voice went on. '*Bundoon Creek Bridge is closed. Anyone not evacuated, do not attempt it now. Repeat, do not attempt to evacuate. Roads are cut to the south. Fire is already impacting to the east. Implement your fire plans but, repeat, evacuation is no longer an option.*'

'We need to get to a refuge centre.' Julie was sitting bolt upright, wide-eyed with horror.

'There isn't one this side of the creek.' He glanced out of the window. 'We're not driving in this smoke. Besides, we have the bunker.' Thank God, they had the bunker.

'But…'

'We can do this, Jules.'

And she settled, just like that. Same old Jules. In a crisis, there was no one he'd rather have by his side.

'The fire plan,' she said. 'I have it.'

Of course she did. Julie was one of the most controlled people he knew. Efficient. Organised. A list-maker extraordinaire.

The moment they'd moved into this place she'd downloaded a Fire Authority Emergency Plan and made him go through it, step by step, making dot-points for every eventuality.

They were better off than most. Bush fire was always a risk in Australian summers and he'd thought about it carefully when he'd designed this place. The house had been built to withstand a furnace—though not an inferno. There'd been fires in Australia where even the most fireproof buildings had burned. But he'd designed the house with every precaution. The house was made of stone, with no garden close to the house. They had solar power, backup generators, underground water tanks, pumps and sprinkler systems. The tool shed doubled as a bunker and could be cleared in minutes, double-doored and built into earth. But still there was risk. He imagined everyone else in the gully would be well away by now and for good reason. Safe house or not, they were crazy to still be here.

But Julie wasn't remonstrating. She was simply moving on.

'I'll close the shutters and tape the windows while you clear the yard,' she said. Taping the windows was important. Heat could blast them inwards. Tape gave them an extra degree of strength and they wouldn't shatter if they broke.

'Wool clothes first, though,' she said, hauling a pile out of her bottom bedroom drawer, along with torches, wool caps and water bottles. Also a small fire extinguisher. The drawer had been set up years ago for the contingency of waking to fire. Efficiency plus.

Was it possible to still love a woman for her plan-making?

'I hope these extinguishers haven't perished,' she said, pulling a wool cap on her head and shoving her hair up into it. It was made of thick wool, way too big. 'Ugh. What do you think?'

'Cute.'

'Oi, we're not thinking cute.' But her eyes smiled at him.

'Hard not to. Woolly caps have always been a turn-on.'

'And I love a man in flannels.' She tossed him a shirt. 'You've been working out.'

'You noticed?'

'I noticed all night.' She even managed a grin. 'But it's time to stop noticing. Cover that six-pack, boy.'

'Yes, ma'am.' But he'd fielded the shirt while he was checking the fire map app on his phone, and what he saw made any thought of smiling back impossible.

She saw his face, grabbed the phone and her eyes widened. 'Rob…' And, for the first time, he saw fear. 'Oh, my…Rob, it's all around us. With this wind…'

'We can do this,' he said. 'We have the bunker.' His hands gripped her shoulders. Steadied her. 'Julie, you came up here for the teddies and the wall-hanging. Anything else?'

'Their…clothes. At least…at least some. And…'

She faltered, but he knew what she wanted to say. Their smell. Their presence. The last place they'd been.

He might not be able to save that for her, but he'd sure as hell try.

'And their fire engines,' he added, reverting, with difficulty, to the practical. 'Let's make that priority one. Hope-fully, the pits are still clear.'

The pits were a fallback position, as well as the bunker. They'd built this house with love, but with clear acceptance that the Australian bush was designed to burn. Many native trees didn't regenerate without fire to crack their seeds. Fire was natural, and over generations even inevitable, so if you lived in the bush you hoped for the best and prepared for the worst. Accordingly, they'd built with care, insured the house to the hilt and didn't keep precious things here.

Except the memories of their boys. How did you keep something like that safe? How did you keep memories in fire pits?

They'd do their best. The pits were a series of holes behind the house, fenced off but easily accessed. Dirt dug from them was still heaped beside them, a method used by those who'd lived in the bush for generations. If you wanted to keep something safe, you buried it: put belongings inside watertight cases; put the cases in the pit; piled the dirt on top.

'Get that shirt on,' Julie growled, moving on with the efficiency she'd been born with. She cast a long regretful look at Rob's six-pack and then sighed and hauled on her sensible pants. 'Moving on... We knew we'd have to, Rob, and now's the time. Clearing the yard's the biggie. Let's go.'

The moment they walked out of the house they knew they were in desperate trouble. The heat took their breath away. It hurt to breathe.

The wind was frightening. It was full of dry leaf litter, blasting against their faces—a portent of things to come. If these leaves were filled with fire... She felt fear deep in her gut. The maps she'd just seen were explicit. This place was going to burn.

She wanted to bury her face in Rob's shoulder and block this out. She wanted to forget, like last night, amazingly, had let her forget.

But last night was last night. Over.

Concentrate on the list. On her dot-points.

'Windows, pits, shovel, go,' Rob said and seized her firmly by the shoulders and kissed her, hard and fast. Making a mockery of her determination that last night was over. 'We can do this, Jules. You've put a lot of work into that fire plan. It'd be a shame if we didn't make it work.'

They could, she thought as she headed for the shutters. They could make the fire plan work.

And maybe, after last night… Maybe…

Too soon. Think of it later. Fire first.

She fixed the windows—fast—then checked the pits. They were overgrown but the mounds of dirt were still loose enough for her to shovel. She could bury things with ease.

She headed inside, grabbed a couple of cases and headed into the boys' room.

And she lost her breath all over again.

She'd figured yesterday that Rob must have hired someone to clean this place on a regular basis. If it had been left solely to her, this house would be a dusty mess. She'd walked away and actively tried to forget.

But now, standing at their bedroom door, it was as if she'd just walked in for the first time. Rob would be carrying the boys behind her. Jiggling them, making them laugh.

Two and a half years old. Blond and blue-eyed scamps. Miniature versions of Rob himself.

They'd been sound asleep when the road gave way, then

killed in an instant, the back of the car crushed as it rolled to the bottom of a gully. The doctors had told her death would have been instant.

But they were right here. She could just tug back the bedding and Rob would carry them in.

Or not.

'Aiden,' she murmured. 'Christopher.'

Grief was all around her, an aching, searing loss. She hadn't let herself feel this for years. She hadn't dared to. It was hidden so far inside her she thought she'd grown armour that could surely protect her.

But the armour was nothing. It was dust, blown away at the sight of one neat bedroom.

It shouldn't be neat. It nearly killed her that it was neat. She wanted those beds to be rumpled. She wanted...

She couldn't want.

She should be thinking about fire, she thought desperately. The warnings were that it'd be on them in less than an hour. She had to move.

She couldn't.

The wind blasted on the windowpanes. She needed to tape them. She needed to bury memories.

Aiden. Christopher.

What had she been thinking, wondering if she could move on? What had she been doing, exposing herself to Rob again? Imagining she could still love.

She couldn't. Peeling back the armour, even a tiny part, allowed in a hurt so great she couldn't bear it.

'Julie?' It was a yell from just outside the window.

She couldn't answer.

'Julie!' Rob's second yell pierced her grief, loud and demanding her attention. 'Jules! If you're standing in that bedroom thinking of black you might want to look outside instead.'

How had he known what she was doing? Because he felt the same?

Still she didn't move.

'Look!' he yelled, even more insistent, and she had to look. She had to move across to the window and pull back the curtains.

She could just see Rob through the smoke haze. He was standing under a ladder, not ten feet from her. He had the ladder propped against the house.

He was carrying a chainsaw.

As she watched in horror he pulled the cord and it roared into life.

'What's an overhanging branch between friends?' he yelled across the roar and she thought: *He'll be killed. He'll be...*

'Mine's the easier job,' he yelled as he took his first step up the ladder. 'But if I can do this, you can shove a teddy into a suitcase. Put the past behind you, Julie. Fire. Now. Go.'

He was climbing a ladder with a chainsaw. Rob and power tools...

He was an architect, not a builder.

She thought suddenly of Rob, just after she'd agreed to marry him. He'd brought her to the mountains and shown her this block, for sale at a price they could afford.

'This can be our retreat,' he'd told her. 'Commute when we can, have an apartment in the city for when we can't.' And then he'd produced his trump card. A tool belt. Gleaming leather, full of bright shiny tools, it was a he-man's tool belt waiting for a he-man. He'd strapped it on and flexed his muscles. 'What do you think?'

'You're never thinking of building yourself?' she'd gasped and he'd grinned and held up a vicious-looking... she didn't have a clue what.

'I might need help,' he admitted. 'These things look scary. I was sort of thinking of a registered builder, with maybe a team of registered builder's assistants on the side. But I could help.'

And he'd grinned at her and she'd known there was nothing she could refuse this man.

Man with tool belt.

Man with ladder and chainsaw.

And it hit her then, with a clarity that was almost frightening. Yesterday when she'd woken up it had been just like the day before and the day before that. She'd got up, she'd functioned for the day, she'd gone to bed. She'd survived.

Life went on around her, but she didn't care.

Yesterday, when she'd told her secretary she was heading up to the Blue Mountains, Maddie had been appalled. 'It's dangerous. They're saying evacuate. Don't go there.'

The thing was, though, for Julie danger no longer existed. The worst thing possible had already happened. There was nothing else to fear.

But now, standing at the window, staring at Rob and his chainsaw, she realised that, like it or not, she still cared. She could still be frightened for someone. For Rob.

But fear hurt. Caring hurt. She didn't want to care. She couldn't. Somehow she had to rebuild the armour. But meanwhile...

Meanwhile Rob was right. She had to move. She had to bury teddies.

He managed to get the branches clear and drag them into the gully, well away from the house.

He raked the loose leaves away from the house, too, easier said than done when the wind was blasting them back. He blocked the gutters and set up the generator so they could use the pump and access the water in the tanks even if they lost the solar power.

He worked his way round the house, checking, rechecking and he almost ran into Julie round the other side.

The smoke was building. It was harder and harder to see. Even with a mask it hurt to breathe.

The heat was intense and the wind was frightening.

How far away was the fire? There was no way to tell. The fire map on his phone was of little use. It showed broad districts. What he wanted was a map of what was happening down the road. He couldn't see by looking. It was starting to be hard to see as far as the end of his arm.

'We've done enough.' Julie's voice was hoarse from the smoke. 'I've done inside and cleared the back porch. I've filled the pits and cleared the bunker. All the dot-points on the plan are complete.'

'Really?' It was weird to feel inordinately pleased that she'd remembered dot-points. Julie and her dot-points… weird that they turned him on.

'So what now?' she asked. 'Oh, Rob, I can't bear it in these clothes. All I want is to take them off and lie under the hose.'

It gave him pause for thought. *Jules, naked under water…* 'Is that included on our dots?' Impossible not to sound hopeful.

'Um…no,' she said, and he heard rather than saw her smile.

'Pity.'

'We could go inside and sit under the air-conditioning while it's still safe to have the air vents open.'

'You go in.' He wouldn't. How to tell what was happening outside if he was inside? 'But, Jules, the vents stay closed. We don't know where the fire is.'

'How can we tell where it is? How close…?' The smile had gone from her voice.

'It's not threatening. Not yet. We have thick smoke and wind and leaf litter but I can reach out my hand and still— sort of—see my fingers. The fire maps tell us the fire's cut the access road, but how long it takes to reach this gully is anyone's guess. It might fly over the top of us. It might miss us completely.' There was a hope.

'So…why not air-conditioning?'

'There's still fire. You can taste it and you can smell it. Even if the house isn't in the firing line, there'll be burning leaf litter swirling in the updraught. On Black Saturday they reckoned there were ember attacks five miles from the fire front. We'd look stupid if embers were sucked in through the vents. But you go in. I'll keep checking.'

'For…how long?' she faltered. 'I mean…'

'For as long as it takes.' He glanced upward, hearing the wind blasting the treetops, but there was no way he could see that far. The smoke was making his throat hurt, but still he felt the need to try and make her smile. 'It looks like we're stuck here for Christmas,' he managed. 'But I'm sure Santa will find a way through. What's his motto? *Neither snow nor rain nor heat nor gloom of night shall stay St Nicholas from the swift completion of his appointed rounds.*'

'Isn't that postmen?' And amazingly he heard the smile again and was inordinately pleased.

'Maybe it is,' he said, picking up his hose and checking pressure. They still had the solar power but he'd already swapped to the generators. There wouldn't be time to do it when…if…the fire hit. 'But I reckon we're all in the same union. Postmen, Santa and us. We'll work through whatever's thrown at us.' And then he set down his hose.

'It's okay, Jules,' he said, taking her shoulders. 'We've

been through worse than this. We both know...that things aren't worth crying over. But our lives are worth something and maybe this house is worth something as well. It used to be a home. I know the teddies and fire engines and wall-hanging are safe but let's see this as a challenge. Let's see if we can save...what's left of the rest of us.'

They sat on the veranda and faced the wind. It was the dumbest place to sit, Julie thought, but it was also sensible. The wind seared their faces, the heat parched their throats but ember attacks would come from the north.

Their phones had stopped working. 'That'll be the transmission tower on Mount Woorndoo,' Rob said matter-of-factly, like it didn't matter that a tower not ten miles away had been put out of action.

He brought the battery radio outside and they listened. All they could figure was that the valley was cut off. All they could work out was that the authorities were no longer in control. There were so many fronts to this fire that no one could keep track.

Most bush fires could be fought. Choppers dropped vast loads of water, fire trucks came in behind the swathes the choppers cleared; communities could be saved.

Here, though, there were so many communities...

'It's like we're the last people in the world,' Julie whispered.

'Yeah. Pretty silly to be here.'

'I wanted to be here.'

'Me, too,' he said and he took her hand and held.

And somehow it felt okay. Scary but right.

They sat on. Surely the fire must arrive soon. The waiting was almost killing her, and yet, in a strange way, she felt almost calm. Maybe she even would have stayed if Rob hadn't come, she thought. Maybe this was...

'We're going to get through this,' Rob said grimly and she hauled her thoughts back from where they'd been taking her.

'You know, those weeks after the boys were killed, they were the worst weeks of my life.' He said it almost conversationally, and she thought: *don't. Don't go there.* They hadn't talked about it. They couldn't.

But he wasn't stopping. She should get up, go inside, move away, but he was waiting for ember attacks, determined to fight this fire, and she couldn't walk away.

Even if he was intent on talking about what she didn't want to hear.

'You were so close to death yourself,' he said, almost as if this had been chatted about before. 'You had smashed ribs, a punctured lung, a shattered pelvis. But that bang on the head... For the first few days they couldn't tell me how you'd wake up. For the first twenty-four hours they didn't even know whether you'd wake up at all. And there I was, almost scot-free. I had a laceration on my arm and nothing more. There were people everywhere—my parents, your parents, our friends. I was surrounded yet I'd never felt so alone. And at the funeral...'

'Don't.' She put a hand on his arm to stop him but he didn't stop. But maybe she had to hear this, she thought numbly. Maybe he had to say it.

'I had to bury them alone,' he said. 'Okay, not alone in the physical sense. The church was packed. My parents were holding me up but you weren't there... It nearly killed me. And then, when you got out of hospital and I asked if you'd go to the cemetery...'

'I couldn't.' She remembered how she'd felt. Where were her boys? To go to the cemetery...to see two tiny graves...

She'd blocked it out. It wasn't real. If she didn't see the

graves, then maybe the nightmare would be just that. An endless dream.

'It was like our family ended right there,' Rob said, staring sightlessly out into the smoke. 'It didn't end when our boys died. It ended…when we couldn't face their death together.'

'Rob…'

'I don't know why I'm saying this now,' he said, almost savagely. 'But hell, Julie, I'm fighting this. Our family doesn't exist any more, I can't get back…any of it. But once upon a time we loved each other and that still means something. So if you're sitting here thinking it doesn't matter much if you go up in flames, then think again. Because, even though I'm not part of your life any more, if I lose you completely, then what's left of my sanity goes, too. So prepare to be protected, Jules. No fire is going to get what's left of what I once loved. Of what I still love. So I'm heading off to do a fast survey of the boundary, looking for embers. It'd be good if you checked closer to the house but you don't need to. I'll do it for both of us. This fire…I'll fight it with everything I have. Enough of our past has been destroyed. This is my line in the sand.'

CHAPTER FOUR

THE SOUND CAME before the fire. Before the embers. Before hell.

It was a thousand freight trains roaring across the mountains, and it was so sudden that they were working separately when it hit. It was a sweeping updraught which felt as if it was sucking all the air from her lungs. It was a mass of burning embers, not small spot fires they could cope with but a mass of burning rain.

Stand and fight… They knew as the rumble built to a roar that no man alive could stay and fight this onslaught.

Julie was fighting to get a last gush of water onto the veranda. A branch had blasted in against the wall and Rob had been dragging it away from the building. She couldn't see him.

He was somewhere out in the smoke, heading back to her. Please, she pleaded. Please let him be heading back to her.

She had the drill in her head. *When the fire hits, take cover in your designated refuge and wait for the front to pass. As soon as the worst has passed, you can emerge to fight for your home, but don't try and fight as the front hits. Take cover.*

Now.

'Rob…' Where was he? She was screaming for him but she couldn't even hear herself above the roar. The heat was blasting in front of the fire, taking the temperature to unbearable levels. She'd have to head for the shelter without him…

Unthinkable!

But suddenly he was with her. Grabbing her, hauling her off the veranda. But, instead of heading towards the bunker, he was hauling her forward, into the heat. 'Jules, help me.'

'Help?' They had to get to the bunker. What else could they do?

'Jules, there are people next door.' He was yelling into her ear. 'There's a woman—pregnant, a mum. She was trying to back her car out of the driveway and she's hit a post. Jules, she won't come with me. We need to make her see sense. Forcibly if need be, and I can't do it by myself.'

And, like it or not, sensible or not, he had her arm. He was hauling her with him, stumbling across their yard, a yard which seemed so unfamiliar now that it was terrifying.

There were burning embers, burning leaves hitting her face. They shouldn't be here. They had to seek refuge. But…

'She's lost…a kid…' Rob was struggling to get enough breath to yell over the roar of impending fire. 'When the car hit, the dog got out. The kid's four years old, chasing his dog and she can't find him. I have to…' But then a blast of heat hit them, so intense he couldn't keep yelling. He just held onto her and ran.

But she wanted to be safe. She wanted this to be over. Why was Rob dragging her away from the bunker?

A child… Four years old? She tried to take it in but her mind wouldn't go there.

And then they were past the boundary post, not even visible now, only recognised because she brushed it as they passed. Then onto the gravel of the next-door neighbour's house. There was a car in the driveway, visible only as they almost ran into it.

She didn't know the neighbours. This house had been owned by an elderly couple when they'd built theirs. The woman had since died, her husband had left to live with his daughter and the house had stood empty and neglected for almost the entire time they'd lived here.

Last night she'd been surprised to see the lights. She and Rob had both registered that there'd been someone there, but then they'd both been so caught up...

And then her thoughts stopped. Through the wall of smoke, there was a woman. Slight. Shorter than she was.

Very, very pregnant.

Rob reached to grab her and held.

'I can't find him.' The woman was screaming. 'Help me! Help me!' The scream pierced even the roar of the fire and it held all the agony in the world. It was a wail of loss and desperation and horror.

'We will.' Rob grabbed Julie's arm, thrust the woman's hand into hers and clamped his own hand on top. 'Julie, don't let go and that's an order. Consider it a dot-point, the biggest one there is. Julie, Amina; Amina, Julie. Amina, Julie's taking you to safety. You need to go with her now. Julie, go.'

'But Danny...' The woman was still screaming.

'I'll find him. Julie, the bunker...'

'But you have to come, too.' Julie was screaming as well. Already they were cutting things so close they mightn't make it. The blackness was now tinged with burning orange, flashes looming out of the blasting heat. Dear God, they had to go—but they had to go together.

But Rob was backing away, yelling back at her over the roar of the fire. 'Jules, there's a little boy.' His voice held a desperation that matched hers. 'He ran to find his dog. I won't let this one die. I won't. Go!'

And his words stopped her screaming. They stopped her even wanting to scream.

She checked for a moment, fought for air, fought for sanity. A wave of wind and heat smashed into her, almost knocking her from her feet. Burning embers were smashing against their clothes.

The woman was wearing a bulky black dress but it didn't hide her late pregnancy. Another child. Dear God…

And they didn't have to wait until the fire front hit them; the fire was here now.

'Jules, go!' Rob was yelling, pushing.

But still… 'I can't…leave you.'

'Danny…' The woman's scream was beyond terror, beyond reason, almost drowning Julie's, but Rob had heard her.

'Jules.' He touched her once, briefly, a hand on her cheek. A touch of reassurance where there was no reassurance to be had. A touch for courage. Then he pushed her again.

'Keep her and her little one safe. You can do this,' he said fiercely. 'But stay safe. I won't lose…more. I'll find him,' he said fiercely. 'Go!'

The woman had to be almost dragged to the bunker. Somewhere out there was her son, and Julie could feel her terror, could almost taste it, and it was nearly enough to drown her own fear.

Left on her own she'd be with Rob, no question. Did it matter if she died? Not much. But she was gripping her neighbour's hand and the woman looked almost to term. Two lives depended on her and Rob had told her what he expected.

And she expected it of herself. That one touch and she knew what she was doing couldn't be questioned.

But by now it was almost impossible to move. She hardly knew where the bunker was. The world was a swirling blast of madness. Trees loomed from nowhere. She could see nothing. How could she be lost in her own front yard?

She couldn't. She wouldn't. She had the woman's hand in a grip of iron and she kept on going, tugging the woman behind her.

Finally she reached the side of the house. There was no vision left at all now. The last of the light had gone. The world was all heat and smoke and fear.

She touched the house and kept touching as she hauled the woman along behind her. The woman had ceased fighting, but she could feel her heaving sobs. There was nothing she could do about that, though. Her only thought was to get to the rear yard, then keep going without deviation and the bunker would be right there.

But Rob…

Don't think of Rob.

There was so much smoke. How could they breathe?

And then the bunker was right in front of her groping arm. She'd been here earlier, checked it was clear. She should have left the door open. Now it was all she could do to haul it wide. She had to let Amina go and she was fearful she'd run.

If it was her little boy out there she'd run.

Christopher. Aiden…

Don't think it. That was the way of madness.

But Amina had obviously made a choice. She was no longer pulling back. Her maternal instincts must be tearing her apart. Her son was in the fire but she had to keep her baby safe. She was trusting in Rob.

Do not think of Rob.

Somehow she managed to haul open the great iron door Rob had built as the entrance to the bunker. The bunker itself was dug into the side of the hill, with reinforced earth on the sides and floor and roof, with one thick door facing the elements and a thinner one inside.

She got the outer door open, shoving the woman inside, fighting to keep out embers.

She slammed it shut behind her and it felt as if she was condemning Rob to death.

Inside the inner door was designed to keep out heat. She couldn't shut that. No way. The outer door would have to buckle before she'd consider it. One sheet of iron between Rob and safety was more than she could bear; two was unthinkable.

The woman was sobbing, crumpling downward. There were lamps by the door. She flicked one on, took a deep, clean breath of air that hardly had any smoke in it and took stock.

She was safe here. They were safe.

She wasn't sure what was driving her, what was stopping her crumbling as well, but she knew what she had to do. The drill. Her dot-points. Rob would laugh at her, say she'd be efficient to the point where she organised her own funeral.

He loved her dot-points.

She allowed herself one tiny sob of fear, then swallowed it and knelt beside the woman, putting her arm around the woman's shoulders.

'We're safe,' she told her, fighting to keep her voice steady. 'You and your baby are safe. This place is fireproof. Rob's designed it so we have ventilation. We have air, water, even food if we need. We can stay here until it's all over.'

'D…Danny.'

'Rob is with Danny,' she said with a certainty she had to assume. But suddenly it wasn't assumed. Rob had to be with Danny and Rob had to be safe. Anything else was unthinkable.

'Rob will have him,' she whispered. 'My...my husband will keep him safe.'

'Danny! Luka!' Why was he yelling? Nothing could be heard above the roar of the fire. He could see nothing. To stay out here and search for a child in these conditions was like searching in hot, blasting sludge. A child would be swallowed, as he was being swallowed.

He'd asked for the dog's name. 'Luka,' Amina had told him through sobs. 'A great big golden retriever my husband bought to keep us safe. Danny loves him.'

So now he added Luka to his yelling. But where in this inferno...?

He stopped and made himself think. The boy had followed the dog. Where would the dog go?

Back to the house, surely. He'd escaped from the car. He'd be terrified. If Danny had managed to follow him...

The heat was burning. He'd shoved a wool cap over his head. Now he pulled it right down over his eyes. He couldn't see anyway and it stopped the pain as embers hit. He had his hands out, blundering his way to the front door.

At least Julie was safe. It was the one thing that kept him sane, but if there was another tragedy out of this day...

He knew, none better, how close to the edge of sanity Julie had been. He knew how tightly she held herself together. How controlled...

He hadn't been able to get past that control and in the end he'd had to respect it. He'd had to walk away, to preserve them both.

If he died now maybe Julie's control would grow even

deeper. The barriers could become impenetrable—or maybe the barriers would crumble completely.

Either option was unthinkable.

Last night he'd seen a glimmer of what they'd once had. Only a glimmer; the barriers had been up again this morning. But he'd seen underneath. How vulnerable…

He could go to her now. Save himself.

And sit in the bunker while another child died?

He had his own armour, his own barriers, and they were vulnerable, too. Another child's death…

'Danny! Luka!' He was screaming, and his screams were mixing with the fire.

'Please…'

Please.

She said it over and over again. She'd found water bottles. She'd given one to Amina, and watched her slump against the back wall, her face expressionless.

Her face looked dead.

Her face would look like that too, Julie thought. Maybe it had looked like that for four years?

She slumped down on the floor beside her. Fought to make her mind work.

What was safety when others weren't safe? When Rob was out there?

'Do you think…?' Amina whispered.

'I can't think,' Julie told her. She took a long gulp of water and realised just how parched she'd been. How much worse for Rob…

'So…so what do we do?' Amina whispered.

'Wait for Rob.'

'Your husband.'

'Yes.' He still was, after all. It was a dead marriage but the legalities still held.

'My...my husband will be trying to reach us,' Amina whispered. 'He's a fly in, fly out miner. He was flying back in last night. He rang from the airport and told us not to move until he got here. I'm not very good in the car but in the end I couldn't wait. But then I crashed.'

'What's his name?' She was trying so hard to focus on anything but Rob.

'Henry,' Amina said. 'He'll come. I know he will. I...I need him.'

You need Rob, Julie thought, but she didn't say it.

And she didn't say how much her life depended on Rob pushing through that door.

Amina's house had caught fire. Dear God, he could see flames through the blackness. The heat was almost unbearable. No, make that past unbearable.

He had to go. He was doing nothing staying here. He was killing himself in a useless hunt.

But still... His hand had caught the veranda rail. He steadied. One last try...

He hauled himself onto the veranda and gave one last yell.

'Danny! Luka!'

And a great heavy body shoved itself at his legs, almost pushing him over.

Dog. He couldn't see him. He could only crouch and hold.

He searched for his collar and found...a hand. A kid, holding the dog.

'Danny!' There was nothing of him, a sliver of gasping fear. He couldn't see. He hauled him into his arms and hugged, steadying for a moment, taking as well as giving comfort. Taking strength.

God, the heat...

'Mama…' the little boy whimpered, burying his face in Rob's chest, not because he trusted him, but to stop the heat.

Rob was holding him with one arm, unbuttoning his wool flannel shirt with the other. Thank God the shirt was oversized. The kid was in shorts and sandals!

He buttoned up again, kid inside, and the kid didn't move. He was past moving, Rob thought. He could feel his chest heaving as he fought for breath. His own breathing hurt.

He had him. Them. The dog was hard at his side, not going anywhere.

He had to get to the bunker. It was way past a safe time for them to get there but there was nowhere else.

Julie would be at the bunker. If she'd made it.

And he had something to fight for. For Rob, the last four years had passed in a mist of grey. He'd tried to get on with his life, he'd built his career, he'd tried to enjoy life again but, in truth, every sense had seemed dulled. Yet now, when the world around him truly was grey and thick with smoke, every one of his senses was alert, intent, focused.

He would make it to the bunker. He would save this kid.

He would make it back to Julie.

Please…

'Hold on,' he managed to yell to the kid, though whether the little boy could hear him over the roar of the flames was impossible to tell. 'Hold your breath, Danny. We're going to run.'

Amina was crying, not sobbing, not hysterical, but tears were running unchecked down her face.

Julie was past crying. She was past feeling. If Rob was safe he'd be here by now. The creek at the bottom of the gully was dry. Even if it had been running it was overhung with dense bush. There was no safe place except here.

She was the last, she thought numbly. Her boys had gone. Now Rob, too?

Last night had been amazing. Last night it had felt as if she was waking up from a nightmare, as if slivers of light were finally breaking through the fog.

She hadn't deserved the light. She might have known…

'Your husband…' Amina managed, and she knew the woman was making a Herculean effort to talk. 'He's… great.'

'I…yeah.' What to say? There was nothing to say.

'How long have you been married?'

She had to think. Was she still married? Sort of. Sort of not.

'Seven years,' she managed.

'No kids?'

'I…no.'

'I'm sorry,' Amina whispered, and the dead feeling inside Julie turned into the hard, tight knot she knew so well. The knot that threatened to choke her. The knot that had ended her life.

'It's too late, isn't it?' Amina whispered. 'They would have been here by now. It's too…'

'I don't know…'

And then she stopped.

A bang. She was sure…

It was embers crashing against the door. Surely.

She should have closed the inner door. It was the last of her dot-points.

Another bang.

She was up, scrambling to reach the door. But then she paused, forcing herself to be logical. She was trying desperately to think and somehow she managed to make her mind see sense. To open the outer door mid-fire would suck every trace of oxygen from the bunker, even if the fire didn't blast right in. She couldn't do that to Amina.

Follow the dot-points. Follow the rules.

The banging must have been flying embers. It must. But if not...

She was already in the outer chamber, hauling the inner door closed behind her, closing herself off from the inner sanctuary. 'Stay!' she yelled at Amina and Amina had the sense to obey.

With the inner door closed it was pitch-dark, but she didn't need to see. She was at the outer door. She could feel the heat.

She hauled up the latch and tugged, then hauled.

The door swung wide with a vicious blast of heat and smoke.

And a body. A great solid body, holding something. Almost falling in.

A huge, furry creature lunging against her legs.

'Get it...get it sh—'

Rob. He was beyond speech. He was beyond anything. He crumpled to his knees, gasping for air.

She knew what he'd been trying to say. She had to get the door shut. She did it but afterwards she never knew how. It felt as if she herself was being sucked out. She fought with the door, fought with everything she had, and finally the great latch Rob had designed with such foresight fell into place.

But still...the smoke... There was no air. She couldn't breathe.

It took effort, will, concentration to find the latch on the inner door but somehow she did. She tugged and Amina was on the other side. As soon as the latch lifted she had it open.

'Danny...' It was a quavering sob.

'He's here,' Rob managed and then slumped sideways into the inner chamber, giving way to the all-consuming black.

Rob surfaced to water. Cool, wondrous water, washing his face. Someone was letting water run over him. There was water on his head. The wool cap was nowhere. There was just water.

He shifted a little and tasted it, and heard a sob of relief.

'Rob...'

'Julie.' The word didn't quite come out, though. His mouth felt thick and swollen. He heard a grunt that must have been him but he couldn't do better.

'Let me hold you while you drink.' And she had him. Her arm was supporting his shoulders, and magically there was a bottle of water at his lips. He drank, gloriously grateful for the water, even more grateful that it was Julie who had him. He could see her by the dim light of the torch lamp. Julie...

'The...the boy...' Maybe it came out, maybe it didn't, but she seemed to understand what he said.

'Danny's safe; not even burned. His mother has him. They're pouring water over Luka's pads. His pads look like your face. You both look scorched, but okay. It's okay, Rob.' Her voice broke. 'You'll live. We'll all live, thanks to you.'

CHAPTER FIVE

How LONG DID they stay in the shelter? Afterwards they tried to figure it out, but at the time they had no clue. Time simply stopped.

The roar from outside built to a crescendo, a sound where nothing could be said, nothing heard. Maybe they should have been terrified, but for Julie and for Amina too, they'd gone past terror. Terror was when the people they loved were outside, missing. Now they were all present and accounted for, and if hell itself broke loose, if their shelter disintegrated, somehow it didn't matter because they were there.

Rob was there.

He roused himself after a while and pushed himself back against the wall. Julie wasn't sure where the black soot ended and burns began. None of his clothes were burned. His eyes seemed swollen and bloodshot, but maybe hers did too. There were no mirrors here.

Amina was cuddling Danny, but she was also cuddling the dog.

The dog had almost cost her son his life, Julie thought wonderingly, but as Amina poured water over Luca's paws and his tail gave a feeble wag of thanks, she thought: *this dog is part of their family.*

No wonder Danny ran after him. He was loved.

Love...

It was a weird concept. Four years ago, love had died. It had shrivelled inside her, leaving her a dried out husk. She'd thought she could never feel pain again.

But when she'd thought she'd lost Rob... The pain was still with her. It was like she'd been under anaesthetic for years, and now the drug had worn off. Leaving her exposed...

The noise...

She was sitting beside the dirt wall, next to Rob.

His hand came out and took hers, and held. Taking comfort?

Her heart twisted, and the remembered pain came flooding back. Family...

She didn't have family. Her family was dead.

But Rob was holding her hand and she couldn't pull away.

She stirred at some stage, found cartons of juice, packets of crackers and tinned tuna. The others didn't speak while she prepared a sort of lunch.

Danny was the first to eat, accepting her offering with pleasure.

'We didn't have breakfast,' he told her. 'Mama was too scared. She was trying to pack the car; trying to ring Papa. I wanted toast but Mama said when we got away from the fire.'

'We're away from the fire now,' she told him, glancing sideways at Rob. She wasn't sure if his throat was burned. She wasn't sure...of anything. But he cautiously sipped the juice and then tucked into the crackers like there was no tomorrow.

The food did them all good. It settled them. *Nothing like a good cup of tea*—Julie's Gran used to say that, and she grinned. There was no way she could attempt to boil water. Juice would have to do as a substitute, but it seemed to be working just as well.

The roaring had muted. She was scarcely daring to hope, but maybe the front had passed.

'It's still too loud and too hot,' Rob croaked. 'We can't open the door yet.'

'My Henry will be looking for us,' Amina said. 'He'll be frantic.'

'He won't have been allowed through,' Rob told her. 'I came up last night and they were closing the road blocks then.'

'You were an idiot for coming,' Julie said.

'Yep.' But he didn't sound like he thought he was an idiot. 'How long have you lived here?' he asked Amina, and Julie thought he was trying hard to sound like things were normal. Like this was just a brief couple of hours of enforced stay and then they'd get on with their lives.

Maybe she would, she thought. After all, what had changed for her? Maybe their house had burned, but she didn't live here anyway.

Maybe more traces of their past were gone, but they'd been doomed to vanish one day. Things were just…things.

'Nearly four years,' Amina said. 'We came just after Danny was born. But this place…it's always been empty. The guy who mows the lawns said there was a tragedy. Kids…' And then her hand flew to her mouth. 'Your kids,' she whispered in horror. 'You're the parents of the twins who died.'

'It was a long time ago,' Rob said quietly. 'It's been a very long time since we were parents.'

'But you're together?' She seemed almost frantic, over-whelmed by past tragedy when recent tragedy had just been avoided.

'For now we are,' Rob told her.

'But you don't live here.'

'Too many ghosts,' Julie said.

'Why don't you sell?' She seemed dazed beyond belief. Horror piled upon horror...

'Because of the ghosts,' Julie whispered.

Amina glanced from Julie to Rob and back again, her expression showing her sheer incomprehension of what they must have gone through. Or maybe it wasn't incomprehension. She'd been so close herself...

'If you hadn't saved Danny...' she whispered.

'We did,' Rob told her.

'But it can't bring your boys back.'

'No.' Rob's voice was harsh.

'There's nothing...' Amina was crying now, hugging Danny to her, looking from Julie to Rob and back again. 'You've saved us and there's nothing I can do to thank you. No way... I wish...'

'We all wish,' Rob said grimly, glancing at Julie. 'But at least today we have less to wish for. A bit of ointment and the odd bandage for Luka's sore paws and we'll be ready to carry on where we left off.'

Where we left off yesterday, though, Julie thought bleakly. *Not where we left off four years ago.*

What had she been about, clinging to this man last night? The ghosts were still all around them.

The ghosts would never let them go.

'We're okay,' Rob said and suddenly he'd tugged her to him and he was holding. Just holding. Taking comfort or giving it, it didn't matter. His body was black and filthy and big and hard and infinitely comforting and she had a huge urge to turn and kiss him, smoke and all. She didn't. She couldn't and it wasn't just that they were with Amina and Danny.

The ghosts still held the power to hold them apart.

* * *

An hour later, Rob finally decreed they might open the bunker doors. The sounds had died to little more than high wind, with the occasional crack of falling timber. The battery-operated radio Rob had dug up from beneath a pile of blankets told them the front had moved south. Messages were confused. There was chaos and destruction throughout the mountains. All roads were closed. The advice was not to move from where they were.

They had no intention of moving from where they were, but they might look outside.

The normal advice during a bush fire was to take shelter while the front passed, and then emerge as soon as possible and fight to keep the house from burning. That'd be okay in a fast-moving grass fire but down in the valley the bush had caught and burned with an intensity that was never going to blow through. There'd been an hour of heat so intense they could feel it through the double doors. Now…she thought they'd emerge to nothing.

'What about staying here while we do a reconnaissance?' Rob asked Amina and the woman gave a grim nod.

'Our house'll be gone anyway; I know that. What's there to see? Danny, can you pass me another drink? We'll stay here until Rob and Julie tell us it's safe.'

'I want to see the burned,' Danny said, and Julie thought this was becoming an adventure to the little boy. He had no idea how close he'd come.

'You'll see it soon enough.' Rob managed to keep the grimness from his voice. 'But, for now, Julie and I are the fearless forward scouts. You're the captain minding the fort. Take care of everyone here, Danny. You're in charge.'

And he held out his hand to Julie. 'Come on, love,' he said. 'Let's go face the music.'

She hesitated. There was so much behind those words.

Sadness, tenderness, and...caring? How many years had they been apart and yet he could still call her *love*.

It twisted her heart. It made her feel vulnerable in a way she couldn't define.

'I'm coming,' she said, but she didn't take his hand. 'Let's go.'

First impression was black and smoke and heat. The wash of heat was so intense it took her breath away.

Second impression was desolation. The once glorious bushland that had surrounded their home was now a blackened, ash-filled landscape, still smouldering, flickers of flame still orange through the haze of smoke.

Third impression was that their house was still standing.

'My God,' Rob breathed. 'It's withstood... Julie, Plan D now.'

And she got it. Their fire plan had been formed years before but it was typed up and laminated, pasted to their bathroom door so they couldn't help but learn it.

Plan A: leave the area before the house was threatened. When they'd had the boys, this was the most sensible course of action. Maybe it was the most sensible course of action anyway. Their independent decision to come into a fire zone had been dumb. But okay, moving on.

Plan B: stay in the house and defend. They'd abandon that plan if the threat was dire, the fire intense.

Plan C: head to the bunker and stay there until the front passed. And then implement Plan D.

Plan D: get out of the bunker as soon as possible and try to stop remnants of fire destroying the house.

The fire had been so intense that Julie had never dreamed she'd be faced with Plan D but now it had happened, and the list with its dot-points was so ingrained in her head that she moved into automatic action.

The generator was under the house. The pump was under there too. If they were safe they could pump water from the underground tanks.

'You do the water, spray the roof,' Rob snapped. 'I'll check inside, then head round the foundations and put out spot fires.' It was still impossibly hard to speak. Even breathing hurt, but somehow Rob managed it. 'We can do this, Julie. With this level of fire, we might be stuck here for hours, if not days. We need to keep the house safe.'

Why? There was a tiny part of her that demanded it. *Why bother?*

For the same reason she'd come back, she thought. This house had been home. It no longer was, or she'd thought it no longer was. But Rob was already heading for the bricked-in cavity under the house where they'd find tools to defend.

Rob thought this place was worth fighting for—the remnants of her home?

Who knew the truth of it? Who knew the logic? All she knew was that Rob thought this house was worth defending and, for now, all she could do was follow.

They worked solidly for two hours. After the initial checks they worked together, side by side. Rob's design genius had paid off. The house was intact but the smouldering fires after the front were insidious. A tiny spark in leaf litter hard by the house could be enough to turn the house into flames hours after the main fire. So Julie sprayed while Rob ran along the base of the house with a mop and bucket.

The underground water tank was a lifesaver. The water flowing out seemed unbelievably precious. Heaven knew how people managed without such tanks.

They didn't, she thought grimly as finally Rob left her

to sentry duty and determinedly made his way through the ash and smoke to check Amina's house.

He came back looking even grimmer than he had when he'd left.

'Gone,' he said. 'And their car… God help them if they'd stayed in that car, or even if they'd made it out onto the road. Our cars are still safe in the garage, but a tree's fallen over the track leading into the house. It's big and it's burning. We're going nowhere.'

There was no more to be said. They worked on. Maybe someone should go back to Amina to tell her about her house, but the highest priority had to be making sure this house was safe. Not because of emotional ties, though. This was all about current need.

Mount Bundoon was a tiny hamlet and this house and Amina's were two miles out of town. Thick bush lay between them and the township. There'd be more fallen logs—who knew what else—between them and civilisation.

'We'll be stuck here till Christmas,' Julie said as they worked, and her voice came out strained. Her throat was so sore from the smoke.

'Seeing as Christmas is tomorrow, yes, we will,' Rob told her. 'Did you have any plans?'

'I…no.'

'Do we have a turkey in the freezer?'

'I should have left it out,' she said unsteadily. 'It would have been roasted by now. Oh, Rob…' She heard her voice shake and Rob's arms came round her shoulders.

'No matter. We've done it. We're almost on the other side, Jules, love.'

But they weren't, she thought, and suddenly bleakness was all around her. What had changed? She could cling to Rob now but she knew that, long-term, they'd destroy each other. How could you help ease someone else's pain when you were withered inside by your own?

'Another half hour and we might be able to liberate Amina,' Rob said and something about the way he spoke told her he was feeling pretty much the same sensations she was feeling. 'The embers are getting less and Luka must be just about busting to find a tree by now.'

'Well, good luck to him finding one,' she said, pausing with her wet mop to stare bleakly round at the moonscape destruction.

'We can help them,' Rob said gently. 'They've lost their house. We can help them get through it. I don't know about you, Jules, but putting my head down and working's been the only thing between me and madness for the last four years. So keeping Amina's little family secure—that's something we can focus on. And we can focus on it together.'

'Just for the next twenty-four hours.'

'That's all I ever think about,' Rob told her, and the bleakness was back in his voice full force. 'One day at a time. One hour at a time. That's survival, Jules. We both know all about it so let's put it into action now.'

One day at a time? Rob worked on, the hard physical work almost a welcome relief from the emotions of the last twenty-four hours but, strangely, he'd stopped thinking of now. He was putting out embers on autopilot but the rest of his brain was moving forward.

Where did he go from here?

Before the fire, he'd thought he had almost reached the other side of a chasm of depression and self-blame. There'd been glimmers of light when he'd thought he could enjoy life again. 'You need to move on,' his shrink had advised him. 'You can't help Julie and together your grief will make you self-destruct.' Or maybe that wasn't what the shrink had advised him—maybe it was what the counselling sessions had made him accept for himself.

But now, working side by side, with Julie a constant presence as they beat out the spot fires still flaring up against the house, it was as if that thinking was revealed for what it was—a travesty. A lie. How could he move on? He still felt married. He still *was* married.

He'd fallen in love with his dot-point-maker, his Julie, eight years ago and that love was still there.

Maybe that was why he'd come back—drawn here because his heart had never left the place. And it wasn't just the kids.

It was his wife.

So... Twenty-four hours on and the mists were starting to clear.

Together your grief will make you self-destruct. It might be true, he conceded, but Julie chose that moment to thump a spark with a wet mop. 'Take that, you—' she grunted and swiped it again for good measure and he found himself smiling.

She was still under there—his Julie.

Together they'd self-destruct? Maybe they would, he conceded as he worked, but was it possible—was there even a chance?—that together they could find a way to heal?

It was time to get Amina and Danny and Luka out of the bunker.

It was dark, not because it was night—it was still mid-afternoon—but because the smoke was still all-enveloping. They'd need to keep watch, take it in turns to check for spot fires, but, for now, they entered the house together.

Rob was holding Amina's hand. He'd been worried

she'd trip over the mass of litter blasted across the yard. Danny was clinging to his mother's other side. Luka was pressing hard against his small master. The dog was limping a little but he wasn't about to leave the little boy.

Which left Julie bringing up the rear. She stood aside as Rob led them indoors and for some crazy reason she thought of the day Rob had brought her here to show her his plans. He'd laid out a tentative floor plan with string and markers on the soil. He'd shown her where the front door would be and then he'd swung her into his arms and lifted her across.

'Welcome to your home, my bride,' he'd told her and he'd set her down into the future hall and he'd kissed her with a passion that had left her breathless. 'Welcome to your Happy Ever After.'

Past history. Moving on. She followed them in and felt bleakness envelop her. The house was grey, dingy, appalling. There were no lights. She flicked the switch without hope and, of course, there was none.

'The cabling from the solar system must have melted,' Rob said, and then he gave a little-boy grin that was, in the circumstances, totally unexpected and totally endearing. 'But I have that covered. I knew the conduit was a weak spot when we built so the electrician's left me backup. I just need to unplug one lot and plug in another. The spare's in the garage, right next to my tool belt.'

And in the face of that grin it was impossible not to smile back. The grey lifted, just a little. Man with tool belt, practically chest-thumping...

He'd designed this house to withstand fire. Skilled with a tool belt or not, he had saved them.

'It might take a bit of fiddling,' Rob conceded, trying —unsuccessfully—to sound modest. 'And the smoke will be messing with it now. But even if it fails completely we have the generator for important things, like pumping water. We have the barbecue. We can manage.'

'If you're thinking of getting up on the roof, Superman…'

'When it cools a little. And I'll let you hold the ladder.' He offered it like he was offering diamonds and, weirdly, she wanted to laugh. Her world was somehow righting.

'Do you mind…if we stay?' Amina faltered and Julie hauled herself together even more. Amina had lost her home. She didn't know where her husband was and Julie knew she was fearful that he'd have been on the road trying to reach her. What was Julie fearful about? Nothing. Rob was safe, and even that shouldn't matter.

But it did. She looked at his smoke-stained face, his bloodshot eyes, his grin that she knew was assumed— she knew this man and she knew he was feeling as bleak as she was, but he was trying his best to cheer them up— and she thought: *no matter what we've been through, we have been through it.*

I know this man. The feeling was solid, a rock in a shifting world. Even if being together hurt so much she couldn't bear it, he still felt part of her.

'Of course you can stay.' She struggled to sound normal, struggled to sound like a friendly neighbour welcoming a friend. 'For as long as you like.'

'For as long as we must,' Rob amended. 'Amina, the roads will be blocked. There's no phone reception. I checked and the transmission towers are down.' He hesitated and looked suddenly nervous. 'When…when's your baby due?'

'Not for another four weeks. Henry works in the mines, two weeks on, two weeks off, but he's done six weeks in a row so he can get a long leave for the baby. He was flying in last night. He'll be frantic. I have to get a message to him.'

'I don't think we can do that,' Rob told her. 'The phones are out and the road is cut by fallen timber. It's over an hour's walk at the best of times down to the highway and frankly it's not safe to try. Burned trees will still be falling. I don't think I can walk in this heat and smoke.'

'I wouldn't want you to, but Henry…'

'He'll have stopped at the road blocks. He'll be forced to wait until the roads are cleared, but the worst of the fire's over. You'll see him soon.'

'But if the fire comes back…'

'It won't,' Rob told her. 'Even if there's a wind change, there's nothing left to burn.'

'But this house…'

'Is a fortress,' Julie told her. 'It's the house that Rob built. No fire dare challenge it.'

'He's amazing,' Amina managed as Rob headed out to do another mop and bucket round—they'd need to keep checking for hours, if not days. 'He's just…a hero.'

'He is.'

'You're so lucky…' And then Amina faltered, remembering. 'I mean… I can't…'

'I am lucky,' Julie told her. 'And yes, Rob's a hero.' And he was. Not her hero but a hero. 'But for now…for now, let's investigate the basics. We need to make this house liveable. It's Christmas tomorrow. Surely we can do something to celebrate.'

'But my Henry…'

'He'll come,' Julie said stoutly. 'And when he does, we need to have Christmas waiting for him.'

Rob made his way slowly round the house, inspecting everything. Every spark, every smouldering leaf or twig copped a mopful of water, but the threat was easing.

The smoke was easing a little. He could almost breathe.

He could almost think.

He'd saved Danny.

It should feel good and it did. He should feel lucky and he did. Strangely, though, he felt more than that. It was like a huge grey weight had been lifted from his shoulders.

Somehow he'd saved Danny. Danny would grow into a man because of what he'd achieved.

It didn't make the twins' death any easier to comprehend but somehow the knot of rage and desolation inside him had loosened a little.

Was it also because he'd held Julie last night? Lost himself in her body?

Julie.

'I wish she'd been able to save him, too,' he said out loud. Nothing and no one answered. It was like he was on Mars.

But Julie was here, right inside the door. And Amina and the kid he'd saved.

If he hadn't come, Julie might not have even made it to the bunker. Her eyes said maybe that wouldn't matter. Sometimes her eyes looked dead already.

How to fix that? How to break through?

He hadn't been able to four years ago. What was different now?

For the last four years he'd missed her with an ache in his gut that had never subsided. He'd learned to live with it. He'd even learned to have fun despite it, dating a couple of women this year, putting out tentative feelers, seeing if he could get back to some semblance of life. For his overtures to Julie had been met with blank rebuttal and there'd been nothing he could do to break through.

Had he tried hard enough? He hadn't, he conceded, because he'd known it was hopeless. He was part of her tragedy and she had to move on.

He'd accepted his marriage was over in everything but name.

So why had he come back here now? Was it really to save two fire engines? Or was it because he'd guessed Julie would be here?

One last hope…

If so, it had been subconscious, acting against the advice of his logic, his shrink, his new-found determination to look forward, to try and live.

But the thing was…Julie was here. She was here now, and it wasn't just the bleak, dead Julie. He could make this Julie smile again. He could reach her.

But every time he did, she closed off again.

No matter. She was still in there, in that house, and he wielded his mop with extra vigour because of it. His Julie was still Julie. She was behind layers of protection so deep he'd need a battering ram to knock them down, but hey, he'd saved a kid and his house had withstood a firestorm.

All he needed now was a battering ram and hope.

And a miracle?

Miracles were possible. They'd had two today. Why not hope for another?

The house was hot, stuffy and filled with smoke but compared to outside it seemed almost normal. It even felt normal until she hauled back the thick shutters and saw outside.

The once glorious view of the bushland was now devastation.

'I don't know what to do,' Amina whimpered and Julie thought: *neither do I.* But at least they were safe; Rob was outside in the heat making sure of it. The option of whimpering, too, was out of the question.

She looked at Amina and remembered how she'd felt

at the same stage in pregnancy. Amina wasn't carrying twins—at least she didn't think so—but this heat would be driving her to the edge, even without the added terrors of the fire.

'We have plenty of water in the underground tank,' she told her. 'And we have a generator running the pumps. If you like, you could have a bath.'

'A bath...' Amina looked at Julie like she'd offered gold. 'Really?'

'Really.'

'I'm not sure I could get in and out.' She gazed down at her bulk and even managed a smile. 'I used to describe it as a basketball. Now I think it's a small hippopotamus.'

'There are safety rails to help you in and out.'

'You put them in when you were pregnant?' It was a shy request, not one that could be snapped at.

'Yes.'

'You and Rob didn't come back here because this is where your boys lived?' Amina ventured, but it wasn't really a question. It was a statement; a discovery.

'Yes.' There was no other answer.

'Maybe I'd have felt the same if I'd lost Danny.' Danny was clinging to her side but he was looking round, interested, oblivious to the danger he'd been in mere hours before. 'Danny, will you come into the bathroom with me?'

But Danny was looking longingly out of the window. He was obviously aching for his adventure to continue, and the last thing Amina needed, Julie thought, was her four-year-old in the bathroom with her.

Luka had flopped on the floor. The big dog gave a gentle whine.

'I'll see to his pads,' Amina said but she couldn't disguise her exhaustion, or her desolation at postponing the promised bath.

'Tell you what,' Julie said. 'You go take a bath and Danny and I will take Luka into the laundry. There's a big shallow shower/bath in there. If he's like any golden retriever I know he'll like water, right?'

'He loves it.'

'Then he can stand under the shower for as long as he wants until we know his pads are completely clean. Then I'll find some burn salve for them. Danny, will you help me?'

'Give Luka a shower?' Danny ventured.

'That's the idea. You can get undressed and have a shower with him if you want.' And Julie's mind, unbidden, was taking her back, knowing what her boys loved best in the world. 'We could have fun.'

Fun... Where had that word come from? Julie McDowell didn't do fun.

'Will Rob help, too?' Danny asked shyly and she nodded.

'When he's stopped firefighting, maybe he will.'

'Rob's big.' There was already a touch of hero worship in the little boy's voice.

'Yes.'

'He made me safe. I was frightened and he made me safe.'

'He's good at that,' Julie managed, but she didn't know where to take it from there.

Once upon a time Rob had made her feel safe. Once upon a time she'd believed safe was possible.

Right now, that was what he was doing. Keeping them safe.

One day at a time, she thought. She'd been doing this for years, taking one day at a time. But now Rob was outside, keeping them safe, and the thought left her exposed.

One day at a time? Right now she was having trouble focusing on one *moment* at a time.

* * *

Rob did one final round of the house and decided that was it; he didn't have the strength to stay in the heat any longer. But the wind had died, there was no fire within two hundred yards of the house and even that was piles of ash, simmering to nothing. He could take a break. He headed up the veranda steps and was met by the sound of a child's laughter.

It stopped him dead in his tracks.

He was filthy. He was exhausted. All he wanted was to stand under a cold shower and then collapse, but the shower was in the laundry.

And someone was already splashing and shouting inside.

He could hear Julie laughing and, for some weird reason, the sound made him want to back away.

Coward, he told himself. He'd faced a bush fire and survived. How could laughter hurt so much? But it took a real effort to open the laundry door.

What met him was mess. Huge mess. The huge laundry shower-cum-bath had a base about a foot deep. It had been built to dump the twins in when they'd come in filthy from outside. The twins had filled it with their chaos and laughter and it was filled now.

More than filled.

Luka was sitting serenely in the middle of the base. The water was streaming over the big dog, and he had his head blissfully raised so the water could pour right over his eyes. Doggy heaven.

Danny had removed his clothes. He was using…one of the twins' boats?…to pour water over Luka's back. Every time he dumped a load, Luka turned and licked him, chin to forehead. Danny shrieked with laughter and scooped another load.

Julie was still fully dressed. She'd hauled off her boots and flannel overshirt but the rest was intact. Dressed or not, though, she was sitting on the edge of the tub, her feet were in the water and she was soaking. Water was streaming over her hair. She was still black but the black was now running in streaks. She looked like she didn't care.

She was helping Danny scoop water. She was laughing with Danny, hugging Luka.

Silly as a tin of worms...

Once upon a time Rob's dad had said that to him. Angus McDowell, Rob's father, was a Very Serious Man, a minister of religion, harsh and unyielding. He'd disapproved of Julie at first, though when Julie's business prowess had been proven he'd unbent towards her. But he'd visited once and listened to Julie playing with the twins at bathtime.

'She's spoiling those two lads. Listen to them. Silly as a tin of worms.'

Right now her hair was wet, the waves curling, twisting and spiralling. He'd loved her hair.

He loved her hair.

How had he managed without this woman for so long?

The same way he'd managed without his boys, he told himself harshly. One moment at a time. One step after another. Getting through each day, one by one.

Julie must feel the same. He'd seen the death of the light behind her eyes. Being together, their one-step-at-a-time rule had faltered. They could only go on if they didn't think, didn't let themselves remember.

But Julie wasn't dead now. She was very much alive. Her eyes were dancing with pleasure and her laughter was almost that of the Julie of years ago. Young. Free.

She turned and saw him and the laughter faded, just like that.

'Rob!' Danny said with satisfaction. 'You're all black. Julie says she doesn't have enough soap to get all the black off.'

'There's enough left.' Julie rose quickly—a little too quickly. Before he could stop himself he'd reached out and caught her. He held her arms as she stepped over the edge of the bath. She was soaking. She'd been using some sort of lemon soap, the one she'd always used, and suddenly he realised where that citrus scent came from. She smelled... She felt...

'You're not clean yet,' he managed and she smiled. She was only six inches away from him. He was holding her. He could just tug...

He didn't tug. This was Julie. She'd been laughing and the sight of him had stopped that laughter.

They'd destroy each other. They'd pretty much decided that, without ever speaking it out loud. Four years ago they'd walked away from each other for good reason.

How could you live with your own hurt when you saw it reflected in another's eyes, day after day? Moment after moment.

A miracle. He needed a miracle.

It's Christmas, he thought inconsequentially. *That's what I want for Christmas, Santa. I've saved Danny. We're safe and our house is safe, but I'm greedy. A third miracle. Please...*

'I'm clean apart from my clothes,' Julie managed, shaking her hair like a dog so that water sprayed over him. It hit his face, cool and delicious. Some hit his lips and he tasted it. Tasted Julie?

'I'll go change if you can take over here,' Julie said. 'Danny, is it okay if Rob comes under the water, too?'

'Yes,' Danny said. 'He's my friend. But you can both fit.'

'I need to find some clean clothes and something your

mum can wear,' Julie told him. 'And some dog food. And some food for us.'

'The freezer…'

'I've hooked it to the generator so I can save the solar power for important stuff,' she said and deliberately she tugged away from him. It hurt that she pulled back. He wanted to hold her. 'Like the lights on the Christmas tree.'

'So we have Christmas lights and there's enough to eat?' he asked, trying hard to concentrate on practicalities.

'If need be, we have enough to live on for weeks.'

'Will we stay here for weeks?' Danny asked and Rob saw a shadow cross Julie's face. It was an act then, he thought, laughing and playing with the child. The pain was still there. She'd managed to push it away while she'd helped Danny have fun but it was with her still. Every time she saw a child…

And every time she saw him. She glanced up at him and he saw the hurt, the bleakness and the same certainty that this was a transient, enforced connection. If they were to survive they had to move on.

He knew it for the truth. It was time it lost the power to hurt.

Miracles were thin on the ground. They'd already had two today. Was it too much to ask for just one more?

How long was frozen food safe? Where was the Internet when she needed it? Finally she decided to play safe. Using the outside barbecue—well, it had been outside but Rob had hauled it under the house during the fire so now it could be wheeled outside again—she boiled dried spaghetti and tipped over a can of spaghetti sauce. The use-by dates on both were well past, but she couldn't figure how they could go off.

'I reckon, come Armageddon, these suckers will survive,' she told Rob, tipping in the sauce.

'We might have to do something a bit more imaginative tomorrow,' Rob told her. Washed and dressed in clean jeans and T-shirt, he'd found her in the kitchen. He was now examining the contents of the freezer. 'Shall I take the turkey out?'

'Surely the roads will be open by tomorrow.'

'Don't count on it,' he said grimly. 'Jules, I've been listening to the radio and the news is horrendous. We're surrounded by miles of burned ground and the fire's ongoing. The authorities won't have the resources to get us out while they're still trying to protect communities facing the fire front.'

'Turkey it is, then,' she said, trying to make it sound light. As if being trapped here was no big deal.

As if the presence of this man she'd once known so well wasn't doing things to her head. And to her body.

She'd known him so well. She *knew* him so well.

One part of her wanted to turn away from the barbecue right now and tug him into her arms. To hold and be held. To feel what she used to take for granted.

Another part of her wanted to leave right now, hike the miles down the road away from the mountains. Sure, it would entail risks but staying close to this man held risks as well. Like remembering how much she wanted him. Like remembering how much giving your heart cost.

It had cost her everything. There was simply…nothing left.

'Can…can I help?' Amina stood at the doorway, Danny clinging by her side. She was dressed in a borrowed house robe of Julie's. She looked lost, bereft, and very, very pregnant.

'Put your feet up inside,' Rob said roughly and Julie

knew by his tone that he was as worried as she was about the girl. 'It's too hot out here already and Julie's cooking. Hot food!'

'You tell me where we can get sandwiches or salad and I'll open my purse,' Julie retorted. 'Sorry, Amina, it's spaghetti or nothing.'

'I'd like to see my house,' she said shyly and Julie winced.

'It's gone, Amina.'

'Burned,' Danny said. The adventure had gone out of the child. He looked scared.

'Yes, but we have this house,' Julie said. 'That's something. You can stay here for as long as you want.'

'My husband will be looking for us,' Amina whispered.

'If he comes next door the first place he'll look will be here.'

'Will Santa know to come here?' Danny asked. His dog was pressed by his side. He looked very small and very frightened. It was his mother's fear, Julie thought. He'd be able to feel it.

'Santa always knows where everyone is,' Rob said, squatting before Danny and scratching Luka's ears. It was intuitive, Julie thought. Danny might well recoil from a hug, but a hug to his dog was pretty much the same thing. 'I promise.'

'He's found us before,' Amina managed, but this time she couldn't stop a sob. 'I can't...we were just...'

'Where are you from?' Rob asked gently, still patting Luka.

'Sri Lanka. We left because of the fighting. My husband... He's a construction engineer. He had a good job; we had a nice house but we...things happened. We had to come here, but here he can't be an engineer. He has to retrain but it's so expensive to get his Australian accreditation. We're working so hard, trying to get the money so he can do the transition course. Meanwhile, I've been working as a cleaner.' She tilted her chin. 'I work for the firm that cleans this house. My job's good. We couldn't believe it when we were able to rent our house. We thought…this is heaven. But Henry has to work as a fly in, fly out miner. He'll be so worried right now and I'm scared he might have tried to get here. If he's been caught in the fire…'

Rob rose and took her hands. She was close to collapse, weak with terror.

'It won't have happened,' he said firmly, strongly, in a voice that Julie hadn't heard before. It was a tone that said: *don't mess with me; this is the truth and you'd better believe me.* 'They put road blocks in place last night. No one was allowed in. I was the last, and I had to talk hard to be let through. If your husband had come in before the blocks were in place, then he'd be here now. He can't have. He'll be stuck at the block or even further down the mountain. He'll be trying to get to you but he won't be permitted. He'll be safe.'

Danny was looking up at Rob as if he were the oracle on high. 'Papa's stuck down the mountain?'

'I imagine he's eating his dinner right now.'

'Where will he eat dinner?'

'The radio says a school has been opened at the foot of the mountains. Anyone who can't get home will be staying at the school.'

'Papa's at school?'

'Yes,' Rob said in that same voice that brooked no argument. 'Yes, he is. Eating dinner. Speaking of dinner… how's it coming along?'

'It's brilliant,' Julie said. 'Michelin three star, no less.'

'I don't doubt it,' Rob said, and grinned at her with the same Rob-grin that twisted her heart with pain and with pleasure. 'Do we have enough to give some to Luka?'

'If Luka eats spaghetti he'll get a very red moustache,' Julie said and Danny giggled.

And Julie smiled back at Rob—and saw the same pain and pleasure reflected in his eyes.

CHAPTER SIX

DANNY AND ROB chatted. It was their saving grace; otherwise their odd little dinner would have been eaten in miserable silence. Too much had happened for Julie to attempt to be social.

Amina was caught up in a pool of misery. Julie's heart went out to her but there was little she could do to help.

She pressed her into eating, with limited success, and worried more.

'When's your baby due?' she asked.

'The twentieth of January.' Amina motioned to Danny. 'We were still in the refugee camp when we had Danny. This was supposed to be so different.'

'It is different.'

'Refugees again,' Amina whispered. 'But not even together.'

'You will be soon,' Julie said stoutly, sending a fervent prayer upward. 'Meanwhile we have ice cream.'

'Ice cream!'

'It's an unopened container, not a hint of ice on it,' she said proudly. 'How's that for forethought? I must have pre-prepared, four years ago.'

There was an offer too good to refuse. They all ate ice cream and Julie was relieved to see Amina reach for seconds.

There was another carton at the base of the freezer. Maybe they could even eat ice cream for breakfast.

Breakfast… How long would they be trapped here?

'Now can I go next door?' Amina asked as the last of the ice cream disappeared.

Rob grimaced. 'You're sure you don't want me to check and report back?'

'I need to see.'

'Me too,' Danny said and his mother looked at him and nodded.

'Danny's seen a lot the world has thrown at us. And his father would expect him to be a man.'

Danny's chest visibly swelled.

Kids. They were all the same. Wanting to be grown-up. Wanting to protect their mum?

It should be the other way round. She should have been able to protect…

'Stop it, Jules,' Rob said in his boss-of-the-world voice, and she flinched. Stop it? How could she stop? It was as if the voices in her head were on permanent replay.

'We need to focus on Santa,' he told her, and his eyes sent her a message that belied his smile. 'Moving on.'

Move on. How could she ever? But here there was no choice. Amina was looking at her and so was Danny. Even Luka… No, actually, Luka was looking at the almost empty ice cream container in her hand.

Move on.

'Right,' she said and lowered the ice cream to possibly its most appreciative consumer. 'Danny, you're going to have to wash your dog's face. Spaghetti followed by chocolate ice cream is not a good look. Meanwhile, I'll see if I can find you some sturdy shoes, Amina, and I have a jogging suit that might fit over your bump. It's not the most gorgeous outfit you might like but it's sensible, and Sensible R Us. Let's get the end of this meal cleared up and then go see if the fire's left anything of your house.'

It hadn't left a thing.

A twisted, gnarled washing line. The skeleton of a washing machine. A mass of smouldering timbers and smashed tiles.

Amina stood weeping. Julie held her and Danny's hands as Rob, in his big boots, stomped over the ruins searching for... Anything.

Nothing.

He came back to them at last, his face bleak. 'Amina, I'm sorry.'

'We didn't have much,' Amina said, faltering. 'My sister...she was killed in the bombing. I had her photographs. That was what I most...' She swallowed. 'But we've lost so much before. I know we can face this too. As long as my Henry is safe.'

'That's a hell of a name for a Sri Lankan engineer,' Rob said and Amina managed a smile.

'My mother-in-law dreamed of her son being an Englishman.'

'Will Australian do instead?'

'It doesn't matter where we are—what we have. It's a long time since we dreamed of anything but our family being safe.'

And then she paused.

The silence after the roar of the fire had been almost eerie. The wind had dropped after the front had passed. There was still the crackle of fire, and occasionally there'd be a crash as fire-weakened timber fell, but there'd been little sound for hours.

Now they heard an engine, faint at first but growing closer.

Rob ushered his little group around Amina's burned car, around the still burning log that lay over their joint driveways and out onto the road. Rob was carrying Danny—much to Danny's disgust, but he had no sensible shoes. And if anyone was to carry him, it seemed okay that his hero should. Thus they stood, waiting, seeing what would emerge out of the smoky haze.

And when it came, inevitably, magically but far too late, it was a fire engine. Big, red, gorgeous.

Julie hadn't realised how tense she'd been until she saw the red of the engine, until she saw the smoke-blackened firefighters in their stained yellow suits. Here was contact with the outside world.

She had a sudden mad urge to climb on the back and hitch a ride, all the way back to Sydney, all the way back to the safety of her office, her ordered financial world.

Ha. As if this apparition was offering any such transport.

'Are you guys okay?' It was the driver, a grim-faced woman in her fifties, swinging out of the cab and facing them with apprehension.

'No casualties,' Rob told her. 'Apart from minor burns on our dog's feet. But we have burn cream. And ice cream. And one intact house.'

'Good for you.' The guys with her were surveying Amina's house and then looking towards their intact house with surprise. 'You managed to save it?'

'It saved itself. We hid in a bunker.'

'Bloody lucky. Can you stay here?'

'Amina's pregnant,' Rob said. 'And her husband will be going out of his mind not knowing if she's safe.'

The woman looked at Amina, noting Danny, noting everything, Julie thought. She had the feeling that this woman was used to making hard decisions.

'We'll put her on the list for evacuation,' she said. 'How pregnant are you?'

'Thirty-six weeks,' Amina whispered.

'No sign of labour?'

'N…no.'

'Then sorry, love, but that puts you down the list. We're radioing in casualties and using the chopper for evacuation, but the chopper has a list a mile long of people with burns, accidents from trying to outrun the fire or breathing problems. And it's a huge risk trying to take anyone out via the road. There's so much falling timber I'm risking my own team being here. Do you have water? Food?'

'We're okay,' Rob told her. 'We have solar power, generators, water tanks, freezers and a stocked pantry. We have plenty of uncontaminated water and more canned food than we know what to do with.'

'Amazing,' the woman told him. 'It sounds like you're luckier than some of the towns that have been in the fire line. We managed to save houses but they're left with no services. Meanwhile, there are houses further up the mountain that haven't been checked. Our job's to get through to them, give emergency assistance and detail evacuation needs for the choppers, but by emergency we're talking life-threatening. That's all we can do— we're stretched past our limits. But we will take your name and get it put up on the lists at the refuge centres to say you're safe,' she told Amina. 'That should reassure your husband. Meanwhile, stay as cool as you can and keep that baby on board.'

'But we have no way of contacting you if anything… happens,' Rob said urgently and the woman grimaced.

'I know and I'm sorry, but I'm making a call here. We'll get the road clear as soon as we can but that'll be late tomorrow at the earliest, and possibly longer. There's timber still actively burning on the roadside. It's no use driving anyone out if a tree's to fall on them, and that's a real risk. You have a house. Your job is to protect it a while longer and thank your lucky stars you're safe. Have as good a Christmas as you can under the circumstances—and make sure that baby stays where it is.'

They watched the fire truck make its cautious way to the next bend and disappear. All of them knew what they were likely to find. It was a subdued little party that picked its way through the rubble and back to the house.

Luka greeted them with dulled pleasure. His paws obviously hurt. Rob had put on burn cream and dressings. They were superficial burns, he reported, but they were obviously painful enough for the big dog to not want to bother his bandages.

Danny lay down on the floor with him, wrapped his arms around his pet's neck and burst into tears.

'My husband wanted a dog to protect us when he was away,' Amina volunteered, and she sounded close to tears herself. 'But Luka's turned into Danny's best friend. Today Luka almost killed him—and yet here I am, thanking everything that Danny still has him. I hope…I hope…'

And Julie knew what she was hoping. This woman had gone through war and refugee camps. She'd be thinking she was homeless once again. With a dog.

Once upon a time as a baby lawyer, Julie had visited a refugee camp. She couldn't remember seeing a single dog.

'It's okay, Amina,' she told her. 'If you've been renting next door, then you can just rent here instead. This place is empty.'

'But…' Rob said.

'We never use it.' Julie cast him an uncertain glance. 'We live…in other places. I know you have a lot to think about and this will be something you and your husband need to discuss together, but, right now, don't worry about accommodation. You can stay here for as long as you want.'

'But don't…don't *you* need to discuss it with your husband?' Amina asked, casting an uncertain glance at Rob.

Her husband. Rob. She glanced down at the wedding ring, still bright on her left hand. She still had a husband—and yet she hadn't made one decision with him for four years.

'Rob and I don't live together,' she said, and she couldn't stop the note of bleakness she could hear in her own words. 'We have separate lives, separate…homes. So I'm sure you agree, don't you, Rob. This place may as well be used.'

There was a moment's pause. Silence hung, and for a moment she didn't know how it could end. But then… 'It should be a home again,' Rob said. 'Julie and I can't make it one. It'd be great if you and Henry and your children could make it happy again.'

'No decisions yet,' Amina urged. 'Don't promise anything. But if we could… If Henry's safe—' She broke off again and choked on tears. 'But it's too soon for anything.'

Rob went off to check the perimeter with his mop and bucket again. They had a wide area of burned grass between them and any smouldering timber. The risk was pretty much over but still he checked.

Amina and Danny went to bed. There was a made-up guest room with a lovely big bed, but Danny had spotted the racing-car beds. That was where he wanted to sleep—so Amina tugged one racing car closer to the other and announced that she was sleeping there, with her son.

She was asleep almost as her head hit the pillow. Had she slept at all last night? Julie wondered. She thought again of past fighting and refugee camps and all this woman had gone through.

Danny was fast asleep too. He was sharing his car-bed with Luka. Julie stood in the doorway and looked at them, this little family who'd been so close to disaster.

Disaster was always so close…

Get over it, she told herself harshly. *Move on.* She needed work to distract herself. She needed legal problems to solve, paperwork to do—stuff that had to be done yesterday.

Rob was out playing fireman but there was no need for the two of them to be there. So what was she supposed to do? Go to bed? She wasn't tired or if she was her body wasn't admitting it. She felt weird, exposed, trapped. Standing in her children's bedroom watching others sleep in their beds… Knowing a man who was no longer her husband was out protecting the property…

What to do? What to do?

Christmas.

The answer came as she headed back down the hall. There in the sitting room was her Christmas tree. Was it only last night that she'd decorated it? Why?

And the answer came clear, obvious now as it hadn't been last night. Because Danny needed it. Because they all needed it?

'Will Santa know to come here?' Danny had asked and Rob had reassured him.

'Santa knows where everyone is.'

That had been a promise and it had to be kept. She wouldn't mind betting Danny would be the first awake in the morning. Right now there was a Christmas tree and nothing else.

Santa had no doubt kept a stash of gifts over at Amina's house, but there was nothing left there now except cinders. Amina had been too exhausted to think past tonight.

'So I'm Santa.' She said it out loud.

'Can I share?'

And Rob was in the doorway, looking at the tree. 'I thought of it while I mopped,' he told her. 'We need to play Father Christmas.'

They could. There was a stash from long ago…

If she could bear it.

Of course she could bear it. Did she make her decision based on emotional back story or the real, tomorrow needs of one small boy? What was the choice? There wasn't one. She glanced at Rob and saw he'd come to the same conclusion she had.

Without a word she headed into their bedroom. Rob followed.

She tugged the bottom drawer out from under the wardrobe, ready to climb—even as toddlers the twins had been expert in finding stuff they didn't want them to find. She put a foot on the first drawer and Rob took her by the waist, lifted her and set her aside.

'Climbing's men's work,' he said.

'Yeah?' Unbidden, came another memory. Their town house in the city. Their elderly neighbour knocking on the door one night.

'Please, my kitten's climbed up the elm outside. He can't get down. Will you help?'

The elm was vast, reaching out over the pavement to the street beyond. The kitten was maybe halfway up, mewing pitifully.

'Right,' Rob had said manfully, though Julie had known him well and heard the qualms behind the bravado.

'Let me call the fire brigade,' she'd said and he'd cast her a look of manly scorn.

'Stand aside, woman.'

Which meant twenty minutes later the kitten was safely back in her owner's arms—having decided she didn't like Rob reaching for her, so she'd headed down under her own steam. And Julie had finally called the fire department to help her husband down.

So now she choked, and Rob glowered, but he was laughing under his glower. 'You're supposed to have forgotten that,' he told her. 'Stupid cat.'

'It's worth remembering.'

'Isn't everything?' he asked obliquely and headed up his drawer-cum-staircase.

And then they really had to remember.

The Christmas-that-never-was was up there. Silently, Rob handed it down. There were glove puppets, a wooden railway set, Batman pyjamas. Colouring books and a blow-up paddling pool. A pile of Christmas wrapping and ties they'd been too busy to use until the last moment. The detritus of a family Christmas that had never made it.

Rob put one of the puppets on his too-big hand. It was a wombat. Its two front paws were his thumb and little finger. Its head had the other fingers stuffed into its insides.

The little head wobbled. 'What do you say, Mrs McDowell?' the little wombat demanded in a voice that sounded like a strangled Rob. 'You reckon we can give me to a little guy who needs me?'

'Yes.' But her voice was strained.

'I'm not real,' the little wombat said—via Rob. 'I'm just a bit of fake fur and some neat stitchery.'

'Of course.'

'But I represent the past.'

'Don't push it, Rob.' Why was the past threatening to rise up and choke her?

'I'm not pushing. I'm facing stuff myself. I've been facing stuff alone for so long...' Rob put down his wombat and picked up the Batman pyjamas. 'It hurts. Would it hurt more together than it does separately? That's a decision we need to make. Meanwhile, we bought these too big for the twins and Danny's tiny. These'll make him happy.'

She could hardly breathe. What was he suggesting? That he wanted to try again? 'I...I know that,' she managed but she was suddenly feeling as if she was in the bunker again, cowering, the outside threats closing in.

Dumb. Rob wasn't threatening. He was holding Batman pyjamas—and smiling at her as if he understood exactly how she felt.

I've been facing stuff alone for so long... She hadn't allowed herself to think about that. She hadn't been able to face his hurt as well as hers.

Guilty...and did she need to add *coward* to her list of failings as well?

'Would it have been easier if it all burned?' Rob asked gently and she flinched.

'Maybe. Maybe it would.'

'So why did you come?'

'You know why.'

'Because it's not over? Because they're still with us?' His voice was kind. 'Because we can't escape it; we're still a family?'

'We're not.'

'They're still with me,' he said, just as gently. 'Every waking moment, and often in my sleep as well, they're with me.'

'Yeah.'

'They're not in this stuff. They're in our hearts.'

'Rob, no.' The pain... She hadn't let herself think it. She hadn't let herself feel it. She'd worked and she'd worked and she'd pushed emotion away because it did her head in.

'Jules, it's been four years. The way I feel…'

'Don't!'

He looked at her for a long, steady moment and then he looked down at the wombat. And nodded. Moving on? 'But we can pack stuff up for Danny?'

'I…yes.'

'We need things for Amina as well.'

'I have…too many things.' She thought of her dressing table, stuffed with girly things collected through a lifetime. She thought of the house next door, a heap of smouldering ash. Sharing was a no-brainer; in fact Amina could have it all.

'Wrapping paper?' Rob demanded. The emotion was dissipating. Maybe he'd realised he'd taken her to an edge that terrified her.

'I have a desk full of it,' she told him, grateful to be back on firm ground.

'Always the organised one.' He hesitated. 'Stockings?'

She took a deep breath at that and the edge was suddenly close again. Yes, they had stockings. Four. Julie, Rob, Aiden, Christopher. Her mother had embroidered names on each.

But she could be practical. She could do this. 'I'll unpick the names,' she said.

'We can use pillowcases instead.'

'N…no. I'll unpick them.'

'I can help.' He hesitated. 'I need to head out and put a few pans of water around for the wildlife, and then I'm all yours. But, Jules…'

'Mmm?'

'When we're done playing Santa Claus…will you come to bed with me tonight?'

This was tearing her in two. If she could walk away now she would, she thought. She'd walk straight out of the door, onto the road down to the highway and out of here. But that wasn't possible and this man, the man with the eyes that saw everything there was to know, was looking at her. And he was smiling, but his smile had all her pain behind it, and all his too. They had shared ghosts. Somehow, Rob was moving past them. But for her… The ghosts held her in thrall and she was trapped.

But for this night, within the trap there was wriggle room. She'd remove names from Christmas stockings. She'd wrap her children's toys and address them to Danny. She'd even find the snorkel and flippers she had hidden up on the top of her wardrobe. She'd bought them for Rob because she loved the beach, she'd loved taking the boys there and she was…she had been…slowly persuading Rob of its delights.

Did he go to the beach now? What was he doing with his life?

Who knew, and after this night she'd stop wondering again. But on Christmas morning the ghosts would see her stuffing the snorkel and flippers in his stocking. He'd head out into the burned bush with his pails of water so animals wouldn't die and, while he did, she'd prepare him a Christmas.

And the ghosts would see her lie in his arms this night.

'Yes,' she whispered because the word seemed all she could manage. And then, because it was important, she tried for more. 'Yes, please, Rob. Tonight…tonight I'd like to sleep with you once more.'

Christmas morning. The first slivers of light were making their way through the shutters Rob had left closed because there was still fire danger. The air was thick with the smell of a charred landscape.

She was lying cocooned in Rob's arms and for this moment she wanted nothing else. The world could disappear. For this moment the pain had gone, she'd found her island and she was clinging for all she was worth.

He was some island. She stirred just a little, savouring the exquisite sensation of skin against skin—her skin against Rob's—and she felt him tense a little in response.

'Good, huh?'

He sounded smug. She'd forgotten that smugness.

She loved that smugness.

'Bit rusty,' she managed and he choked on laughter.

'Rusty? I'll show you rusty.' He swung up over the top of her, his dark eyes gleaming with delicious laughter. 'I've been saving myself for you for all this time...'

'There's been no one else?'

She shouldn't have asked. She saw the laughter fade, but the tenderness was there still.

'I did try,' he said. 'I thought I should move on. It was a disaster. You?'

'I didn't even try,' she whispered. 'I knew it wouldn't work.'

'So you were saving yourself for me too.'

'I was saving myself for nobody.'

'Well, that sounds a bit bleak. You know, Jules, maybe we should cut ourselves a little slack. Put bleakness behind us for a bit.'

'For today at least,' she conceded, and tried to smile back. 'Merry Christmas.'

'Merry Christmas to you, too,' he said, and the wickedness was back. 'You want me to give you your first present?'

'I...'

'Because I'm about to,' he said and his gorgeous muscular body, the body she'd loved with all her heart, lowered to hers.

She rose to meet him. Skin against skin. She took his

body into her arms and tugged him to her, around her, merging into the warmth and depth of him.

Merry Christmas.

The ghosts had backed off. For now there was only Rob, there was only this moment, there was only now.

They surfaced—who could say how much later? They were entwined in each other's bodies, sleepily content, loosely covered by a light cotton sheet. Which was just as well as they emerged to the sound of quiet but desperate sniffs.

Danny.

They rolled as one to look at the door, as they'd done so many times with the twins.

Danny was in the doorway, clutching Luka's collar. He was wearing a singlet and knickers. His hair was tousled, his eyes were still dazed with sleep but he was sniffing desperately, trying not to cry.

'Hey,' Rob said, hauling the sheet a little higher. 'Danny! What's up, mate?'

'Mama's crying,' Danny said. 'She's crying and crying and she won't stop.'

'That'll be because your house is burned and your dad's stuck down the mountain,' Rob said prosaically, as if this was the sort of thing that happened every day. 'I guess your dad won't be able to make it here for a while yet, so maybe it's up to us to cheer her up. What do you think might help?'

'I don't know,' Danny whispered. 'Me and Luka tried to hug her.'

'Hugs are good.' Rob sat up and Julie lay still and watched, trying not to be too conscious of Rob's naked chest, plus the fact that he was still naked under the sheet, and his body was still touching hers and every sense…

No. That was hardly fair because she was tuned to Danny.

She'd been able to juggle…everything when they were a family. She glanced at her watch. Eight o'clock. Four years ago she'd have been up by six, trying to fit in an hour of work before the twins woke. Even at weekends, the times they'd lain here together, they'd always been conscious of pressure.

Yeah, well, both of them had busy professional lives. Both of them thought…had thought…getting on was important.

'You know, hugs are great,' Rob was saying and he lay down again and hugged Julie, just to demonstrate. 'But there might be something better today. Did you remember today is Christmas?'

'Yes, but Mama said Santa won't be able to get through the burn,' Danny quavered. 'She says…Santa will have to wait.'

'I don't think Santa ever waits,' Rob said gravely. 'Why don't you go look under the Christmas tree while Julie and I get dressed? Then we'll go hug your mama and bring her to the tree too.'

'There might be presents?' Danny breathed.

'Santa's a clever old feller,' Rob told him. 'I don't think he'd let a little thing like a bush fire stop him, do you?'

'But Mama said…'

'Your mama was acting on incorrect information,' Rob told him. 'She doesn't know Australia like Julie and I do. Bush fires happen over Australian Christmases all the time. Santa's used to it. So go check, but no opening anything until we're all dressed and out there with you. Promise?'

'I promise.'

'Does Luka promise, too?'

And Danny giggled and Julie thought she did have senses for something—for someone—other than Rob.

To make a child smile at Christmas… It wasn't a bad feeling.

Actually, it was a great feeling. It drove the pain away as nothing else could.

And then she thought…it was like coming out of bleak fog into sunlight.

It was a sliver, the faintest streak of brilliance, but it was something that hadn't touched her for so long. She'd been grey for years, or sepia-toned, everything made two-dimensional, flat and dull.

Right now she was lying in Rob's arms and she was hearing Danny giggle. And it wasn't an echo of the twins. She wasn't thinking of the twins.

She was thinking this little boy had been born in a refugee camp. His mother had coped with coming from a war-torn country.

She'd wrapped the most beautiful alpaca shawl for Amina, in the softest rose and cream. She knew Amina would love it; she just knew.

And there was a wombat glove puppet just waiting to be opened.

'Go,' she ordered Danny, sitting up too, but hastily remembering to keep her sheet tucked around her. 'Check out the Christmas tree and see if Rob's right and Santa's been. I hope he's been for all of us. We'll be there in five minutes, and then we need to get your mama up and tell her things will be okay. And they will be okay, Danny. It's Christmas and Rob and I are here to make sure that you and your mama and Luka have a very good time.'

They did have a good time. Amina was teary but, washed and dressed in a frivolous bath robe Rob had once given Julie, ensconced in the most comfortable armchair in the living room, tears gave way to bemusement.

Julie had wrapped the sensible gifts, two or three each, nice things carefully chosen. Rob, however, had taken wrapping to extremes, deciding there was too much wrapping paper and it couldn't be wasted. So he'd hunted the house and wrapped silly things. As well as the scarf and a bracelet from Africa, Amina's stocking also contained a gift-wrapped hammer, nails, a grease gun—*'because you never know what'll need greasing',* Rob told her— and a bottle of cleaning bleach. They made Amina gasp and then giggle.

'Santa thinks I might be a handyman?'

'Every house needs one,' Rob said gravely. 'In our house I wear the tool belt but Santa's not sexist.'

'My Henry's an engineer.'

'Then you get to share. Sharing a grease gun—that's real domestic harmony.'

Amina chuckled and held her grease gun like it was gold and they moved on.

Julie's stocking contained the nightdress she'd lusted after four years before and a voucher for a day spa, now long expired. *Whoops.*

'The girls at the spa gift-wrapped it for me four years ago,' Rob explained. 'How was I to know it had expired?' Then, 'No matter,' he said expansively. 'Santa will buy you another.'

He was like a bountiful genie, Julie thought, determined to make each of them happy.

He'd made her happy last night. Was it possible…? Did she have the courage…?

'You have another gift,' Rob reminded her and she hauled her thoughts back to now.

Her final gift was a wad of paper, fresh from their printer. Bemused, she flicked through it.

It was *Freezing—the Modern Woman's Survival Guide,*

plus a how-to manual extolling the virtues of ash in compost. He'd clearly got their printer to work while she'd gift-wrapped. He'd practically printed out a book.

She showed Amina and both women dissolved into laughter while Rob beamed benevolently.

'Never say I don't put thought into my gifts,' he told them and Julie held up the spa voucher.

'An out-of-date day spa?'

'They cancel each other out. I still rock.'

They chuckled again and then turned their attention to Danny.

Danny was simply entranced. He loved the pyjamas and his fire engine but most of all he loved the wombat puppet. Rob demonstrated. Danny watched and was smitten.

And so was Julie. She watched the two of them together and she thought: *I know why I fell in love with this man.*

I know why I love this man?

Was she brave enough to go there?

As well as snorkel and flippers—which Rob had received with open enjoyment before promising Danny that they could try them out in the bath later—Julie had given Rob a coat—a cord jacket. She remembered buying it for him all those years ago. She'd tried it on herself, rushing in her lunch hour, last-minute shopping. It had cost far more than she'd budgeted for but she'd imagined it on Rob, imagined holding him when he was wearing it, imagined how it'd look, faded and worn, years hence.

She should have given it to him four years ago. Now he shrugged himself into it and smiled across the room at her and she realised why she hadn't given it to him. Why she'd refused to have contact with him.

She was afraid of that smile.

Was she still? Tomorrow, would she...?

No. Tomorrow was for tomorrow. For now she needed

to watch Danny help Luka open a multi-wrapped gift that finally revealed a packet of biscuits scarily past their use-by date. Oatmeal gingernuts. 'They'll be the closest thing Santa could find to dog biscuits,' Rob told Danny.

'Doesn't Santa have dog biscuits at the North Pole?'

'I reckon he does,' Rob said gravely. 'But I think he'll have also seen all this burned bush and thought of all the animals out here who don't have much to eat. So he might have dropped his supply of dog biscuits out of his sleigh to help.'

'He's clever,' Danny said and Rob nodded.

'And kind.'

He's not the only one, Julie thought, and her heart twisted. Once upon a time this man had been her husband. If she could go back…

Turn back time? As if that was going to happen.

'Is it time to put the turkey on?' Rob asked and Julie glanced at him and thought *he's as tense as I am.* Making love didn't count, she thought, or it did, but all it showed was the same attraction was there that had always been there. And with it came the same propensity for heartbreak.

He was still wearing his jacket. He liked it. You could always tell with Rob. If he loved something, he loved it for ever. And she realised that might just count for her too.

Whether she wanted that love or not.

Switch to practical. 'We still need to use the barbecue,' she said. 'We don't have enough electricity to use the oven.'

'That's us then,' Rob said, puffing his chest. 'Me and Danny. Barbecuing's men's work, hey, Dan?'

'Can my wombat help?'

'Sure he can.'

'I'm not sure what we can have with it,' Julie said. 'There doesn't seem to be a lot of salad in the fridge.'

'Let me look at what you have,' Amina said. 'I can cook.'

'Don't you need to rest?'

'I've had enough rest,' Amina declared. 'And I can't sleep. I need to know my husband's safe. I can't rest until we're all together.'

That's us shot then, Julie thought bleakly. For her family, together was never going to happen.

They ate a surprisingly delicious dinner—turkey with the burned-from-the-freezer bits chopped off, gravy made from a packet mix and couscous with nuts and dried fruit and dried herbs.

They had pudding, slices fried in the butter she'd bought with the bread, served with custard made from evaporated milk.

They pulled bon-bons. They wore silly hats. They told jokes.

But even Danny kept glancing out of the window. He was waiting for his father to appear.

So much could have happened. If he'd tried to reach them last night… All sorts of scenarios were flitting through Julie's mind and she didn't like any of them.

Once catastrophe struck, did you spend the rest of your life expecting it to happen again? Of course you did.

'He'll be fine.' Astonishingly, the reassurance came from Amina. Had she sensed how tense Julie was? 'What you said made sense. He'll be at the road block. And, as for the house… We've seen worse than this before. We'll survive.'

'Of course you will.'

'No, you have to believe it,' Amina said. 'Don't just say it. Believe it or you go mad.'

What had this woman gone through? She had no idea. She didn't want to even imagine.

'I'd like to do something for you,' Amina said shyly. 'If

you permit… In the bathroom I noticed a hair colour kit. Crimson. Is it yours?'

'Julie doesn't colour her hair,' Rob said, but Julie was remembering a day long ago, a momentary impulse.

She'd be a redhead for Christmas, she'd thought. Her boys would love it, or she thought they might. But of course she hadn't had time to go to a salon. On impulse she'd bought a do-it-yourself kit, then chickened out at the last minute—of course—and the kit had sat in the second bathroom since.

'I'm a hairdresser,' Amina said, even more shyly. 'In my country, that's what I do. Or did. My husband has to retrain here for engineering but there are no such requirements for hairdressing, and I know this product.' She gazed at Julie's hair with professional interest. 'Colour would look good, but I don't think all over. If you permit, I could give you highlights.'

'I don't think…'

'Jules,' Rob said, and she heard an undercurrent of steel, 'you'd look great with red highlights.'

She'd hardly touched her ash-blonde curls for four years. She tugged them into a knot for work; when they became too unruly to control she'd gone to the cheap walk-in hairdresser near work and she'd thought no more about it.

Even before the boys died… When had she last had time to think about what her hair looked like?

When she'd met Rob she'd had auburn highlights. He'd loved them. He'd played with her curls, running his long, strong fingers through them, massaging her scalp, kissing her as the touch of his fingers through her hair sent her wild…

Even then she hadn't arranged it herself. Her mother had organised it as a gift.

'I bought this voucher for you, pet. I know you don't

have time for the salon but you need to make a little time for yourself.'

Her parents were overseas now, having the holiday of a lifetime. They wouldn't be worried about her. They knew she'd be buried in her work.

They'd never imagine she'd be here. With time…

'I don't think…'

'Do it, Jules,' Rob said and she caught a note of steel in his voice. She looked at him uncertainly, and then at Amina, and she understood.

This wasn't about her. Rob wasn't pushing her because he wanted a wife…an ex-wife…with crimson highlights. He was pushing her because Amina needed to do something to keep her mind off her burned house and her missing husband. And she also needed to give something back.

She thought suddenly of the sympathy and kindness she'd received during the months after the boys' deaths and she remembered thinking, more than once: *I want to be the one giving sympathy. I want to give rather than take.*

Amina was a refugee. She would have been needing help for years. Now, this one thing…

'I'd love highlights,' she confessed and Amina smiled, really smiled, for the first time since she'd met her. It was a lovely smile, and it made Danny smile too.

She glanced at Rob and his stern face had relaxed.

Better to give than receive? Sometimes not. Her eyes caught Rob's and she knew he was thinking exactly the same thing.

He'd have been on the receiving end of sympathy too. And then she thought of all the things he'd tried to make her feel better—every way he could during those awful weeks in hospital, trying and trying, but every time she'd pushed him away.

'Don't get soppy on us,' Rob said, and she blinked and

he chuckled and put his arm around her and gave her a fast, hard hug. 'Right, Amina, we need a hair salon. Danny, I need your help. A chair in the bathroom, right? One that doesn't matter if it gets the odd red splash on it.'

He set them up, and then he disappeared. She caught a glimpse of him through the window, heading down to the creek, shovel over his shoulder.

She guessed what he'd be doing. He'd left water for wildlife, but there'd be animals too badly burned…

'He's a good man,' Amina said and she turned and Amina was watching her. 'You have a good husband.'

'We're not…together.'

'Because of your babies?'

'I…yes.'

'It happens,' Amina said softly. 'Dreadful things…they tear you apart or they pull you together. The choice is yours.'

'There's no choice,' she said, more harshly than she intended, but Danny was waiting in the bathroom eyeing the colouring kit with anticipation, and she could turn away and bite her lip and hope Amina didn't sense the surge of anger and resentment that her words engendered.

Get over it… It was never said, not in so many words, but, four years on, she knew she was pretty much regarded as cool and aloof. The adjectives were no longer seen as a symptom of loss—they simply described who she was.

And who she intended to be for the rest of her life?

Thinking ahead was too hard. But Rob was gone, off to do what he could for injured wildlife, and Danny was waiting in the bathroom and Amina was watching her with a gaze that said she saw almost too much.

Do something.

Back in the office, she'd be neck-deep in contracts.

It was Christmas Day.

Okay, back home, she'd have left her brother's place

after managing to stay polite all through Christmas dinner and now she'd be back in her apartment. Neck-deep in contracts.

But now…neck-deep in hair dye?

'Let's get this over with,' she muttered and Amina took a step back.

'You don't have to. If you don't want…'

She caught herself. If Rob came back and found her wallowing in self-pity, with her hair the same colour and Amina left alone…

See, there was the problem. With Rob around she couldn't wallow.

Maybe that was why she'd left him.

Maybe that was selfish. Maybe *grief* was selfish.

It was all too hard. She caught herself and forced a smile and then tried even harder. This time the smile was almost natural.

'Rob is a good man,' she conceded. 'But he needs a nicer woman than me. A happier one.'

'You can be happier if you try,' Amina told her.

'You can be happy if you have red hair,' Danny volunteered and she grinned at his little-boy answer to the problems of the world.

'Then give me red hair,' she said. 'Red hair is your mum's gift to me for Christmas, and if there's one thing Christmas needs it's gifts. Are you and Luka going to watch or are you going to play with your Christmas presents?'

'Me and Luka are going to watch,' Danny said, and he wiggled his glove puppet. 'And Wombat. Me and Luka and Wombat are going to watch you get happy.'

Almost as soon as they started, Julie realised that agreeing to this had been a mistake.

Putting a colour through her hair would have been a relatively easy task—simply applying the colour, leaving it to take and then washing it out again.

Amina, though, had different ideas. 'Not flat colour,' she said, just as flatly. 'You want highlights, gold and crimson. You'll look beautiful.'

Yeah, well, she might, but each highlight meant the application of colour to just a few strands of hair, then those strands wrapped in foil before Amina moved to the next strands.

It wasn't a job Amina could do sitting down. She also didn't intend to do a half-hearted job.

'If I put too much hair in each foil, then you'll have flat clumps of colour,' she told Julie as she protested. 'It won't look half as good. And I want some of them strong and some diluted.'

'But you shouldn't be on your feet.' She hadn't thought this through. Amina was eight months pregnant, she'd had one hell of a time and now she was struggling.

She looked exhausted. But…

'I need to do this,' Amina told her. 'Please…I want to. I need to do something.'

She did. Julie knew the worry about her husband was still hanging over her, plus the overwhelming grief of the devastation next door. But still…

'I don't want you to risk this baby,' she told her. 'Amina, this is madness.'

'It's not madness,' Amina said stubbornly. 'It's what I want to do. Sit still.'

So she sat, but she worried, and when Rob appeared as the last foil was done she felt a huge wash of relief. Not that there was anything Rob could do to help the situation but at least…at least he was here.

She'd missed him…

'Wow,' Rob said, stopping at the entrance to the bathroom and raising his brows in his grimy face. 'You look like a sputnik.'

'What's a sputnik?' Danny demanded.

'A spiky thing that floats round in space,' Rob told him. 'You think we should put Julie in a rocket launcher and send her to the moon?'

Danny giggled and Amina smiled and once again there was that lovely release of tension that only Rob seemed capable of producing. He was the best man to have in a crisis.

'Amina's exhausted, though,' Julie told him. 'She needs to sleep.'

'You need to keep those foils in for forty minutes,' Amina retorted. 'Then you need a full scalp massage to get the colour even and then a wash and condition. Then I'll rest.'

'Ah, but I'm back now,' Rob said, and Julie knew he could see the exhaustion on Amina's face. He'd have taken in her worry at a glance. 'And if anyone's going to massage my wife it's me. Forty minutes?' He glanced at his watch. 'Amina, I came to ask if there was anything precious, any jewellery, anything that might have survived the fire that you'd like us to search for. The radio's saying it may rain tonight, in which case the ash will turn to concrete. Sputnik and I could have a look now.'

Julie choked. *Sputnik?* She glanced in the mirror. She was wearing one of Rob's shirts, faded jeans, and her head was covered in silver spikes. Okay, yep. Sputnik.

'I could be a Christmas decoration instead,' she volunteered. 'One of those shiny spiky balls you put on top of the tree.'

'You'll be more help sifting through ash. I assume you can put a towel around the spikes—the wildlife has had

enough scares for the time being without adding aliens to
the mix. Amina, is that okay with you?'

'I will look,' Amina said but Rob caught her hands. He
had great hands, Julie thought inconsequentially. He was
holding Amina and Julie knew he was imparting strength,
reassurance, determination. All those things…

He was a good man. Her husband?

'The ground's treacherous,' he told her. 'Your house is a
pile of ash and rubble and parts of it are still very hot. Julie
and I have the heavy boots we used to garden in, we have
strong protective clothing and we're not carrying a baby.
You need to take care of your little one, and of Danny.
We won't stay over there for long—it's too hot—but we
can do a superficial search. If you tell us where to look…'

'Our bedroom,' Amina told him, meeting his stern gaze,
giving in to sense. 'The front bay window…you should see
the outline. Our bed started two feet back from the window
and was centred on it. The bed was six foot long. On either
side of the bed was a bedside table. We each had a box…'

'Wood?' Rob asked without much hope.

'Tin.'

'Well, that's possible. Though don't get your hopes up
too much; that fire was searing and tin melts. We'll have
a look—but only if you try and get some rest. Danny, will
you stand guard while your mum sleeps?'

'I want to help with the burn.'

'There'll be lots of time to help with the burn,' Rob
said grimly. 'But, for now, you need to be in charge of
your mother. Go lie down beside her, play with your toys
while she sleeps, but if she tries to get up, then growl at
her. Can you do that?'

Danny considered. 'Because of the baby?'

'Yes.'

'Papa says I have to look after her because of the baby.'

'Then you'll do what your papa asked?'

'Yes,' Danny said and then his voice faltered. 'I wish he'd come.'

'He will come,' Rob said in a voice that brooked no argument. 'He will come. I promise.'

CHAPTER SEVEN

'IT SHOULD HAVE been ours.' Julie stood in the midst of the devastation that was all that was left of Amina's house, she glanced across at their intact home and she felt ill.

'Fire doesn't make sense,' Rob told her, staring grimly round the ruin.

'No. And I understand that it was your design that saved it. But Amina's house was…a home.'

'Our place will be a home again. If we rent it out to them, Amina will make it one. I suspect she's been making homes in all sorts of places for a long time.'

'I know. Home's where the heart is,' Julie said bleakly. 'They all say it. If you only knew how much I hate that saying.'

'We're not here for self-pity, Jules,' Rob said, hauling her up with a start. He sounded angry, and maybe justifiably. This was no time to wallow. 'If it rains, then there'll be little chance of finding anything. Let's get to it.' He handed her a pair of leather gloves and a shovel. 'Watch your feet for anything hot. Sift in front of you before you put your feet down. Don't go near anywhere that looks unstable.'

There wasn't much that looked unstable. The house had collapsed in on itself. The roof was corrugated iron, but Rob must have been here before, because it had been hauled off site.

The bedroom. They could see the outline of the bay window.

'You focus on either side of where the bed would have been,' Rob told her. 'I'm doing a general search.'

What a way to spend Christmas afternoon. Overdressed, hot, struggling to breathe with the wafts of smoke still in the air, her hair in spikes, covered by a towel, squatting, sifting through layer upon layer of warm ash…

She found the first tin almost immediately. It had melted—of course it had—but it had held enough of its shape to recognise it for what it was.

Who knew what was inside? There was no time now to try and open it. She set it aside and moved to the other side of where the bed would have been and kept on searching.

And was stopped in her tracks by a whoop.

She looked up and Rob was standing at the rear of the house, where the laundry would have been. He'd been shovelling.

'Jules, come and see.'

She rose stiffly and made her way gingerly across the ruin.

It was a safe. Unmistakably it was a safe and it must be fireproof, judging by the fact that it looked intact, even its paintwork almost unscathed.

'It must have been set in the floor,' Rob said. 'Look, it's still in some sort of frame. But I can get it out.'

'Do you think Amina knew it was there?'

'Who knows? But we'll take it next door. How goes the tin hunt?'

'One down.'

'Then let's find the other.' He grabbed her and gave her a hard unexpected hug. 'See, good things can happen. I just hope there's something inside that safe other than insurance papers.'

'Insurance papers would be good.'

'You and I both know that's not important. And we have five minutes to go before sputnik takes off. Tin, Jules, fetch.'

And, amazingly, they did fetch—two minutes later their search produced a tin box even more melted than the first. Three prizes. Rob brought the barrow from their yard, then they heaved the safe into it and carted it back. 'I feel like a pup with two tails,' Rob said.

Julie grinned and thought: *fun*.

That had been fun. She'd just had fun with Rob. How long since…?

She caught herself, a shaft of guilt hitting her blindside as it always did when she started forgetting. She had no right…

They parked their barrow on the veranda and went to check on Amina. She was fast asleep, as was Danny, curled up beside her. Luka was by their bedside, calmly watchful. The big dog looked up at them as if to say: *What's important enough to wake them up?*

Nothing was. But the foils had to come off.

'I can take them off myself,' Julie said, but dubiously, because in truth they were now overdue to come off and, by the time she took off every last one, the fine foils would be well overdone. What happened if you cooked your hair for too long? Did it fall out? She had no idea, and she had no intention of finding out.

'I'll take them out,' Rob said and looked ruefully down at himself. 'Your beautician, though, ma'am, is filthy.'

'In case you hadn't noticed, your client is filthy too. Can you imagine me popping into a high-class Sydney salon like this?'

'You'd set a new trend,' Rob told her, touching her foils with a grin. 'Smoked Sputnik. It'd take off like a bush fire.'

'Of course it would,' she lied. She'd reached the bathroom now and looked at the mirror. 'Ugh.'

'Let's get these things off then,' he said. 'Sit.'

So she sat on the little white bathroom stool, which promptly turned grey with soot. Rob stood behind her and she watched in the mirror as he slid each foil from her hair.

He worked swiftly, dextrously, intently. He was always like this on a job, she remembered. When he was focused on something he blocked out the world.

When he made love to her, the world might well not exist.

He was standing so close. He smelled of fire, of smoke, of burned eucalyptus. His fingers were in her hair, doing mundane things, removing foils, but it didn't feel mundane. It felt…it felt…

Too soon, the last of the foils was gone, heaped into the trash. Her hair was still spiky, looking very red. Actually, she wouldn't mind if it was green, she thought, as long as she could find an excuse to keep Rob here with her. To stretch out this moment.

'I can…' Her voice wobbled and she fought to steady it. 'I can go from here. I'll shower it off.'

'You need a full scalp massage to even the colour,' Rob told her, but his voice wasn't steady either. It was, however, stern. 'I'm Amina's underling. She's given us orders. The least we can do is obey.'

'I can do it by myself.'

'But you don't have to,' he said, and he bent and touched her forehead with his mouth. It was a feather touch, hardly a kiss, just a fleeting sensation, but it sent shivers through her whole body. 'For now, just give in and forget about facing things alone.'

So she gave in. Of course she did. She sat perfectly still while Rob massaged her scalp with his gorgeous, sensuous fingers and her every nerve ending reacted to him.

He was filthy, covered with smoke and ash. If you met this man on a dark night you'd scream and run, she thought, catching his reflection in the mirror in the split second she allowed herself to glance at him. For she couldn't watch. Feeling him was bad enough…or good enough…

Good was maybe too small a word. Her entire body was reacting to his touch. Any more and she'd turn and take him. She wanted…

'Conditioner,' Rob said, only the faintest tremor cutting through the prosaic word. 'Amina said conditioner.'

'It's in the shower.'

'Then I suggest,' he said, bending down so his lips were right against her ear, 'that we adjourn to the shower.'

'Rob…'

'Mmm?'

'N…nothing.'

'No objections?'

'We…we might lock the door first.'

'What an excellent idea,' he said approvingly. 'I have a practical wife. I always knew I had a practical wife. I'd just forgotten…'

And seemingly in one swift movement the door was locked and she was swept into his arms. He pushed the shower screen back with his elbow and deposited her inside.

It was a large shower. A gorgeous shower. They'd built it…well, they'd built it when they were in love.

It was wide enough for Rob to step inside with her and tug the glass screen closed after them.

'Clothes,' he said. 'Stat?'

'Stat?'

'That's what they say in hospitals in emergencies. Oxygen here, nurse, stat.'

'So we need clothes?'

'We don't need clothes. If this was a hospital and I was a doctor, that's what I'd be saying. Nurse, my wife needs her clothes removed. Stat.'

'Rob...'

'Yes?'

She looked at him and she thought she needed to say she wasn't his wife. She should say she didn't have the courage to take this further. She was too selfish, too armoured, too closed.

But he was inches away from her. He smelled of bush fire. His face was grimy and blackened. As was she.

The only part of her that wasn't grimy or blackened was her hair. Crimson droplets were dripping onto the white shower base, mixing with the ash.

How much colour had Amina put in? How had she trusted a woman she didn't know to colour her hair?

Rob was standing before her, holding her.

She trusted this man with all her heart, and that was the problem. She felt herself falling...

Where was her armour?

She'd find it tomorrow, she told herself. This was an extraordinary situation. This was a time out, pretend, a disaster-induced remarriage that would dissolve as soon as the rest of the world peered in. But for this moment she was stranded in this time, in this place...

In this shower.

And Rob was tugging her shirt up over her head and she was lifting her arms to help him. And then, as the shirt was tossed over the screen, as he turned his attention to her bra, she started to undo the buttons of his shirt.

Her hands were shaking.

He took her hands in his and held. Tight. Hard. Cupping her hands, completely enfolding them.

'There's no need for shaking, Jules. I'd never hurt you.'

'I might…hurt you.'

'I'm a big boy now,' he told her. 'I can take it.'

'Rob, I need to say…this is for now. I don't think…I still can't think…'

'Of course you can't.' He held her still. 'But for now, for this moment, let's take things as they come. Let our bodies remember why we fell in love. Let's start at the beginning and let things happen.'

And then he kissed her, and that kiss made her forget every other thing. Everything but Rob.

Water was streaming over them. Somehow they managed to stop, pull back, give themselves time to haul their clothes off and toss them out, a sodden, stained puddle to be dealt with later.

Everything could be dealt with later, Julie thought hazily as she turned back to her beautiful naked Rob. For now there was only Rob. There was only this moment.

Water was running in rivulets down his beautiful face, onto his chest, lower. He was wet and glistening and wonderful. His hands were on the small of her back, drawing her into him, and the feel of wet hands on wet skin was indescribably erotic.

For now there was no pain. There was no yesterday. There was only this man, this body. There was only this desire and the only moment that mattered was now.

'You think we should have a nap now, too?' Rob asked.

Somehow they were out of the shower, sated, satisfied, dazed.

Maybe she should make that almost satisfied, Julie thought. Rob was drying her. She was facing the mirror, watching him behind her. The feel of the towel was indescribably delicious.

He pressed her down onto the bathroom stool and started drying her hair. Gently. Wonderfully.

If she could die now, she'd float to heaven. She was floating already.

'If we go anywhere near the bed I can't be held responsible for what happens,' she managed and Rob chuckled. Oh, she remembered that chuckle. She'd forgotten how much she'd missed it.

How much else had she forgotten?

Had she wanted to forget…all of it?

'Maybe you're right. But maybe it's worth not being responsible,' Rob growled. 'But I want to see your hair dry first.'

Her hair. She'd had colour foils put in. Every woman in her right senses regarded the removing of colour foils with trepidation, hoping the colour would work. For some reason Julie had forgotten all about it.

'It looks good wet,' Rob said, stooping and kissing her behind her ear. 'Let's see it dry.'

She tried to look at it in the mirror. Yeah, well, that was a mistake. Rob was right behind her and he was naked. How was a woman to look at her hair when her hairdresser was…Rob?

'I…I can do it,' she tried but he was already hauling the hairdryer from the cabinet. This place was a time warp. Everything had simply been left. It had been stupid, but coming back here four years ago had been impossible. She'd simply abandoned everything…which meant she had a hairdryer.

And, stupid or not, that had its advantages, she decided, as Rob switched on the dryer and directed warm air at her hair. As did the solar panels he'd installed on the roof and the massive bank of power batteries under the house.

They had electricity, and every cent they'd paid for such a massive backup was worth it just for this moment. For the power of one hairdryer.

She couldn't move. Her body seemed more alive than she could remember. Every nerve was tingling, every sense was on fire but she couldn't move. She was paralysed by the touch of his hands, by the warmth of the dryer, by the way he lifted each curl and twisted and played with it as he dried it.

By the way he watched her in the mirror as he dried.

By the way he just…was.

He was lighting her body.

He was also lighting her hair. Good grief, her hair…

It was almost dry now, and the colours were impossible to ignore. They were part of the same magical fantasy that was this moment, but these colours weren't going to go away with the opening of the bathroom door.

What had happened?

She'd bought auburn highlights, but what Amina had done… She must have mixed them in uneven strengths, done something, woven magic…because what had happened *was* magic.

Her mousey-blonde hair was no longer remotely mouse. It was a shiny mass of gold and chestnut and auburn. It was like the glowing embers of a fire, flickering flames on a muted background.

Rob was lifting her curls, watching the light play on them as he made sure every strand was dry. Her hair felt as if it was their centre. Nothing else mattered.

If only nothing else mattered. If only they could move on from this moment, forgetting everything.

But she didn't want to forget. The thought slammed home and she saw Rob's eyes in the mirror and knew the thought had slammed into him almost simultaneously. They always had known what each other was thinking.

One mind. One body.

'Jules, we could try again,' he said softly, almost as if

talking to himself. 'We've done four years of hell. Does it have to continue?'

'I don't see how it can't.'

'We don't have to forget. Going forward together isn't a betrayal. Does it hurt, every time you look at me, because of what we had?'

'No. Yes!'

'I've seen a shrink. There I was, lying on a couch, telling all.' He smiled down at her and lifted a curl, then letting it drop. 'Actually, it was a chair. But the idea's the same. I'm shrunk.'

'And what did he…she…tell you?'

'She didn't tell me anything. She led me round and round in circles until I figured it out. But finally I did. Four people weren't killed that day, though they can be if we let them.'

'You can live…without them?'

'There's no choice, Jules,' he said, his voice suddenly rough. 'Look at us. It's Christmas, our fourth Christmas without them, yet it's all about two little boys who are no longer here. Out there is a little boy who's alive and who needs us to make him happy. We can help Amina be happy, at least for the day. We can do all sorts of things, make all sorts of people happy if we forget we're the walking dead.'

'I'm not…'

'No. You're not the walking dead. Look at your hair. This is fun hair, fantastic hair, the hair of a woman who wants to move forward. And look at your body. It's a woman's body, Jules, your body, and it gives you pleasure. It still can give you pleasure. Maybe it could even give you another child.'

'No!'

'Are you so closed?'

'Are you? You said you've been seeing other women?'

'I said I've been trying,' he said, and once again his fingers started drifting in her curls. 'The problem is they're not you.'

'You can't still love me.'

'I've never stopped.'

'But there's nothing left to love.' She was sounding desperate, negative, harsh. She'd built up so much armour and he'd penetrated it. It was cracking and she was fighting desperately to retain it. If it shattered…how could she risk such hurt again? She felt as if she was on the edge of an abyss, about to fall.

'Jump,' Rob said softly. 'I'll catch you.'

But she had to keep trying. She had to make him see. 'Rob, there are so many women out there. Undamaged. Women who could give you a family again.'

'Are you offering me up for public auction? I'm not available,' he said, more harshly still. 'Julie, remember the first time we came here? Deciding to camp? Me nobly giving you our only single air bed, then the rain at two in the morning and you refusing to move because you were warm and dry and floating?'

'I did move in the end.'

'Only because I tipped you off into six inches of water.'

'That wasn't exactly chivalrous.'

'Exactly. The thing is, Jules, that with you I've never felt the need to be chivalrous. What happens between us just…happens.'

'You did rescue the kitten…sort of.'

'That's what comes of playing the hero. You end up laughing.'

'I didn't laugh at you.'

'No,' he said and he stooped and took her hands in his. 'You laugh with me. Every time I laugh, I know you're laughing too. And every time I'm gutted it's the same.

That's what's tearing me apart the most. I've known, these last four years, that you haven't been laughing. Nor have you been gutted because I would have felt it. You've just been frozen. But I want you, Jules. I want my lovely, laughing Julie back again. We've lost so much. Do we have to lose everything?'

He was so close. His hands enfolded hers. It would be so easy to fall...

But it was easier to make love to him than what he was asking her now. She remembered that closeness. That feeling that she was part of him. That even when he drove her crazy she understood why, and she sort of got that she might be driving him crazy too.

They'd fought. Of course they'd fought. Understanding someone didn't mean you had to share a point of view and often they hadn't.

She'd loved fighting with him and often she hadn't actually minded losing. A triumphant Rob made her laugh.

But to start again...

Could she?

She so wanted to, but...but...

She was like the meat she had taken out from the freezer, she thought tangentially. On the surface she was defrosting but at her core there was still a deep knot of frozen.

If she could get out of here, get away from Rob, then that core would stay protected. Her outer layers could freeze again as well.

Was that what she wanted?

'Jules, try,' Rob said, drawing her into his arms and holding her. 'You can't waste all that hair on legal contracts. Waste it on me.'

'What do you think I'm doing now?'

'But long-term? After the fire.'

'I don't know.' The panic was suddenly back, all around

her—the panic that had overwhelmed her the first time she'd walked into the twins' empty bedroom, the panic that threatened to bring her down if she got close to anyone. The abyss was so close…

'I won't push you,' Rob said.

'So making love isn't pushing?'

'That wasn't me,' he said, almost sternly. 'It was both of us. You know you want me as much as I want you.'

'I want your body.'

'You want all of me. You want the part that wants to be part of you again. The part that wants to love you and demands you love me back.'

'Rob…I can't!' How could she stop this overwhelming feeling of terror? She wanted this man so much, but…but…

She had to make one last Herculean effort. One last try to stay…frozen.

'It's…time to get dressed,' she managed, and he nodded and lifted his fingers through her curls one last time.

'I guess,' he said ruefully, achingly reluctant. 'But let's try. Let the world in, my Julie. Let Amina see what her magic produced.'

'Only it's not magic,' she whispered. 'We can't cast a happy-ever-after spell.'

'We could try.'

'We could destroy each other.'

'More than we already have?' He sighed. 'But it's okay. Whatever you decide has to be okay. I *will not* push.' He kissed her once again, on the nape of her neck, and it was all she could do not to turn and take him into her arms and hold him and hold him and hold him. She didn't. The panic was too raw. The abyss too close.

But he was twisting a towel around his hips. It nearly killed her to see his nakedness disappear. If the world wasn't waiting…

Someone was banging on the front door. Luka started barking.

The world was indeed waiting. It was time to dress. It was time to move on.

Rob reached the front door first. He'd hauled jeans on and left it at that. Amina and Danny must be still asleep, or waking slowly, because only Luka was there, barking hysterically.

The knocking started again as he reached the hall, but for some reason his steps slowed.

He didn't want the world to enter?

Maybe there was a truck outside, emergency personnel offering to take them down the mountain, evacuate them to safety. The authorities would want everyone off the mountain. This place was self-sufficient but most homes were dependent on essential services. That first truck had been the precursor to many. The army could even have been called in, with instructions to enforce evacuation.

He didn't want to go.

Well, that was dumb. For a start, Amina desperately needed evacuation. It wasn't safe for an eight months pregnant woman to be here, with no guaranteed way out if she went into labour. With the ferocity of the burn and the amount of bushland right up to the edges of the roads, normal traffic would be impossible for weeks. So many burned trees, all threatening to fall... They needed to get out as soon as it was safe to go.

And yet...and yet...

And yet he didn't want to leave.

Maybe he could send Amina and Danny away and keep Julie here.

As his prisoner? That was another dumb thought. He couldn't keep her against her will, nor would he want to, but, even so, the thought was there. The last twenty-four hours had revealed his wife again. He knew she was still hurting. He knew that breaking down her armour required a miracle, and he also knew that once they were off the mountain, then that miracle couldn't happen. She'd retreat again into her world of finance and pain.

'She has to deal with it in her own time.' The words of his shrink had been firm. *'Rob, you've been wounded just as much as she has, but you're working through it. For now it's as much as you can do to heal yourself. You need to let Julie go.'*

But what if they could heal together? These last hours had shown him Julie was still there—the Julie he'd loved, the Julie he'd married.

But he couldn't lock her up. That wasn't the way of healing and he knew it.

What was? Holding her close? She'd let him do that. They'd made love, they'd remembered how their bodies had reacted to each other, yet it had achieved…nothing.

Could he keep trying? Dare he? These last years he'd achieved a measure of peace and acceptance. Would taking Julie to him open the floodgates again? Would watching her pain drive him back to the abyss? Only he knew how hard it had been to pull himself back to a point where he felt more or less at peace.

He knew what his shrink would say. *Move away and stay away. Leave the past in the past.*

Only the past was in their shared bedroom, with hair that glistened under his hands, with eyes that smiled at him with…hope? If he could find the strength… If, some-how, he could drag her to the other side of the nightmare…

Enough of the introspection. The knocking contin-ued and he'd reached the door. He tugged it open, Luka launched himself straight out—and into the arms of a guy standing on the doorstep.

The man was shorter than Rob, and leaner. He looked in his forties, dark-skinned and filthy. He looked…haggard. His eyes were bloodshot and he hadn't shaved for a couple of days. He was leaning against the door jamb, breathing heavily, but as Luka launched himself forward he grabbed him and held him as if he was drowning.

He met Rob's eyes over Luka's great head, and his look was anguished.

'Amina?' It was scarcely a croak.

'Safe,' Rob said quickly. 'And Danny. They're both here. They're safe. You're Henry?' He had to be. No one but Amina's husband could say her name with the same mix of love and terror.

'Yes. I am. I went…next door. Oh, God, it's…'

'We got them here before the house went up,' Rob said, speaking quickly, cutting through Henry's obvious terror. 'They're tired but well. They're asleep now but they've been as worried about you as you seem to be about them. They're safe.'

The man's knees sagged. Rob grabbed the dog and hauled him back, then took Henry's elbows under his hands, holding him up. He looked beyond exhaustion.

'They're safe,' he said again. 'I promise. Happy Christmas, Henry. I know your house is burned and I'm sorry, but things can be replaced. People can't. Everything else can wait. For now, come in and see your wife.'

And Henry burst into tears.

After that things seemed to happen in a blur.

There was a whimper behind him. Rob turned and Amina was there, staring in incredulity. And then somehow she was in Rob's place, holding her husband, holding and holding. Weeping.

And then Danny, flying down the hall. 'Papa…' He was between them, a wriggling, excited bundle of joy. 'My Papa's come,' he yelled to anyone who'd listen and then he was between them, sandwiched, muffled but still yelling. 'Papa, our house burned and burned and Luka was lost and I was scared but Rob found me and then we hid in a little cave and we've been here for lots and lots and Santa came and we had turkey but we didn't have chocolates. Mama had them for us but they've been burned as well, but Mama says we can get some more. Papa, come and see my presents.'

Rob backed away and then Julie was beside him, in her gorgeous crimson robe with her gorgeous crimson hair, and she was sniffing. He took her hand and held and it felt…right.

They finally found themselves in the kitchen, watching Henry eat leftover Christmas lunch like he hadn't eaten for a week—but he still wasn't concentrating on the food. He kept looking from Amina to Danny and back again, like he couldn't get enough of them. Like he was seeing ghosts…

His plane last night, a later one than Rob's, had been diverted—landing in Melbourne instead of Sydney because of the smoke. He'd spent the night trying to get any information he could, going crazy because he couldn't contact anyone.

This morning he'd flown into Sydney at dawn, hired a car, hit the road blocks, left the car, dodged the road blocks and walked.

It didn't take any more than seeing his smoke-stained face and his bloodshot eyes to tell them how fraught that walk had been. And how terror had stayed with him every inch of the way.

But he was home. He had his family back again. Julie watched them with hungry eyes, and Rob watched Julie and thought that going back was a dream. A fantasy. He couldn't live with that empty hunger for ever.

'We've plenty of water. Go and take a bath,' he told Henry, and Danny brightened.

'Luka and I will help,' he announced and they disappeared towards the bathroom, with the sounds of splashing and laughter ensuing. Happy ever after...

'I'll go get dressed,' Julie said, sounding subdued, and Amina touched her hair.

'Beautiful.'

'Yes. Thank you.'

'Don't waste it,' Amina said sternly with a meaningful glance at Rob, and Julie flinched a little but managed a smile.

'I promise I won't wear a hat for months.'

Which wasn't what Amina had meant and they all knew it but it was enough for Julie to escape.

Which left Amina with Rob.

'You love her still,' she said, almost as if she was talking of something mundane, chatting about the weather, and Rob had to rerun the words in his mind for a bit before he could find an answer.

'Yes,' he said at last. 'But our grief threatened to destroy us. It's still destroying us.'

'You want...to try again?'

'I don't think we can.'

'It takes courage,' she whispered. 'So much courage. But you...you have courage to spare. You saved my son.'

'It takes more than courage to wake up to grief every morning of your life.'

'It's better than walking away,' she said softly. 'Walking away is the thing you do when all else fails. Walking away is the end.'

'Amina…'

'I shall cook dinner,' she announced, moving on. 'Food is good. Food is excellent. When all else fails, eat. I need to inspect this frozen-in-time kitchen of yours.'

'You need to rest.'

'I have rested,' she said. 'I have my husband back. My family is together and that's all that matters. We need to move on.'

Christmas dinner was a sort of Middle Eastern goulash made with leftover turkey, couscous, dried herbs, packet stock and raisins. It should have tasted weird—half the in-gredients were well over their use-by dates—but it tasted delicious. The house had a formal dining room but no one was interested in using it. They squashed round the kitchen table meant for four, with Luka taking up most of the room underneath, and it felt right.

Home, Rob thought as he glanced at his dinner com-panions. That was what this felt like. Outside, the world was a bleak mess but here was food, security, togetherness.

Henry couldn't stop looking at Amina and Danny. From one to the other. It was like he was seeing a dream.

That was what looking at Julie felt like too, Rob thought. A dream. Something that could never be.

But still… Henry had made a quick, bleak foray across to the ruins of his house and came back grimly determined.

'We can build again,' he'd said. 'We've coped with worse than this.'

Building again… Could he and Julie? A building needed foundations, though, Rob thought, and their foundations hardly existed any more. At least, that was what Julie thought. She thought their foundations were a bed of pain,

of nightmares. Could he ever break through to foundations that had been laid long before the twins were born?

Did he have the strength to try?

'You have our safe,' Henry said as the meal came to
an end and anxiety was in his voice again. 'You said you
managed to haul it out.'

'I did,' Rob told him. 'I'm not sure whether the contents
have withstood the fire.'

'It's built to withstand an inferno. And the contents…
it's not chocolate.'

'I'd like some chocolate,' Danny said wistfully, but there
was ice cream. Honestly, wrapped containers might cope
with a nuclear blast, Rob thought as they sliced through the
layers of plastic to ice cream that looked almost perfect.

But Amina didn't want any. She was looking exhausted
again. Julie was watching her with concern, and Rob
picked up on it.

'You want to go back to bed?' he asked her. 'All of you.
Henry's had a nightmare twenty-four hours and you've
made us a feast of a Christmas dinner. You've earned some
sleep.'

'I'm fine,' Amina said, wincing a little. 'I just have a
backache. I need a cushion, that's all.'

In moments she had about four and they moved into
the living room, settled in the comfortable lounge suite…
wondering where to go from here.

He'd quite like to carry Julie back to the bedroom, Rob
thought. It was Christmas night. He could think of gifts
he'd like to give and receive…

But Danny had slept this afternoon, and he was wide
awake now. He was zooming back and forth across the
floor with his new fire truck. In Danny's eyes, Christmas was still happening. There was no way he was going
calmly to bed, and that meant the adults had to stay up.

Henry was exhausted. He'd slumped into his chair, his face still grey with exhaustion and stress.

Amina also looked stressed. The effort of making dinner had been too much for her. She had no energy left.

Rob sank to the floor and started playing with Danny, forming a makeshift road for his fire engine, pretending the TV remote was a police car, conducting races, making the little boy laugh. Doing what he'd done before...

It nearly killed her. He was doing what she'd seen him do so many times, what she'd loved seeing him do.

Now he was playing with a child who wasn't his.

He was *getting over it*?

Get over it. How many times had those words been said to her? 'It'll take time but you will get over it. You will be able to start again.'

She knew she never would, but Rob just might. It had been a mistake, coming back here, she thought. Connecting with Rob again. Reminding themselves of what they'd once had.

It had hurt him, she thought. It had made him hope...

She should cut that hope off right now. There was no chance she could move on. The thought of having another child, of watching Rob romp with another baby... It hurt.

Happy Christmas, she thought bitterly. This was worse than the nothing Christmases she'd had for the last few years. Watching Rob play with a child who wasn't his.

She glanced up and saw Amina was watching her and, to her surprise, she saw her pain reflected in the other woman's eyes.

'Are you okay?' she asked. 'Amina...?'

'It's only the backache,' she said, but somehow Julie knew it wasn't. 'Henry, the safe... Could you check? I need to know.'

'I'll do it in the morning,' Henry said uneasily but Amina shook her head.

'I need to see now. The television…does it work?'

'We have enough power,' Rob told her. 'But there won't be reception.'

'We don't need reception. I just need to see…'

'Amina, it'll hurt,' Henry said.

'Yes, but I still need to see,' she said stubbornly. 'Henry, do this for me, please. I need to see that they're still there.'

Which explained why, ten minutes later, Rob and Henry were out on the veranda, staring at a fire-stained safe. The paint had peeled and charred, but essentially it looked okay.

'Do you want to open it in privacy?' Rob asked, but Henry shook his head.

'We have nothing of value. This holds our passports, our insurance—our house contents are insured, how fortunate is that?'

'Wise.'

'The last house we lost was insured too,' Henry said. 'But not for acts of war.'

'Henry…'

'No matter. This is better. But Amina wants her memories. Do you permit?'

He wasn't sure what was going on but, two minutes later, Henry had worked the still operational combination lock and was hauling out the contents.

Papers, documents…and a couple of USB sticks.

'I worried,' Henry said. 'They're plastic but they seem okay. It would break Amina's heart to lose these. Can we check them on your television?'

'Of course. Julie and I can go to bed if you want privacy.'

'If it's okay with you,' Henry said diffidently, 'it's better to share. I mean…Amina needs to…well, her history seems more real to her if she can share. Right now she's hurting. It would help…if you could watch. I know it'll be dull for you, other people's memories, but it might help. The way Amina's looking… Losing our house. Worrying about me. The baby… It's taken its toll.'

'Of course we can watch.' It was Julie in the doorway behind them. 'Anything that can help has to be okay by us.'

The television worked. The USB worked. Ten minutes later they were in Sri Lanka.

In Amina and Henry's past lives.

The files contained photographs—many, many photographs. Most were amateur snaps, taken at family celebrations, taken at home, a big, assorted group of people whose smiles and laughter reached out across distance and time.

And, as Julie watched her, the stress around Amina's eyes faded. She was introducing people as if they were here.

'This is my mother, Aisha, and my older sister Hannah. These two are my brothers. Haija is an architect like you, Rob. He designs offices, wonderful buildings. The last office he designed had a waterfall, three storeys high. It wasn't built, but, oh, if it had been… And here are my nieces and nephews. And Olivia…' She was weeping a little but smiling through tears as the photograph of a teenage girl appeared on the screen, laughing, mocking the camera, mischief apparent even from such a time and distance. 'My little sister Olivia. Oh, she is trouble. She'll be trouble still. Danny, you remember how I told you Olivia loves trains?' she demanded of her son. 'Olivia had a train set, a whole city. She started when she was a tiny child, wanting and wanting trains. "What are you interested in those for?" my father asked. "Trains are for boys." But Olivia wanted and wanted and finally he bought her a tiny train and a track, and then another. And then our father helped her build such a city. He built a platform she could raise to the roof on chains whenever my mother wanted the space for visitors. Look, here's a picture.'

And there they were—trains, recorded on video, tiny locomotives chugging through an Alpine village, with snow-covered trees and tiny figures, railway stations, tunnels, mountains, little plastic figures, a businessman in a bowler hat endlessly missing his train…

Danny was entranced but he'd obviously seen it before. 'Olivia's trains,' he said in satisfaction and he was right by the television, pointing to each train. 'This green one is her favourite. Mama's Papa gave it to her for her eighth birthday. Mama says when I am eight she'll try and find a train just like that for me. Isn't it lucky I'm not eight yet? If Mama had already found my train, it would have been burned.'

'Do you…still see them?' Rob asked cautiously.

Amina smiled sadly and shook her head. 'Our house was bombed. Accidentally, they said, but that's when Henry and I decided to come here. It's better here. No bombs.'

'Bush fires, though,' Rob said, trying for a smile and, amazingly, Amina smiled back at him, even as she put her hand to her obviously aching back.

'We can cope with what we have to cope with,' she said simply. She looked back at the television to where her sister was laughing at her father. Two little steam engines lay crashed on their side on the model track, obviously victims of a fake disaster. 'You get up and keep going,' she said simply. 'What choice is there?'

You can close down, Julie thought. *You can roll into a tight ball of controlled pain, unbending only to work.* That was what she'd done for four long years.

'Would you like to see our boys?' Rob asked and her eyes flew wide. What was he saying? Shock held her immobile and it was as if his voice was coming from the television, not from him. But, 'I'd like to show you our sons,' he was saying. 'They're not here either, but they're still in our hearts. It'd be great to share.'

No. No! She wanted to scream it but she couldn't.

'Would you like us to see them, Julie?' Amina asked shyly, tentatively, as if she guessed Julie's pain. As she must. She'd lost so much herself.

'We lost our boys in a car accident four years ago,' Rob told Henry. 'But it still feels like they're here.'

'But it hurts Julie?' Amina said. 'To talk about them? To see them? Is it better not?'

Yes, Julie thought. *Much better.* But then she looked at Rob, and with a shock she realised that his face said it wasn't better at all.

His expression told her that he longed to talk about them. He longed to show these strangers pictures of his sons, as they'd shown him pictures of their family.

'It's up to Jules, though,' Rob said. 'Julie, do you know where the disc is of their birthday?'

She did, but she didn't want to say. She never spoke of the boys. She never looked at their photographs. They were locked inside her, kept, hers. They were dead.

'Maybe not,' Amina said, still gently. 'If Julie doesn't want to share, that's her right.'

Share…share her boys… She wanted to say no. She wanted to scream it because the thought almost blindsided her. To talk about them…to say their names out loud…to act as if they still had a place in her life…

To see her boys on the screen…

'Jules?' Rob said gently and he crossed the room and stooped and touched her chin with his finger. 'Up to you, love. Share or not? No pressure.'

But it was pressure, she thought desperately, and it was as if the pressure had been building for years. The containment she'd held herself in was no longer holding.

To share her boys… To share her pain…

Rob's gaze was on her, calmly watchful. Waiting for the yay or nay.

No pressure.

Share… Share with this man.

A photo session, she thought. That was all he was asking. To see his kids as they'd been when they'd turned two. How hard was that?

'Don't do it if it hurts,' Amina whispered and Julie knew that it would hurt. But suddenly she knew that it'd hurt much more not to.

They were her boys. Hers and Rob's. And Rob was asking her to share memories, to sit in this room and look at photographs of their kids and let them come to life again, if only on the screen. To introduce them, to talk of them as Amina had talked of her family.

'I…I'll get it,' she said and Rob ran a finger the length of her cheek. His eyes said he did understand what he was asking, and yet he was still asking.

His gaze said he knew her hurt; he shared it. He shared…

She rose and she staggered a little, but Rob was beside her, giving her a swift, hard hug. 'I love that video,' he said but she knew he hadn't seen it for four years. It had been hidden, held here in limbo. Maybe it was time…

She couldn't think past that. She gave Rob a tight hug in return and went to fetch the disc.

* * *

And there they were. Her boys. It had been the most glorious birthday party, held here on the back lawn. All the family had been here—her parents, Rob's parents, their siblings, Rob's brother's kids, Rob's parents' dog, a muddle of family and chaos on the back lawn.

A brand-new paddling pool. Two little boys, gloriously happy, covered in the remains of birthday cake and ice cream, squealing with delight. Rob swinging them in circles, a twin under each arm.

Julie trying to reach Aiden across the pool, slipping and sprawling in the water. Julie lying in the pool in her jeans and T-shirt, the twins jumping on her, thinking she'd meant it, squealing with joy. Rob's laughter in the background. Julie laughing up at the camera, hugging her boys, then yelling at Rob's dad because the dog was using the distraction to investigate the picnic table.

The camera swivelled to the dog and the remains of the cake—and laughter and a dog zooming off into the bushes with half a cake in his mouth.

Family…

She'd thought she couldn't bear it. She'd thought she could never look at photographs again, but, instead of crying, instead of withering in pain, she found she was smiling. Laughing, even. When the dog took off with the cake they were all laughing.

'Luka wouldn't do that,' Danny decreed. 'Bad dog.'

'They look…like a wonderful family,' Amina said and Rob nodded.

'They are.'

They were. She'd never let them close. She'd seen her remaining family perfunctorily for the last four years, when she had to, and she'd never let anyone talk of the boys.

'Aiden and Christopher were…great.'

She said their names now out loud and it was like turning a key in a rusty lock. She hadn't said their names to anyone else since…

'They're the best kids,' Rob said, smiling. He was gripping her hand, she realised, and she hadn't even noticed when he'd taken it. 'They were here for such a short time, but the way they changed our lives… You know, in the far reaches of my head, they're still with me. When I get together with my parents and we talk about them, they're real. They're alive. I understand why you need your family tonight, Amina. For the same reason I need mine.'

Julie listened, and Rob's words left her stunned. His words left her in a limbo she didn't understand. Like an invitation to jump a crevice…but how could she?

The recording had come to an end. The last frame was of the twins sitting in their pool, beaming out at all of them. She wanted to reach out and touch them. She felt as if her skin was bursting. That she could look at her boys and laugh… That she could hold Rob's hand and remember how it had felt to be a family…

'Thank you for showing us,' Henry said, gravely now, and Julie thought that he knew. This man knew how much it hurt. He'd lost too, him and Amina, but now he was tugging his wife to her feet, holding her…moving on.

'We need to sleep,' he said. 'All of us. But thank you for giving us such a wonderful, magical Christmas. Thank you for saving my family, and thank you for sharing yours.'

They left.

Rob flicked the television off and the picture of their boys faded to nothing.

Without a word, Rob went out to the veranda. He stood at the rail and stared into the night and, after a moment's hesitation, Julie followed. The smouldering bushland gave no chance of starlight but, astonishingly, a few of the solar lights they'd installed along the garden paths still glowed. The light was faint but it was enough to show a couple of wallabies drinking deeply from the water basins Rob had left.

'How many did you put out?' Julie said inconsequentially. There were so many emotions coursing through her she had no hope of processing them.

'As many containers as I could find. I suspect our veranda was a refuge. There are droppings all over the south side. All sorts of droppings.'

'So we saved more than Amina and Danny and Luka.'

'I think we did. It's been one hell of a Christmas.' He hesitated. 'So…past Christmases…Julie, each Christmas, each birthday and so many times in between, I've tried to ring. You know how often, but I've always been sent straight through to voicemail. I finally accepted that you wanted no contact, but it hasn't stopped me thinking of you. I've thought of you and the boys every day. But at Christmas…for me it's been a day to get through the best way I can. But, Julie, how has it been for you? I rang your parents. The year after…they said you were with them but you didn't want to talk to me. The year after that they were away and I couldn't contact you.'

How to tell him what she'd been doing? The first year she'd been in hospital and Christmas had been a blur of pain and disbelief. The next her parents had persuaded her to spend with them.

Doug and Isabelle were lovely ex-hippy types, loving their garden, their books, their lives. They'd always been astonished by their only daughter's decision to go into law and finance, but they'd decreed anything she did was okay by them. Doug was a builder, Isabelle taught disadvantaged kids and they accepted everyone. They'd loved Rob and their grandsons but, after the car crash, they'd accepted Julie's decision that she didn't want to talk of them, ever.

But it had left a great hole. They were so careful to avoid it, and she was so conscious of their avoidance. That first Christmas with them had been appalling.

The next year she'd given them an Arctic cruise as a Christmas gift. They'd looked at her with sadness but with understanding and ever since then they'd travelled at Christmas.

And what had Julie been doing?

'I work at Christmas,' she said. 'I'm international. The finance sector hardly closes down.'

'You go into work?'

'I'm not that sad,' she snapped, though she remembered thinking if the entire building hadn't been closed and shut down over Christmas Day she might have. 'I have Christmas dinner with my brother. But I do take contracts home. It takes the pressure off the rest of the staff, knowing someone's willing to take responsibility for the urgent stuff. How about you?'

'That's terrible.'

'How about you?' she repeated and she made no attempt to block her anger. Yeah, Christmas was a nightmare. But he had no right to make her remember how much of a nightmare it normally was, so she wasn't about to let him off the hook. 'While I've been neck-deep in legal negotiations, what have you been doing?'

'To keep Santa at bay?'

'That's one way of looking at it.'

'I've skied.'

It was so out of left field that she blinked. 'What?'

'Skied,' he repeated.

'Where?'

'Aspen.'

She couldn't have been more astounded if he'd said he'd been to Mars. 'You hate the cold.'

'I hated the cold. I'm not that Rob any more.'

She thought about that for a moment while the stillness of the night intensified. The smell of the smoke was all-consuming but…it was okay. It was a mist around them, enveloping them in a weird kind of intimacy.

Rob in the snow at Christmas.

Without her.

Rob in a life without her.

It was odd, she thought numbly. She'd been in a sort of limbo since the accident, a weird, desolate space where time seemed to stand still. There was no future and no past, simply the piles of legal contracts she had in front of her. When she'd had her family, her work had been important. When she hadn't, her work was everything.

But, meanwhile, Rob had been doing…other stuff. Skiing in Aspen.

'Are you any good?' she asked inconsequentially and she heard him smile.

'At first, ludicrous. A couple of guys from work asked me to go with them. I spent my first time on the nursery slopes, watching three-year-olds zoom around me. But I've improved. I pretty much threw my heart and soul into it.'

'Even on Christmas Day?'

'On Christmas Day I pretty much have the slopes to myself. I ski my butt off, to the point where I sleep.'

'Without nightmares?'

'There are always nightmares, Jules,' he said gently. 'Always. But you learn to live around them.'

'But this Christmas—you didn't go to Aspen?'

'My clients finished the house to die for in the Adelaide Hills. They were having a Christmas Eve party. My sister asked me to join her tribe for Christmas today.

I'd decided…well, I'd decided it was time to stay home. Time to move on.'

Without me? She didn't say it. It was mean and unfair. She'd decided on this desolate existence. Rob was free to move on as best he could.

But…but…

He was right here, in front of her. Rob. Her beloved Rob, who she'd turned away from. She could have helped…

Or she could have destroyed him.

He reached out and touched her cheek, a feather touch, and the sensation sent shivers through her body. *Her Rob.*

'Hell, Julie, how do we move on from this?' His voice was grave. Compassionate. Loving?

'I don't know,' she whispered. 'I can't think how to escape this fog.'

There was a moment's hesitation and then his voice changed. 'Escape,' he said bitterly. 'Is that what you want? Do you think Amina was escaping by coming here?'

'I don't know.'

'Well, I do,' he said roughly, almost angrily. 'She wasn't escaping. She was regrouping. Figuring out how badly she and her family had been wounded, and how to survive. And look at her. After all she's been through, back she goes, to her memories, to talking about the ones she loves. You know why I wasn't going to Aspen this Christmas? Because I've finally figured it out. I've finally figured that's what I want, Jules. I want to be able to talk about Aiden and Christopher without hurting. Call it a Christmas list if you want, my Santa wish, but that wish has been with me for four years. Every day I wake up and I want the same thing. I want people to talk of Christopher and Aiden like Amina does of her family. I want to admit that Christopher bugged me when he whined for sweets. I want to remember that Aiden never wanted me to go the bathroom by myself. I want to be able to say that you sometimes took all the bedcovers…'

'I did not!'

'And the one time I got really pissed off and pinned them to my side of the bed you ripped them. You did, too.'

'Rob!'

'Don't sound so outraged.' But then he gave a rueful smile and shrugged. 'Actually, that's okay. Outrage is good. Anything's good apart from silence. Or fog. We've been living with silence for years. Does it have to go on for ever?'

'I'm…safe where I am.'

'Because no one talks about Aiden or Christopher? Or me. Do they talk about me, Julie, or am I as dead to you as the boys are?'

'If they did talk…it hurts.'

But he was still angry. Relentless. The gentle, compassionate Rob was gone. 'Do you remember the first time we climbed this mountain?' he demanded, and he grabbed her hand and hauled her round so she was facing out to where the smoke-shrouded mountain lay beyond the darkened bush. 'Mount Bundoon. You were so unfit. It was mean of me to make you walk, but you wanted to come.'

'I only did it because I was besotted with you.'

'And I only made you come because I wanted you to see. Because I knew it was worth it. Because I knew you'd think it was worth it.' His hand was still holding hers, firm and strong. 'So you struggled up the track and I helped you…'

'You pushed. You bullied!'

'So I did and you got blisters on blisters and we hadn't taken enough water and we were idiots.'

'And then we reached the top,' she said, remembering.

'Yeah,' he said in satisfaction and hauled her against

him. 'We reached the top and we looked out over the gorge and it's the most beautiful place in the whole world. Only gained through blisters.'

'Rob...'

'And what do you remember now?' he demanded, rough again. 'Blisters?'

'No.'

'So? Does my saying Aiden's name, Christopher's name, my name—does it hurt so much you can't reach the top? Because you know what I reckon, Jules? I reckon that saying Aiden's name and Christopher's, and talking of them to each other, that's the top. That's what we ought to aim for. If we could start loving the boys again...to-gether...could we do that, Jules? Not just now? Not just for Christmas? For ever?'

And she wanted to. With every nerve in her body she wanted to.

'Do you know what I've done every Christmas?' he asked, gently now, holding her, but there was some-thing implacable about his voice, something that said he was about to say something that would hurt. 'And every birthday. And so many times in between...I've taken that damned recording out and watched it. And you know what? I love it. I love that I have it. I love that my kids—and my Julie—can still make me smile.'

'You...you have it?' She was stammering. 'But to-night...I had to find the disc.'

'That's because tonight had to be your choice. I have a copy. Jules, I've made my choice. I'm living on, with my kids, with my memories and I've figured that's the way to survive. But you have to do your own figuring. Whether you want to continue blocking the past out for ever. Whether you want to let the memories back in. Or maybe...maybe whether you dare to move forward. With me or without. Julie, I still want you. You're still my wife. I still love you, but the rest…it's up to you.'

The night grew even more still. It was as if the world was holding its breath.

He was so close and he was holding her and he wanted her. All she had to do was sink into him and let him love her.

All she had to do was love in return.

But what did she have to give? It'd be all one way, she thought, her head spinning. Rob could say he loved her, he could say he still wanted her but it wasn't the Julie of now that he wanted. It was the Julie of years ago. The Julie she'd seen on replay. Today's Julie was like a husk, the shed skin of someone she had once been.

Rob deserved better.

She loved this man; she knew she did. But he deserved the old Julie and, confused or not, dizzy or not, she knew at some deep, basic level that she didn't have the energy to be that woman.

'Jules, you can,' he said urgently, as if he knew what she was thinking—how did he do that? How did he still have the skill?

How could she still know him when so much of her had died?

She wanted him, she ached for him, but it terrified her. Could she pretend to be the old Julie? she wondered. Could she fake being someone she used to be?

'Try for us,' Rob demanded, and his hands held her. He tugged her to him, and she felt…like someone was hauling the floor from under her feet.

Rob would catch her. Rob would always catch her.

She had to learn to catch herself.

'Maybe I should see the same shrink,' she managed. 'The one who's made you brave enough to start again.'

'The shrink didn't make me brave. That's all me.'

'I don't want…'

'That's just it. You have to want. You have to want more than to hide.'

'You can't make me,' she said, almost resentfully, and he nodded.

'I know I can't. But the alternative? Do you want to walk away? Once the road is reopened, once Christmas is over, do you want to go back to the life you've been existing in? Not living, existing. Is that what you want?'

'It's what I have to want.'

'It's not,' he said, really angry now. 'You can change. Ask Danny. His Christmas list was written months ago. Amina said he wanted a bike but he got a wombat instead and you know what? Now he thinks that's what he wanted all along.'

'You think I can be happy with second best? Life without our boys?'

'I think you can be happy. I think dying with them is a bloody waste.'

'There's no need…'

'To swear? No, I suppose not. There's no need to do anything. There's no need to even try. Okay, Jules, I'll back off.'

'Rob, I'm…'

'Don't you dare say you're sorry. I couldn't bear it.'

But there was nothing to say but sorry so she said nothing at all. She stood and looked down at her feet. She listened to the soft scuffles of the wallabies out in the garden. She thought…she thought…

'Please?'

And the outside world broke in. The one word was a harsh plea, reverberating through the stillness and it came from neither of them. She turned and so did Rob.

Henry was in the open doorway, his hands held out in entreaty.

'Please,' he said again. 'Can either of you…do either of you know…?'

'What?' Rob said. 'Henry, what's wrong?'

'It's Amina,' Henry stammered. 'She says the baby's coming.'

CHAPTER EIGHT

ALL THE WAY to the bedroom Julie hoped Henry might be mistaken. They reached the guest room, however, and one look told her that there could be no mistake about this. Amina was crouched by the bed, holding onto the bed post, clinging as if drowning. She swung round as Julie entered and her eyes were filled with panic.

'It can't come. It's too early. I can't…last time it was so… I can't do this.'

Right. Okay.

'And it's breech,' Amina moaned. 'It was supposed to turn; otherwise the doctor said I might need a Caesarean…'

Breech! A baby coming and breech! Things that might best have been known when the fire crew was here, Julie thought wildly. They'd had that one chance to get away from here. If they'd known they could have insisted on help, on helicopter evacuation. Amina would surely have been a priority. But now…it was nine o'clock on Christmas night and they'd already knocked back help. What was the chance of a passing ambulance? Or a passing anything?

They were trapped. Their cars were stuck in the garage. The tree that had fallen over the driveway was still there, huge and smouldering. It had taken Henry almost twelve hours to walk up from the road blocks and he'd risked his life doing so.

'The phone…' she said without much hope, and Rob shook his head.

'I checked half an hour ago.' He rechecked then, flipping it from his pocket. 'No reception. Zip. Jules, I'll start down the mountain by foot. I might find someone with a car.'

'I didn't see an occupied house all the way up the mountain.' Henry shook his head. 'The homes that aren't burned are all evacuated. Amina, can't you stop?'

Amina said something that made them all blink. Apparently stopping was not on the agenda.

'What's wrong with Mama?' It was Danny, standing in the hall in his new Batman pyjamas. The pyjamas Julie had bought for her sons. The pyjamas that she'd thought would make her feel…make her feel…

But there wasn't time for her to feel anything. Danny's voice echoed his father's fear. Amina looked close to hysterics. Someone had to do something—now.

She was a lawyer, Julie thought wildly. She didn't do babies.

But it seemed she had no choice. By the look of Amina, this baby was coming, ready or not.

Breech.

'You'll be fine,' she said with a whole lot more assurance than she was feeling. 'Rob, take Danny into the living room and turn on a good loud movie. He had a nap this afternoon; he won't be sleepy. Isn't that right, Danny?'

'But what's wrong with Mama?'

She took a deep breath and squatted beside the little boy. Behind her, Henry was kneeling by his wife—remonstrating? For heaven's sake—as if Amina could switch anything off. And Danny looked terrified.

And suddenly Julie was done with terror. *Enough.*

'Danny, your mama is having a baby,' she told him.

'There's nothing to worry about. There's nothing wrong, but I suspect this is a big baby and your mama will hurt a bit as she pushes it out.'

'How will she push it out?'

'Rob will tell you,' she said grandly, 'while he finds a movie for you to watch. Won't you, Rob?'

'Um…yeah?' He looked wild-eyed and suddenly Julie was fighting an insane desire to grin. A woman in labour or teaching a kid the facts of life—what a choice.

'And your papa and I will help your mama,' she added. But…

'No.' It was Amina, staring up at them, practically yelling. 'No,' she managed again, and this time it was milder. 'It's okay, Danny,' she managed, making a supreme effort to sound normal in the face of her son's fear. 'This is what happened when I had you. It's normal. Having babies hurts, but only like pulling a big splinter out.' *As if*, Julie thought. *Right*.

'But Papa's not going to stay here.' Amina's voice firmed, becoming almost threatening, and she looked up at Julie and her eyes pleaded. 'Last time…Henry fainted. I was having Danny and suddenly the midwives were fussing over Henry because he cut his head on the floor when he fell. Henry, I love you but I don't want you here. I want you to go away.'

Which left…Julie and Rob. They met each other's gaze and Julie's chaotic thoughts were exactly mirrored in Rob's eyes.

Big breath. No, make that deep breathing. A bit of Zen calm. Where was a nice safe monastery when she needed one?

'Give us a moment,' she said to Amina. 'Henry, no fainting yet. Help Amina into bed, then you and Danny can leave the baby delivering to us. We can do this, can't we, Rob?'

'I...'

'*You* won't faint on me,' she said in a voice of steel.

'I guess I won't,' Rob managed. 'If you say so—I guess I wouldn't dare.'

She propelled him out into the passage and closed the door. They stared at each other in a moment of mutual panic, while each of them fought for composure.

'We can't do this,' Rob said.

'We don't have a choice.'

'I don't have the first clue...'

'I've read a bit.' And she had. When she was having the twins, the dot-point part of her—she was a lawyer and an accountant after all, and research was her thing—had read everything she could get her hands on about childbirth. The fact that she'd forgotten every word the moment she went into labour was immaterial. She knew it all. In theory.

'You're a lawyer, Jules,' Rob managed. 'Not an obstetrician. All you know is law.'

And she thought suddenly, fleetingly: *that's not all I have to be.*

Why was it a revelation?

Weirdly, she was remembering the day she'd got the marks to get into law school. Her hippy parents had been baffled, but Julie had been elated. From that moment she'd been a lawyer.

Even when the twins were born...she'd loved Rob to bits and she'd adored her boys but she was always a lawyer. She'd had Rob bring files into hospital after she'd delivered, so she wouldn't fall behind.

All you know is law...

For the last four years law had been her cave, her hiding place. Her all. The night the boys were killed they'd been running late because of her work and Rob's work.

Rob had started skiing, she thought inconsequentially and then she thought that maybe it was time she did something different too. Like delivering babies?

The whole concept took a nanosecond to wash through her mind but, strangely, it settled her.

'We don't even have the Internet,' Rob groaned.

'I have books.'

'Books?'

'You know: things with pages. I bought every birth book I could get my hands on when the twins were due. They'll still be in the bookcase.'

'You intend to deliver a breech baby with one hand while you hold the book in the other?'

'That's where you come in, Rob McDowell,' she snapped. 'From this moment we're a united team. I want hot water, warm towels and a professional attitude.'

'I'm an architect!'

'Not tonight you're not,' she told him. 'It's still Christmas. You played Santa this morning. Now you need to put your midwife hat on and deliver again.'

She'd sounded calm enough when she'd talked to Rob but, as she stood in front of her small library of childbirth books, she felt the calm slip away.

What...? How...?

Steady, she told herself. *Think*. She stared at the myriad titles and tried to decide.

Not for the first time in her life, she blessed her memory. Read it once, forget it never. Obviously she couldn't remember every detail in these books—some parts she'd skimmed over fast. But the thing with childbirth, she'd figured, was that almost anyone could do it. Women had been doing it since time immemorial and they'd done it without the help of books. Ninety-nine times out of a hundred there were no problems; all the midwife had to do was encourage, support, catch and clean up.

But the one per cent…

Julie had become just a trifle obsessive in the last weeks of her pregnancy. She therefore had books with pictures of unthinkable outcomes. She remembered Rob had found her staring in horror at a picture of conjoined twins, and a mother who'd laboured for days before dying. *Extreme Complications of Pregnancy.* He'd taken that book straight to the shredder, but she had others.

Breech, she thought frantically, fingering one title after another. There were all sorts of complications with breech deliveries and she'd read them all.

But…but…

Ninety-nine per cent of babies are born normally, she told herself and she kept on thinking of past reading. *Breech is more likely to be a problem in first time mothers because the perineum is unproven.* Or words to that effect? She'd read that somewhere and she remembered thinking if her firstborn twin was breech it might be a problem, but if the book was right the second twin would be a piece of cake regardless.

'You're smiling!'

Rob had come into the living room and was staring at her in astonishment.

'No problem. We can do this.' And she hauled out one of the slimmest tomes on the shelf, almost a booklet, written by a midwife and not a doctor. It was well thumbed. She'd read it over and over because in the end it had been the most comforting.

She flicked until she found what she was looking for, and there were the words again. *If the breech is a second baby it's much less likely to require intervention.* But it did sound a warning. *Avoid home birth unless you're near good medical backup.*

There wasn't a lot of backup here. One architect, one lawyer, one fainting engineer and a four-year-old. Plus a first aid box containing sticking plasters, tweezers and antiseptic.

Breech... She flipped to the page she was looking for and her eyes widened. Rob looked over her shoulder and she felt him stiffen. 'My God...'

'We can do this.' *Steady*, she told herself. *If I don't stay calm, who will?* 'Look,' she said. 'We have step by step instructions with pictures. It's just like buying a desk and assembling it at home, following instructions. Besides, if we need to intervene, we can, but it says we probably won't need to. It's big on hands off.'

'But if we do? You know me and kit furniture—it always ends up with screws left over and one side wonkier than the other. And look what it says! If it's facing upward, head for hospital because...'

'There's no need to think like that,' she snapped. 'We need to stay positive. That means calm, Rob.' And she thought back, remembering. 'Forget the kit furniture analogy. Yes, you're a terrible carpenter but as a first time dad you were great. You are great. You need to be like you were with me, every step of the way. No matter how terrified I was, you were there saying how brave I was, how well I was doing, and you sounded so calm, so sure...'

'I wasn't in the least sure. I was a mess.'

'So you're a good actor. Put the act on again.'

'This isn't you we're talking about. Jules, I could do it when I had to.'

'Then you have to now.' She took a long, hard look at the diagrams, committing them to memory. Hoping to heaven she wouldn't need them. 'Amina has us. Rob, together we can do this.'

'Okay.' He took a deep breath while he literally squared his shoulders. 'If you say so, maybe we can.' Then suddenly he tugged her to him and hugged her, hard, and gave her a swift firm kiss. 'Maybe that's what I've been saying all along. Apart we're floundering. Together we might...'

'Be able to have a baby? Do you have those towels warming?' The kiss had left her flustered, but she regrouped fast.

'Yes, ma'am.'

'I'll need sterilised scissors.'

'I already thought of that. They're in a pot on the barbecue. So all we need is one baby.' He cupped her chin and smiled down at her. 'Okay, Dr McDowell, do you have your dot-point plan ready? I hope you do because we're in your hands.'

Breech births were supposed to be long. Weren't they? Surely they were supposed to take longer than normal labours, but no one seemed to have told Amina's baby that. When Rob and Julie returned to her room she was mid-contraction and one look at her told them both that this was some contraction. Surely a contraction shouldn't be as all-consuming if it was early labour.

Henry and Danny were looking appalled but Henry was looking even more appalled than his son. He'd fainted at Danny's birth, but then refugees did it tough, Rob thought, and who knew what the circumstances had been? Today he'd literally walked through fire to reach his family. He must be past exhaustion. He'd cut him some slack—and, besides, if Henry left with Danny, it would be Henry who'd have to explain childbirth to his son.

He put his hand on Henry's shoulder and gripped, hard. 'We can do this, mate,' he said. 'At least, Julie can and I'm here to assist. Julie suggested I take Danny into the living room and turn on a movie. If it's okay with Amina, how about you take my place? We have a pile of kids' movies. Pick a loud, exciting one and watch it until you both go to sleep. Hug Luka and know everything's okay. Danny, your mama's about to have a baby and she needs to be able to yell a bit while she does. It's okay, honest, most mamas yell when they have babies. So if you hear yelling, don't you worry. Snuggle up with your papa and Luka, and when you wake up in the morning I reckon your mama will have a baby to show you. Is that okay, Henry?'

'I'll stay,' Henry quavered. 'If you want me to, Amina…'

'Leave,' Amina ordered, easing back from the contraction enough to manage a weak smile at her husband and then her son. 'It's okay, sweetheart,' she told Danny. 'This baby has to push its way out and I have to squeeze and squeeze and it's easier for me if I can yell when I squeeze. Papa's going to show you a movie and Julie and Rob are going to stay with me to take care of the baby when it's born.'

'Can I come back and see it—when it's born?'

'Yes.'

'And will it be a boy?'

'I don't know,' Amina told him. 'But, Danny, take your papa away because I have to squeeze again and Papa doesn't like yelling. You look after Papa, okay?'

'And watch a movie?'

'Yes,' Amina managed through gritted teeth. Julie got behind Henry and practically propelled him and his son through the door and closed it behind them, and it was just as well because Amina was true to her word.

She yelled.

* * *

Hands off. Do not interfere unless you have to. That was the mantra the little book extolled and that was fine by Julie because there didn't seem to be an alternative.

She and Rob both washed, scrupulously on Julie's part, the way she'd seen it done on television. Rob looked at her with her arms held out, dripping, and gave a rueful chuckle. 'Waiting for a nurse to apply latex gloves?'

'The only gloves I have are the ones I use for the washing-up. I'm dripping dry,' she retorted and then another contraction hit and any thought of chuckling went out of the window.

'Hey,' Rob said, hauling a chair up by Amina's bedside. 'It's okay. Yell as much as you want. We're used to it. You should have heard Julie when she had the twins. I'd imagine you could have heard her in Sri Lanka.'

'But…but she knows…what to do? Your Julie?'

'My Julie knows what to do,' Rob told her, taking her hand. 'My Julie's awesome.'

And how was a woman to react to that? Julie felt her eyes well, but then Rob went on.

'My Julie's also efficient. She'll help you get through this faster than anyone I know. And if there's any mucking around she'll know who to sue. She's a fearsome woman, my Julie, so let's just put ourselves in her hands, Amina, love, and get this baby born.'

Which meant there was no time for welling eyes, no time for emotion. There was a baby to deliver.

By unspoken agreement, Rob stayed by Amina's side and did what a more together Henry should have done, while Julie stayed at the business end of the bed.

The instructions in her little booklet played over and over in her head, giving her a clear plan of action. How close? Julie had no clue. She couldn't see the baby yet but, with the power of these contractions, it surely wouldn't be long before she did.

She felt useless, but at the other end of the bed Rob was a lot more help.

'Come on, Amina, you can do this. Every contraction brings your baby closer. You're being terrific. Did anyone ever teach you how to breathe? You do it like this between contractions…' And he proceeded to demonstrate puffing as he'd learned years before in Julie's antenatal classes. 'It really works. Julie said so.'

Julie had said no such thing, she thought. She'd said a whole lot of things during her long labour but she couldn't remember saying anything complimentary about anything.

And Amina was in a similar mood. When Rob waited until the next contraction passed and then encouraged Amina to puff again, he got told where he could put his puffing.

'And it's breech,' she gasped. 'Julie doesn't know about breech.'

'Julie knows everything,' Rob declared. 'Memory like a bull elephant, my Julie. Tell us the King of Spain in 1703, Jules.'

'Philip Five,' Julie said absently.

'Name a deadly mushroom?'

'Conocybe? Death caps? How many do you want?'

'And tell me what's different about breech?'

'I might have to do a little rotating as the baby comes out,' Julie said, trying to sound as if it was no big deal.

'There you go, then,' Rob approved as Amina disappeared into another contraction. 'She knows it all. This'll be a piece of cake for our Julie.'

Only it wasn't. Rob had managed to calm Amina; there no longer seemed to be terror behind the pain, but there was certainly a fair bit of terror behind Julie's façade of competence.

One line in the little book stood out. *If the baby's presenting face up then there's no choice; it must be a Caesarean.*

Any minute now she'd know. *Dear God…*

Her mind was flying off at tangents as she waited. Was there any other option? They couldn't go for help. They couldn't ring anyone. For heaven's sake, they couldn't even light a fire and send out smoke signals. If it was face up…

'And my Julie always stays calm,' Rob said, and his voice was suddenly stern, cutting across the series of yelps Amina was making. 'That's what I love about her. That's why you're in such good hands, Amina. Are you sure you don't want to puff?'

Amina swore and slapped at his hand and a memory came back to Julie—she'd done exactly the same thing. She'd even bruised him. The day after the twins were born she'd looked at a blackening bruise on her husband's arm, and she'd also seen marks on his palm where her nails had dug in.

Her eyes met his and he smiled, a faint gentle smile that had her thinking…*memories can be good.* The remembrance of Rob's comfort. Her first sight of her babies.

The love…

Surely that love still deserved to live. Surely it shouldn't be put away for ever in the dusty recesses of her mind, locked away because letting it out hurt?

Surely Rob was right to relive those memories. To let them make him smile…

But then Amina gasped and struggled and Rob supported her as she tried to rise. She grasped her knees and she pushed.

Stage two. Stage two, stage two, stage two.

Face up, face down. *Please, please, please...*

There was a long, loaded pause and Amina actually puffed. But still she held her knees while the whole world seemed to hold its breath.

Another contraction. Another push.

Julie could see it. She could see...what? *What?*

A backside. A tiny bottom.

Face down. *Oh, God, face down. Thank you, thank you, thank you.* She glanced up at Rob and her relief must have shown in her face. He gave her a fast thumbs-up and then went back to holding, encouraging, being...Rob.

She loved him. She loved him with all her heart but now wasn't the time to get corny. Now was the time to try and deliver this baby.

Hands off. That was what the book said. *Breech babies will often deliver totally on their own.*

Please...

But they'd been lucky once. They couldn't ask for twice. Amina pushed, the baby's bottom slid out so far but as the contraction receded, so did the baby.

Over and over.

Exhaustion was starting to set in. Time for Dr Julie to take a hand? Did she dare?

Another glance at Rob, and his face was stern. He'd read the book over her shoulder, seen the pictures, figured what was expected now. His face said: *do it.*

So do it.

She'd set out what she'd need. Actually, she'd set out what she had. The book said if the head didn't come, then forceps might be required. She didn't actually have forceps or anything that could be usefully used instead.

Please don't let them be needed. It was a silent prayer said over and over.

Don't think forward. One step at a time. First she had to deliver the legs.

Dot-point number one. Carefully, she lubricated her fingers. One leg at a time. One leg…

Remember the pictures.

'Jules is about to help your baby out,' Rob said, his voice steady, calm, settling. 'Next push, Amina, go as far as you can and then hold. Puff, just like I said. Keep the pressure on.'

Next contraction… The baby's back slid out again. Deep breath and Julie felt along the tiny leg. What did the book say? *Manoeuvre your finger behind the knee and gently push upward. This causes the knee to flex. Hold the femur, splint it gently with your finger to prevent it breaking. This should allow the leg to…*

It did! It flopped out. *Oh, my…*

Calm. Next. Dot-point number two.

The other leg was easier. Now the baby could no longer recede. *Manoeuvre to the right position. Flex.*

Two legs delivered. She was almost delirious with hope. *Please…*

Dot-point number three. *Gently rotate the baby into the side position to allow delivery of the right arm.* Easier said than done but the illustrations had been clear. If only her hands weren't so slippery, but they had to be slippery.

'Fantastic, Jules,' Rob said. 'Fantastic, Amina. You're both doing great.'

She had the tiny body slightly rotated. Enough? It had to be. Her finger found the elbow, put her finger over the top, pressured gently, inexorably.

An arm. She'd delivered an arm. The dot-points were blurring, but she still had work to do. She was acting mostly on instinct, but thank God for the book. She'd write to the author. No, she'd send the author half her kingdom. All her kingdom.

She suddenly thought of the almost obscene amount of money she'd been earning these past years and thought...

And thought there was another arm to go and then the head, and the head was...

'Jules. We're doing great,' Rob growled and she glanced up at him and thought he'd seen the shiver of panic and he was grounding her again.

He'd always grounded her. She needed him.

Her hands held the tiny body, took a grip, lifted as the book said, thirty degrees so the left arm was in position for delivery. She twisted as the next contraction eased. The baby rotated like magic.

She found the elbow and pushed gently down. The left arm slithered out.

Now the head. *Please, God, the head.* She didn't have forceps. She wouldn't have the first clue what to do with forceps if she had them.

'Lift,' Rob snapped and he was echoing the book too. 'Come on, Jules, you know what the book says. Come on, Amina. Our baby's so close. We can do this.'

Our baby...

It sounded good. It sounded right.

'Next contraction, puff afterwards, ease off until Jules has the baby in position,' Rob urged Amina, and magically she did.

Amina was working so hard. Surely she could do the same.

She steadied. Waited. The next contraction passed. Amina puffed, Rob held her hand and murmured gentle words. 'Hold, Amina, hold, we're so close...'

Do it.

She held the baby, resting it on her right hand. She manoeuvred her hand so two fingers were on the side of the tiny jaw. With her other hand she put her middle finger on the back of the baby's head.

It sounded easy. It wasn't. She lifted the baby as high as she could, remembering the pictures, remembering…

So much sweat. She needed…she needed…

'You're doing great, Jules,' Rob said. 'Amina, your baby's so close. Maybe one more push. This is fantastic. Let's do this, people. Okay, Jules?'

'O…Okay.' She nodded. She'd forgotten how to breathe. *Please*…

'Okay, Amina, push,' Rob ordered and Amina pushed—and the next second Julie had a healthy, lusty, slippery bundle of baby girl in her arms.

She gasped and staggered but she had her. She had Amina's baby.

Safe. Delivered.

And seconds later a tiny girl was lying on her mother's tummy. Amina was sobbing with joy, and a new little life had begun.

After that things happened in a blur. Waiting for the afterbirth and checking it as the book had shown. Clearing up. Watching one tiny girl find her mother's breast. Ushering an awed and abashed Henry into the room, with Danny by his side.

Watching the happiness. Watching the little family cling. Watching the love and the pride, and then backing out into the night, their job done.

Julie reached the passage, leaned against the wall and sagged.

But she wasn't allowed to sag for long. Her husband had her in his arms. He held her and held her and held her, and she felt his heart beat against hers and she thought: *here is my home.*

Here is my family.

Here is my heart.

'Love, I need to check the boundaries again,' he said at last, ruefully, and she thought with a jolt: *fire.* She hadn't thought of the fire for hours. But of course he was right. There'd still be embers falling around them. They should have kept checking.

'We should have told Henry to check,' she managed.

'Do you think he would have even seen an ember? You take a shower. I'll be with you soon.'

'Rob…' she managed.

'Mmm?'

'I love you,' she whispered.

'I love you too, Dr McDowell.' He kissed her on the tip of the nose and then put her away. 'But then, I always have. All we need to do now is to figure some way forward. Think of it in the shower, my Jules. Think of me. Now, go get yourself clean again while I rid myself of my obstetric suit and put on my fireman's clothes. Figuring roles for ourselves… This day's thrown plenty at us. Think about it, Jules, love. What role do you want for the rest of your life?'

And he was gone, off to play fireman.

While Julie was left to think about it.

There was little to think about—and yet there was lots. She thought really fast while she let the water stream over her. Then she towelled dry, donned her robe and headed back out onto the veranda.

Rob was just finishing, heading up the steps with his bucket and mop.

'Not a single ember,' he announced triumphantly. 'Not

a spark. After today I doubt an ember would dare come close. Have I told you recently that we rock? If I didn't think Amina might be asleep already I'd puff out my chest and do a yodel worthy of Tarzan.'

'Riiiight…'

'It's true. In fact I feel a yodel coming on right this minute. But not here. Do you fancy wandering up the hill a little and yodelling with me?'

And it was such a crazy idea that she thought: *why not?* But then, she was in a robe and slippers and she should…

No. She shouldn't think of reasons not to. *Move forward.*

'That's something I need to hear,' she said and grinned. 'A Tarzan yodel… Wow.' She grabbed his mop, tossed it aside, took his hand and hauled him out into the night.

'Jules! I didn't mean…'

'To yodel? Rob McDowell, if you think I'm going through what we've gone through without listening to you yodel, you're very much mistaken.'

'What have I done?' But Rob was helpless in her hands as she hauled him round the back of the bunker, up through the rocks that formed the back of their property, along a burned out trail that led almost straight up—it was so rocky here that no trees grew, which made it safe from the remnants of fire—and out onto a rock platform where usually she could see almost all over the Blue Mountains.

She couldn't see the Blue Mountains tonight. The pall of smoke was still so thick she could hardly see the path, but the smoke was lifting a little. They could sometimes see a faint moon, with smoke drifting over, sending them from deep dark to a little sight and back again. It didn't matter, though. They weren't here to see the moon or the Blue Mountains. They were here…to yodel.

'Right,' Julie said as they reached the platform. 'Go ahead.'

'Really?'

'Was it all hot air? You never meant it?'

He chuckled. 'It won't be pretty.'

'I'm not interested in pretty!'

'Well, you asked for it.' And he breathed in, swelled, pummelled his chest—and yodelled.

It was a truly heroic yodel. It made Julie double with laughter. It made her feel…feel…as if she was thirteen years old again, in love for the first time and life was just beginning.

It was a true Tarzan yodel.

'You've practised,' she said accusingly. 'No one could make a yodel sound that good first try.'

'My therapist said I should let go my anger,' he told her. 'It started with standing in the shower and yelling at the soap. After a while I started experimenting elsewhere.'

'Moving on?'

'It's what you have to do.'

'Rob…'

'I know,' he said. 'You haven't. But you will. Try it yourself. Open your mouth and yell.' And he stood back and dared her with his eyes. He was laughing, with her, though, not at her. Daring her to laugh with him. Daring her to yodel?

And finally, amazingly, it felt as if she could. How long had it been since she'd felt this free? This alive? Maybe never. Even when they were courting, even when the twins were born, she'd always felt the constraints of work. The constraints of life. But now…

Rob's hands were exerting a gentle pressure but that pressure was no constraint. She was facing outward into the rest of the world.

She was facing outward into the rest of her life.

'Can you do it?' Rob asked, and he kissed the nape of her neck. 'Not that I doubt you. My wife can do anything.'

And she could. Or at least maybe she could.

Deep breath. Pummel a little.

Yodel.

And she was doing it, yodelling like a mad woman, and she took another breath and tried again and this time Rob joined her.

It was crazy. It was ridiculous.

It was fun.

'We've delivered a Christmas baby,' Rob managed as finally they ran out of puff, as finally they ran out of yodel. 'A new life. And we're learning Christmas yodelling duets! Is there nothing we're not capable of? Happy Christmas, Mrs McDowell, and, by the way, will you marry me? Again? Make our vows again? I know we're not divorced but it surely feels like we have been. Can we be a family? Can we take our past and live with it? Can we love what we've had, and love each other again for the rest of our lives?'

And the smoke suddenly cleared. Everything cleared. Rob was standing in front of her, he was holding her and the future was hers to grasp and to hold.

And in the end there was nothing to say except the most obvious response in the whole world.

'Why, yes, Mr McDowell,' she whispered. 'Happy Christmas, my love, and yes, I believe I will marry you again. I believe I will marry you—for ever.'

CHAPTER NINE

A RETAKING OF weddings vows shouldn't be as romantic as the first time around. That was what Julie's mother had read somewhere, but she watched her daughter marry for the second time and she thought: *what do 'they' know?*

People go into a second marriage with their eyes wide open, with all the knowledge of the trials and pitfalls of marriage behind them, and yet they choose to step forward again, and step forward with joy. Because they know what love is. Because they know that, despite the hassles and the day-to-day trivia, and sometimes despite the tragedy and the heartache, they know that love is worth it.

So Julie's mother held her husband's hand and watched her daughter retake her vows, and felt her heart swell with pride. They'd ached every step of the way with their daughter. They'd ached for their grandsons and for the hurt they'd known their son-in-law must be feeling. But in the end they'd stopped watching. Julie had driven them away, as she'd driven away most people in her life. But somehow one magical Christmas had brought healing.

It was almost Easter now. Julie had wanted to get on with their lives with no fuss, but Rob wasn't having any part of such a lame new beginning. 'I watch people have parties for their new homes,' he'd said. 'How much more important is this? We're having a party for our new lives.'

And they would be new lives. So much had changed.

They'd moved—Julie from her sterile apartment in Sydney, Rob from his bachelor pad in Adelaide—but they'd decided not to move back to the Blue Mountains. Amina and Henry were in desperate need of a house—*'and we need to move on,'* they'd told them.

Together they'd found a ramshackle weatherboard cottage on the beach just south of Sydney. They'd both abandoned their jobs for the duration and were tackling the house with energy and passion—if not skill. It might end up a bit wonky round the edges, but already it felt like home.

But... *Home. Home is where the heart is,* so somehow, some way, it felt right that their vows were being made back here. On the newly sprouting gardens around Amina and Henry's home in the Blue Mountains, where there was love in spades. Amina and Henry had been overjoyed when Rob and Julie had asked to have the ceremony here.

'Because your love brought us together again,' Julie had told Amina. 'You and Henry, with your courage and your love for each other.'

'You were together all the time,' Amina had whispered, holding her baby daughter close. 'You just didn't know it.'

Rob and Julie were now godparents. More. They were landlords and they were also sponsoring Henry through retraining. There'd be no more working in the mines. No more long absences. This family deserved to stay together.

As did Julie and Rob.

'I asked you this seven years ago,' the celebrant said, smiling mistily at them. She must have seen hundreds of weddings, but did she mist up for all of them? Surely not. 'But I can't tell you the joy it gives me to ask you again. Rob, do you take Julie—again—to be your lawful wedded wife, to love and to cherish, in sickness and in health, forsaking all others, for as long as you both shall live?'

'I do—and the rest,' Rob said softly, speaking to Julie and to Julie alone. 'Beyond the grave I'll love you. Love doesn't end with death. We both know that. Love keeps going and going and going, if only we let it. Will we let it? Will we let it, my love?'

'Yes, please,' Julie whispered, and then she, too, made her vows.

And Mr McDowell married Mrs McDowell—again— and the thing was done.

Christmas morning.

Julie woke early and listened to the sounds of the surf just below the house. She loved this time of day. Once upon a time she'd listened to galahs and cockatoos in the bush around their house. Now she listened to the sounds of the waves and the sandpipers and oystercatchers calling to each other as they hunted on the shore of a receding tide.

Only that wasn't right, she told herself. She'd never lain in bed and listened to the sounds of birds in the bush. She'd been too busy working. Too busy with her dot-points.

But now… They'd slowed, almost to a crawl. Her dot-points had grown fewer and fewer. Rob worked from home, his gorgeous house plans sprawled over his massive study at the rear of the house. Julie commuted to Sydney twice a week, and she, too, worked the rest of the time at home.

But they didn't work so much that they couldn't lie in bed and listen to the surf. And love each other. And start again.

She'd stop commuting soon, she thought in satisfaction. She could maybe still accept a little contract work, as long as it didn't mess with her life. With her love.

With her loves?

And, unbidden, her hand crept to her tummy, where her secret lay.

She couldn't wait a moment longer. She rolled over and kissed her husband, tenderly but firmly.

'Wake up,' she told him. 'It's Christmas.'

'So it is.' He woke with laughter, reaching for her, holding her, kissing her. 'Happy Christmas, wife.'

'Happy Christmas, husband.'

'I have the best Christmas gift for you,' he said, pushing himself up so he was smiling down at her with all the tenderness in the world. 'I bet you can't guess what it is.'

She choked on laughter. Last night he'd driven home late and on the roof rack of his car was a luridly wrapped Christmas present, complete with a huge Christmas bow. It was magnificently wrapped but all the wrapping in the world couldn't disguise the fact that it was a surfboard.

'I have no idea,' she lied. 'I can't wait.'

They'd come so far, she thought, as Rob gathered her into his arms. This year would be so different from the past. All their assorted family was coming for lunch, as were Amina and Henry and their children. For family came in all sorts of assorted sizes and shapes. It changed. Tragedies happened but so did joys. Christmas was full of memories, and each memory was to be treasured, used to shape the future with love and with hope and memories to come.

And dot-points, she thought suddenly. There were—what?—twenty people due for lunch. Loving aside, smugness aside, she had to get organised. Dot-point number one. Stuff the turkey.

But Rob was holding her—and she had her gift for him.

So: *soon*, she told her dot-point, and proceeded to indulge her husband. And herself.

'Do you want your present now?' she asked as they finally resurfaced, though she couldn't get her mind to be practical quite yet.

'I have everything I need right here.'

'Are you sure?'

'What more could a man want?'

She smiled. She smiled and she smiled. She'd been holding this secret for almost two weeks and it had almost killed her not to tell him, but now… She tugged away from his arms, then kissed him on the nose and settled on her back. And tugged his hand to her naked tummy.

She could scarcely feel it herself. Could he…? Would he…?

But he got it in one. She saw his eyes widen in shock. He was clever, her husband. He was loving and tender and wise. He was a terrible handyman—her kitchen shelves were a disaster and she was hoping her dad might stay on long enough to fix them—but a woman couldn't have everything.

Actually, she did. She did have everything. Her husband was looking down at her with awe and tenderness and love.

'Really?' he whispered.

'Really.'

And she saw him melt, just like that. A blaze of joy that took her breath away.

Joy… They had so much, and this baby was more. For it was true what they said: *love doesn't die*. The memories of Christopher and Aiden would stay with them for ever—tender, joyous, always mourned but an intrinsic part of her family. Their family. Hers and Rob's.

'Happy Christmas, Daddy,' she murmured and she kissed him long and hard. 'Happy Christmas, my love.'

'Do you suppose it might be twins again?' he breathed, awed beyond belief, and she smiled and smiled.

'Who knows? Whoever it is, we'll love them for ever.

Like I love you. Now, are you going to make love to me again or are you going to let me go? I hate to mention it but I have all these dot-points to attend to.'

'But here is your number one dot-point,' he said smugly, and gathered her into his arms yet again. 'The turkey can wait. Christmas can wait. Number one is us.'

* * * * *

SNOWED IN AT
THE RANCH

CARA COLTER

To my daughter, Cassidy:
Love you forever

CHAPTER ONE

TY Halliday was beyond exhaustion. The driving mix of sleet and snow had soaked through his oilskin slicker hours ago. Icy water was sluicing off the back of his hat's brim, inside his upturned collar and straight down his spine.

The horse stumbled, as exhausted as his rider, dark setting in too fast.

But beneath all the discomfort, Ty allowed himself satisfaction. He'd found the entire herd. The three cows that shuffled along in front of him were the last of them.

It had been sixteen hours, roughly, since he'd found the broken fence, the cougar tracks. He counted himself lucky most of the herd had petered out and allowed themselves to be herded home, long before these three.

Tracks in fresh snow told the story of the herd splitting in a dozen different directions, the cougar locking in on these three, finally giving up and prowling away down Halliday Creek. These cows, in a panic, had kept on going, almost to the summer range, way up the mountain.

Below him, Ty could see the lights of his house winking against the growing darkness. It made him impatient for hot food, a stiff drink, a scalding shower and his bed.

But the horse, Ben, was young and had already demonstrated great heart, had given everything he had, and
so Ty did not push him, but let the young gelding set his
own pace down a trail that was slick with new snow.

Finally, finally, the cows were back with the herd,
the pasture fences secured, Ben fed and watered. Ty
followed a path from the barn, worn deep by a hundred years of Halliday boots, to where the "new" house
sat on the top of a knoll of land, in the shadow of the
mountain behind it.

The house was called new because it shared the property with the "old" homestead place, which his father
had built for his first wife twenty-five years before Ty
had been born.

Ty swayed on his back porch, his hand going to the
doorknob.

Where it froze.

What had he heard?

Silence.

He cocked his head, listening hard, but heard only
the lonely whistle of a December wind under the rafters of the house.

Ty felt he was suffering the delusions of a man who
had pushed himself to his limit, and then a mile or two
beyond it.

But he was frowning now, thinking of the lights inside his house that had winked him home. He lived
alone. He was pretty damned sure that he had not left
any lights on when he'd left way before dawn this morning.

The sound came again, and he took a startled step
back, nearly tumbling down his back-porch steps.

The sound was definitely coming from *inside* his house. It was an almost shockingly happy sound. His tired mind grappled with it. He hadn't had a television for years. He didn't own a computer. Had he left the radio on?

No. He had not turned on anything this morning, some distress note in the faraway bawl of a cow letting him know something had been amiss. He had scrambled out of bed and out of the house in total darkness and in a hurry.

There was only one thing that made a sound like the one he had just heard.

And there was absolutely no chance it was coming from inside *his* house.

No, it was exhaustion. An auditory hallucination. Ears straining, picking up noises that did not exist.

Just as Ty was about to dismiss the sound he thought he had heard as a figment of an exhausted mind—clearly it was impossible—it came again. Louder. A babbling sound, like cold creek water tinkling over the first thin shards of ice.

And even though he was not a man with much experience in such things, Ty knew exactly what it was.

There was a baby inside his house.

Ty backed off his porch on silent feet, took a deep breath, felt a need to ground himself. He paused at the corner of his house, surveying the rolling land of the foothills, black against the midnight-blue of a rapidly darkening sky.

Snow-crusted pasture rolled away from him, beyond that a forested valley, all of it ringed by the craggy magnificence of the Rocky Mountains. The rugged sweep of his land soothed him, though it was not "safe." A man could die—or be injured—in this country fast and hard. The arrival of the cougar was a case in point, though getting wet and lost in December was far more dangerous than an old mountain lion.

Still, for all its challenges, if ever a place was made to put a man's soul at ease, wasn't it this one? He had gone away from here once, and nearly lost himself.

The baby's happy squawking from inside the house was revving up a notch and he felt the simple shock of it down to his wet, frozen toes inside his boots.

A baby?

The truth be told, the danger of the cougar that had passed through his pastures appealed to him more than the mysterious presence of an infant inside his house.

Ty moved along the side of the house until he stood at the front. At the top of a long, long drive that twisted endlessly up the valley from Highway 22—sometimes called The Cowboy Trail—a car was parked in the gravel turnaround.

It was not the kind of car anyone in these parts would be caught dead driving.

No, folks around here favored pickup trucks, diesel, big enough to haul cattle and horses and hay. Trucks that could be shifted into four-wheel drive as the seasons changed and the roads became more demanding. People around here drove vehicles that were big, muddy and ugly.

No one Ty knew drove a car like this: bright red, shaped like a ladybug, impractically low to the ground.

Cute.

No surprise that a baby seat sat in the back, cheerfully padded with a bright fabric that had cartoon dogs and cats on it.

Ty placed his hand on the hood. Cold. The car had been here for a time.

He checked the plate. Alberta. A Calgary parking sticker was in the left-hand corner of the windshield. Not so far from wherever home was, then, maybe one and a half, two hours, if the roads had been good.

It would be easy enough to slide open the door and find the paperwork, but when he tried the door, it was locked. Under different circumstances he might have seen that as hilarious. Locked? He allowed his eyes to sweep the unpopulated landscape again. Against what?

He turned back to the house. Then he saw his front window.

For the second time in less than five minutes, Ty felt himself stumble backward in shock. His sense of being in an exhausted state of distorted reality increased. He made himself stand very still, squint through the sleet and snow, demanding *it* go away.

It was a Christmas tree. And it was real, because when he blinked hard and looked again, it was still there. Behind plate glass, bright lights winked against dark boughs, sent little splashes of color onto the gathering snow in his front yard.

He checked his driveway again, seeking familiar landmarks. Turned and studied his house, reassured himself that had been *his* pasture the cows had been shepherded into, *his* barn where he had put up his horse.

His eyes went back to the tree.

As far as Ty knew, there had never been one set up in the new Halliday house.

Or at least not in the twenty-six years he had lived here.

And in Ty's exhausted mind, a single, vulnerable hope crept in, a wish that he had made as a small boy.

Maybe his mother had come home.

He shook off the thought, irritated that it had somehow breached the wall of his adult world. Wishes were for children, and there had been no chance of his ever coming true, thanks to his father.

In his tired mind it did not bode well that the car in the yard, and the baby in his house, and the tree in his window had stirred something up that was better left alone, that he had not given any power to for years.

He went around to the back door again, habit more than anything else. In these parts the front door was rarely used, even by company. The back entrance was built to accommodate dirty boots and jackets, hats, gloves, bridles hung indoors in cold weather to keep the bits warm.

Ty Halliday took a deep breath, aware that the pit of his stomach felt exactly as it had in his days on the rodeo circuit when you gave that quick nod, the chute door opened, and suddenly you were riding a whirling explosion of bovine motion and malice.

He put his hand on the doorknob and felt it resist his flick of the wrist. At first he thought it was stuck, but then in an evening where he could have done without one more shock, he was shocked again. His door was locked.

Okay. Maybe one of his neighbors was playing a practical joke on him. Unlocked doors invited pranks. It was a tightly knit community and they all loved to have a laugh. Melvin Harris had once come home to find a burro in his living room. When Cathy Lambert had married Paul Cranston some of the neighbors had snuck into their house and filled every single drawer with confetti. They'd been married six years, and sometimes you still saw a piece of it sticking to one of Cathy's sweaters.

Ty lifted a worn welcome mat and found a rusty key. Sometimes he locked up if he was going to be away for a few days.

He slid the key in the door and let himself in, braced for some kind of battle, but what greeted him was enough to make him want to lay down his weapons.

His house, which he had always seen primarily as providing shelter, felt like *home*.

First, it smelled good. There was a light perfume in the air, woman, baby, underlying the smell of something wonderful cooking.

Second, the sound was enough to break every barrier a man had placed around his heart—and Ty would be the first to admit in his case, that was many. The baby was now chortling with glee.

Ty took the bridle he had slung over his shoulder and hung it on an empty peg. Then he took off his wet gloves and tossed them on the floor. He slid his sodden feet from muddy boots, and then took a deep breath— gladiator entering the ring to face unexpected horrors— and went up the stairs off the landing and surveyed his kitchen.

A fat baby with a shock of impossibly curly red hair sat dead center of Ty's kitchen on a blanket surrounded by toys. The baby, a boy, if the dump trucks and fire engines that surrounded him were any indication, was gurgling joyously.

The baby turned at his entrance, regarded him solemnly with gigantic soft brown eyes.

Instead of looking alarmed by the arrival of a big, irritated stranger, whose long Aussie-style riding coat was dripping water on the floor, the baby's eyes crinkled happily, and the joyous gurgling increased.

"Papa," he shouted.

Ty said a word he was pretty sure it was against the law to use in the presence of babies.

Or ladies.

Not that she looked like a lady, exactly. Through a wide archway, the kitchen opened onto the living room, and first a crop of hair as curly as the baby's appeared from behind the boughs of the tree. And then eyes, like the baby's, too, large and soft and brown, startled now.

Startled?

It was *his* house.

Cute. Just like the car. She had a light dusting of freckles across a delicate nose, curly hair the color of liquid honey in a jar. At first, he thought she had a boyish build, but Ty quickly saw her curves were just disguised in a masculine plaid shirt.

She didn't have on a speck of makeup and was one of those rare women who didn't need it, either.

"Who are you?" she demanded, a tiny tremor in her voice.

What kind of question was that to be asked in his own house? He could tell, from the way her eyes skittered around—looking for something to hit him with if he moved on the baby or her—that she was not just startled, she was scared. Any remaining thought that this might be a prank disappeared.

Her pulse beat frantically in the hollow of her slender neck.

Ty had to fight, again, the notion that he was somehow dreaming, and that he was going to wake up very soon. He didn't like it one little bit that exhaustion would make it way too easy to appreciate this scene.

That exhaustion was making some childhood wish try to push out of a dark corner of his mind.

Annoyed with himself—a man who believed in his strength and his determination, a man who put no faith at all in wishes—Ty planted his legs firmly apart, folded his arms over his chest.

She darted out from behind the tree, dropped the tangle of Christmas tree lights that were in her hand and grabbed a lamp. She yanked it off the side table and stood there holding it like a baseball bat.

Ty squinted at her. "Now, what are you going to do with that?" he asked mildly.

"If you touch my baby or me, you'll find out!"

The lamp was constructed out of an elk antler. It was big and heavy and it was already costing her to hold it up. It made him very aware of how small she was.

He had to fight to get beyond the exhaustion and the irritation that came with the weariness, to the same calm energy he tapped into to tame a nervous colt. He thought of the locked car and the locked back door.

He said, "I'm way more scared of a baby than that lamp. Especially one who calls me Papa."

He thought maybe her hold on the lamp relaxed marginally.

"How did you get into my house?" she demanded. "I locked the door."

"I used a key," he said, his voice deliberately quiet, firm, calm. "I happen to have one. I'm Ty Halliday. And last time I looked, this was my place."

The lamp wavered. Doubt played across her features for a second. Then she brought her weapon back up to batting position, glaring at him.

"Why don't you put that down?" he suggested. "Your arms are starting to shake. We both know I could take it from you if I had a mind to."

"Just try it," she warned him.

It was a little bit like an ant challenging an aardvark, but somehow he didn't think pointing that out to her was going to help the situation, and he reluctantly admired her spunk.

Something yanked on the hem of his coat. He looked down. The baby had crawled over and had grabbed a fistful of the wet oilskin of Ty's jacket. He was pulling himself up on it.

"Papa!" he crowed.

"Don't touch him!"

"Believe me, I'm not going to."

In a flash, she had set down the lamp, crossed the room, pried her baby's fist loose of his jacket and scooped him up into her arms.

This close he could smell them both. Her scent was subtle. Some flower. Lilac? No. Lavendar. It was mingled with baby powder. He wasn't sure how he recognized either of those scents, not common to his world, but he did, and it felt as if they were enveloping him.

She took a step back, eyeing him warily.

"You're in the wrong place," he said. "This really is my house. I'm cold and I'm wet and I'm dead tired, so let's get this sorted out so you can move on and I can go to bed."

Apparently the fact that he wanted to get rid of her rather than steal either her baby or her virtue reassured her in some way.

She pondered him. "If this is really your house, what's in the top drawer in the kitchen?"

"Knives and spoons and forks."

"That's in the top drawer of every kitchen!"

"You asked the question," he reminded her.

"Okay, second drawer."

He closed his eyes. "I'm losing patience," he warned her, but then gave in. The sooner he got that scared look off her face, the sooner she would realize her error and get on her way.

"Tea towels, once white, now the color of weak tea. One red oven glove with a hole burned right through it. Next drawer—potato masher, soup ladle, rolling pin, hammer for beating the tough out of rough cuts of beef."

Her eyes widened. "Oh, God," she whispered.

"How long have you been here that you know what's in my drawers?"

Her eyes shifted guiltily and made him wonder exactly what other drawers she had been investigating.

He swore softly. "Have you made it as far as my bedroom?"

"Oh, God," she said again.

The fear drained out of her, leaving her looking pale and shaky. She actually wobbled on her feet.

"Don't faint," he said. "I don't want to have to catch the kid."

"Oh," she said sharply, drawing herself up, annoyed,

"I am not going to faint. What kind of weak ninny do you take me for?"

"Weak ninny? How about the kind that reads *Jane Eyre?* How about the kind who is lost in the country, setting up housekeeping in someone else's house?" he said smoothly.

The truth was he liked her annoyance better than the pale, shaky look. He decided it would be good, from a tactical standpoint, to encourage annoyance.

"You don't look like you would know the first thing about *Jane Eyre,*" she said.

"That's right. Things are primitive out here in the sticks. We don't read and can barely write. When we do, we use a tablet and a chisel."

"I'm sorry," she said, blinking hard. "Now I've insulted you. I've moved in to the wrong house and I've insulted you. But I'm not going to faint. I promise. I'm not the fainting kind."

"Reassuring," he said drily. "And just for the record, I'm not easily insulted. It would take a lot more than the insinuation that I'm not up on my literary classics."

She sucked in a deep, steadying breath. "This isn't the McFinley residence, is it?"

Her face was crumpling, all the wariness and defiance seeping out of it. It was worse than pale and shaky.

He had the most ridiculous notion of wanting to comfort her, to move closer to her, pat her on the shoulder, tell her it would be all right.

But of course, he had no way of knowing if it would be all right, and he already knew if you moved too fast around a nervous colt, that little tiny bit of trust you had earned went out the window a whole lot faster than it had come in.

"But you know the McFinleys?" she asked, the desperation deepening in her voice. "I'm housesitting for them. For six months. They've left for Australia. They had to leave a few days before I could get away...."

He shook his head. He had the horrible feeling she was within a hairsbreadth of crying. Nervous colts were one thing. Crying women were a totally different thing. Totally.

The baby had sensed the change in his mother's tone. His happy babbling had ceased. He was eyeing his mother, his face scrunched up alarmingly, waiting for his cue.

One false move, Ty warned himself, and they would both be crying.

Ty checked the calendar in his mind. It was six days before Christmas. Why did a woman take her baby and find a new place to live six days before Christmas?

Running.

From what, or from whom, he told himself firmly, fell strictly into the none-of-his-business category.

"Mona and Ron?" Her voice faded as she correctly read his expression.

He was silent.

"You've never heard of them," she deduced. She sucked in another deep breath, assessing him.

Ty watched, trying not to let amusement tug at his mouth, as she apparently decided he was not an ax murderer, and made the decision to be brave.

She moved the baby onto her hip and wiped her

hand—she'd been scared enough to sweat?—on slacks that weren't made for riding horses. Like the shirt, the slacks emphasized the surprising lushness of such a slight figure.

All the defiance, all the I'll-lay-my-life-down-for-my-baby drained out of her. She looked wildly embarrassed at having been found making herself at home in someone else's house. Still, blushing, she tried for dignity as she extended her hand.

"I'm Amy Mitchell."

The blush made her look pretty. And vulnerable. He didn't want to take her hand, because despite her effort to be brave she still looked a breath away from crying, and the baby was still watching her intently, waiting.

"Mrs. Mitchell," he said, even though she wore no wedding band. He took her hand.

Ty knew instantly why he had resisted taking it. Amy Mitchell's hand in his felt tiny, soft beyond soft. The touch of her hand, his closeness to her, made him aware of his bleak world in ways that made him uncomfortable.

Her eyes were not brown, as he had initially thought from across the room, but a kaleidoscope of greens and golds, shot through with rich, dark hints of coffee color.

Now that she didn't feel she had her back against the wall, with a home invader coming at her, her eyes were soft and worried. Her honey-in-a-jar hair was scattered about her face in a wild disarray of curls that made him want to right it, to feel its texture beneath his fingertips.

Ty Halliday's world was a hard place. There was no softness in it, and no room for softness, either. There

was no room in his world for the tears that shone, un-
shed, behind the astounding loveliness of her eyes; there
was no room in his world for the bright, hopeful lights
of the Christmas tree.

The baby, eyes shifting from him to his mother and
back again, suddenly relaxed. "Papa," he cooed, and
leaned away from his mommy, reaching for Ty.

Ty took a defensive step backward.

There was no room in his world for such innocence
or trust. All these things were as foreign to Ty as an ex-
otic, unvisited land.

He realized he was still holding Amy Mitchell's hand.
She realized it, too, and with a deepening blush, slipped
it from his.

"I can't believe this," she muttered. "I have GPS."

She said that as if her faulty system or reading of it
was the cause of the stain moving up her cheeks, instead of her awareness of him.

And maybe it was.

But he didn't think so.

Still, he focused on the GPS, too, something safe in
a room that suddenly seemed fraught with dangers of
a kind he had never considered before.

The faith city folk put in their gadgets never failed to
astound him, but aware she was still terrifyingly close
to the tear stage, he tried to think of a way to phrase it
that wouldn't wound her.

"It wouldn't be the first time GPS got people into
trouble in this country," he said after some thought.

"Really?"

Obviously, she was pleased that hers was not an isolated case of being misled by her global positioning system, and he could have left it at that.

Instead, he found the worry lines dissolving on her forehead encouraging enough to want to make them—and the possibility of tears—disappear altogether.

"One of the neighbors found an old couple stranded in George's Pass last year. They'd been on the news. Missing for a week."

But instead of being further reassured that her mistake was not all that uncommon, Amy looked aghast. He remembered the locked doors and saw her considering other scenarios. Disastrous possibilities flashed through her eyes as she considered what could have happened to her if she had followed her GPS instructions somewhere other than his driveway.

Which just served as a reminder that he could not really be trusted with soft things or a woman so frightened of life she locked everything all the time and was ready to defend herself with a lamp if need be.

She marshaled herself and turned away from him. She plunked the baby down on his padded rear and began to whip around the room, picking up baby things, putting them in a pile. Given the short amount of time she had been here, the pile grew to a mountain with astonishing swiftness.

"I'm terribly sorry, Mr. Halliday. We'll go right away. I'm so embarrassed."

If he had thought she was blushing before, that had only been a hint of the main event.

Amy Mitchell was turning a shade of red that matched some of the lights on the tree. Was that a smile tickling around the edges of his mouth? He tried to remember the last time he had smiled.

Sunshine Sketches of a Little Town had made him smile, he decided. He'd reread that a week or so ago.

No doubt his current good cheer was because his visitor was so intent on leaving. There was no need to tell her to pack her baby and get the hell out of his house. She was doing it all on her own.

"It will take me a minute to gather my things," she said, all business and flurrying activity. "I'll leave the groceries."

"Groceries?"

"Oh, I stocked the fridge. I thought I was going to be living here, after all."

"You're not leaving the groceries," he said.

"Oh, no, really. You didn't have a thing in your fridge. That's part of why I thought I was in the right place. Nothing in the fridge, no tree up, no socks on the floor."

She *had* been in his bedroom.

"Really, I didn't think anyone had lived here recently." She shot him a look that was faintly accusing and faintly sympathetic. "It certainly didn't look as though anyone lived here."

"I don't need your groceries," he said a bit more tightly than he intended. He was so hungry, and whatever she had in the fridge would be better than the tin of stew he had planned on opening. But to admit that might invite more sympathy, and he definitely didn't need her sympathy.

So his place looked unlived in. So it wasn't going to be the featured house on *Cozy Country Homes*. So what? It was a place to hang his hat and lay his head. He didn't need more than that.

Or at least he hadn't felt as if he had for a long, long time. But there it was again, unwanted, uninvited emotion whispering along his spine.

Yearning. A wish he had managed to bury deep to have something that he did not have.

"I started to unpack. I've got some things in the bedroom," she explained as she scurried around the room, the remnants of her embarrassment making her awkward. She dropped a baby puzzle on the floor, and the wooden pieces scattered.

He just knew she had been in there, in his bedroom. And he knew, suddenly, why it bothered him, too. That could move yearning in a whole other direction if he let it, which he wasn't going to.

He hadn't allowed himself feelings for a long, long time. It must be the Christmas tree, the baby, the scents, the astonishing discovery of a woman in his house, his own exhaustion, making him oddly vulnerable, making him aware of a hole a mile deep where his soul should be.

He watched Amy Mitchell, on her hands and knees, picking up the pieces of the puzzle, stuffing them into a box. Out of the corner of his eye he could see the baby roll off his rear end onto all fours.

With startling speed and unsettling determination, he crawled across the floor, making a beeline for Ty.

Ty stepped out of his way. The baby followed like a heat-seeking missile locked on target.

"Papa!" he yelled.

"Where is his papa?" he asked, deftly sidestepping the baby one more time.

CHAPTER TWO

"So, that's what they call the Texas two-step," Amy said, rocking back on her heels to watch, after something in Ty's tone had made her look up from where she was gathering the puzzle pieces.

"It's not funny. Tell him to stop it."

But it was funny, watching the big cowboy trying, not without desperation, to evade the determined baby. She giggled.

The cowboy glanced at her, glared, shifted away from the baby. "Don't laugh," he warned her.

"I'm sorry. It just looks as if you'd be completely unfazed by almost anything life threw at you. And you're running from a baby!"

"I am not running," he said tersely. "Call him off."

She did laugh then. Ty glared at her, stepped away from the baby. He had waltzed around half the living room.

"Just stop and pick him up," Amy managed to advise between snorts of laughter. "He thinks it's a game."

Oh, it felt good to laugh. She knew it was partly re-action to the situation she found herself in, a release from the fear she had felt when she had been startled by the big cowboy appearing in a home she'd already been busy making hers. But life had been such a serious affair for far too long.

The tall cowboy glaring at her warningly only seemed to make it more impossible to control her rising mirth.

"Now you want me to pick him up? Before you were going to hit me with a lamp if I even looked at him."

"That was when I thought you were the intruder," she said, wiping at her eyes. "Now I know it's me who is the intruder. If you pick him up and cuddle him for a few seconds, he'll lose interest."

"Cuddle?"

"You mustn't say that as if I'm asking you to get friendly with a rattlesnake!"

"It was the word *cuddle* that I took offense to!"

"A threat to your masculinity, is it?"

"I'm wet. I'm dirty."

"You're scared."

He looked at her darkly, and then heaved a sigh.

"Terrified," he admitted, and the laughter, recently tamed, burst free again. It still felt good to release the tension that had been building in her since Ty Halliday had set her world upside down by coming in the back door of the house she had been assuming was going to be all hers for the next six months.

The tiniest smile tugged at the edges of that hard mouth, and her laughter died. Nothing in her entire existence—she'd lived all over the world, gone to university, married into a well-to-do society family—had prepared her for a man like Ty Halliday.

In a world filled with illusions, the man was absolutely, one hundred per cent real. He had physical power

and presence. He was as big as an oak tree, and just as
solid. He had seemed to fill the room, to charge the air
in it with a subtle hiss of dark sensuality. There was
something about him standing there, all cowboy, that
was equal parts menace and romance.

There was toughness in the chiseled angles of his
dark whisker-shadowed face, something uncompro-
mising about the set of his chin, the muscle that jerked
along his jawline, the hard lack of humor around the
line of his lips.

He was handsome—Amy was not sure she had ever
seen eyes that color, a flinty blue sapphire—almost
beyond words, but his good looks were of the un-
touchable variety. He wore solitude, self-reliance, as
comfortably as he wore that past-his-knees, dark, dripping Australian-style riding coat that emphasized the
broadness of his shoulders and the impossible length
of his legs.

"If you pick him up, the chasing-papa game will be
over," she said, though suddenly she was not at all sure
she wanted to see her baby in those strong arms.

She needn't have worried. Ty Halliday was not picking up anyone's baby. He stepped away, Jamey followed,
crowing demandingly.

"At least stop and pat him on the head and say hello
to him. His name is Jamey, with a *Y*."

"The *Y* part is important?"

"Very important," she said solemnly. It marked one
of the few occasions she had stood up to her husband
and her in-laws. They had wanted James. She had not.
She had thought *Jamey* was a wonderful compromise.
They had not. But for once, she had stood firm.

"Just try it," she said encouragingly.

Ty stopped, contemplated the situation. Jamey pitched himself into the hesitation, grabbed the hem of the wet coat and pulled himself up.

"Papa."

Looking very much as if he was reaching out to a full-grown tiger, Ty rested a reluctant hand on Jamey's nest of red curls.

"Hey. Little fella. Jamey."

"Papa," Jamey crooned, leaned into the jacket without letting go, and plopped his thumb in his mouth.

"Why does he think I'm his papa, for heaven's sake?"

"Don't take it personally. He calls every man that."

"Why? Where is his papa?"

Ty looked at her then, and his gaze seemed uncomfortably all-seeing.

"Are you running from something?" he asked softly.

She actually shivered from the fierce look that crossed his face. She told herself not to take it personally. He would just be one of those men with a very traditional set of values, thinking women and children—much as he disliked the latter—were in need of his extremely masculine self for protection.

Amy hated that the old-fashioned notion actually filled her with the oddest sense of comfort.

"What would make you think I'm running from something?" she hedged, because of course that was uncomfortably close to the truth.

"Less than a week before Christmas, and you're looking for a new home?"

"It's just the timing," she said. "The McFinleys wanted to be in Australia by Christmas."

He did not look convinced, but he did not look as if he cared to pursue it, either.

"Where's his papa?" he asked again, patting Jamey—who was showing absolutely no sign of losing interest in him—with surprising gentleness, on the head.

"I'm a widow," she said quietly. "Jamey's father was killed in an accident three months after he was born. It's nearly nine months ago now."

Some shadow passed over his face and through the depths of those amazing sapphire eyes. She felt as if Ty Halliday could clearly see the broken place in her.

She could feel his awkwardness. It was obvious from his house that he was a man alone in the world, and had been for a long time. There was not a single feminine touch in this place. It was also obvious he was a man allergic to attachments. There were no pictures, no family photographs. There was no ring on his finger.

On arriving, she had thought the McFinleys had taken their personal touches down so that she could put up her own and feel more at home. But she had not even asked herself about the unlocked door, the lack of curtains, or throw rugs or little lace dollies. She had not asked herself about the dresser still filled with neatly folded clothes.

Now, feeling his eyes on her, Amy knew it was way beyond this solitary cowboy's skill level to know what to say to her. She was touched when he tried.

"That seems to fall squarely into the life-is-unfair department," he said gently.

She lifted her chin. "I stopped expecting life to be fair a long time ago."

He frowned. "No, you didn't."

"Pardon me?"

"That sounds like something I would say. And you're not like me."

"And what are you like?"

"Cynical. World-weary."

"That's me exactly!" she protested.

A small smile teased the devastating curve of his lips. "No, it's not," he said. "You just wish it was. It's evident from looking at you, you are nothing of the sort."

"You can't possibly know that about me on such a short acquaintance."

"Yes, I can."

"How?" she demanded, folding her arms over her chest, some defense against what he was seeing. No, what he *thought* he was seeing.

She was not the naive girl she had once been, so reliant on the approval of others, begging for love, so desperate for a place to call home that it had made her overlook things she should have seen. Amy Mitchell was on a new path now.

She was going to be fully independent. She was not going to rely on anyone else to make a home for her and her baby.

Looking after the McFinley house, venturing so far from the familiar, expanding her website, Baby Bytes, into a viable business from there, were all part of her new vision for her life.

She hated it that a complete stranger thought he could see through it.

She hated it even more that her first day of her new life was turning into something of a fiasco.

Thankfully, no one but Ty Halliday ever needed to know.

She had called her in-laws as soon as she stepped in the door to let them know she had arrived safely.

She had heard her mother-in-law's disapproval, so like her son's had been.

"For heaven's sake, Amy, give up this harebrained scheme. John and I are delighted to look after you and Jamey. Delighted."

Delighted to control and criticize her, just like their son had done. Delighted to keep her dependent on them. She shivered. Wouldn't they love to see the predicament she was in now?

But they never had to know. In a little while she would be where she was supposed to be, none the worse for the wear, no one to question her competence.

"By the way," she said, "before I forget, I owe you money for a phone call. My cell phone wouldn't work here. Now, how can you know so much about me?"

"No one with a truly jaded soul would offer me money for a phone call I wouldn't even know you made for a month. And no one truly fed up with life arrives at a new home and makes it their first priority to put up a Christmas tree," he said.

"Oh."

"I don't even know where you found this stuff. The tree is obviously too big to have arrived in your shrimpy little car."

That shrimpy little car was the first major purchase she had ever made on her own. Her mother-in-law, not aware that Baby Nap had just signed up to be a sponsor on the website, had not thought it was a sensible use of funds.

"I prefer to think of it as sporty," Amy said proudly. The car was part of the new independent her!

"Sporty. Shrimpy. There is no way a Christmas tree arrived in the trunk of it."

"The tree was in your basement."

He turned and scanned her face, looking for a lie. "This tree was in *my* basement?"

"Along with all the decorations and lights and such."

"No kidding." He whistled, long and low. "Who would buy an artificial tree when there are a million real ones two steps out the back door?"

"So you usually have a real tree?" she asked.

He snorted. "We've never had a tree up in this house."

"But why?" she whispered, horrified by his revelation.

He looked at her and shook his head. "You want me to believe you're cynical when you cannot imagine a world with no Christmas tree, a world without fluffy white kittens, a world without fresh baked chocolate chip cookies?"

"Is it for religious reasons?" she asked solemnly.

He threw back his head and laughed then, but it was not a nice laugh.

"Religion is as foreign to this house as Christmas trees. And now, Miss Cynical, you look like you took a wrong turn and ended up in the devil's den."

At least he had dropped the *Mrs*.

Amy was aware she should let it go. And couldn't. "I just can't believe you never had a Christmas tree. Why?"

"It wasn't a big deal. My mom left when I was about

the same age as your little guy. It was just me and my dad. Christmas was just another day, filled with hard work and the demands of the ranch."

She felt appalled, and it must have shown on her face.

"Don't get me wrong. The neighbors always had us for dinner."

That did not make her feel any less appalled. "Your mom left you?" She knew she shouldn't have asked, but she couldn't help it. She thought of what it would take to make her leave Jamey.

And the only answer she could come up with was death.

He was irritated by her question, and it was clear he had no intention of answering her. He rolled his shoulders, and she could tell he hated that he had said anything about himself that might be construed as inviting sympathy. She offered it nonetheless.

"I guess I'm not the only one life has been unfair to," she said softly into his silence.

He wouldn't look at her. He shook free of Jamey, again and moved over, looked in one of the boxes. He shuffled through some old ornaments and a Christmas tree star.

And then he took his hand out and stared at it.

He was holding a packet of letters, yellow with age, tied with a blue ribbon. He swore, his voice a low, animal growl of pain.

Amy froze, stared at him wide-eyed.

"Sorry," he muttered, and rubbed his brow with a tired hand. "Sorry."

"What's wrong?" she asked, and she knew instantly,

from the way his expression closed, that he couldn't bear it that she could see something was wrong.

He shoved the letters into a deep pocket on his jacket.

"I've just come home from a real devil of a day to find my house invaded by a lamp-wielding stranger with a baby who wants to call me Papa. What's wrong? Why, nothing!"

"I'm sorry," Amy said. "I really am. I'm leaving as fast as I can."

And she meant it.

There was something about him that was so alone it made her ache. It made her want to lay her hand on the thickness of that powerful wrist and say to him, *Tell me.*

But if he did, if he ever confided in her, she knew instinctively it would change something irrevocably and forever.

Like her plan for a new life.

Still, looking into his closed face, she knew she was in no danger from his confidences.

He kept things to himself.

He did not lean.

He did not rely.

He was the last of a dying breed, a ruggedly independent man who was entirely self-sufficient, confident in his own strength to be enough to get him by in an unforgiving environment.

He was totally alone in the world, and he liked it that way.

She was leaving. She did not need to know one more single thing about him.

He moved to the window, away from Jamey's relentless pursuit. He looked out and sighed.

"I don't think life is quite done being unfair to either one of us," he said, his voice deep, edged with gravel and gruffness.

"What do you mean?"

"Come and see for yourself."

Amy moved beside him and was stunned to see that while she had been decorating the tree, oblivious, a storm had deepened outside the window. The snow was mounding on his driveway, like heaps of fresh whipped cream. Already the gravel road that twisted up to the house was barely discernible from the land around it.

His eyes still on the window, not looking at her, he said, "Mrs. Mitchell?"

"Amy."

"Whatever. You won't be going anywhere tonight."

"Not going anywhere tonight?" Amy echoed. But she *had* to. She had to correct her mistake, hopefully before anyone else found out.

The urgency to do so felt as if it intensified the moment he said she wasn't going anywhere.

If there was one thing Amy Mitchell was through with, it was being controlled. It was somebody telling her what to do. It was being treated as an inferior rather than an equal.

And she fully intended to make that clear to Mr. Ty Halliday. He wasn't going to tell her what to do.

"I *have* to go," she said.

"This isn't the city. Going out in that isn't quite the same as going to the corner store for a jug of milk. If you get in trouble—"

"And you think I will."

"—and I think there's a chance you might, it can turn deadly."

She shivered at that.

"There's not a lot of people out here waiting to rescue you if you go in the ditch or off the road, or get lost some more or run out of gas."

"I'm a very good driver," she said. "I've been driving in winter conditions my whole life."

"*Urban* winter conditions," he guessed, and made no effort to hide his scorn. "I don't think that's a chance you want to take with your baby."

"You're probably overstating it."

"Why would I do that?" he asked, and his eyebrows shot up in genuine bewilderment.

Yes, why would he? He had made it plain her and Jamey's being here was an imposition on him. The possibility startled her that he wasn't trying to control her, that he was only being practical.

"The native people have lived in this country longer than both of us," he continued quietly. "When they see this kind of weather, they just stop wherever they are and make the best of it. They don't think about where they want to be or what time they should be there and who might be waiting for them. They stay in the moment and its reality and that's why they don't end up dead the way somebody who is married to their agenda might."

Amy saw, reluctantly, how right he was. This was the kind of situation that had made her husband, Edwin, mental. And her in-laws. Delayed flights. Dinner late. Any wrench in their carefully laid plans sent them off the deep end.

This was her new life. If she just applied the same

old rules—if she rigidly adhered to her plan—wasn't she going to get the same old thing? Feeling uptight and harried and like she had somehow failed to be perfect?

What if instead she saw this as an opportunity to try something new, a different approach to life? What if she relaxed into what life had given her rather than trying to force it to meet her vision and expectation?

What if she acted as if she was free? What if she just made the best of whatever came?

Her desire to protest, to have her own way, suddenly seemed silly and maybe even dangerous, so she let it dissipate.

And when it was gone, she looked at Ty Halliday, standing in the window, his coat drawn around him, his handsome face remote, and she was not sure she had ever seen anyone so alone.

At any time of year, that probably would have struck her as poignant.

But at Christmas?

What did it mean that he had never put up a Christmas tree, not even when he was a child? That seemed unbearably sad to her, and intensified that sense she had of him being terribly and absolutely alone in the world.

What if she used these altered circumstances to make the best of it? What if she made the best of it by giving him an unexpected gift? What if she overcame her own hurt, the unfairness of her own life, and gave this stranger a gift?

A humble gift. A decorated tree.

Wasn't that really what Christmas was all about? When she had left the safety of her old world behind her this morning, she hadn't been running away from something, as he had guessed.

No, she hoped she was running toward something. Hadn't she hoped she was moving toward something she had lost? Some truth about who she really was? Or maybe about who she wanted to be? About the kind of life she wanted to give her baby?

She did not want to be so wrapped up in her own grievances she could not be moved by the absolute aloneness of another human being.

She took a deep breath.

"Okay," she said, "I guess I could stay. Just for the night."

He turned and looked at her, one eyebrow lifted, as if amused she thought she had a choice.

"In the morning," he said with the annoying and quiet confidence of a man who was accustomed to being deferred to, "I'll see that you get where you're going."

I'll look after you.

Maybe it was the fury of the storm that made that seem attractive. Or maybe, Amy thought, she had an inherent weakness in her character that made her want to be looked after!

"I can clearly see it makes sense to avoid going out in the storm tonight, but no thank you to your offer to show me the way in the morning. I am quite capable of looking after myself."

The wind gusted so strongly that it rattled the glass of the window, hurled snow against it. Nature, in its unpredictable wrath, was reminding her that some things were going to be out of her control.

But not, she reminded herself, how she handled those

things. And so she would be a better person and finish decorating this tree, her gift to a stranger, before she left here tomorrow and never looked back. It would not matter to her if he didn't show appreciation.

Somewhere in his heart he would feel the warmth of the tree and the gesture, and be moved by it.

She slid him another glance, and saw the man was dead on his feet. And that he was soaked from the top of his dripping cowboy hat to his wet socks. He hadn't driven up in a vehicle.

"You were out in that," she said, and was ashamed by how thoroughly she had made it all about her.

He glanced at her and seemed to find her concern amusing. "That's my world," he said with a touch of wryness. "Besides, it wasn't that bad then."

"You're starving," she guessed. "And frozen."

He said nothing, a man accustomed to discomfort, to pitting his strength against whatever the world brought him, and expecting to win. Ty Halliday was obviously a man entirely used to looking after himself.

So, since she was stuck here anyway, she would make the best of it, and this would become part of her gift to him.

"I've got a chicken potpie in the oven. I'll make a salad while you go shower. Everything should be ready in twenty minutes."

Her take-charge tone of voice was probably spoiled somewhat by the fire she felt creep up her cheeks after she mentioned the shower.

The very thought of him in the shower, steam rising off a body that she could tell was hard-muscled and powerful, made something hot and sweet and wildly uncomfortable unfold inside of her.

He regarded her for a moment too long. She suspected he wanted to refuse even this tiniest offer to enter his world. But then he sniffed the air like a hungry wolf and surrendered to the fact she was already in his world. He turned away.

"Thanks," he said gruffly. "It smells good."

She could tell it was not easy for him to accept her offer, but obviously, like her, he knew he had to just try and make the best of an awkward situation.

He went by her, and his scent overrode that of the potpie in the oven. He smelled of wet oilskin, wild horses, pure man, and his aroma enveloped her. And then he was gone. Amy waited until she heard a door down the hallway snap shut before she went and sank down on her knees beside her baby. She was aware her knees were trembling.

The wrong house?

Her clothes, her partially unpacked suitcase, were spread out on Ty Halliday's bed!

It all seemed as if it might be a terrible omen. She had set out on the road this morning to a brand-new life.

She had not listened to the objections of her family or her in-laws.

She was done with the stuffiness of it all. She was done with being stifled. Lectured. Patronized.

This morning, she had felt joy unfurl in her for the first time in a long time. Amy had followed her heart instead of her head.

But where had it led her?

Amy tried to still the trembling of her knees and her heart by picking up Jamey and settling him on her lap.

"Papa?" he asked, a plaintive whisper, his eyes glued to the place where Ty Halliday had disappeared down the hallway.

"No, sweetie, not Papa." There was no sense telling Jamey, yet again, there was no papa. In all his nearly a year of wisdom, even though his father had been gone for longer than he had been in Jamey's life, Jamey had become determined to have what his little pals at play school had—a daddy.

"Papa," Jamey insisted, leaning back into her and putting his thumb in his mouth.

Amy heard the shower turn on in another part of the house and was horrified to feel a heated blush move up her cheeks.

Good grief! She had set out this morning on a mission. To find herself. Her real self. Who she was genuinely meant to be.

She could not let the first obstacle—no matter that he was large and intimidating—make her feel as if she was on the wrong road!

She had to act the part of the confident woman she was determined to become. That woman ran her own business and her own house and was not always flinching from put-downs.

Amy refused to go any further down that road, feeling guilty as always, for acknowledging she might not have been completely satisfied with the life her husband had given her.

Out loud, quietly, she said, "I will not be a schoolgirl who blushes at the thought of a man in the shower."

But, of course, the man in that shower was not any man.

Could anything prepare a woman for the kind of raw magnetism Ty Halliday radiated?

Could anything prepare a woman for a man who moved with such unconscious grace, as fluid as water, so at home with his own power? Could anything prepare a woman for that kind of pure masculine energy, the kind that felt like a force field around him, sizzling, faintly but alluringly dangerous?

Could anything prepare a woman for the strength that radiated out from under the brim of that soaked hat, from underneath that wet slicker like a palpable force?

The answer was no.

But she reminded herself firmly of her mission.

Tomorrow she would be back on the right road. Tonight she would decorate that tree as her gift to a stranger. She would cook him a hot meal. That was it.

Tomorrow her quest would resume. She was on a journey. She was determined to find out who she really was, and what really mattered. She had lost sight of both things since her marriage.

And Ty Halliday was just an uncomfortable—and brief—detour from that quest. Amy put down her baby and went to rummage through Ty's ill-equipped kitchen.

Amy made a vow. She resolved not to let his shocking appeal alter her focus. She put Jamey on his blanket surrounded by his toys and checked the chicken potpie she'd put in the oven earlier for their supper.

She frowned. The pie was not cooking properly, and she suspected the oven was not producing the correct heat for the temperature it was set at. She turned it up, and the oven made a protesting noise. The oven seemed decidedly cranky.

"Just like its owner," she muttered.

"Papa," Jamey supplied.

"Precisely." And then she realized she could not start agreeing, even casually, with Jamey labeling Ty as his papa.

"Don't call him that, sweetie. He's not your papa."

"Umpa?"

"No, not your grandpa, either. Call him—" The oven made another noise, and she went and opened the door and peered in. The burner was red-hot and making a hissing sound.

"Oh, damn," she said, and turned it back down.

"Odam," Jamey repeated.

"Sure," she said distractedly, "call him that."

The oven looked after, and papa renamed something Jamey could pronounce, Amy turned to the salad.

In every place in the world where her family had moved to, Amy, to her career-oriented mother's bewilderment, had always found sanctuary in the kitchen. She loved to cook.

As she was ripping and washing lettuce, she heard the water shut off in the bathroom and had a renegade thought about naked wet skin and steam.

And then, as if her thoughts were too hot to handle, the smoke alarm started to shriek.

She turned from the sink to see smoke was roiling out of the oven.

Jamey, startled, began to wail along with the smoke alarm.

Amy donned the red oven mitt with the hole burned

right through it, and opened the oven door a crack. Just as she had suspected, the potpie had boiled over onto the burner.

She shut the oven off and slammed the door. She opened the kitchen window, and picked up her howling baby.

"Hey. Hey, little man, it's okay."

But it wasn't. Because just then, through the haze of smoke that filled the kitchen, Ty appeared.

Ty scanned the room, every muscle taut. Amy could have sworn he was prepared to lay down his life for her and Jamey, two near strangers. A strange emotion clawed at her throat.

Then, when Ty saw there was no emergency, he stood down. Instantly. He went from ready to relaxed in a second, though a certain level of annoyance marred his altogether too handsome features.

But while Ty relaxed, Amy felt as if her nerve endings were singing with tension. It wasn't just that he had been prepared to lay down his life for them, either.

No, Ty Halliday was nearly naked, clad only in boxer shorts.

And if the smoke alarm had not been going off before, it certainly would have started now. Because Ty Halliday was nearly naked. Even his feet were sexy!

He was everything she had imagined he would be, only about a hundred times off the scale of where her imagination went to.

His dark slashing eyebrows, the dark shadow of whiskers on his face, had made her think his hair would be dark under the cowboy hat he had worn.

But he was blond, his wet hair the color of antique pieces of gold in a just opened treasure chest.

But the astonishing color of his hair held her attention for only a millisecond. He was lean and strong and his skin was flawless. His arms, corded with muscles of honed steel, were deeply tanned, a color that didn't go away, apparently, even in these long days of winter. His legs were equally powerful-looking: long, straight, made to curve around a horse, or a bucking bull, or…

She couldn't go there. Instead, she let her hungry gaze go to his chest, deep and smooth. His shoulders were impossibly broad and his stomach a perfect washboard of rippling, hard muscle. Ty was just way too hot to handle, and as the smoke detector continued to shriek, Amy was aware her own five-alarm fire had started going off deep inside of her.

She dared look at the boxers. Her mouth fell open.

Ty Halliday was wearing bright red boxer shorts, low, snugged over his flat hips and the taut lines of his lower belly. And what were his red boxer shorts covered with?

Santa, his sleigh and twelve reindeer. She presumed twelve reindeer, because she really shouldn't count.

She didn't want to appear too interested, but she could not draw her eyes away until she had read the words that were also dancing across the shorts.

Have you been naughty or nice?

For the second time that day, she started to laugh. She laughed so hard the tears squirted from her eyes.

Or maybe that was the smoke.

Ty folded those gorgeous muscled arms over an equally gorgeous muscled chest, planted his long, muscled legs far apart.

If it weren't for the shorts, he would definitely have the intimidating presence she was fairly certain he was aiming for.

"I don't see what's so funny," he yelled over the screaming alarm, the baby howling and her laughter.

"You don't?" she gasped.

"No, I don't," he said sternly.

"Ty Halliday, you have some Christmas spirit, after all." She pointed. "You just keep it well hidden."

CHAPTER THREE

Ty followed her pointing finger, unfolded his arms and looked down at himself.

He said three words in a row that made the baby stop yelling for a moment, and stare at him with wide-eyed wariness.

He would have appreciated a little wide-eyed wariness from Amy, but she was smirking mirthfully.

"Oh, my," she said silkily. "Are you blushing?"

"No." He folded his arms again, leveled a warning look at her, which she ignored.

"Yes, you are."

"You're bluffing. There's no way you can tell through all this smoke what color my face is. But you can take my word for it, Amy, I haven't blushed since I was ten or eleven years old."

Amy. He contemplated that. How had Mrs. Mitchell become Amy so quickly?

Marching by her with as much dignity as he could muster, Ty grabbed a towel from the drawer he had described to her earlier. He went and stood under the smoke detector and flailed at it until the rush of air created by the tea towel infused it with enough fresh air to shut off.

Still laughing, she went across the kitchen, scooped up the baby and covered his tearstained face with kisses. He hiccupped several times, and then stopped crying, abruptly, as if someone had pulled a switch.

The silence was blessed.

"Don't believe him," she told the baby. "Nobody *stops* blushing when they're eleven. That's when they start."

Ty ordered himself not to show the slightest curiosity. But, despite the order, he heard himself saying skeptically, "You remember what made you blush at eleven?"

"Of course."

He ordered himself not to pursue it. He heard himself say, "And?"

"The cruelty of boys, of course. First bra. The back strap being snapped."

He did not want to be thinking about her with her first bra. Or any bra at all. But once a man's mind went to those places it was tougher than wrestling an ornery steer to bring it back in line.

Black and slinky? Red and sexy? White and sporty? He hardened his features as she squinted at him.

"You're right," she decided. "I don't think you are blushing. So, what made you stop blushing at the tender age of eleven?"

He was standing in his kitchen in his underwear, being encouraged to exchange confidences with a perfect stranger. He ordered himself to go get dressed.

Instead, he said, "I was raised by a man, around a family of men, a couple of old ranch hands who were as tough and as hard as two buckets of old nails. The hands seemed to consider it part of their job to educate me, no matter how embarrassing the information they imparted was.

"I was toughened up on incessant teasing, prank-pulling and roughhousing. Those guys considered it their sacred and sworn duty to ferret out any form of weakness in me and snuff it out before it blossomed. Believe me, by the time I was ten or eleven, I'd learned absolute control over my reactions to everything."

He'd said way too much. She looked horrified and fascinated, as if she had met a man raised by wolves.

Which, of course, was probably not that far off the mark.

So, no, he knew he was not blushing. Though if ever a situation called for embarrassment it was this one!

Ty had just stepped out of the shower when he'd heard the smoke detector going off. He'd gone into rescue mode, some deep instinct he didn't know he had kicking in. There was a baby and a woman in his house, and if the place was on fire, he had to get them out.

But even in hero mode, he wasn't running out there naked.

And so he'd opened his bottom drawer—he was into the stuff he *never* wore because he hadn't gotten at the laundry for a while—and randomly picked something to shove on.

Now, his adrenaline still pumping, even though it was obvious his house was not on fire and no one needed him to be a hero, he looked down at his choice of attire again.

He said the three words again. Jamey commenced howling.

Amy and Jamey gave him identical looks of accusation, though hers was tempered by that tiny smile that wouldn't quit, and that kept drawing Ty's eyes back to the full, luscious curve of her plump bottom lip.

"Oh, I get it," she said. "You swear instead of blush. Very manly."

She was being sarcastic!

"There, there," she said, patting the baby's plump shoulder. It seemed it would be ineffectual against the tears and hollering, but both subsided almost instantly, and Jamey burrowed deep into his mother's shoulder.

Then he peered at Ty with yet more accusation, put his thumb in his mouth and took a long pull on it.

"Odam," he said through his thumb, and then slurped contentedly.

"See?" Ty said approvingly. "It's what men do. They swear. Your baby just said 'damn.'"

"He did not swear!" she said indignantly.

"Mild, but still a cuss. Good boy."

"Stop it. He wasn't cursing. I think he may be calling on the Viking god."

"Ha! You're telling me your baby is versed in Viking mythology?" Ty realized he was enjoying this little interchange.

She shrugged as if it was a possibility. That damned smile was still tickling along the luscious lines of her lips.

"I mean, I'm all for embracing Viking ways," he said. "No Christmas."

"Tell your shorts you don't like Christmas." She looked as though she was going to start laughing again. Her laughter was one of the nicest sounds he had ever heard. He felt it could be like a drug, making him weak when he needed to be strong.

But even so, a man had to defend himself. "Just to set the record straight, for your information, I didn't buy these for myself. We do a gift exchange with the neighbors. It's mostly gag gifts."

"All right," she said soothingly, "I get it. Christmas spirit only by accident in the Halliday household."

He nodded his confirmation. "And just while I'm setting the record straight, his name is Odin."

She looked baffled.

"The Norse god, worshipped by the Vikings. Odin. Not Odam."

Her mouth fell open.

He knew he had said quite enough, but he didn't even bother ordering himself to stop, because he felt as if he couldn't.

"Also, while we're setting the record straight, I'm not just some dumb cowboy who fell off the hay wagon yesterday."

Why was he saying this? She didn't need to know this!

Obviously, there had been no one around except the horses and cows to talk to for a very long time. Too long. His mouth felt as if it was running like a river that had been let loose of a dam.

"I read," he said, "I read all the time. I read everything I can get my hands on."

"Have you really read *Jane Eyre?*"

He wasn't going to stand here in his underwear making confessions about his reading material. He felt

annoyed enough with himself that he had told her something so integral to who he was.

There it was again, his childhood, rising like a ghost.
A lonely little boy longing for his mother, reading his
pain away despite the fact that he had been teased un-
mercifully for it. It had never stopped him, though,
maybe even driven him deeper into his passion for
books.

When he said nothing, her eyes went round. "You
have!"

He said nothing, turned on his heel, went into his
room and got dressed. If he chose more carefully than
normal, he wasn't admitting that to anyone, least of all
not himself.

Dinner was delicious, ambrosia to a man who ate out
of a can and a freezer, unless one of the neighbors took
pity on him and delivered a casserole. Ty had ordered
himself not to say one more revealing thing to Amy, but
he needn't have worried. She didn't bring up the subject
of his reading material.

She had her hands full with the baby. Ty did not have
a great deal of experience being around babies, eating,
or otherwise.

Ty had no high chair in his house, so the squirming
Jamey was on his mother's lap, seemingly doing his
best to dodge the spoon his mother held for him and
eat with his hands.

Between food being thrown on the floor to exuberant shouts of "oops" and food being smashed to a chant
of "Odam," the baby kept his mother hopping and Ty
thoroughly entertained.

"Wow," Ty said, when the baby's bowl was finally

empty. "I don't know if any of that got in his mouth. There's goo in his ears, eyes and nose, and between his toes, and all over you, but as far as I could see not a single crumb made it to his mouth. Not that he looks undernourished."

She brushed crumbs off her blouse and shook them out of her hair, then rose, baby on her hip, and began to clear plates.

"Stop it. I'll do that."

For a moment, she looked as if she was going to protest, but then she looked at the baby, and his head-to-toe covering of chicken potpie.

"Are you sure you don't mind? I could pop him in the bath before bed. You don't mind if I put him in your tub?"

"Of course not. Thank you for the dinner. It was the best thing I've had in a long time."

"You're welcome. Come on, Jamey, bath time."

After he'd cleared the dishes, he took a quick look through the open door of the bathroom and said goodnight to them both. Ty was done, physically finished, and worried his exhaustion might get him blabbing again. He did not want a quiet moment alone with her once the baby was in bed.

Jamey, wet and pink, was now as covered with bubbles as he had been with chicken potpie. He leaned forward, arms upstretched, making loud smacking noises.

"He wants a kiss."

"He might as well learn now that what he wants and what he gets are two different things."

"Did you learn that from the ranch hands?" she shot back at him.

"Yeah. I did. The cowboy way. And it has stood me in good stead, too."

"I can clearly see you radiate happiness," she said sweetly.

He gave her a sour look and went into his bedroom, away from *that* look in her eyes, knowing and sympathetic. Well, he had no one to blame but himself, blabbing his life history to her.

From behind his closed bedroom door, Ty slipped off his jeans and rolled into bed. He could hear the bath noises. Someone was obviously *radiating* happiness.

The baby's bath time was imbued with the same level of enthusiasm and joy as eating had been. There was gleeful chortles, splashing, motorboat noises, gurgles, clapping and games.

Ty tried putting his pillow over his head.

All it did was muffle the happiness that had invaded his house.

And then the invaders were in the bedroom beside his. Ty had moved Amy's suitcase off his bed and in there. He only had two bedrooms, so she was going to have to share the space she had set up for the baby. There was a twin bed, she had a playpen set up with a little nest of pale blue blankets and stuffed toys in its confines for the baby to sleep in.

Ty realized how thin the walls were. He gave up on the pillow. She didn't ever have to know he was eavesdropping on story time.

She read three stories, and Ty found himself hanging on every word. He recognized the stories, ones he had begged the kindergarten teacher to lend him, in love with stories from the first encounter. That teacher had been a kind woman, and lent the little motherless boy all the books he could haul home.

He had shown his father the books hopefully, but his dad had looked baffled by them. He'd flipped through them impatiently, looking at the pictures of little creatures dressed in human clothes and living in human houses with amazed dismay. Then he'd shoved the precious books back at Ty.

"I don't have time for make-believe," he'd said gruffly.

And so, carefully, greedily, looking at pictures and sounding out the words to *Curious George* and others by himself in his bed at night, long after his exhausted father had gone to sleep, he would read by flashlight.

Only years later did Ty figure out his father's reading skills were only rudimentary. His father had always known Halliday Creek Ranch would be his life, just as it had been his father's before that. He had not seen a use for education, and school had been a painful experience for him, one he could not wait to leave behind.

Now, listening to the stories, Ty wondered if his father had *wanted* to read to him. He dismissed the thought as quickly as it came.

Amy finished the bedtime stories with a tale Ty had not heard, called *Love You Forever,* and Ty felt the emotionally evocative words pull on someplace in him like a gathering storm.

He could hear her putting the baby in the playpen, imagined her covering him with a blanket. There was not a single protest.

And then he knew why.

She had saved the best for last.

She began to sing Jamey lullabies. Her voice was clear and true, shining like stars coming out in an evening sky.

And suddenly Ty's heart was heavy, and his eyes were heavy, and her soft voice was soaring in his ears. A yearning was sitting on his chest like a weight. It was for a wish unrealized. It was for all the things that had never been.

And that he had long since accepted would never be.

He slept when the songs were done, instantly and deeply, the sleep of an exhausted man.

When he awoke in the morning, he was aware of two things. First, it had snowed through the night, and probably hard. The house had that quiet to it, outside sounds of cattle and birds and horses muffled by a layer of snow on the ground and on the roof.

Second, he was intensely and instantly aware he was not in the house by himself. He was not sure why that awareness was so sharp. The child and the woman were making no sound, almost certainly still asleep in these predawn hours that he habitually woke in.

So, how did he know? The smells from last night's dinner, the chicken potpie scorched on the burner and the baby's bath lingering in the air?

No, those smells seemed to be gone, replaced by more tempting ones. Ty was sure he could faintly smell popcorn, and something else. Surely she hadn't got to baking after she'd put the baby to bed?

But more than smells, he knew it was being a man alone that had made him sensitive to the presence of others in his house. He could feel it tickling along his skin, almost as if the notes from her song had left something shivering in the air long after her voice had died away and both he and the baby had slept.

Ty rose quickly, dressed quietly and went on silent feet from his room.

The house was still, as he had known it would be, the guest room door slightly ajar.

He tiptoed through to the kitchen, put on coffee. He would take a travel mug with him, go outside and do chores without awakening his visitors. When he got back they would be up, and he could help her pack her stuff in her little car and wave at her as she went down the driveway.

She'd probably ask for an email address so she could keep in touch. And he didn't have one, so that would be the end of that.

He turned to the back porch, but a flicker of light drew his attention to the living room.

He froze, stared, moved forward.

Last night, when he had gone to bed, the tree had been at the same stage as when he had walked in the evening before. The lights had been on it, but nothing else.

Now, as if Santa's elves had appeared in the night, it had been transformed into a glorious thing. The lights had been left plugged in and winked with bright cheer. The star shone like a beacon from the top of it.

Astoundingly, the tree had been completely decorated.

Ty could barely see the offensive artificial branches there was so much stuff on the tree. He was sure those few scant boxes of decorations could not have filled the branches like this.

Almost against his will, he was drawn closer.

He had smelled popcorn. Strings of it were looped around the tree. And he *had* smelled baking. Because she had made up for the lack of ornaments by hanging cookies. He stepped closer again. The cookies were shaped like round ornaments, and like trees, and like Christmas parcels, all decorated with different colors of icing and sprinkles of candy.

It occurred to Ty that Amy must have arrived with all the things needed to make such intricate cookies stuffed into her little car, intent on making the perfect Christmas for her little boy.

And then, sometime yesterday, her intention had shifted.

She hadn't done this for Jamey.

They were leaving. They were leaving today.

No, she must have been up half the night doing this for him. Why? Ty thought he had made it clear that he did not invest in the sentiment of it all.

And that was probably why. She had been driven to show him what he was missing.

Great. He had managed to invoke her pity.

He tried to harden his heart to it, but it didn't work. Ty was shocked by how the gift of it wiggled by his customary cynicism, and made him feel a deep sense of humility.

Ty reached out, pulled one of the cookies off the tree, bit into it. It was delicious. He allowed a small smile. Perfect for him. An edible tree.

The chores needed doing, and he turned to leave all this magic behind him. He needed space around him— his space—to clear his head. And then he saw her.

Amy Mitchell was not in the guest room. She had fallen asleep in the big easy chair, curled up, her legs underneath her, her chin down on her neck. Her curls were flat in places and standing straight up in others. Her shirt was gaping open at the throat. The book he'd been reading and had left on a side table was spread out, open across her chest.

Had his choice of books told her something about him? He'd never been to university, but last year he had come across a reading list and was making his way through it. He moved Homer's *The Iliad* gently from her breast.

There was a blanket in a basket beside the chair and he hesitated. And then he took it and unfolded it, tucked it around her with a tenderness that astounded him. He fought off an impulse to touch those crazy curls.

He was glad she would be gone soon.

There was nothing in him that knew anything about being with a woman like this. She had seen his world was a hard place, with no soft edges, and made him the gift of the tree. Trying to show him something, or save him from something.

It didn't really matter which, because there was nothing in him that knew about the sensitivity and softness that would be required to appreciate a woman like this.

She represented everything he could not have.

And everything he had convinced himself he did not want, until he had heard her voice singing to the baby last night, woken up to the remarkably gentle gift of the tree. And he suspected that was her intention.

To let him have a glimpse at a softer world. To make him know he was missing something.

He turned his back on her swiftly. The thing about what she was offering him—once a man tasted that, he could start craving it. Craving was weakness.

He yanked on his boots, hat and coat, out of sorts now as he went out the back door. There he paused, stunned by what he saw. He had known from the muffled sounds this morning that it had snowed.

Nothing could have prepared him for how much.

The accumulated snow, when he stepped off his back stair, was nearly at his knee. In his lifetime, he had not seen so much snow in one dump. And the dump wasn't over. Though no snow was falling at the moment, the sky was leaden, the mountains obscured by thick, ominous cloud. He sniffed the air and could smell the threat. There was more snow coming.

He plowed a path with his boots, around the side of his house, to the front. He surveyed his driveway, though he had already known what he would see.

Her car was somewhere under a mound of snow that was precisely the same size and shape as an igloo.

It would take a hard day of plowing with his tractor to make his driveway reappear from under a stretch of snow that rolled clear to the mountains. And with more snow coming, was there any point in tackling that task?

Besides, beyond his driveway would the roads be open? Possibly. He would be able to turn on the radio and find out.

But what if the roads were open? A big truck with four-wheel drive and a driver with more guts than brains could get through on them.

But Ty felt as if it would border on criminal to allow her and the baby to leave in these conditions.

These conditions. The reality hit him.

Snowed in.

Ty remembered "snow" days from when he was a kid. Days the school bus couldn't get through on the roads. And since then, every few years there would be a day or two when he didn't get to the driveway with the plow and was stuck on the place.

It was never a big deal. He always had a freezer full of beef, a pantry stocked with tinned goods.

But now he had unexpected guests. And if felt like a very big deal, indeed. How long was she going to be here?

With a sinking heart, he realized it was going to be another day, at the very least.

He reminded himself the native people, so in tune with this land and the larger picture, would say just to make the best of it.

But when he thought of her singing to the baby, and that tree in his house, her gentle gift to him, and when he thought of how he felt tucking the blanket around her, he knew how easy it would be to feel attached to them.

That had really been his unspoken motto through much of his life: No Attachments.

He refused even to own a dog, the most pragmatic of men, he didn't see a cute little puppy. He saw how it was going to end.

Amy was stuck here. He was stuck with her. It was his job now to make sure they all got out of it with no one getting hurt.

He had to be indifferent to her. He had to. Not for his sake, but for hers. A long time ago, when he'd run wild on the rodeo circuit, a girl had told him, tearfully,

Cowboy, you are the kind of guy who breaks hearts. Because you don't have one.

So he just had to be himself, which was a heartless bastard. That shouldn't be too difficult for him. When he was able to get the driveway clear, Amy Mitchell would be so glad to get gone, that little car would go down the road as if it had been shot from a catapult.

As he was finishing up his chores, the snow had started again. The flakes were huge and wet, nearly obliterating his house from his view.

He came in the back door, knowing he had to tell her the bad news quick and get it over with. He glanced up from the porch and saw Amy sitting at the kitchen table. She looked pale, and her eyes smarted with tears.

At first he thought she must have already figured out she wasn't going anywhere. But then something about her stillness, and the look on her face, made him take the stairs two at time.

The frying pan was on the stove, turned off, half-cooked bacon in it.

"What happened?"

Mutely, she held one hand toward him, the fingers of her other hand circling a wrist that was as tiny, her bones as fragile as a sparrow's.

"I—I—I never used that kind of pan before. I didn't realize the handle would get so hot."

"What the—" he glanced at the hundred-year-old cast-iron frying pan, and then looked at her hand.

Across the palm was a welt, angry-looking and puckered, the imprint of the pan handle scorched into her skin like a brand.

He went on his knees in front of her, but when he

reached out to take her hand, to get a better look, she yanked it away.

"I might have to go to the hospital," she said, her effort at bravery diminished somewhat by the fact her whole body was trembling.

"Let me look."

She didn't want to trust him. Smart girl. But there was no one else, and so he captured her hand, held it firm, studied the burn. Bad, but not hospital bad, which given the condition of the roads was a good thing.

"Stupid of me," she said in a wooden voice.

He looked up from her hand.

"Just like coming here by accident. Dumb. It's what they all expect, and they're all right."

It occurred to him it wasn't because she hadn't trusted him that she hadn't wanted to show him her hand.

It was because she was afraid of being judged. Found stupid.

For a guy who didn't have a heart, he was surprised by where he felt that.

"Who?" he said quietly.

And then she was crying, big fat tears slithering down her cheeks.

"Everybody. My husband, his parents, my parents. Everybody treats me like I can't ever do anything right. Can't be trusted to make good decisions."

Considering how he had dreaded the thought of her crying when it had almost happened yesterday, considering he had a fully formulated plan that had *heartless bastard* at its core, Ty surprised himself by not bolting for the door.

Instead, inwardly, calmly, he acknowledged it would take a stronger man than he was to be indifferent to her.

Her palm still lay across his hand. He lifted it to his lips and blew gently on the burn. She went very still, and he looked up at her.

"Hey," he said, "it's going to be okay."

"It hurts so bad."

He wasn't quite sure if she meant the burn, or everyone's low expectations of her. He remembered seeing something in her face when she had said she was a widow, a torment of some kind. He'd thought it was because of her loss. Now he wondered if it wasn't a loss of a different sort instead.

"I'll fix it."

And he wasn't quite sure what he meant by that, either. The burn, or the wounded place in her that was so much deeper than the burn.

The burn would be easy.

And surely Ty had enough self-knowledge to know he could not be trusted with the other?

And then, even though his jacket was cold and wet with melting flakes of snow, she put her arms around his neck.

He felt her uninjured hand, warm and soft, trace the coldness of the exposed skin on the back of his neck. The other she held away from him. She leaned forward and put her forehead against his, drew in a deep trembling breath. He stiffened.

For a moment he froze, uncertain what to do with all this pain and all this trust.

And then the certainty came. As naturally as breathing, he put his arms around her and pulled her close into him, so close that he could feel her heart beating against the oilskin of the jacket. So close that her tears slithered down his neck along with melting snow.

And he held her, and then, something in him surrendered. He did what he realized he had wanted to do since the moment he had first seen her peeking at him from behind his tree.

He ran his fingers through her hair, and felt the tangles dissolve under his touch. She pulled back from him slightly, looked him in the face, and then leaned forward and kissed him lightly on his lips.

"Thank you," she said huskily.

For what? All he'd managed to do, so far, was break his vow to himself to keep his distance, to keep them all safe from the treachery of attachment.

He reeled back from her, scrambled to his feet. She looked as though she was going to cry even harder, of course. She was probably realizing she'd just done something *really* dumb.

He resisted the urge to wipe his lips. It wouldn't do what he wanted anyway. It wouldn't remove the sweet, clean taste of her.

That was branded on his mind as surely as the frying pan had left a mark on her delicate skin.

In the guest bedroom, the baby started to cry. If someone had told him yesterday he would welcome a baby crying, Ty would have scoffed.

But now it was just the diversion from all this intensity that he needed.

"I'll get him," he said.

"No, I can—"

"No, you can't." He sounded really stern and cold,

which was a good thing. Rebuilding his fences. "I don't want you to touch anything until I've got a dressing on the burn. When you are in a remote location like this, the wound generally isn't the problem. It's infection. Think of *Lonesome Dove*."

Yeah, he ordered himself, think of Lonesome Dove. *Not her lips.*

"*Lonesome Dove?*"

"On my top twenty list of good books." Why had he said that? She did not need to know he had a top twenty list. She did not need to know one more thing about him! He was pretty sure that's how attachments were formed, these little bits of information knitting together into a chain.

Kissing didn't help, either.

"I only have the vaguest notion what you are talking about." Was she staring at his lips? With *longing?*

Buck up, cowboy.

"It's not the arrow that finishes the main character, it's infection. I'll get the baby."

"Yesterday, you didn't even want to pick him up!" she reminded him. "You could barely give him a pat on the head."

"Well, yesterday I didn't have to. Today, I do."

Ty left her, shrugged off his coat and boots in the porch, and then went to the bedroom door and looked in at the baby.

Jamey had hauled himself up on the rails of the playpen, and was jumping up and down, howling his outrage at being imprisoned.

"Hey, that's enough out of you."

Jamey stopped jumping up and down and stopped

howling. He smiled, and made a little goo-goo sound, instantly charming.

"Papa Odam," he declared. His arms shot out. "Up."

Ty went in. This was how old he had been when his mother had walked out the door and scarcely looked back. Or at least that was what he had believed. Until the letters.

Is this what his father had felt that day?

Terrified? As if he'd been left in charge of something breakable and didn't have a clue what to do?

"Up." It wasn't a request, the charm dissolving. It was a command.

"Are you always so bossy?" he said to the baby.

Ty felt a nudge of sympathy for his dad, just like he had felt last night when he'd heard Amy reading stories and wondered if his dad had wanted to read to him.

Funny that he would feel sympathy when the letters had resurfaced. Rationally, that should make him angry all over again.

He thought of Amy singing last night, and seeing the tree, and putting the blanket on her this morning. He thought of her tears and his hands in her hair. He thought of the exquisite softness of her lips taking his.

"Up!"

"All right, already."

Taking a deep breath, he leaned over and picked up the baby.

It was not a tender moment. The baby stank to high heaven.

And yet as that stinky baby snuggled into him, Ty was aware for the first time that that long ago girl who had accused him of not having a heart, had not been right after all.

Because he did have a heart. He could feel it beating as Jamey pressed deeper against him, sighed happily, as if it were a homecoming.

It was that he had built walls around it, an impenetrable fortress.

It was obviously Amy's fault, even before the complication of her lips touching his, that the walls were being compromised, the fortress being threatened. Softness was flowing through the barriers like water onto parched earth. Allowing that softness in was why, without warning, he felt sympathy for a man he had barely spoken to for years.

And he didn't know how, in the end, any of this could possibly be a good thing.

CHAPTER FOUR

WHAT had she done?

Amy sank back in her chair, listened to the gruff masculine melody of Ty talking to Jamey down the hallway in the guest bedroom.

She had kissed him. She had kissed Ty Halliday. That's what she had done. There were excuses of course: the pain of the burn had knocked down her normal quota of reserve. Still, she waited for regret to swim around her like a shark sensing blood. Giving in to the temptation to taste his lips was just more evidence of her stupidity.

But the regret did not come.

How could she regret that? Taking his lips in hers had felt like a conscious decision, entirely empowering. And she could still feel the shiver of pure sensation. She thought she might remember it as long as she lived.

She was leaving, anyway. As soon as the roads were passable, she would be gone. So what did it matter that, when he had put his arms around her, she had felt for the first time in a long, long time as if she had fallen and there had been a net waiting to catch her?

That's what the kiss had been about.

Pure gratitude.

Instead of agreeing with her that she had indeed been stupid about burning herself, about winding up here when she needed to be somewhere else, his voice had been deep and calm and reassuring.

Hey, it's going to be okay.

Instead of pointing out to her all the different ways she could have avoided the situation, and all the trouble she had caused, he had just said, simply, *I'll fix it.*

If something other than gratitude had shivered to life in that brief second when her lips had touched his and her world had tilted crazily, so what? Again, she was leaving. Whatever else had been there—some primal awareness, some wrenching hunger—would have no opportunity to blossom to life.

Whatever *that* had been, he had felt it, too. Right down to the toes of his wet cowboy boots. He'd pulled away from her as if he'd got a jolt form a cattle prod.

Amy chided herself. She should have the decency at least to be embarrassed. But she did not feel embarrassed.

She felt, again, oddly and delightfully empowered. That big, self-assured cowboy was just a little bit afraid of what had happened between them. He had built a world where he had absolute control, and it could be nothing but a good thing for that attitude to be challenged now and then!

Ty came back into the kitchen with Jamey. The baby looked ridiculously happy to find himself in Ty's arms.

There was something terrifyingly beautiful about seeing a tiny child in the arms of such a man.

It was a study in contrasts. The man's skin etched by sun and wind and a hint of rough, dark whisker, the baby's skin as tender as the fuzzy inside of a creamy rose petal. The man had easy certainty in his own rugged strength, the baby was like a melting puddle of skin and bone. The man's eyes held shadows, the baby's innocence. The man's mouth was a stern line of cynicism, the baby's a curve of pure joy.

And of course, the man was totally self-reliant, the baby totally the opposite. And in this moment, Ty had assumed the mantle of responsibility for the baby's reliance.

It surprised her that, given his reluctance to hold the baby yesterday, Ty looked relatively comfortable with his little charge. He dodged the pudgy finger trying to insert itself in his nose with the ease and grace of a bullfighter who had done it all a thousand times.

Then Amy caught a whiff of her charming offspring. She was amazed that Ty had him in the crook of his arm, nestled against his chest, that Jamey wasn't being held at arm's length like a bomb about to go off.

"I don't expect you to deal with *that,*" she said.

"Oh, really?" He raised that dark slash of a brow at her. "Who do you expect to deal with it?"

That silenced her. Who did she expect to deal with it? Her hand felt as if it was on fire. It actually hurt so bad that she felt nauseous. She was not sure she could do a one-handed diaper change, even if she could fight through the haze of physical pain. And then there *was* the question of infection.

Ty set Jamey down on the baby blanket, still spread out on the kitchen floor. "Where's his stuff? You'll have to give me step-by-step instructions."

She directed Ty to the diaper bag, watched him set it

down on the floor and get down on his knees between the baby and the bag.

"Prepare yourself," she said. "This is not going to be pretty."

Ty leveled a look at her. "Lady, I've been up to my knees in all kinds of crap since I was old enough to walk. I've watched animals being born, and I've watched them die. And I've seen plenty of stuff in between that wasn't anything close to pretty. So if you think there's anything about what's about to happen that would faze me, you're about as wrong as you can get."

"I'm just saying men aren't good at this."

"Look, there are things a man *wants* to be good at."

Did his eyes actually linger on her lips as he said that before he turned his attention to the diaper bag?

"In my world," he informed her, digging through the bag, "a man wants to be good at throwing a rope. He wants to be good at riding anything that has four legs. He wants to be good at turning a green colt into a reliable cow horse."

His words were drawing rather enticing pictures in her mind.

"He wants to be good at starting a fire with no matches and wet wood. He wants to be good with his fists if he's backed into a corner and there is no other way out. He wants to be good at tying a fly that will call a trout out of a brook."

"This—" he gestured at her son, lying down, legs flaying the air and releasing clouds of odor "—is not something any man aspires to be good at. The question is, can he get the job done?"

"I may have stated it wrong. I simply meant it's not something men do well."

"Are you going to be grading me on this?"

Suddenly, Amy *needed* to share it, as if it was a secret burden she had carried alone for too long. She suddenly needed another person's perspective.

"My late husband, Edwin, changed Jamey's diaper twice. Twice. Both times it was a production. Clothes peg on the nose, gagging, brown blotches on the walls, the floor, the baby and his Hugo Boss shirt. The diaper was finally on inside out and backward to the declaration of 'good enough.'"

Edwin's efforts, she remembered, had always been good enough. Hers, not so much. She had asked him to do less and less. Amy had hoped for something else. In her marriage. And especially with the baby. Shared trials. Magical moments. Much laughter.

The pain of the remembered disappointment felt nearly as bad as the pain in her hand.

Ty glanced at her sharply, as if he was seeing something she had not intended for him to see.

"Twice?" he said. "And the baby was three months old when he died?"

She nodded.

"And he managed to be put out both times?"

She nodded again. "But he was a CEO of a corporation," she said. "Strictly white collar."

"I got that at the Hugo Boss part," he said drily. "And you know what? His perception of his own importance is a damn poor excuse."

She had wanted this perspective. Needed desperately

to know it wasn't her, expecting too much, being un-reasonably demanding.

But now that she had it, she felt a guilty need to de-fend her husband.

"He was a busy, important man. I'm afraid he had better things to do than change a diaper."

She remembered asking Edwin to do it. Insisting. Getting *that* look. All she had wanted was for him to empathize with her life. She had wanted him to be more hands-on with the baby. She had wanted him to appre-ciate what she did every day. Maybe she wasn't even sure what she had wanted.

But whatever it was, Edwin's annoyed look down at his shirt, and his *Are you happy now?* had not been it.

Ty rocked back on his heels and looked at her hard. She felt as if every lonely night she had spent in her marriage was visible for him to see.

"You know what?" he said, his voice a growl of pure disgust, "I'm beginning to really dislike Edwin."

Her sense of guilt deepened. Why had she brought this up? "He was not a bad person because he didn't like changing diapers," she said. "That would make a huge percentage of the world's population bad people."

"It's not about the diapers," he said quietly. "It's about what you said earlier, too. As if you having an accident and burning your hand made you stupid. It's about him making you feel like you were less than him."

She was stunned by that. Her relationship with Edwin had never been defined quite so succinctly.

She had been so alone with her feeling of deficiency, questioning herself.

"He's dead," she reminded Ty primly, the only defense left that she could think of.

"Yeah, well, that doesn't automatically elevate him to sainthood."

She thought of the shrine being built in his parents' living room. In conversation, the new and improved version of Edwin was what her in-laws insisted on remembering and immortalizing.

And her guilt intensified at how relieved she was that someone—anyone—could see something else.

She changed the subject abruptly, feeling as if she was going to throw herself at him all over again. It was just wrong to be feeling this much kinship over a diaper change, of all things.

He rummaged through the bag, held up a diaper for her inspection. At her nod, he said, "Check."

He laid out her whole checklist of items in a neat line on the blanket: baby wipes, petroleum jelly, baby powder and the diaper.

"Isn't that how soldiers take apart weapons?" she asked.

"Precisely," he said, pleased by the analogy.

"Okay. Now you lay him down and take off his pajamas. They're Onesies—

"Whatsies?"

"Onesies, one-piece jumpers, so you undo all the snaps down the front and right down his leg and slip him out."

"Like slipping a banana out of a peel," he said. "It's even yellow."

"Well, yes, kind of—"

"Except bananas don't leak, uh, brown blotches." He grimaced, but there was no gagging, no drama.

In one swift movement he had plump limbs out of the pajamas, and had them off. In another move, he slipped off the soiled diaper. He dispensed with both items with nary a flinch.

Jamey kicked wildly, and Ty caught the little feet easily in one hand.

"Hey," he warned, "cut it out." But it was a mild warning. He also did not flinch from cleaning Jamey up. He was methodical and thorough, and as he had promised, unfazed by the task. The minefield of petroleum jelly and diaper tabs did not claim him as a victim.

In fact, in short order, the baby was in a new diaper, gurgling happily and kicking his legs.

Ty picked up the messy items and disappeared. The diaper went out the back door, and then she heard him washing his hands in the bathroom.

When he came back, he had a new Onesies and had snitched one of the cookies off the tree. He slipped the baby into the new jammies, and handed the cookie to him.

"That should keep him busy while I look at your hand. I put the banana peel in the sink to soak the brown blotches until we have time to run a load of laundry."

She wasn't running a load of laundry. She was *leaving*. The need to go was feeling increasingly urgent.

Because watching him, and the apparent ease with which he adapted to what life threw at him—a baby and a woman invading his bachelor cave and the woman now nearly completely incapacitated—she felt sudden awareness of the tall self-assured cowboy shiver up her spine.

As he came and sat in the chair opposite her, and then pulled it so close their knees were touching, she was totally aware of Ty Halliday as pure man.

"Let me see your hand again."

This time she just gave it to him willingly, watched as he took it and steadied it on his own knee. He bent his head over it, and she felt a deep thrill at his physical closeness. His scent filled her world—clean, mysterious, masculine. The overhead kitchen light danced in the rich, pure gold of his hair.

His touch was exquisite.

After inspecting the damage thoroughly, he surrendered her hand back to her and got up. She followed him with her eyes as he reached up above his fridge and retrieved a first-aid kit.

Amy felt as if she was in a lovely altered state of awareness where she could appreciate the broadness of his shoulders, the narrowness of his hips, the slight swell of his rear under the snug fit of his jeans, the impossible length of his legs.

He turned back to her, his expression one of complete calm and utter confidence.

He knew what to do. And he was not the least bit afraid or hesitant to do it.

It struck her, as he moved back toward her, his grace and strength unconscious, that Ty had all the ingredients that had made men men since the beginning of time.

As he sat back down, she saw the intensity of his focus in the amazing sapphire of his eyes. She saw him as a warrior, a hunter, a protector, an explorer, a cowboy and a king.

Obviously, changing diapers and dressing wounds had not been in his plan for the day.

But Ty Halliday had no whine in him. No complaint.

What she saw was a stoic acceptance of what it meant to be a man, an unconscious confidence in his ability to rise to any occasion and do what needed to be done, whether that was putting in long hours doing rugged ranch work, or whether it was nursing something—or someone—injured.

The diaper had not been pretty. Neither was her wound.

And yet he did not shirk from either one. She suspected there was very little he would not face head-on.

She was not sure why, but that simple competence left her almost breathless with awe, tingling with a physical awareness of him, and of the space he was taking up in her world.

On the kitchen table that was beside them he again laid things out with the precision of a solider taking apart a familiar weapon. From the first-aid kit he removed individually packaged disinfectant wipes, antibiotic ointment, gauze pads, gauze wrap, scissors, tiny metal clips.

He surveyed the lineup of materials, remembered something, got up and reached into the cabinct above the fridge again. He came back with one more thing.

Amy gasped when he set it down, her awareness of his considerable masculine charm competing with this latest item. At the very end of his line of first-aid items, he had added a very large needle, attached to an even larger syringe.

"What's that for?" she asked.

"Penicillin. Don't worry about it." He picked up her hand, cradled it in his. With his other hand and his teeth, he opened a package and removed an antiseptic wipe from it.

She barely registered that. She was not sure she had ever seen such a large needle. She gulped. "You can't just give a person a needle, you know."

He swabbed the burn.

"You can't?" he asked, unconcerned. She watched him as he tore open a second antiseptic wipe with his teeth and cleaned the whole area again. She glanced back at the needle.

"You have to be a doctor."

"I didn't know that." He tossed aside the used wipes, opened the tube of ointment, squeezed some out onto the palm of her hand.

Gently, he smoothed the ointment over the burn.

At any other time, she might have appreciated the gentle certainty of his touch. But she couldn't seem to take her eyes off that needle, and its place in the lineup.

"Or at least a nurse."

"I've given thousands of needles." He inspected her hand, and then satisfied, covered the burn with a gauze pad, item number three. The needle and syringe were item number seven and he was making his way steadily toward them.

"Thousands?" she asked with jittery skepticism.

"Literally. Thousands. To cows and horses, but I'm pretty sure the technique is the same. Or similar."

He took the roll of gauze, item number four, and began to unwind it firmly around the pad in the palm of her hand.

"It isn't," she told him. "It's not the same technique. It's not even similar."

"How do you know? How many horses have you given needles to?" He was making a neat figure eight over her burned palm, around her thumb and up her wrist. He went around and around, his movements smooth, sure, mesmerizing.

"Well, none. I haven't actually ever given a needle to anything. But it just makes sense that giving one to a person and an animal are totally different things."

She heard a certain shrill nervousness in her voice.

In contrast, his was low and calm. "Don't worry, Amy, I'm not going to hurt you."

"On purpose," she said. "You might by accident."

He glanced up at her sharply. She had a woozy sense of not being at all sure they were still talking about the needle.

"I'll try not to."

No promises, she noticed.

He picked up the scissors, item number five, cut the gauze wrap. She glanced over at the table. He was nearly done.

He picked up the little metal clips, item number six, pulled the end of the gauze wrap firm on top of her wrist and inserted the teeth of the clips into the thickest place on the gauze. He gave his handiwork a satisfied pat.

"You can't just give a person penicillin," she said, staring at what remained in his neat lineup on the table—number seven, the syringe and needle. "You need a prescription for it!"

"Okay."

She eyed him suspiciously. He seemed to acquiesce

just a little too easily. She watched narrowly as he methodically repacked the first aid kit. He picked it up, and almost as an afterthought, picked up the huge needle and syringe. He stowed them all back in the cupboard above the fridge.

"Oh!" she said, and let out a huge breath of relief. "You never planned on using the needle! You scared me on purpose."

"Dressing a burn hurts like hell. I prefer to think of it as a distraction," he said, and then he smiled.

His smile was absolutely devastating. It took him from stern and formidable to boyishly charming in a blink.

She looked down at her hand. He had distracted her on purpose, and she honestly didn't know if she was grateful or annoyed by how gullible she was, but the smile made it impossible to be annoyed with him no matter how annoyed she was at herself.

And she realized the syringe and needle had indeed been a distraction. But that distraction had existed in the background. In the foreground had been the exquisiteness of his touch, his strength so tempered by gentleness, that pleasure and pain had become merged into a third sensation altogether.

And that third sensation scorched through her, more powerfully than the burn.

It was desire.

She wanted to kiss him again. Harder this time. Longer.

She had to get away from here. She was just in the baby stages of getting her life back in order. This was no time for kissing and all the complications that kissing could bring.

She'd known this man less than twenty-four hours. What was she thinking? The truth? She wasn't thinking at all. She was falling under some kind of spell, an enchantment that had been deepened by tasting him, and then by the drugging sensuality of his easy smile.

He had a tea towel in his hand now. "Sorry. I don't have a real sling. I'll improvise with this."

"I don't need a sling!" Imagine how close to her he'd have to get to put that on!

"It'll be better if we immobilize your hand. If we don't, you'll be surprised by how often you want to use it. You could just try it for today."

"But I won't be able to drive if my arm is in a sling."

His gaze slid away from her before he turned back, opened his palm and held out two white pills.

"You generally need a prescription for these, too. We're a long way from an emergency ward here. We take some liberties."

"I really won't be able to drive if I take those." *Or,* she added to herself, *keep my head about me.*

"No, you won't."

"Then I'd better not."

"Ah, well, there's something I have to tell you. The driveway isn't passable. I'm going to turn on the radio and see what the roads are like, not that it really matters if you can't get out of the driveway." He glanced to the window. "Don't get your hopes up. It's snowing again."

Her eyes drifted to the window. Snowing again was an understatement. The window looked as if it had been washed with white paint, the snow beyond it was so thick light could barely penetrate. She felt panic surge in her.

This terrible wave of affection had been building in her since he had changed Jamey. Shamefully, it had grown even more when he'd said he disliked her husband.

That sensation of someone having her back had deepened the emotion she was feeling for him.

And now that he had dressed her hand so gently, with such skill, distracting her from the pain, she felt a terrible danger from the desire that was beating like a steady pulse at the core of her being.

"You can't possibly mean I can't get out of here!" She knew she was saying it like it was his fault. She knew it wasn't.

His silence was answer.

"But for how long?" she asked, her voice shrill with desperation.

"It won't be long," he said in a tone one might use trying to divert a small child from having a temper tantrum. She was done with his diversions.

"That isn't a real answer."

"I don't have a crystal ball. I don't have a real answer."

"If you were going to guess?" she pressed him.

He hesitated. "I'd say tomorrow. If it stops snowing in the next hour or so I can get the driveway plowed by then. I'll put on the radio and get the weather forecast."

"I'm trapped," she whispered.

"Well, not limb-in-leg-hold-trap trapped, but not-going-anywhere-today trapped." He sounded just a little tongue-in-cheek. He clearly did not understand the gravity of this situation!

Her new life, her new plan for herself was being threatened by him. It was being threatened and she had been here less than twenty-four hours. She'd kissed a man she barely knew and wanted to do it again.

What kind of mess would she be in forty-eight hours from now?

Maybe she would be ripping off his clothes and chasing him around the kitchen. Not that she was that type.

Good heavens, she had never been that type.

But she was well aware that the "type" she had been—pleasing other people in the hope they would play their role in her fantasy of the perfect home and family—had not brought her one iota of happiness. Not one.

That realization left her wide-open to being pulled down the road of temptation.

"But there could be an emergency!" she said, knowing there had to be a way out of here if the stakes were high enough.

"An emergency? What kind of emergency?"

The thought that there might be an emergency of the magnitude that he could not handle seemed to take him totally by surprise.

"Like a medical emergency. Not a little burn, either. What if something happens to Jamey? What if he gets sick and has a temperature of one hundred and three? What if he fell down the steps and broke his neck?"

Ty rocked back on his heels and regarded her with just a trace of exasperation. He held out the white pills. "If you don't take these, I think I might," he said, his tone dry.

"You have to think of the possibilities!"

"No, I don't. There are millions of possibilities. That is way more thinking than I care to do. The phone is working. The power is on. We have heat and food. We could probably get a helicopter in if a real emergency happened. It won't."

"How can you know that?" She was slightly mollified that they could get a helicopter in, even as she was aware the real danger she needed to escape was something else entirely.

He shrugged. "I just know."

And, despite herself, she believed him. He knew his world inside out and backward. He trusted himself in it and that made her, however reluctantly, trust him, too. She was the wild card in all this, not him. Imagine her, Amy Mitchell, being a wild card.

Still, taking the pills seemed like it would threaten her control just a little too completely, so she pushed them aside just as the phone rang.

He got up and got it. He listened for a moment, and then without a word, brought her the receiver. The line of his mouth was turned downward, and he raised an eyebrow at her.

How could it be for her?

Puzzled, she took it.

"Amy, what is going on? Are you with a man?"

Ah. The miracles of modern technology. Yesterday, when her cell phone had not worked, she had called from here. The number must have come up on her mother-in-law, Cynthia's, caller ID unit.

"Hello, Cynthia. Please calm down, everything is fine."

"What do you mean everything is fine! And do not
tell me to calm down in that snotty tone of voice, young
lady. You have my grandson and you are with a man.
Who is that man?"

Somehow, everything Amy was running from was in
that strident tone. Judgment. Lack of trust. Disapproval.

"He's—" Amy glanced at him. The explanation
seemed complicated. And would confirm every single
thing Cynthia already thought. Amy really wasn't ready
to admit she had lost her way yet, especially not to her
supercritical, always ready to pounce mother-in-law.
If towels not folded correctly could bring that pinched
look of pained forbearance, how much worse was this
going to be?

Amy took a deep breath and turned away from Ty
so she didn't have to see his reaction to what she was
about to say. "I'm having trouble with the laundry. He's
the washer repairman."

"How come the washer repairman is answering the
phone?" Cynthia asked, her voice shrill and full of suspicion.

"Uh, how come he answered the phone? Uh—" And
suddenly, Ty was standing in front of her. He held out
his hand.

It would be downright cowardly to give him the
phone and let him handle her mother-in-law.

She looked into his eyes, saw the man she was trusting with her life and the life of her baby, and surrendered the phone.

He took it and winked at her. *Winked!*

"This is the washer repairman," he said, his voice

solemn. "We are having an emergency. Brown blotches. It's not a good time to talk."

And then he hung up the phone, crossed his arms and gazed at Amy.

"She's going to phone right back," Amy warned him.

The phone started to ring.

Ty reached behind Amy's back and pulled the plug from the wall.

There was so much he could say. But he didn't. And there was so much she could say, but she didn't, either.

She giggled. And then giggled again.

He smiled, and then he laughed. His laughter was possibly the most beautiful sound she had ever heard. It was rich and clean and without any kind of mockery in it. No reprimand about lying. No advice about how to handle her pushy mother-in-law.

The laughter flowed out of him, like water tumbling over rocks, and suddenly with absolutely no warning a sweet feeling of absolute freedom filled Amy.

For the first time since she had married Edwin, Amy did not feel trapped at all. She savored the irony of that. She was trapped, really, by all the snow.

"You know what, Amy?" Ty finally said, wiping at his eyes. "I think it's time to have some fun."

"No offense," she said, wiping at her eyes, too, "but you don't look like you know that much about having fun."

His eyes went to her lips and locked there. That slow smile played across the sinfully sensuous line of his mouth.

He moved very close to her. His lips were so close to her ear, she could feel the heat of his breath on her skin.

"I guess," he growled, "that would depend on how you defined fun."

CHAPTER FIVE

AMY was staring at him, and Ty could tell she was actually holding her breath, waiting for him to suggest something really fun, and perhaps a little naughty, like maybe tasting each other's lips again.

And while that would definitely be fun, the repercussions of such foolishness—even allowing the thought into his brain for three or four red-hot seconds—seemed truly dangerous.

Besides, he could tell she was not that kind of girl. But he could also tell it probably wouldn't take much of a shove to move her in that direction.

She was impossibly uptight, and when a string was pulled that taut, it was the easiest thing in the world to break. Plus, he had sensed something in that kiss that had made him pull back sharply from it.

Hunger. Raw and powerful. Had it been all his? Or had there been plenty of hers, too?

So, no, tempting as it might have been to follow the road that had opened up when she had kissed him, he had something else in mind for fun. He wasn't taking the low road. For goodness' sake, she had decorated a Christmas tree for him. Having any kind of naughty fun with her would be like fooling around with one of Santa's elves.

No, with the baby looking on a PG rating would be the best thing for everyone.

"The most fun a person can ever have on this earth?" he asked her, adding to himself *at least in the wholesome category.*

"Yes?" she breathed.

"Playing with a horse."

"Oh." She definitely looked disappointed. There was a wildcat in her waiting to be unleashed, and Ty wasn't quite sure if he envied or pitied the man who was going to be the one to unleash that.

"I'm actually, er, terrified of horses."

"I kind of figured." He watched her fiddle nervously with the dressing around her hand.

"What?" Her head flew up. "How would you figure that?"

"Hmm, let's see. You're scared of your car getting stolen and your house being broken in to. You're petrified of needles. Being snowed in has opened a whole world of dreadful possibilities that you never even considered before. And you're terrified of whoever that was on the phone."

"My mother-in-law."

He wondered if she was still Amy's mother-in-law since the husband was dead, but decided now was not the time to debate the technicalities of it.

They were stuck here together.

What if taking the high road meant he could show her one small thing? She had given him that Christmas tree. What if he gave her something in return?

What if he could show her there was nothing to be afraid of?

Given how filled she was with terror, he saw it was something of a miracle that she had packed up that baby in the middle of winter and headed into the unknown.

A miracle, or one desperate last-ditch effort to save herself, to truly live.

But if she could not tame all that fear, he saw the outcome as being predictable. Just as a horse went back into a barn that was engulfed in flames, Amy would go right back to what was familiar, no matter how uncomfortable that was. And that voice on the phone, shrill and demanding, asking him who he was without even saying hello? That would be plenty uncomfortable.

Ty had told Amy he had no religion. But the truth was, you could not live in a place like this, so close to the formidable majesty of nature, without seeing the order of things, that life unfolded with reason, that sometimes the smallest things that appeared random at first ended up being connected to a larger picture.

Was there a possibility that Amy Mitchell had arrived on his doorstep, not by accident, but for a reason?

If that was true, he had to get beyond his petty need to protect his comfortable little world. Rise above his own fears.

But then his eyes went to her lips.

Starting with that one.

What if he could give her one small gift and help her find the fearless place in her? To do that, he was going to have to require more of himself, he was going to have to be more and do better.

"Come on. Get the baby ready."

"Maybe you should just go ahead without us. I can find things to do inside. It looks like a perfect day to bake bread."

She really didn't want to do this. At some level, she was figuring it out. Saying yes to him right now was going to put the way she lived her whole life at stake.

The incentive of fresh-baked bread nearly killed his new vow to be a better man.

"Are you using the promise of fresh-baked bread to distract me? Just like I used that needle to distract you? Because, really, fresh-baked bread to a bachelor is like offering water to someone lost in the desert."

Was that his life? Was he lost in the desert? He had never thought so before. This little bit of a thing was shaking up his life way beyond what her size should warrant!

He took in her look of relief.

"So," she said, "that's settled. I'll bake bread. You'll go play with horses. We'll both have fun, in our own ways."

"No."

"No?"

"I don't know that much about baking bread, but I'm pretty sure you need two hands to do it."

She looked, dismayed, at her wrapped hand.

"I told you we should put a sling on it as a reminder you are on the injured list. How about if you come play with me, and then I'll come play with you?"

"You'll help me bake bread?" Did she sound slightly skeptical?

"I've already demonstrated my great ability to catch

on with Mr. Splotchy over there. I hope baking bread is more fun than that."

"Well, it has to be more fun than that, but somehow I can't see you enjoying it. It's not very manly."

He laughed. "It would take more than helping to bake bread to threaten my masculinity. Do we have a deal?"

"I don't know."

That was an improvement over an out-and-out no.

"You know," he challenged her softly, "if you can learn to deal with a horse…"

She nodded.

"Your mother-in-law will be a piece of cake."

She went very still. She looked like a woman standing at the edge of a cliff, looking at the water below, deciding.

She jumped.

"Okay," she said, "I'm in."

And then she laughed again. And so did he. And she let him put her arm in a sling, which made him have to fight with his demons all over again. One kiss, right on the tender nape of that neck, where he was knotting the sling.

An hour later, he was congratulating himself because he had managed to fight off temptation and now they were all standing safely at the round corral, in his world.

Amy was wearing a bright toque with a fuzzy pompom on top and one of his jackets to accommodate the sling. She had one arm in the sleeve, the other tucked safely inside the jacket. The jacket, a plaid logger's coat came to his upper thigh when he wore it. On her it was past her knees.

It made her look adorable, small and lost, like an orphan standing on a street corner waiting for someone to take her home.

It had taken forever to get the baby into a snowsuit, but Jamey was in it now and looked like a bright blue marshmallow—felt like one, too—nestled into the curve of Ty's arm.

"So, this is Ben," Ty said as they all stood at the rail, looking at the horse in the round corral behind the barn.

The flakes were still dancing down around them, huge and unrelenting. Jamey kept bending over backward trying to catch snowflakes on his tongue, grumbling and yelling when they hit him in the eyes instead.

Ben was the horse Ty had ridden the day before. He was a good horse, young, part mustang, a red roan, with about the softest eyes Ty had ever seen on a horse.

"He's a two-year-old, which is basically a baby in horse years."

"He seems very large for a baby," Amy said cautiously. "His size alone makes me nervous."

"He'll be nervous if you're nervous. That's the secret about horses. They are looking to you for leadership. He *wants* you to lead him. We should go ahead and get in there with him."

"I don't know. He's so big. He could kill us."

"It's funny you should say that, because that's exactly what he's afraid of, too. Death by predator."

He was holding the baby, so when he went through the rails, she followed. Whether she would have if he didn't have the baby, Ty wasn't sure.

"The road's closed," she reminded him in a terrified whisper. "What if something happens?"

"Something is going to happen," he promised. "Pure magic. Stick close to me, walk as if you're a king."

"I'm the wrong sex to be a king," she muttered.

He was committed to wholesome. He didn't even want her using that word right now. "He doesn't know that, and a princess won't do."

"You better know what you're doing."

"Oh, I do." He took them to the center of the paddock. He ignored Ben, who had watched them enter the corral with a certain shy caution. Then the horse circled them on feet muffled by snow, and was now tiptoeing along behind them.

Ty turned. Amy, stuck to him like glue, turned with him.

"Ah! I didn't know he was right behind us!" She went to take a step back as the horse pulled up short, but Ty had anticipated it and placed a hand in the middle of her back.

"Don't step back from him," he instructed softly. "Hold your ground. He is reading every single thing about you. He can probably tell your heart is beating too fast. So don't step back. Because if you do, he'll take that as a weakness, that you are less than him, and so he will move forward, claim your space, try to dominate you."

She froze and stared at Ty. He saw the light of understanding go on in the amazing depths of her hazel eyes.

"Oh, my," she whispered, "if that doesn't sound like the story of my life!"

"That's the thing about watching someone with a horse," he told her quietly. "You can tell every single thing about them. How you interact with a horse is exactly how you interact with life."

"Oh, dear."

"Whether you know it or not," Ty finished, "you are telling people how to treat you all the time. Come. Come closer."

He went and stood right at the horse's neck. The baby did not have her hesitancy. He reached eagerly for the horse, buried pudgy fingers in the silken strands of Ben's mane. He cooed his love and approval.

Ty leaned close and blew a gentle breath in the colt's wide nostril. It blew back and he breathed in the scent.

"Try that."

Amy hesitated, studied not the horse, but him, and decided to give him a most fragile gift. She trusted him.

She leaned forward and blew.

And then Ben blew back.

"Breathe it in," Ty said. "Breathe it in. That breath is what you have in common, the thread that connects you both to life. Breathe him in. Can you feel what he is? His essence?"

"His breath is so sweet," she said, awed.

She turned and looked at Ty. Her eyes were shining with that moment of discovery. He knew he had her.

"Okay, now we're going to make the decision it's time for him to leave, so push his shoulder now, and raise your right hand."

The horse moved away from them and out to the perimeter of the corral.

"Keep your eye on his hip, keep your hand up, step toward him."

Fluidly, the horse broke into a relaxed canter and circled them, throwing up great puffs of snow.

"I didn't make him do that!" Amy said, awed.

"Prove to yourself that you did. Back up, lower your right hand and raise your left, and then move one step toward him again."

"I don't have a left!" she reminded him, and wagged her empty sleeve at Ty.

He moved behind her, laughing, and physically lowered her right hand. There was the sweet temptation of her neck again.

"Back up," he instructed.

The horse planted his feet as she backed up, and then Ty picked up the empty sleeve and waved it. Ben swiveled in one graceful move at the switch of hands. He cantered the other way.

"He's so beautiful," Amy said. "I feel as if I'm in a movie."

The horse was beautiful, but his beauty was eclipsed by hers. Her curls were sticking out from under that silly hat, her cheeks were flushed from cold and exhilaration, her eyes were shining. A smile, so genuine it would have outshone the sun, if there had been any sun, played across her lips.

Seeing her with the horse told Ty exactly who she was.

And he knew how right he had been to take the high road with her, to fight the temptation of placing a kiss on the soft curve of her lips or her exposed neck.

Because she was beautiful and soft and gentle to her very core.

In other words, exactly the kind of woman that a

rough-and-tumble guy who had known way too many hard knocks could do a lot of damage to.

Still, enchanted with her reaction to all of this, Ty talked her through the sequence a few more times. Her face was absolutely glowing as she began to understand the horse was responding to her slightest move.

"Everyone and everything is responding to us all the time, at some level. Sometimes it's so subtle we don't know what we've told them."

For instance, her kiss had told him she was hungry. But her eyes were saying she wasn't ready.

"Okay, lower your hand—" he let her empty sleeve fall "—and move your eyes to his shoulder."

The horse skidded to a halt. He turned in, his eyes riveted on her. "Step back."

She did, and the horse came into her, dropped his head in front of her in submission that was not surrender.

"Scratch his ears. And his forehead. Say something to him."

"Ben, I think I'm in love with you."

Her voice was husky and sweet, and it seemed to him a man could die to hear such words coming from her.

But his next instructions, intended for the horse, were instructions he needed to heed himself.

"Now turn and walk away."

Not that he could. Not while they were snowed in here together, but there were many ways to walk away.

And he should know because he'd done most of them at one time or another.

"I don't want to walk away," she said, stroking Ben's

nose with soft reverence. "I want to stay like this forever."

Yup, she was the kind of girl who could turn a man's thoughts to forever.

"Sometimes it's better to play hard to get. Turn and walk away," he said more firmly.

She shot him a look, and then did as he asked.

"Don't look back."

"I can feel him," she said. "Ohmygosh, he's breathing right down my neck. Is he following me?"

"Like a dog."

She moved a little faster. She slowed down. She turned, she doubled back on herself. The horse stayed right with her, taking her cues effortlessly, devoted to her as his new leader.

Finally, Ty allowed her to turn and pet Ben some more.

"You were right," she breathed. "Oh, Ty, that was the most fun ever."

"Actually, the most fun is still to come. You think you might like to ride him?"

"Oh," she said, "I don't know."

"I'll ride him, and then you can decide."

He went into the barn and retrieved the tack. He showed her how to brush the horse, was aware of how intent her attention was on him as he saddled and bridled the young colt.

He got on in an easy swing. Now Ty was completely in his world. He felt his own energy and the energy of the colt merging. He felt the balance between them.

He didn't so much ride the horse as dance with him. A few gentle laps around the paddock at a walk, and reversing direction, at a trot. And then, he let the rein loose, gave the slightest pressure with his knees.

The colt moved into an easy lope. He slid him to a halt with pressure and signals that no one could see, that were strictly between him and the horse. They loped the other way.

He glanced at Amy. She was awestruck.

He'd done enough for one day. But what guy didn't love a girl looking at him like that?

He nudged Ben forward, toward the place of freedom. The horse moved out of a lope into a hard gallop. Ty leaned forward, drinking in the air and the scent of the colt. Peripherally he was aware of Amy and the baby in the center.

And it was all one.

A wonderful blur of oneness.

It was a vulnerable moment of choice. He could show her all of who he was, or he could hold back something.

But wasn't the purpose to make her want to be who she truly was?

He dropped the loop of the reins over the saddle horn, and spread his arms wide and tilted his chin up, closing his eyes against the falling snow.

It was complete trust.

Not just in himself. Not just in the horse. Not just in her reaction to all this.

It was complete trust in life.

He lost himself in it, came back only reluctantly. He took up the reins again, and then he stopped and rode the horse into the center, where she was staring at him.

"I have never seen anything like that," she said. "Not ever. I will never forget it as long as I live."

It was like a promise, and he knew he had succeeded in giving her something.

He was aware he had taken a giant risk. He had shown her exactly who he was, and then he knew it had been worth it.

"I want that," she said. "I want to go to that place, be in that place, live in that place."

He bent down and brushed her curls from her face with a gloved fingertip. He realized the baby was probably getting very heavy for her to manage with one arm. He took the baby from her arms and set him in the saddle in front of him. They took a few turns around, and Ty thought of his father again, how some of his earliest memories were of this.

Sitting in the saddle in front of his dad, beginning to understand the language not just of horses, but of his life.

Was it the first time he had consciously realized the gift his father had given him?

What was it about her that was making him see his life in different ways?

He reminded himself of the goal. For her to see her life in a different way. He rode back to her, pulled his leg out of the far stirrup, slid out of the saddle with the baby still in his arms.

"Well, I guess if that's what you want," he said, "you better get on. Because you can't start the trip without finding your ride."

"I don't think I could get on with two good arms," she said doubtfully. "We should wait until I can use both arms. We should wait until it's not snowing. We should—"

"You can always wait. You can always wait until everything is perfect and all the stars line up. But you're going to miss a whole lot of what life is trying to give you right now."

"What if I fall? What if I wreck my other arm. What if—"

He put his finger gently to her lips, and then he set the baby down. He picked her up, two hands around her waist, and lifted.

She was so light that he held her for a moment, like a dancer, or a pairs skater starting a lift.

And then he twisted ever so slightly and put her in the saddle.

"Pick up Jamey," she said. She was clinging to the saddle horn with her visible hand. "He could get stepped on!"

He picked him up, but not before giving her a look that let her know it was his watch, and no babies were getting stepped on on his watch. That horse would not move a muscle without Ty's okay, or some instruction from her.

"I don't want you to be afraid anymore. That's what I want you to take from this. That's what I want you to remember forever. Now pick up the rein with your good hand. Attagirl. Just squeeze him ever so gently with your legs and then release."

The horse walked out. And in front of his eyes, Ty watched as Amy's fear dissolved into something else.

And this time Ty knew he was going to be the one never to forget.

"Whoa, boy," she said a while later as he helped her down, and she watched him strip the saddle and blanket off the horse. "Baking bread is not going to be able to compete with this in the fun department."

"It's going to be whatever we make it," he told her.

And then he looked at the sky. There was no sign of the snow letting up. None. If anything, it seemed to be snowing harder than when they had first come out.

And so there was no sign of their forced togetherness coming to an end.

And that, too, would be whatever they made it.

Ty's house still smelled of fresh-baked bread, even though it had been more than twenty-four hours since they had made it.

The smell alone made his mouth water.

"Do you want some toast," he said, "and jam?"

The baby was bathed and in bed. Ty sprawled out on the couch, his arm thrown up over his forehead, his eyes closed.

Amy turned from the window. "You have not stopped eating since I got here!"

"You have not stopped cooking since you got here."

"We," she reminded him.

"No man who has been cooking for himself as long as I have could resist that bread. Amy, it is the best thing I've ever tasted."

That was not exactly true. The best thing he had ever tasted had been her lips, and after the best part of three days in each other's company, he was fighting himself constantly.

"It's all in the kneading," she said, glanced again at him, something hot flashing through her eyes when he deliberately flexed his kneading muscles for her.

"How do you do this all by yourself?" he asked a few minutes later, coming back into the living room with a plate heaped with toast. "It's utterly exhausting. Who knew a baby was so much work?"

He took a bite, closed his eyes and sighed. Then he reopened them.

"You can't make it stop snowing by standing there."

"I stopped wishing it would stop after you beat me at Scrabble last night. It has to last at least until the re-match. Do you want to set it up for tonight?"

He was happy to see the consistently worried look was gone, even though the continuation of the snow-fall meant she wasn't going anywhere tomorrow, either.

He had turned on the radio with supper. What was going on outside his window was a part of what was being called the Storm of the Century. Some of the secondary roads were closed, including The Cowboy Trail, 22, which his driveway joined.

"Honestly, Amy? I'm too tired to pit my wits against you. How do you do it by yourself?"

They were moving back and forth between their two worlds seamlessly. She and the baby had come with him today to do chores. They had all squeezed into the cab of his tractor as he moved large bales into the pas-ture for his cows. Then they had played with the horse again. Despite not being able to use her one hand, she had executed a pretty passable trot.

Inside, it was her world. She loved to cook. She had shown him how to make bread and cookies, a simple cream soup. The baby was an unbelievable amount of work: diaper and clothing changes, baths and feedings. How did she manage all this by herself?

"It never seems like work to me," she said and came and sat down in the chair opposite him. "It's what I always wanted. Babies. A cozy kitchen. Bread baking."

This was getting easier all the time, too, conversation flowing between them with the ease of old friends.

"What made you want that?" he asked.

She turned and smiled at him. "I know. I know. It's a hopelessly traditional, old-fashioned vision in a modern world. It's not what my parents hoped for me at all."

"Really?" He sensed she was going to trust him with some parts of herself that she did not reveal often.

He needed to be worthy of that trust. He closed his eyes, so he wouldn't look at her lips, and pulled his plate of toast close so that the scent would override hers.

"My parents were both business analysts. Their skills were sought after all over the world. I grew up in Germany, Japan, California, France.

"We always lived in the best houses in the best neighborhoods, but it never felt like home. I don't ever remember having a home-cooked meal, unless our current house came with staff, which they sometimes did. And then it was hardly roast beef and potatoes. Baked Sockeye salmon with a lemongrass sauce.

"I was always in private schools with loads of activities, depending which country we were in. I'm something of a reluctant expert at figure skating, gymnastics, badminton, swimming and soccer. But really, from the youngest age, I remember craving home.

"I craved a sense of family. I was an only child who wanted six brothers and sisters. It was probably unrealistic, my vision based on watching TV families, reading magazines. But unrealistic or not, I started cooking and baking when I was about thirteen. And I had my own ideas about what I wanted my room to look like, wherever we were, and it did not mesh with the designer's idea of *teenage girl.* I wanted homemade crafts on the walls, a crocheted blanket.

"It was my mother's worst nightmare."

Ty laughed. "At thirteen you were crocheting blankets and baking cookies, and that was your mother's worst nightmare? She wouldn't have wanted to know me at thirteen."

"Oh! Tell me about that!"

"Stealing sips of whiskey. Smoking behind the barn. Sneaking out of the house. Taking the truck without permission. Terrorizing the neighborhood girls." He felt the ripple of sympathy for his dad again.

"I'm not saying one more word about my boring childhood!"

"Please?" he wheedled. "I like hearing about you at thirteen."

"I'm not sure why. I taught myself how to cook and crochet. I got a sewing machine and learned to sew. My mother was appalled by my fascination with all things domestic. I had my own little world."

"Boys?" he asked.

"Terrified of them, while writing secret love letters to the ones I liked best. Never mailed, of course."

"Of course." He laughed. He could see her as just that kind of girl: sweet and shy, the kind guys, dumb prisoners to raging hormones that they were, overlooked again and again.

"We were back in Canada when I finished high school—still no boyfriend—and by then, I was dreaming of babies to fill up my little fantasy cottage. But I did what my parents wanted. I went to university in Calgary, as per my mother's plans, but in my second year a boy had finally shown interest in me.

"Poor guy. Before he knew what had happened, I had him cast in the starring role of my secret fantasy. I dropped out to get married. My parents, surprisingly, approved of Edwin, possibly because his family owned a company that traded on the New York Stock Exchange.

"Edwin was still going to university, so we lived with his parents."

"You were newlyweds and you lived with his parents?"

"Actually, at first it seemed as if I was in heaven. His mother was like Martha Stewart on steroids."

"Martha who?"

"Stewart. She has a television show. And a magazine. She's the world's leading expert on all things domestic, from removing wine stains from white linen to making Halloween punch with the illusion of a dismembered hand floating in it."

"Terrifying," he said drily.

"The Halloween punch or Martha?"

"Both. You were telling me about your in-laws."

"They had lived in the same house for twenty-five years."

"That's not long. There have been Hallidays on this place for over a hundred."

Maybe he shouldn't have said that. Amy got a distinctly dreamy look on her face.

"For somebody like me who never had a home, a family in the same place for so long was like a fairy tale coming true. And then it was all about cooking, and stunning crafts, and décor, and creating an environment that whispered sweet welcome.

"But somewhere along the line, I realized it was all about how everything looked, and not about how it felt. Cynthia's perfect home, her perfectly cooked meals, her crystal collections and towels folded in precise thirds—everything looked so perfect and felt so plastic.

"And, I'm afraid that describes my marriage, too. I thought it was the house, so as soon as Edwin finished university, I wanted to move out. But he said it was too much pressure. He'd been appointed CEO of one of the family companies, and that was his life.

"Honestly, I felt as if I was back with my parents. He worked. I was invisible. I thought the baby would help."

"Ah."

"It helped *me*. I didn't feel so alone. I finally had something to live for." She said softly, reluctantly, "It was not what I had hoped my marriage would be."

"My first clue—living with his parents. My second clue—he *wanted* to live with his parents. Pretty hard to chase each other around the house shrieking with *amour* when Mommy and Daddy are looking on."

"We managed to make a baby," she said primly.

"Miracle of miracles."

"I've never said this to another living soul."

He said nothing, waiting.

"The baby was wonderful. Other than that, I've never felt so lonely. My own parents had decided to retire. You know how the type A personality retires? Mountain trekking in Nepal."

"Not there for you."

"You want to hear something ironic? They built an orphanage in Africa."

"And you were practically an orphan."

"I didn't mean to sound like I wanted pity. I had absolutely everything growing up."

"You didn't sound like you wanted pity," he assured her.

"So, almost by accident, after Jamey was born, I started this little website on the internet called Baby Bytes. I never even told Edwin, my parents, his parents. It was so precious to me, and I knew I couldn't handle the put-downs or the patronizing or the criticism or the input.

"Edwin was killed in an accident very shortly after that. He was coming home from work late. He'd had a few drinks and hit a telephone pole.

"I feel like my little company kept me going, gave me back an identity when I was suffocating in everyone's expectations. Their expectations actually felt even more stifling after he died.

"I was supposed to behave like the grieving widow for the rest of my life. Live with his parents. Gratefully accept their help and their gifts.

"When the house-sitting opportunity came up, I knew I had to take it. To make the break. Baby Bytes has started to make money, and I know I can take it to the next level."

"Tell me about it."

She gave him a wary look, as if she was deciding whether or not to tell him the color of her underwear.

"It's just a website. It's free for people to use, mostly young moms. It's got recipes on it for everything from making bread to making your own baby food. And I put up patterns for clothes and homemade toys. Photography tips. I have little contests for cute baby pictures and best names. Nobody is more surprised than me by the number of people using the site."

She ducked her head, as if waiting for him to mock her success.

"I think that's great," he said, and he meant it.

"It's kind of like the Martha Stewart of the baby world," she said, her tone self-disparaging.

He hated that. When no one else put her down, she did it herself.

"I like how you are blending different worlds," he told her. "Using high tech to showcase things you value."

He was aware that was what they had been doing for the past few days, too. Blending worlds. Moving back and forth between each other's worlds with a growing amount of comfort.

"I started putting out feelers," she confided shyly, "and a couple of the big baby companies, like Baby Nap, have committed to taking out ads on it. It's going to give me a very comfortable living within a year."

"So you have your parents' business acumen, too. That's amazing. You must be very proud."

"I'm scared."

"No, you're not. You were scared, but today and yesterday you played with a horse. And now you don't have to be scared anymore. Not of anything."

"Anything?" she whispered. She took a deep breath, and turned, and looked at him with those amazing, beautiful eyes. "How about the fact it's still snowing?"

"I think we'll survive."

"It's the twenty-first of December today. How about the fact I may be spending Christmas with you?"

"It's just another day. You can celebrate it however you want when you leave."

She looked at him long and hard, as if he was clearly missing the point. She drew in another deep breath.

He had to have known this was coming. He had to have sensed it in their growing comfort with one another, the effortless way he had become her extra hand, the enthusiastic way she was embracing his world.

But somehow her next words shocked him completely. Completely.

"How about the way I'm starting to feel about you, Ty Halliday? How about that?"

CHAPTER SIX

Ty leaped up off the couch as if he'd accidentally sat on a hot ember. He nearly dumped his plate.

"Like I said, I'm exhausted. Done in. I have to go to bed."

Amy squinted at him narrowly. This was a repeat of when she had kissed him! He was letting her know, in no uncertain terms, he was not interested in her in *that* way.

"I'm going to have to figure out a way to get to my dad tomorrow," he said as if he had to rush off to bed and think hard about that.

"Your dad?" she asked, astounded.

"He and his lady friend live on the old Halliday homestead place. It's a few miles from here. I'd better make sure they're stocked up."

Amy felt shocked. She'd assumed Ty was alone in life. Really alone. As alone as any person she had ever met. But his dad lived a few miles away, and he'd never even mentioned it?

She suddenly felt embarrassed that she had blurted out her whole life story to him. In fact, over the past three days, she had revealed quite a bit about herself.

But he hadn't! She had just assumed they were getting to know each other, but in actual fact he'd been getting to know her.

Enough to know he wasn't interested in *that* way. She watched him take off down the hall to his room, heard the finality in the way the door snapped closed.

Ty Halliday was telling her to back off and that was his right.

It was the situation here that had made her feel so instantly enamored with him. It was seeing him laughing with Jamey, frowning over the Scrabble board, kneading bread until his arm muscles rippled, looking after her hand with such tenderness, stepping up to the plate to uncomplainingly shoulder every single thing she couldn't do because of her injury.

But the kicker had been to see Ty Halliday on a horse. It went beyond horsemanship.

It went straight to spirit.

She had witnessed the grace and the power of man and horse melt into one seamless entity.

Watching Ty ride was going to that place she had been to so rarely: a place of being fully engaged, fully connected, fully alive.

And she thought she might as well just die now if she did not learn how to get there, too.

But it was precisely the same mistake she had made before. She was looking for a hero, someone to rescue her from her life.

And Ty would certainly fit anyone's definition of a hero. Seeing him in his element and watching the ease with which he had slipped into hers, given the forced closeness of their circumstances, her total reliance on him, it was natural that she would be feeling things with a strange and sizzling intensity.

It was not unlike a hostage bonding with their captor.

And if there was one thing she was done with, it was being taken hostage. She had to take responsibility for her own life. No more waiting to be rescued.

Knowing exactly what she had to do, she marched into the kitchen.

The phone was still unplugged from the wall.

So, despite the physical closeness of his father, Ty really was more alone than most people. She doubted he had even given a thought to his phone being unplugged—him being unable to be reached—since he had pulled that thing from the wall. If he was concerned about his father, why didn't he phone him?

None of her business, she told herself firmly. She was in no position to advise Ty on family matters when she had allowed her own to become such a mess.

Now, taking a deep breath, Amy plugged the telephone back in and dialed the familiar number. She was aware her heart was beating too fast. She was aware that all her life she had been telling people how to treat her.

Now she had ridden a horse. Now she had breathed his essence deep inside her. Now she had to step up and claim her own space.

"Hello, Cynthia, it's Amy."

"I have been so worried! I was within a hairbreadth of calling the police."

Cynthia's tone was wounded, and of course she would not have called the police. It was just her way of letting Amy know she felt her negligence was nearly criminal. She bit back the impulse to apologize.

Instead, she pictured walking up to that horse and not giving an inch.

"Cynthia," she said firmly, "while I appreciate your concern, I'm fine. Jamey is fine. I just wanted to let you know we won't be there for Christmas dinner. You've probably seen on the news that the roads are closed out this way. I'm at the end of a long driveway. It's going to take a while to dig out."

"But where are you? The call display still says Halliday, not McFinley. You said you were house-sitting for people called McFinley. I've called the number listed for them in the phone book. And there is no answer. And there is no answer at the house you called from with the so-called washer repairman. So where are you? And who was that man who answered the phone? Please don't play me for the fool. I know it wasn't a washer repairman. Have you met someone on the internet? It's not safe!"

A thousand explanations ran through Amy's head, and then feeling sweet relief she realized she did not have to make any of them.

"Cynthia, I need you to listen carefully. I love you and I appreciate your concern for me and for Jamey. But I am an adult woman. I do not need to report to you."

"Please just come back!"

"I won't be coming back. Not to live there."

"But John and I are in such a comfortable position to look after you."

"I don't want to be looked after."

"Think of Jamey! We are in a far better position to give him everything he could ever want than you will ever be!"

There it was, what was always there: the underlying lack of faith in her.

"Cynthia, I want to be respected. I want to look after myself."

There was a long pause. "Really, Amy, this is no time to make a philosophical stand. The well-being of my grandson is at stake."

Truer words had never been spoken. And Amy did not want to teach her son that she could not stand on her own two feet, that she was a dependent personality without the guts or the wherewithal to make it on her own.

Ty Halliday had just done her a big favor by rejecting her interest in him! He'd set her back on the correct path.

"Jamey will miss you on Christmas. We'll come for a visit as soon as the weather permits." As she hung up on her mother-in-law, Amy felt she had never been more on her own path.

She heard Ty get up in the morning, rustling around. She had the feeling he was trying very hard not to wake her.

And the woman she had been when she first arrived probably would have rolled over and pretended to sleep until he left the house, leaving her to nurse her wounded ego.

But she was not that woman anymore. She got out of bed, looked out her window for a moment, then donned her dressing gown and went into the kitchen.

Ty was actually glaring at the coffeepot, drumming the countertop with impatient fingers waiting for it to brew. The radio was on at a very low volume next to him.

He looked up at her, looked away, clearly not happy

to see her. He removed the pot and stuck his travel mug directly under the drip.

She ordered herself to face it head-on. "Look, Ty, I just looked out my window. Still snowing. We're going to be stuck here together for a few more days."

He nodded, put the cup to his lips. "Yeah, I saw the snow, too. The road reports are the only thing on the radio. Some roads are open, but there are travel advisories on them and the weather warnings haven't been lifted."

"So, you're stuck with me."

He winced and rolled his shoulders uncomfortably, but didn't argue with her blunt wording.

"Ty, I don't want you to feel uncomfortable in your own home. I'm not going to break into pieces because you made it clear you don't find me attractive. You've done me a favor, actually. I should be all done looking for heroes."

He choked on the coffee. He set down the cup. He stalked over to her.

"Don't find you attractive? Are you crazy?"

She looked up at him, drank in the fire in those sapphire eyes, the way his pulse beat in his throat, the tight line of his jaw.

"I find you way too attractive, Amy."

"You do?" For a moment, she felt her whole world start to shift, but then she reminded herself that the new Amy Mitchell needed to be more cynical, more pragmatic. "Or you're just saying that?"

His mouth fell open. His eyes spit blue sparks of pure heat. "I don't just say things. How can you not know that about me?"

"We hardly know each other at all. It feels as if we do because of how we've been forced together, but I shouldn't have said what I said last night. It put you in an awkward position. But don't worry, I don't plan to moon over you."

He moved in closer, his eyes still burning with a deep blue flame, like the one that hovered over the hottest part of a fire. And then his hand moved, almost as if it were against his will, and his finger traced the line of her mouth before his hand went to the back of her head and buried itself in her curls. He drew her close.

The blue fire that had been in his eyes sizzled briefly in the small space between them, singeing the air, making her lips tingle.

"Oh, Amy," he whispered, and then he took her lips with his.

Inferno.

It was everything she had known it would be, and it was so much more.

As his lips, remarkably soft, astoundingly sensual, claimed hers, her world made the final melt into his.

The touch of his lips intensified, took charge and then surrendered to her. He was gentle, and fierce and hungry. He was tender and ruthless, taking and giving.

It seemed to her his kiss asked her not to submit to him, but to be worthy of him. And so she gave back. Everything. For the first time in her life, she gave every single thing she was. Her gentleness. Her fury. Her hunger. Her uncertainty. Her yearning. Her dreams. Her strength.

When it seemed as if there would be nothing left of

either of them except smoldering ash, Ty pulled back from her.

He took a step back. His shoulders were heaving as he raked his hand through his hair, tossed her a troubled look.

She took a step toward him, not ready to let go.

He took a step back from her.

"Amy, we are in a complicated situation here. It is incredibly intense. Giving in to this will only make it way more complicated. That's what I was trying to tell you last night when I walked away. Now, I'm going to my dad's. I'll be gone a couple of hours and that should give me a chance to cool off and put my head back on straight."

Terrible to be so thrilled that she was responsible for the fact he did not have his head on straight.

"How are you getting to your dad's in all this snow? Why don't you just phone him?"

"It's complicated."

"Hmm. For a simple cowboy you seem to have a complicated life."

"Some days are worse than others." His eyes trailed to her lips, and then moved swiftly away. He jammed his coffee mug back under the drip, waited for it to fill partially, then took a huge swig. He was going to burn his mouth on that coffee if he didn't watch out.

"I've got a sleigh. I'll hook up a couple of the big horses to it, put a few supplies in, in case he needs them."

"I'm coming."

"I just said we need to cool off."

"I'll try to keep my hands off you. But, Ty, I am not missing a genuine sleigh ride for anything."

Ty looked torn, but then he gave in. It was not like him to give in so easily, and she felt her heart warm as much as it had for the kiss. He *wanted* to share this experience with her and Jamey. Their worlds were not yet finished melting together.

"Now, what do you think your dad might need? We'll bring him the last loaf of fresh bread and—"

"He doesn't need the last loaf of fresh bread," Ty said sourly.

"Ty! We can always make more."

But he still looked sour as she found a box and with her good hand started loading a few basic supplies, including the fresh bread, into it. Jamey woke, and without being asked, Ty disappeared down the hall.

When he came out the baby had already been changed and was in a fresh Onesies.

An hour later, with Ty carrying Jamey in his little blue snowsuit, they made their way down to the barn. The snow was still coming. But did it seem a little lighter this morning?

Handing Jamey to her at the barn, Ty left them. He returned with two horses, one lead rope in each hand, and brought them through the open barn doors. The horses were absolutely huge, golden-colored with heavy white manes and tails, and white feathers around their feet.

"Their feet must be as big as pie plates!" she said.

Maybe her awareness had been heightened by that kiss, but every single thing seemed to shimmer this morning.

She was so aware: Ty in a sheepskin-lined jean jacket, dark cowboy hat, leather gloves, looking strong and rugged and calm and self-assured—the quintessential cowboy. And the horses: clouds of breath, the warm smell of them, the squeak and jingle of the leather harnesses as Ty got them ready.

"Can I breathe in their noses?" she said. "The way I did with Ben?"

He cast her a glance from under the shadowed brim of his cowboy hat. After that kiss she was aware of him trying frantically to rebuild walls. But she did not miss the quiet satisfaction that passed through his eyes that she was not afraid of these huge horses.

She went and stood at their shoulders, breathed in their wonderful scent, let Jamey pet and stroke and coo and call out in excitement.

But all the time, she was so aware of how Ty was with the horses. She had promised not to moon over him, but really, how could she stop herself?

Besides, he was very focused on what he was doing, ignoring her. This was second nature to him. Ty worked around the huge animals with confidence and unconscious grace, entirely certain of himself. He talked to them as he quickly brushed them out, his tone low and soothing, his voice sending shivers up and down her spine.

The harnesses seemed complicated, and yet Ty's manner was easy. Putting a harness on a horse was no different for him than checking the air pressure on a tire or the dipstick on the oil was for most men.

And yet watching a man doing mundane vehicle maintenance could never have this kind of pull to it.

Watching Ty get the horses ready, his hands gliding along strong muscles, working buckles, untangling
leather straps, was like watching something extraordinarily and breathtakingly beautiful. It was a symphony
of motion and energy.

When he had the horses harnessed, he led them out
into the snow. Bells jingled on the big leather collars
and the snow kicked out in huge puffs from their feath-
ered feet.

There was a lean-to attached to the barn, and in it
was a huge lump under a blue tarp. He dropped the
reins for the horses.

"Stand," he commanded, and the huge horses stood
quietly, while he went and removed the tarp.

Again, she felt as if she was in a state of heightened
awareness, because the sleigh was so pretty it made her
eyes smart with tears.

It was possibly the most Christmassy thing she had
ever seen. It was painted bright red, with a black leather
front seat and shiny runners.

Expertly, Ty backed the horses toward the hitch.
Again, watching his confidence and efficiency of
motion took her breath away. Once the horses were
hitched, he took the baby, helped her up onto the seat
and climbed up beside her.

He took up the reins. "Hang on." He made a click-
ing noise. The sleigh lurched as it moved from the dry
ground under the roof to the snow outside the lean-to.
And then it was gliding along, the huge horses plowing
effortlessly through the deep snow, tossing their heads,
moving into a huge-gaited trot.

Ty directed them up the hill to the house, dropped

the reins and told the horses to stand. He made several trips: the box of supplies, baby things, warm blankets which he stowed behind the seat. And then lastly he came out with several square items wrapped in towels.

"I threw a couple of bricks in the oven this morning after you said you were coming. Just tuck them around you and Jamey."

She did and the sensation of warmth on this chilly day was incredible. The sensation of being cared about was even more incredible.

Though, she reminded herself, he would have denied it. If she questioned it, she was sure he would say it was something he would do for anyone.

Ty got back in the driver's seat, took up the reins and moved the sleigh down the slope of his hill, where his driveway once had been. At the bottom of the hill, he turned along a wooden fence line.

"This is called a pioneer fence," he said. "My great-grandfather built it."

The snow falling was even lighter now, and the horses settled into the task at hand, bells jingling, their great strength breaking a path through the snow effortlessly. The runners on the sleigh made a hissing noise on the ground. The baby laughed and all those sounds became part of the magic of a world muffled by snow.

"I think," Amy whispered, "this may be the most beautiful moment of my whole life."

Ty shot her a look that clearly said *sheltered,* but it didn't matter. The horse-drawn sleigh followed the fence for a while, and then Ty turned and they wove their way through open fields, then through a small forested stretch. When they came out the sun had burst through and was glinting off the pristine snow.

But it wasn't white. It was like the earth was covered in sparkling diamonds with blue fire at their core.

"Don't get your hopes up about the snow stopping," Ty said.

But somewhere along the way, Amy realized, all that had shifted. She didn't want it to stop. She wanted it to snow forever, to stay in this world of the two of them, and the baby, and Scrabble and baking bread together, and squeezing into the cab of his tractor and playing with horses.

"Why do you say that?"

"I can taste more snow on the air."

She stared at him. "You can taste snow on the air?"

"Sure, try it."

And so she stuck out her tongue, and tasted nothing. And then she breathed the air in through her mouth. Still nothing.

And then she noticed his shoulders shaking with suppressed mirth.

"You can't taste it!" she said, thumping him firmly on the arm.

He rubbed his arm with pretend hurt. "Yes, I can. But I also heard it on the radio. Slight clearing today, more snow coming."

And somehow the tension that had been created by that kiss dissipated, and there was something playful and comfortable in the air between them.

"You want to try driving the horses?" he asked.

"Really? How can I with one hand?"

"We'll figure it out."

Amy was so aware that woman she had been when she'd arrived would have shrunk back from this. Would have seen everything that could go wrong: horses stampeding, sleigh overturning.

Now she felt eager for the new experience, warmed that Ty offered it to her, trusted her not to screw up.

Ty took the baby and passed her the reins into her one hand. She could feel the power of the horses singing through the leather. She laughed out loud. She was aware of Ty watching her, a small smile tickling across the line of his lips.

A woman could start living to make that man smile, to make that light go on in his eyes!

"Just keep your hand steady, just like that. We're going that way." He reached over and pulled ever so slightly on the inside rein, his hand brushing hers, and then staying there.

Amy suspected the horses knew exactly where they were going, but it was so much fun anyway, like taking a trip into the past. This is what life had once been, there had been a beautiful simplicity to it, moments that were slower and lovelier. She felt as if her whole body was humming with awareness.

Though, of course, Ty was a big part of that. His shoulder brushing hers, his gloved hand resting on her mitten, the baby happy in his lap, his face relaxed and happy, his laughter frequent.

She couldn't taste snow coming, but somehow the taste of him, the way his lips had been on hers, was still with her, woven into the magic of the day.

Woven into who she was becoming, and who she would always be, now.

They moved up a hill, crested it, traveled along the ridge for a bit, and then he took the reins back from her as they headed down through a small copse of trees.

When they came out of the trees, they were partway down a valley, in rolling open pasture. Spread below them was a scene from a Christmas card: an old barn, wood grayed from weather, sagging from age and hard use.

And there was a house.

It was a two-story log house, the logs weathered as gray as the barn. A low porch wrapped around the entire place. Smoke curled out of a river rock chimney.

Amy could see bright curtains in the windows and cheerful light inside. Even from here she could see an immense wreath on the front door, and the porch railings decorated with festive red bows.

"Stop, Ty, please stop."

He sent her a puzzled look, but did as she asked. She passed him the baby and climbed from the sled, stood in the snow, gazing down at the house below her.

The horses turned their heads to look at her, curious about the stop.

"Stand."

Ty came with Jamey and stood beside her.

"What is it?" he asked quietly.

She took in a deep breath, looked at him, this self-assured man holding her baby as if it was second nature to him.

She debated telling him. It made her feel as if she was showing him something that would make her so vulnerable.

But, she reminded herself, the new Amy was courageous.

And that didn't just mean taking the reins.

It meant risking showing people your heart. It meant doing that, even though she was risking rejection—again. She felt compelled to tell him who she really was.

"Oh, Ty," she breathed, "all my life I dreamed of home. All my life. And that is what I dreamed of." She gestured to the scene below them.

He could have done anything. He could have been impatient. Or mocked her. But instead, she felt his hand on her shoulder, the gentle squeeze of fingers under his gloves.

He gave her his silence and let her drink her fill of the beautiful scene. And then he helped her back on the sleigh and they made the final descent to the house.

As they got closer, it got better. Ty pulled the big horses to a halt at the wide steps that went up to the front door. There was actually a hitching post there, and he got down from the sleigh, fastened the horses, and then came back and took Jamey before helping her down.

The wreath on the door was thick, lush with different types of boughs all woven together. It had a huge plaid bow on it, and country ornaments—rocking horses and snowmen with cowboy hats—peeked out from under the boughs. There was a little wooden word buried in the bows.

Wish.

As they went up the steps, she could smell the fragrance of the wreath. It reminded her of how close it was to Christmas. Despite the tree at Ty's house, she had not been able to achieve any kind of Christmassy feeling there.

The door opened before they knocked, and Amy's sense of somehow coming home was complete. A woman stood there, diminutive, white-haired, her face etched, not with surprise, but with kindness.

Behind her wood floors glowed with the patina of age, and a fireplace, hung with socks, crackled with bright welcome. *Wish*. This was exactly what Amy had always wished for.

"Ty!" the woman said, "what a nice surprise."

"Beth."

Amy turned to him, taken aback by something cold in his tone and in his eyes. This is what she should have known all along: Ty was not interested in being part of Amy's picture of perfection.

"Oh, my word," Beth said reverently, holding out her arms. If she had noticed Ty's coldness, she did not acknowledge it. "You've brought us a baby."

Ty handed off the baby into the eager arms, turned around and clattered back down the steps.

"Hunter, look! Ty's come and he's brought company. Come in. Come in."

Amy stepped in the door. And saw Ty's father. She would have known it was him instantly, not so much because they looked alike but because of the way he held himself. He was extraordinarily handsome even though his hair was white as snow and his features were weathered. He was in a wheelchair, but even so, he exuded power, his energy was like a brilliant light in the room.

His features were stern, and there was wariness in his dark eyes, but when he saw the baby it melted. Beth brought Jamey to him, and he held out his arms and took him. Amy had never seen a man so at ease with a baby. Certainly Edwin had never acquired this ease, and her father-in-law was like a stick man when he found Jamey in his arms.

But Ty's father was obviously a man who knew a great deal about babies.

My mother left when I was about that age.

Ty came back in the door and set the box of supplies inside of it. "I thought you might be needing a few things."

Their eyes locked, the young man and the old.

Hunter spoke, his tone proud. "We were just fine."

The tension was raw in the room, and Amy suddenly understood why Ty had not phoned and had acquiesced so easily to her coming.

His offer to help would have been refused. And he had brought her because she would provide the distraction.

"I'm Amy Mitchell," she said, kicking off her boots. Her hand was taken by Beth.

"Amy, I'm Beth, and this is Hunter."

She went over to Ty's dad. She loved how he was with the baby. He was already engrossed in removing the snowsuit, and Jamey was enthralled with him.

"Papa, papa, papa," he crowed as if he had met a long-lost love.

She extended her hand, and it was swallowed in one that was rough textured and as strong as his son's. His eyes searched her face, and then he let go of her hand, a small smile playing the stern line of his mouth.

"I'm Hunter Halliday."

"Tea or coffee?" Beth called.

Ty was still standing at the door, holding the first box of supplies. He looked as if he planned to just drop it off and leave!

"Tea," Amy said. She wasn't leaving this place for as long as she could help it. The sensation of coming home had intensified, not diminished, since she had come in that door.

Ty made a growling noise deep in his throat. "I'll see to the horses." And then he turned and went back out the door.

Amy loved it at the old homestead. She loved the handmade throw rugs on the wide-planked floors, the scarred centuries-old harvest table, the crackling fire in the fireplace. She loved the worn furniture and the paned windows. She loved the cat curled up on the hearth. She loved the smell in the air, the tart scent of the pine boughs, a hint of wood smoke, the delicious aroma of something baking.

She shrugged off her coat, and Beth made a fuss about her bandaged hand and clucked sympathetically when Amy told her what had happened.

"I was a nurse before I retired. Do you mind if I look at it?"

Baby in his lap, Hunter wheeled over to the table. So, while he found a set of keys and entertained the baby with them, Amy sat down and Beth looked at her hand.

"Ty did a great job on this. It looks fine. I'll just change the dressing."

Amy was aware she was in the company of strangers, and yet she felt safe and loved and entirely at home.

Ty stood in the doorway, surveying the scene, his face impassive. "What do you need done?" he said to Beth.

His father answered. "I can do it myself."

Ty blew out an impatient breath, went back out the door. A few seconds later they heard an ax thumping into wood. It managed to sound quite angry.

"So," Beth said, setting a teapot on the table—most likely antique—and scones steaming from the oven, "what brings you to Halliday Creek Ranch, Amy?"

And while Hunter broke scones into bits and fed them to Jamey, who opened his mouth and cooed like a small eager bird, she found herself telling them. And not feeling the least ashamed of her ineptitude with the GPS device.

Beth and Hunter seemed to think her descending by accident on Ty was one of the most hilarious stories they had ever heard.

When Ty came back through the door, his arms loaded with freshly split wood, he found them all laughing. Looking like thunder, he dumped the wood in the wood box by the fireplace and went back out the door.

They heard the angry bite of the ax blade into wood again.

The next hour was a delight of laughter and easy conversation. But in the background Amy was aware of Ty's seething presence. Ty chopped wood and filled the wood box to overflowing. Then he climbed up on the porch roof and cleared snow. When he was done that, they could see him out the window, heaving snow off the path to the garage.

When he finally came back in, he had worked himself into such a sweat that steam rose off him.

"Amy, we should go."

"I was hoping you'd stay for lunch," Beth said.

"Maybe another time," Ty said. Polite. Terse.

His father glanced at him.

And Amy saw clearly a whole gamut of emotions going through the elder Halliday's eyes. Pride. And something deeper than pain. Sorrow.

How could Ty be like this? So stubborn? So indifferent to the pain he was causing people?

What had happened between this father and son? And was there any chance, any chance at all, that maybe she could help fix it? So that they all could experience a Christmas miracle?

CHAPTER SEVEN

"What happened to your dad?" Amy asked.

The horses were more eager to get home than they had been to leave, and it was necessary to have a firm hand on the reins to keep them in check. The snow was falling lightly again, too.

Ty glanced at her. He was aware that she hadn't wanted to leave his dad and Beth, aware of the reproving look she had cast at him when he'd refused lunch.

His father had worked his charm on her. The old bastard could be charming when he set his mind to it. He'd never been short of female companionship.

"He's an old-style cowboy," Ty said, stripping his voice of any emotion. "They bronced out horses. Throw a saddle on a green colt, let him buck it out, put it to work right away, work the knots out as you go. It's dumb. And dangerous. But you could never tell my dad anything. He knew it all. And then one day he met a horse who had more buck than he had stick."

"It must be very hard on a man who lived like that to make the adjustment to being in a wheelchair," Amy said.

Her voice begged him to show some sympathy.

Instead, he just shrugged.

"What's wrong between you two, Ty?"

Her voice was so soft, her eyes so warm. Inviting him to lay it at her feet. Inviting him to share his burdens.

He had seen that word *wish* peeking out from the dark green of Beth's wreath.

And he was aware, in a very short time, that's what Amy had done to his world. Breathed life into a wish he thought he had managed to kill a long time ago.

With her Christmas tree and her filling his house with the smells of baking, with her enthusiasm to try new things, with her soft voice, and her wit and her intelligence, and her unguarded tenderness toward the baby, she was making him wish for a different life.

But he'd done that when he was a kid. Wished and wished and wished.

Around Christmas, he had wished even harder. There was magic in the air. And joy. Unexpected gifts. In these country communities, Christmas was a big deal. Community events, baking marathons, sleigh rides, home decorating contests, neighbors gathering, tables groaning under the weight of food.

He and his father had always been included in everything. They had so many invitations for Christmas dinner they were always left with a hard choice of where to go.

But instead of soothing him, being included in other people's family Christmases had only made Ty more aware of his own lack, so aware of the warmth and good cheer that other people's families brought them.

And so he had wished harder.

But his wishes had never come true. And then, the night his father had given him that pack of letters, when he was seventeen, that place in him that had fostered hope had died.

Or at least he thought it had.

Now he could clearly see that an ember of that hope had remained. He could clearly see that Amy could fan it back to life.

But he had no desire to have it live again, to be open to the world of pain and disappointment that empty wishes brought.

"Amy," he said, his voice deliberately cold, "don't go there."

She flinched as if he had slapped her, and he wanted to take it back. He wanted to tell her everything.

But it felt like a weakness.

And there was no room for weakness in a world without hope. None at all. And yet he found the recrimination in her eyes hard to bear. Maybe if he showed her those letters and told her all of it, maybe then she would get it.

He hazarded a glance at her. Jamey was fast asleep, snuggled into her breast.

Amy was a picture of softness.

She was looking at the world, snow falling again, the steam coming from the horses' nostrils in giant puffs, with a certain rapt attention, as if it was all miraculous.

"There's absolutely no chance I'm going to get away before Christmas, is there?" she asked, worried.

Maybe she was getting it after all, figuring out she was going to be spending Christmas with him, and that he was hard-hearted and a Christmas grinch, and it wasn't going to be much fun at all.

"It doesn't look like it," he said.

"Then I have a lot to do to get ready," she said. "Tomorrow is Christmas Eve!"

He saw he had misread her worry. It wasn't about having Christmas with him. It was about making Christmas what she wanted it to be. She was determined to have Christmas wherever she was.

"Don't get too uptight about it," he said. "It's just another day."

"No, Ty," she said firmly. "It isn't."

He dropped her off at the house, carrying the baby in for her. And then he took the horses down to the barn. It didn't take him long to get them unharnessed, and to do his evening chores.

It didn't take him long at all, and yet when he came back the transformation of his house had already started.

"Ty, before you take your coat off, could you go cut me some boughs? I'd love to bring the scent in here. I can make a simple centerpiece for the table with tree boughs and a candle."

Tell her no, Ty ordered himself. But he found he couldn't. It wasn't as if it was her choice to be here. She was stuck here. She wanted to make the best of it. For her baby.

Heaving a big sigh, Ty went back outside and began cutting boughs.

"I didn't need that many," she said when he came back in.

Nonetheless, she looked delighted as she spread out the boughs on the kitchen counter and began to sort through them.

"Do you smell them, Ty?" she asked, smiling over her shoulder.

"Yeah."

"Take off your coat. Come help me. Darn this burned hand. I can't do anything."

Again, he knew he should say no. For his own self-preservation, it seemed imperative.

But he didn't want to be the one to put out the light in her face. And it was true. She was going to need his help.

If she had enough time with him, he would eventually manage to snuff out her light, he was sure. But for right now, why not just be the better man? Reach deep inside and make it not about him, but about her and Jamey?

"Okay," he said gruffly. "Show me what to do."

And as she showed him, something in him relaxed. He allowed her enthusiasm to touch him. And then, he gave himself over to it.

They decorated the house with boughs until the scent filled every corner. Then they ate, bathed the baby, read bedtime stories together, the baby between them on the narrow bed in the guest room grabbing at pages.

When Jamey was finally in bed, she started ticking things off on her fingers. "So, Christmas Eve. I want to make a gingerbread house. I want that to be one of Jamey's and my traditions. His grandmother, Cynthia, makes the most gorgeous gingerbread creations. Last year, we did a little village together. Maybe I should start the gingerbread tonight." She glanced at the clock, worried that she was running out of time.

"I am pretty sure there is nothing in my kitchen to make a gingerbread house, never mind a gingerbread village."

"Oh, I brought everything I need."

"Where the heck did you hide the trailer you must have hauled behind that car to get all your stuff here?"

"I'm very organized. I have a talent for spatial relationships. I bet I could figure out how to get an elephant inside that car if I had to."

"Let's hope you never have to," he said deadpan.

"We could be done in an hour. The cookie part. And then it will be cool enough to cut it and make the house tomorrow."

"I don't want to make gingerbread." A man had to put his foot down, or he'd be swept up in her world before he quite knew what had hit him. The truth was, he didn't want to make gingerbread tonight. Or tomorrow, either. A gingerbread village? No thanks to that much Christmas hokiness.

"I could probably do it myself," she said, but doubtfully, glaring down at her wrapped hand with accusation. "I will do it myself."

"Oh, never mind. I'll give you a hand." It was a surrender.

"You will?"

"One house. No village." But not a complete surrender.

They were not done in an hour. His cranky oven burned the first batch of gingerbread black. Finally, the gingerbread, perfect and golden-brown, was cooling on his kitchen counter.

"There," Amy said, satisfied. "I'm out of your hair. Do whatever you would normally do. Pretend I'm not here."

Good idea. He went into the living room, settled in his chair and picked up his book.

His house smelled overpoweringly of pine boughs and gingerbread. There was a Christmas tree in his living room. And baby toys all over the floor.

And then there was Amy, sitting across from him, looking out the window. "Still snowing."

"Uh-huh." He scrunched lower in his chair, furrowed his brow. But try as he might, he could not pretend she wasn't there. And who knew when he might have an opportunity like this again?

"What the heck is a dactylic hexameter?"

She looked thoughtful. "I have no idea."

And then they were both laughing.

"I always read two books at once," he told her. "One that's really hard, and one for pure enjoyment."

She came and sat beside him, and he read a few passages of the epic poem to her.

She wrinkled her nose. "Could we try the pure enjoyment one?"

"I'm so happy you asked," he said, and then he went and got *Lonesome Dove* and read her his favorite part of that. And somehow they were talking and talking and talking, and they fell asleep on the couch with her head nestled against his chest.

He woke up to her stirring against him.

She opened her eyes, looked at him groggily, and then smiled the most beautiful smile he had ever seen.

"It's Christmas Eve," she said, as round-eyed and full of wonder as a child.

"Technically, that would be tonight."

She thumped him on his chest with her small fist, a good-natured reprimand.

"We have so much to do! We have to make the gingerbread house. Jamey will love helping with that." Suddenly, she went very still. "Do you have a turkey? That should come out of the freezer today."

"I don't have a turkey. Sorry."

"A chicken, then?"

"Sorry, my freezer is full of what I raise, which is beef."

"Somehow I can't imagine a big steak for Christmas dinner," she said.

"I can."

He got the thump again. Funny, the things that could make a man realize he was losing control.

He went out and did the chores. When he came back in, Jamey was awake and needing tending, and Amy was champing at the bit to get her gingerbread house made.

Then with her instructions, he was taking the sheets of gingerbread and cutting them.

"Now, we make a house."

He did not want to think of making a house with Amy. It felt as if thoughts could make him weak instead of strong.

"We use this icing to glue it all together."

Carefully, Ty cut the sheets of cookie into squares. Even being careful, a nice chunk broke off. It was a reminder that he could not be trusted to make any kind of a house with anyone.

He popped the broken piece into his mouth, passed some to the grasping baby.

"Hey, it's not to eat," she said, and he popped a piece into her open mouth to silence her.

Focused intently, he took the slabs of cookie and stood four of them up, leaning on each other to form rough walls. Then, pleased, he put another on top.

"Well?" He stood back and surveyed his house.

"It doesn't look like a house, Ty."

"What does it look like?"

"I don't know. A box."

"I'll fix the roof." He took another piece of gingerbread, took a bite out of it, and then made a slanted roof instead of a flat one.

"I told you, it's not to eat! Did you have to take a bite out of the roof? It looks like—"

"Hansel and Gretel have been here," he decided happily. It looked like the whole thing was leaning, ready to topple over. He slathered the joints liberally with the icing glue. It got all over the place, including his hands. He handed the wooden spoon to Jamey, who merrily chewed the end and then bashed the kitchen counter with it.

She eyed the house critically after he'd made the changes. "Now it looks like a shed."

"Perfect. Just what I planned. A manger for Christmas."

The thump again.

"Hey, I'm a cowboy, not a construction guy."

And not anyone who could be trusted to make a house with her.

He made a few adjustments. "It will look fine once we add a few windows."

But of course it didn't look fine. Jamey had to "help"

decorate, and the jelly beans and jujubes that didn't make it into his mouth were rather mutilated by the time they made it onto the house.

She stepped back from it.

She surveyed the house: listing badly, part of the roof broken, misshapen candies on it, and then she looked at her baby, sticky with icing and gingerbread, and then she looked at Ty.

And it was as if that scent that filled his house and made it home was right inside of him when she looked at him like that.

She started to laugh. "It's perfect," she declared.

Amy stared at the house, and let the feeling it was giving her fill her up. Perfection.

It was not the kind of house Cynthia made—perfect miniatures from a Swiss village. In fact, it looked only remotely like a house.

It had a bite out of the roof. The candies were sliding in icing down the walls into a heap at the bottom. The whole thing was tilting quite badly to one side, and looked as if it might fall right over.

And for all that it looked wrong?

It had never felt so right. Christmas had never felt so right as it did in this moment, sharing a room with that big golden-haired cowboy, watching his eyes tilt with laughter as he used his finger to clean icing off Jamey's nose.

Her other Christmas Eve activities were perfect, too. Ty dug an old sled out of the barn, so they went down the hill in front of his house, sinking in the deep snow, inching along, tumbling and laughing. The snow also was not quite right for making a snowman, not nearly sticky enough, and they ended up with a lumpy pile with an old cowboy hat sitting on top of it, two rocks for eyes and a carrot for a nose.

What the snow was perfect for was snow angels, and they soon covered that entire slope with the imprints of their bodies.

Her feeling of having the most perfect day ever solidified.

Darkness fell. The baby went to bed. She locked herself in her bedroom, door closed. She had not been able to find wrapping paper, but there had been a huge roll of butcher's paper.

She had Christmas shopped a little for Jamey back in Calgary, so one-handed, she managed to get a chunky little train and some cars wrapped. Then she wrapped a few of his old toys, knowing full well he would not know the difference.

Now, what for Ty? She crept out of her room and retrieved his oven gloves. She cut her red toque, and a towel she had brought with her, and managed to patch the hole in the one. She wrapped it up. And then she went thought her suitcase, found the two books she had brought with her and wrapped those up for him.

Funny, humble little gifts.

That filled her with the Christmas spirit.

And when she came out, she had little brown paper wrapped packages, the wrapping lumpy and terrible, which she put under the tree with great and gleeful pride.

"Now," she told Ty, who was stretched out on the living-room sofa, nearly asleep, "I'm going to make us some hot chocolate. And then we can sing Christmas carols."

He snorted, but didn't say no.

Amy was in the kitchen, stirring a vat of hot chocolate when the phone rang.

"Hey, can you get that?" he called from the living room.

She picked it up, was thrilled with the caller and the invitation.

"That was Beth," Amy said, standing in the doorway. "She realized I was going to be here for Christmas Day. She invited us over for dinner. They have turkey."

"We were just there," he pointed out, something stubborn in the set of his jaw, a shield over his eyes.

"Surely you would have been joining them for Christmas dinner?" she asked.

He said nothing.

"You wouldn't go and be with your own father on Christmas Day? You'd rather sit here by yourself?"

Again he said nothing.

"I want to go. I have Christmas presents for them." She went and stood in front of him, folded her arms over her chest.

"How could you possibly have that?"

"I made them something. I already told her we would go."

"You shouldn't have done that. I'm not going there for Christmas."

"But—"

"I'm not arguing with you. And it's not open for discussion."

"Oh! Now you sound just like Edwin!"

She could tell he didn't like that one little bit.

"Look," he said, his tone cool. "We are not husband and wife. We are not even a couple. So we don't have to discuss decisions."

Regardless of the truth in that, Amy was not going to be the woman she had been with Edwin. Never again. Just deferring to him, trying to make him happy, avoiding confrontation, even when the price of that avoidance had been the loss of her own identity and her own soul.

"You're absolutely right. We don't have to discuss decisions. I'll go without you," she decided.

His mouth formed a grim line. "And how are you going to do that?"

"I'll take the little sled we used to toboggan with today. And I'll follow the track we made with the horses."

"With one hand?" he said with satisfied skepticism.

"That's all I need to pull Jamey on the sleigh," she said stubbornly.

His mouth fell open. "What happened to the girl who was afraid of her own shadow?"

Her eyes went to his lips.

He had happened to her. And she was a girl no more. She was a woman, and she was one who knew her own mind.

And this is what her own mind knew, standing there on Christmas Eve having her first fight with Ty Halliday.

The woman she had become was in love with him. Enough to believe, even given the stubborn cast of his features, that a Christmas miracle could still happen.

She went and sat beside him on the couch, covered his hand with her good one.

"Tell me what's wrong between you and your dad," she said, again.

She needed desperately to know that he felt he could trust her. She was aware that it was the only gift she wanted from him. And she wanted to give him the gift of not being so alone. That's what she had wanted to give him from the moment she had set up that tree for him.

And her hopes hung between them, in the silence, waiting for his answer.

CHAPTER EIGHT

Ty felt her weight settle on the sofa beside him. He was surprised. He had used anger to keep people away from him for a long, long time.

Maybe he had used anger because it felt so much more powerful than what lurked right beneath the anger.

Sadness. A well of sadness so deep and so profound a man could drown in it, if he let himself.

But now Amy was beside him, and he felt that if he went down into that sadness, and it seemed like it would drown him, she would throw him the rope.

Crazy to think this little speck of a woman could save him.

Crazy to think he needed saving at all.

But he was suddenly so aware that he did. That he was alone and that he was lonely and that it was going to stay that way forever if he didn't take the risk of telling someone.

The old cowhands had a favorite expression that they had used liberally on him when he was growing up and made mistakes.

If ya always do what ya always did, y'all always git what ya always got.

And suddenly, Ty was aware of wanting something different. A new chance at his old life.

He was aware he was giving in to the temptation of wishing. He took a deep breath and hoped he wasn't going to be sorry.

"I told you already my mom left. I was a little older than Jamey, eighteen months or so. I don't remember it. My dad wouldn't say anything about it. Then or now. He didn't talk about her. It was pictures of his first wife, Ruth-Anne, who had died, in his wallet and on the mantel. Until I was four or five I thought the woman in the pictures must have been my mom.

"Then one day she phoned. My mother phoned. She said she wanted to take me to Disneyland but my dad wouldn't let me go.

"And then I never heard another word from her, ever. And my dad would just get this look on his face whenever I tried to bring it up. And believe me, I tried to bring it up. Because I had a mother! She was out there, somewhere. She wanted to take me to Disneyland.

"I was convinced she'd just show up one day. That I'd come home from school and come in the door and there she'd be. With a tray full of chocolate chip cookies. Or the Christmas tree up and decorated." He smiled a touch at that.

"My dad and I lived in this world that was pure guy. Horses and cattle, hard work and cowhands.

"But we were invited for dinner lots. And I'd see this other world. Where people had curtains on the windows, and there wasn't a tractor engine in pieces on the kitchen table, and a newborn calf on a blanket in front of the stove. They had nice dishes and their houses smelled like good things cooking, not motor oil and horses.

"And then I went to school. There's a thing called Mother's Day that I had been blissfully unaware of. Everybody makes a little plaster cast of their hand for Mom, or sticks macaroni on a plate with glue and paints it silver to make a wall hanging.

"Sometimes, if it was slow season on the ranch, I'd go home on the school bus with one of the other kids. Their handprints and macaroni art were hung on the wall. I stuck mine in a box I put it under my bed to give to my mom when she showed up.

"My friends' moms would fuss over me. Cut my hair if it was too long, mend my jeans, send me home with cookies.

"Christmas was the worst time to be a kid with no mom. Every other house looked the way this house looks tonight and never has before.

"Everybody had trees up, and socks hanging by the fire and stacks of presents. Kids talked about Santa. Sheesh! Santa? My dad told me that was a bunch of baloney when I was two.

"My dad's idea of a present? New leather work gloves. I got all the clothes I needed every year for Christmas—a pair of jeans, a couple of new shirts, and a new pair of boots.

"I don't want it to sound like I didn't appreciate it, but I wanted something else—a new book, or some music or a game. Something fun. Maybe even frivolous.

"In my mind, I was inventing a fantasy mother. She was a little bit of everybody's mom. Pretty like Mrs. Campbell, could make lemon meringue pie from scratch like Jody Wentworth's ma, she thought long and hard about just the right gifts, like Julia Farnstead. When I snitched my dad's whiskey, she'd ground me, like Mrs. Holmes, not make me clean stalls. And then after a couple of days of being grounded, she'd forget all about it, not have me up to my ass in crap for the next hundred years.

"I guess I was building kind of a head of steam against my dad even before it happened. We were butting heads. I was drinking and smoking and carousing, and he was pretty damn unhappy about it.

"Then, when I was seventeen, I came in one day, and he was at the kitchen table with his head in his hands, and this pack of letters in front of him.

"And he looked at me and said word had just got to him that my mother had passed.

"And he handed me these letters, said he had been waiting on the right time to give them to me, and it had just never seemed like it was it.

"I've never been so mad in my whole life. Killing mad. But he got up and left, and I took those letters and read them, and the fury just built.

"My mom loved me. She'd written me letters. And he'd never given them to me. Not a single one. Not even when he saw me pining away on Mother's Day, and on my birthday and at Christmas."

Ty thought he should stop then. His fury felt fresh and dangerous.

"Then what happened?" Amy's soft voice prodded him to go on.

"I packed my bags that night and left."

"At seventeen?" She was aghast.

"Quit school. Slept under a bridge the first couple of nights. Got hungry. But never hungry enough to come back. Finally, I found work on a ranch. I ended up riding a bit on the rodeo circuit.

"Wild years," he said with a shake of his head. "An angry young man taking out his anger on the world.

"And losing myself a little more every day. Taking stupid risks with broncs and bulls and life in general.

"Then I got a call my dad's been hurt bad in an accident. And I came home. We didn't really speak. He gave me the deed to the ranch, said it was mine now and he expected me to man up and look after it.

"And I did. End of story."

He waited now. For her to do the wrong thing. To prove to him his trust had been totally misplaced, that it had been a mistake to tell her.

He waited for her to give him some Pollyanna advice. To make him hate her by giving him sympathy.

But she did nothing at all. She sat there, and after a while she leaned her head against his chest.

And she whispered, "Oh, Ty. Oh, Ty."

Quite frankly, it made him feel as if he wanted to bawl his damned eyes out, which was what he'd been scared of all along.

But he put his hand to her hair and stroked it, and that sensation of fury disappeared, and so did the feeling he might lose control of his emotions.

Instead, a sweet sense of not being alone filled him.

She was absolutely silent, and yet he could sense her feeling for him. They stayed together like that in a wordless place of being utterly and beautifully joined, until his eyes felt heavy. He gave in to something. And he slept.

When he awoke, his heart felt tender. He carefully shifted out from under the weight of Amy's resting head, let her down gently on the sofa. Then he went to the back door and put on his jacket and went outside into the cold night air. It had stopped snowing, finally. He could see the great expanse of stars over his head.

He went to the barn and into the tack room, and got down the little saddle he had used as a small child. It seemed impossibly tiny now.

He wanted to give something to Jamey. And something to her. He didn't want them to wake up in the morning to no gifts from him, when clearly she'd been busy all day making sure everyone was getting something from her.

So in the cold of the tack room, under a bare light-bulb he worked long into the night cleaning and oiling the old, old saddle.

And when he was done, he went up to the house. Amy had got up off the sofa and gone to bed. It was past midnight—Christmas morning actually—and he was glad she had not waited up for him. He felt fragile. Some untouched part of him bruised.

He set the saddle aside and then took his most precious possession and wrapped it for her.

He put the saddle with a clumsy bow and the carefully wrapped copy of *Lonesome Dove* under the tree.

He realized he was giving away things that really mattered to him.

And that he didn't feel sad. Still, fragile, almost raw, but not sad.

He felt lighter than he had in years.

In the morning, she cried when she saw the saddle for Jamey. And cried even harder when she unwrapped the book.

He felt a little lump in his throat, too, when he found his oven mitts had been repaired. He squinted at the repair job. If he was not mistaken, the repair had been executed at the expense of her little red toque. And she had surrendered the two books she had brought with her to him. He hadn't read either of the authors before, but she promised him the books were not chick lit.

And then the real magic of Christmas happened. Jamey was put in front of a small pile of gifts, wrapped in butcher's paper.

He was thrilled that he was allowed to rip and tear. The contents of the first package spilled out—she had wrapped up his little wooden puzzle for him.

"Regifting," Ty said with a shake of his head.

"What would you know about regifting?" She laughed.

Jamey was way more interested in the paper anyway. He shredded it, and then moved on to his next package. A pair of Onesies fell out.

"Is that an elf suit?"

"I bought it before I came. Isn't it cute? He can wear it over to your dad's this afternoon."

Something in him froze. He'd told her everything. Surely, she didn't think he was going to go over there!

He'd trusted her. He'd thought she got it.

Now, looking at her, he wondered what he had expected. For her to choose a side? And for it to be his side?

To be understood, he realized. His expectation, his *wish* had been to be understood.

He had trusted her with his deepest hurt. He had told her about the man who had stolen Christmas mornings like this one from him. It was as if she hadn't heard a word, lost in her Pollyanna world. If she had heard what he was saying, she would know he didn't want to be around his father.

She was helping Jamey unwrap another parcel, taking a teddy bear from it, wagging it at him.

She didn't even know she had hurt him. Which was good. She never had to. It had stopped snowing. If he worked at it, today could be her last day here.

For a hallelujah moment it felt very flat.

"I'm going to go feed the horses and cows," he said. "Then I'm going to make a start on the driveway."

"It's Christmas!"

"I know." He deliberately turned his back on the magic that had very nearly caught him with its spell.

"I've got to check the turkey," Beth said.

It was a perfect Christmas moment: fire blazing in their hearth, Beth murmuring about the turkey, Hunter Halliday holding Jamey on the old wooden rocking horse he and Beth had given them.

It was the perfect Christmas, except for one thing: as soon as they had arrived, Ty had cast a glance toward the house, then headed for the machine shed. Moments later they had all heard a tractor start up.

"He's not coming in," Hunter said, casting her a glance. "You might as well relax."

"He'll come in for dinner, won't he?"

"I don't know. I doubt it."

"It's Christmas," she whispered. "I had hoped something would happen."

"Something did happen," Hunter said.

She liked him so much. She didn't know why he had kept those letters from Ty. But she also didn't know why Ty didn't just ask him. There had to be a reason. When she saw Hunter playing with Jamey she felt she could see who he really was.

And it was a man who loved deeply and completely, not someone intent on stealing his son's happiness.

Why couldn't Ty see that?

"You said something happened," she said to Hunter. "What?"

"You said he gave your baby his saddle."

"Yes, he did. I don't know why. It's not like I have a pony."

"Don't ever get a pony!" Hunter said. "Mean-spirited little rascals! Now, let me tell you about a gift like a saddle. It's not a saddle. It's a wish for your little boy. It's a hope that his future holds a good horse. Long rides. Camping under starry skies. The companionship of hard men who have your back. Someone to teach you to be a man."

Amy felt tears in her eyes. "You gave him that saddle once, didn't you?"

"And my daddy gave it to me."

"We can't take it then! It's a family heirloom."

"It's not about the saddle, Amy. It's about the wish. Ty hasn't made one of those for a very long time. So, maybe while you were waiting for one miracle, another came in the back door."

"Ty told me you didn't have any religion," she said.

"Don't need religion to see a miracle. Take me in this chair. I think I see some pity in your eyes."

She was embarrassed. "I just see the man you once were and know it has to be hard for you."

"Here's the thing—when I got hurt, Beth was my nurse in the hospital. Wouldn't have met her unless it happened.

"And here's the other thing—that boy of mine was killing himself on anger and self-pity and I didn't know how to bring him home.

"So, I could have my legs, but no Beth. And I could have my legs, but I would have put my son in the ground by now. So I can't walk. Maybe I didn't get the miracle I wanted, but I sure as hell got the one I needed. Lost my legs. Found my heart, got my boy back."

The tears that clouded Amy's eyes began to fall. She wiped at them.

"Don't go crying, now. Beth'll have my hide."

"Dinner's ready." Beth called. "Amy, will you tell Ty?"

She pulled on her boots and coat and followed the freshly plowed drive. He was a long way down it, and she waved her hands at him.

He turned off the tractor.

"Come eat. Beth has put a lot of work into dinner."

He looked as though he was going to refuse, but then didn't. She wanted the man he had been last night. So open to her. But he wasn't. He was remote and closed, and she wanted to weep at her loss. After a while, Amy wished he had stayed outside on the tractor.

He was ruining everything with his sour look and his terse way.

And right after dinner, he wanted to leave, even though Beth had the cards out and Amy thought it would make Christmas absolutely perfect to stay and play cards and laugh and get to know each other deep into the night.

The sleigh ride home didn't even seem magical. Jamey was crabby until he finally went to sleep.

"Your dad really cares about you," she finally said. "I think it's time to bury your hatchets."

"Yeah, in each other's skulls," he muttered.

"Stop it!"

He squinted ahead silently.

"Have you ever just asked him? Why would he do that? Why would he keep those letters from you?"

"Do you think any reason why would be good enough?" he asked quietly. "I've been watching you with your baby. I see what that relationship between a mother and a child is. If it was you and Jamey, could any reason someone kept him from you be enough?"

"You need to forgive him," she said softly, imploringly.

"Don't presume to know what I need. And you don't seem like any kind of expert on forgiveness yourself."

"That's not true," she said. "I have forgiven Edwin."

"Edwin?" he snorted. "It's not Edwin you haven't forgiven. It's yourself. You were so sold on your own fantasy world that you put the blinders on when it came to the man you picked. Because you wanted something so badly. That's what you can't forgive."

She felt stunned by how clearly he had seen her.

And by the truth of it.

And by the fact that making a mistake on Edwin had not killed that fantasy at all. Here she was, in love again!

Still willing to overlook glaring faults—his stubbornness, his hard heart—to have her fantasy. Of home. And family. And love.

"You know I could overlook a lot of faults, Ty, but you being mean to a cripple? That speaks to your character!"

"Yeah, well, if my dad ever heard you call him a cripple, you'd be off his Christmas list, too."

"You're missing the point."

"No. You're missing the point. Why would I care if you overlooked my faults or not? That would imply some kind of vision for the future. And I don't have one. Not with you."

That hurt! And she saw that he had intended for it to hurt. But as mad as it made her, he was absolutely right.

She had no business thinking about a future that included him. She had a lot of work to do. All of it on herself.

As they pulled up to his barn he glanced over.

"Well, would you look at that?"

She looked and saw a long line of headlights moving slowly up the driveway.

"Neighbors," he said. "Plowing me out."

"Does that mean I can leave?"

Why did he hesitate before he answered? "Yeah, you can leave."

"Good!"

She grabbed Jamey and, ignoring the pain in her

hand, leaped off the sled. She could not bear Ty touching her, helping her. She was going to be off the Halliday Creek Ranch before he even unhitched the horses.

CHAPTER NINE

Ty knew as soon as he walked in the house that she was gone. He could feel the emptiness even before he saw all the things had been taken.

He had tried to drive her off with those last cruel words.

He went to his front window, and could see her little red car going down his freshly plowed driveway. He could see she had it so packed full of stuff that she couldn't even see out her back window.

Ty fought the desire to go after her, to follow her at a safe distance, to make sure she didn't get lost again, to make sure she made it safely to her destination.

But wouldn't it be better for all involved if she didn't know how much he cared? He didn't ever want her to come back here. Because how could you not pick up the gauntlet she had laid down? He would have to be a better man if he wanted a future with her.

And then he saw them.

He didn't know where they had come from. He thought he had stuffed those letters in his riding jacket pocket.

But there they were on the kitchen counter, the envelopes yellow, that blue ribbon tied around them.

He went and touched them. He told himself just to throw them out. That nothing could be gained by reading them again.

Except, he had been seventeen when he'd read them last.

And full of emotion. Anger. Bewilderment. The loss of something he had held on to and wished for his whole childhood.

He took the letters, tossed them on his dresser and went to bed. The first thing he thought of in the morning was Amy. The second was Jamey.

The third, before he was even out of bed, was the letters.

Suddenly, he knew he needed to read these letters now, not as a kid, but as a man.

He took them, went and made coffee, sat in his house that was too quiet and too empty, and pulled out the first letter.

An hour later, he set the last one down, squeezed the bridge of his nose hard between his thumb and his index finger.

When he was seventeen, he had read these letters and he had been as blind as Amy had been when she married her husband, he had wanted something so badly.

All he had seen was his mother's love for him and how his father had thwarted him. Now, older, wiser, he saw something completely different.

Every letter started with the same line.

Hi, Ty. Are you missing me?

And now he saw what he had not seen all those years ago. Not once did she say she was missing him. Not once. And that little blue ribbon held a dozen letters, which averaged out to less than one a year. The letters rambled on about things that would hold no interest to a child, *her* shopping trips, *her* travels, *her* concerns with weight, and hairdos and gym routines and boyfriends.

As an adult, Ty saw things he had overlooked when he'd first read them. He saw a certain sly undermining of his father: claims she wrote lots of letters and that his father probably withheld them. That she sent cards and gifts for his birthday or Christmas, but she was sure his father could not be trusted to pass them on.

How could he have missed this when he first read those letters?

And then he realized, he hadn't. At some level he had recognized the truth staring straight at him.

He'd been abandoned. And she didn't care about him. Not even a little bit.

And at seventeen, he hadn't been able to handle what that had opened up inside of him. So much easier to be angry at his father. So much more powerful a feeling than to face the sadness of it all. To face the real ending of his wish. If he could convince himself that she was the one who had been wronged, then she could still be the good person he had imagined.

He remembered, as a kid, hearing the word *amnesia* for the first time. That such a condition existed had made him ecstatic. It would explain everything. And excuse everything.

Now, having reread the letters, Ty saw the truth. His mother had walked out. She hadn't cared about the child she had had. She had not thought about him, or wondered about him, or dreamed of coming to tuck him in or make him cookies. She had not had amnesia. His father had played only the smallest role in her abandonment of her child.

At seventeen, he had not been able to face that reality. Amy was right.

Kind, gentle, sweet Amy was right.

He needed to ask his dad the one simple question. Why? And he realized why it had been so hard to do that. Because part of him had known it had nothing to do with his dad. He was pretty sure he knew the answer, but he had to ask it anyway. It was time to man up.

He was glad his road was clear and he could drive to the old homestead place. It felt as if taking the sleigh there would pull what was left of his heart right out of his chest. All he would think of was her, and her awe of the experience, and that little baby with them.

When he arrived, he knocked on the door and his father told him to come in. He was obviously alone. Of course, it was the first day in several that the roads had been open. Beth was no doubt taking advantage of it to restock the household.

His father looked eagerly over his shoulder. "Where are Amy and Jamey?"

"Gone. The roads opened. And I doubt if she'll be back. She was good and mad when she left."

His father nodded. "Karma's a bitch," he said.

"Amy didn't think I'd given you a fair shake. She said all I had to do was ask."

"So you're only here because Amy thinks you should be?"

"No. I'm here because I think I should be."

His dad nodded, satisfied.

"Why?" Ty asked softly. "Why didn't you give those

letters to me? I read them again. I think I know the answer, but it's time to hear your side of it. I should have
asked a long time ago."

Ty tossed the letters down in front of his father. He
watched as his father picked them up with worn hands,
turned them over, something resigned in his face, but
strong, too, ready to weather the storm.

"Were there more of these?" Ty asked.

"No. I tied up everything that came with a ribbon to
give to you. Someday."

"Were there cards and gifts? For my birthday? For
Christmas?"

"No, son. There weren't. Not ever."

It was as he had suspected when he'd read the letters; a lie contrived to cast a bad light on his father. Or
maybe to convince a child—not that hard to do—that
she was not the negligent one.

He dropped into the chair across from his father. "I
need you to tell me."

His dad glanced at him, and something flickered in
his eyes. Ty was ashamed that he was able to recog-
nize it as hope.

"Tell me about my mother," he said softly.

And his father sighed and glanced at him again, then
nodded. "All right. But maybe I need to tell you about
me first. I'm just a simple man, Ty. Hardly been off
this ranch, don't have a whole lot in the tool kit to help
me handle things that are complicated. I think you figured out I'm not really a man of letters. School was
hard for me."

"Yeah, I figured that out," Ty said.

"I was married before your mama, you know that."

"For the longest time I thought Ruth-Anne was my mother," he said. "That's whose picture you had on the mantel and in your wallet."

He was taken now with the look on his father's face, an almost dreamy look at the mention of Ruth-Anne.

"We were sweethearts from middle school. We got married right out of high school. I was only eighteen. You know that never should have worked, but damn, it did. We thought we were going to have us a pile of kids, but for whatever reason, she couldn't. I suspect now it was a warning that something was wrong, but that warning took twenty-five years to play out.

"Aw, Ty, twenty-five of the best years. Working together. Playing together. Filling all those spaces where the kids would have been with each other."

Ty was staring at his father, trying not to let his jaw drop.

"She died of cancer after we'd been married twenty-five years. I can't even tell you about that kind of pain, so bad it was a mercy when she finally went. And then my world opened up to a whole new kind of pain. I didn't know what to do with it. She'd been my earth. Everything.

"So I drank and lived hard and reckless and on the very edge, hoping the man upstairs would get the message and take me, too.

"But he dint. Nope. Those years are a blur of bad living, like attending a never-ending party in hell. I hooked up with your mama. Oh, boy. I'd met a woman who could match my hard living and raise me some. Her name was Millicent, though she never went by anything but Millie.

"And then, just like that, the party was over. She told me she was pregnant."

He cast Ty a long sideways, measuring look.

"I want to know it all," Ty said, reading reluctance in his father's expression.

His father nodded, as if deciding something. "She said she'd decided to get an abortion. She said she'd had an abortion before. That it was no big deal."

His father's hands were clenching and unclenching unconsciously. "No big deal?" he whispered. "Me and Ruth-Anne would have done anything to have a baby. And now I was going to throw one away? It just went against my grain. Nothing in the way I was raised prepared me for a notion like that.

"I knew, that second, the party was over. The self-pity was over. I had a job to do, and I'd better step up to the plate and do it. I convinced Millie to marry me and have the baby.

"We moved back out here to the ranch. It had been neglected for quite some time. I nearly lost the place, and I was aware I could still lose it if I didn't knuckle down. The work was unending. You know what it's like now. It was ten times worse then. Trying to build a herd, every fence and building falling down. I wasn't young anymore, I was in my mid-forties by then."

His voice drifted away for a moment. "I'd been partying in hell before, now I was just in hell. No party. Your mama, she couldn't stand this place. She was lonely and restless and bored. She wouldn't come work with me, like Ruth-Anne had always done, so she'd sit in the house. She didn't cook a meal or clean a floor. She just watched her soaps on TV and brooded on things to fight about.

"By the time I'd drag my sorry ass through the door after putting in a fourteen or fifteen-hour day, she'd be ready. That woman could fight about anything. If I said it looked like rain, she'd say snow, and the war was on.

"I thought it was my fault. Working too hard, not paying enough attention to her. I thought it might be because she was pregnant and hated everything about that state. She didn't see herself as growing the most beautiful thing on earth. She saw herself as fat and ugly. And I'm ashamed to say I got tired of trying to convince her otherwise.

"She started accusing me of having a girlfriend on the side. I'd walk in, so tired and wet and dirty I could barely keep my feet, and she'd come and sniff my neck. Claim she could smell a woman on me. And I'm ashamed to say, I got tired of that pretty damn quick, too.

"And then you came along. God almighty, Ty, I ain't saying this just because you were mine, but you were the most beautiful baby ever born. Golden hair, like a little lion, and bright eyes, and this lusty voice. Powerful for a baby. I just stood in amazement of you from the first second."

Again, the hesitation, the sideways look. But Ty had read the letters. He had already guessed this part.

"Tell me," he said.

"Aw, Ty, it's what I never wanted to tell you. You've seen cows who reject their calves? Basically, she was indifferent to you. She was aghast at the idea of breast-feeding. That was for *animals*.

"I'd come in from a hard day, and it was more of the same. She thought I'd been seeing someone. And she'd start screaming it was my turn to look after the baby, my turn to change diapers and feed you.

"As if it was a burden," his father said, soft, still shocked by it. "It was no burden. Hell, Ty, you were what I lived for. Those moments when I came in and picked you up and saw after what you needed. And then I'd take you and plant you right in the middle of my chest, and we'd both fall fast asleep on that sofa.

"After Ruth-Anne died, I'd pretty much given up on love. And Millie had soured me even more. But when you and I would fall asleep on that couch, I believed in love again.

"I came home one day early, and one of the ranch hands was coming out of the house. He wouldn't look me in the face, muttered something about Millie calling him about the plumbing.

"I was so fed up, I was beyond caring what she did. I can see now that just added to the problems. The more I didn't care, the more she tried to make me care. She thought she could make me jealous, but all it did was make me worry she might be neglecting you.

"So I got myself one of those kangaroo pouch things and popped you in it. My saddle bags were filled with diapers and formula. You literally were on a horse before you could walk. If I had a real hard day lined up, I'd drop you off with one of the neighbor ladies.

"One day we came home and she was gone. She'd smashed every single dish in the house and every picture frame, she'd cut up all my clothes, but she was gone.

"And I didn't feel nothing but relief.

"I tried to be a good dad, but when I think about it, I probably wasn't. I wasn't much of a talker. And I was strict as all get-out, like that would make it seem like I knew what I was doing when I didn't. Scared to let you know how much I loved you, like it might turn you into a sissy boy or something.

"I knew you longed for a mama. Anytime we went to a neighbor's you were scouting out a female to attach yourself to. And I figured that was enough. I mean, our friends and our neighbors circled the wagons around me and especially around you. You were raised by every woman in this whole community, which is probably why you turned out half-decent.

"It was four years before I heard from her. Just phones up one day as if she suddenly remembered she had a little boy. Told me her and her new husband wanted to pick you up and take you to Disneyland.

"Like I said at the beginning. I was just a simple man. I didn't know what to do with a complicated situation. But I didn't really trust your mama. Once she had you, what if she just disappeared with you? And I sure as hell wasn't sending you to Disneyland with a man I'd never met.

"So, I told her no, and then she asked to talk to you. I knew how bad you wanted a mama, so against my better judgment I put you on the phone. When you got off, you were looking daggers at me and screaming that you wanted to go to Disneyland with your mama.

"You wanted a mama so badly, and now one had magically appeared. But all I could see was trouble and broken hearts, so after that when she phoned I'd say you were at a neighbor's or something. It wasn't often.

Once or twice a year, then not for several years in a row. Same with the writing. A letter here and there once she figured out you were old enough to read, I guess. I opened the first few of her letters, and I knew nothing had changed. It was all about her. Suddenly, you were old enough that she could try and use you to fill up that horrible hole inside of her.

"And right or wrong, I wasn't having it. I told myself when you were old enough to sort it out for yourself, I'd tell you about it. But somehow the time never seemed right, because you always seemed so hungry for a mama that I knew you would never see her for what she was.

"I tried to protect you. And I doubt I did it right, and yet if I had the same choice to make again, I would make the same one. So how can I even say I'm sorry?"

"Why didn't you just tell me? Dad, all these years. Lost."

"They weren't lost, son. You had a chance to step out of my shadow, to become the man I always knew you would be. Every father and son goes through it. I did with my own daddy and had no excuse for it, either."

It hurt him that his father had held faith in him through all these years of stubborn distance. He felt tears pricking at the back of his eyes.

"And the last few years gave me something, too," his father said. "All those years, you were my first responsibility. Love had banged me up pretty good. Then when I got hurt, I was alone, and Beth was alone, and—" He shrugged. "Beth tells me now, your mama was probably sick. Bi-Polaroid."

"Bipolar," Ty said softly. It made sense. It fit with

what he had read in the letters, the manic pages of writing, followed by months, even years of silence.

"The way I see it I had Ruth-Anne. And she was earth. And I had Millie and she was fire. Beth was and is like a cool drink of water on a hot day."

"Did you ever wonder if I was yours?" Ty asked softly. "I mean, it sounds as if she might have played it hard and fast."

His father looked genuinely shocked. "Of course not! You're way too stubborn to be anyone else's. Besides, you are now, and always have been, my sky, so bright it nearly hurts my eyes to look at you.

"Once I had a narrow view on life and wouldn't have put stock in such things, but now I see I've had a life of perfect balance, earth and fire, water and sky.

"I don't have any regrets, Ty. Your mother brought me you. This chair brought you back to where you belong."

"All these years," Ty said. He knew now it wasn't his father he'd had to forgive at all. It was his mother.

And in some part of him, he had probably known that all along.

"You go after that girl who was here. You go after her and that little boy. They both need you. If you don't mind my saying so, it's time to grow up, Ty. You ain't a little boy pining after your mama anymore. There's nothing like someone needing you to make a man grow up."

"I don't even know if she'd have me, Dad. She'd resent the implication that she needed me."

"Now you're talking nonsense. To their great detriment, women just love us Halliday men. They'll put up with quite a bit from us. See what we could be, see the diamond underneath all that coal, and get damned determined to mine it. She needs you, all right. And you need her."

Amy looked out the window of the McFinley house. It was a nice house, custom-built on a small acreage some twenty miles from the Halliday Creek Ranch. The views were not as sweeping as the ones from Ty's front window—she could see the neighbors' place—and it lacked the charm of the homestead.

It was a typical January day in southern Alberta—bright blue skies and teeth-numbing cold.

"A good day to bake bread," she told herself out loud, as if that could ward off the loneliness. Jamey was napping. Terrible to wish he would wake up so that the huge emptiness inside her could be filled with his laughter and gurgles, his energy and motion.

Perhaps she was imagining it, but he, too, seemed subdued.

One of the things he had got for Christmas, when they had made it to Cynthia's, was a farm set, with buildings and horses and cows.

Jamey had a favorite horse. He called it Ben. And when he played with it, he mournfully and softly called Papa Odam over and over again.

So she knew she would not bake bread. The memories of the last time she had baked bread, Ty laughing beside her, putting his muscle into the kneading, were just too intense.

For a while, she acknowledged, being snowed in with

Ty, having Christmas at the homestead place, she had touched what she had always wanted.

It had filled her to overflowing. It had been better than the dream.

Now, despite this beautiful home, despite her internet business taking off and filling most of her waking hours, she could not outrun the feeling. The feeling of loss.

She had spent six days on the Halliday Creek Ranch.

She felt as if she was mourning it more profoundly than the loss of her husband. Of course, that dream had already been shattered.

Her time at the ranch had breathed hope into her when she had convinced herself all hope was gone.

And now, gazing out the window at the icy beauty of the landscape, she felt as though all hope was gone again.

Somehow, she thought he would have called.

As deeply in the thrall of all those good memories as she was.

And somehow, she was not sure how, she had found the courage and pride not to call him. Especially as she read *Lonesome Dove,* savoring every word, feeling some connection to Ty as she read it.

But no, it was time for her to make it on her own. Time for her to stand on her own two legs. Time for her to forgive herself all her mistakes by drawing power from who she was now, what she could accomplish, her considerable strengths and talents.

"So, cookies it is," Amy said, forcing herself to move from the window. "Chocolate chip."

The doorbell rang as she was taking the last of them from the oven.

She went and opened it. The most adorable teenage girl she had ever seen stood there. She was about thirteen, owlish behind glasses. She had an armful of books, and flashed a shy smile that revealed braces.

"Mrs. Mitchell?"

"Yes?"

"I'm Jasmine Nelville. Ty Halliday sent me to babysit. He said to tell you I have my babysitting certificate, and that I can give you references. I've been babysitting for two years."

Amy looked at her visitor, stunned. She noticed a car in the driveway, and realized it was Jasmine's mother, who waved and drove away.

"Right now?" she stammered.

"I think he's right behind us. Of course, he's hauling, so that takes longer."

"Hauling?"

"Is that the baby?" Jasmine said when a wail filled the house.

"Jamey. He's just waking up from his nap."

Jasmine brushed by her, set down her books and followed the sound. With Amy trailing dazedly behind her, she went into the bedroom and picked Jamey out of his crib.

"Oh!" she said blissfully. "What a handsome boy."

Jamey preened.

"Mrs. Mitchell, you need to get ready. Dress warm. And he said to tell you to wear sensible boots."

"But—" She heard clanking and thumping and a big, diesel engine. She went to her front window and watched as Ty jumped out of the cab of his truck, went and opened the back door of the trailer he was pulling.

One horse, saddled, backed out. And then Ben, also saddled.

The rational part of her knew that she should say no to this. He hadn't even called. He didn't even know if she wanted to go with him.

But the rational part of her could hardly be heard above the singing of her heart. It was not time to be rational. She had been rational all her life. Even when she had chosen Edwin, it had been a rational decision based on what she wanted, and on what he seemed to be.

Stable. Safe. From a good family. Able to provide.

That was what she needed to forgive. The great injustice she had done Edwin when she had chosen him for what he was, instead of who he was.

And that man outside, calmly tightening cinches, waiting for her?

She knew exactly who he was. Exactly. She ran for her coat and her boots and raced out the door.

He looked up and saw her coming, smiled at her over the top of the saddle, and then came around the horse and opened his arms.

She flew into them. And he lifted her high and swung her around, and then set her down and gazed at her like a man who had crossed the desert and she was his drink.

"What are you doing here?" she asked, breathless.

"Why, Miss Amy, isn't it obvious?"

"Not really."

"I've come a-courting."

"Oh!" she said, suddenly shy.

"You're an old-fashioned girl in a new-fangled world. So with your permission, I'm going to do this in an old-fashioned way. I'm going to wine you, and dine you and bring you flowers. I'm going to sweep you right off your feet."

Was there any point telling him he already had? No. Why miss the fun?

He helped her onto the horse. He told her it was an old mare named Patsy and he called her dead-broke.

But it didn't matter. She would have felt no fear being put on a fire-snorting, head-tossing, feet-dancing stallion right now.

They rode out the McFinleys' driveway and down a snowy road. He rode right beside her, asking her about Jamey and the house and Baby Bytes.

And she asked him about Beth and his dad, and as they rode, he told her all of it. About reading the letters and reconciling with his father.

"Been working hard at being the man you'll expect me to be," he said.

The skies were so bright, and the air so crisp. They rode for nearly an hour and then he found a way down to a frozen river, and set a picnic blanket out in the snow. From his saddle bags, he removed hot chocolate and sandwiches on bread that was flat and might have tasted quite terrible if he had not mentioned he had made it himself.

He took out a book of poetry and read to her. He looked up at her, mischief winking in his sapphire eyes.

"It's on the first-year university reading list," he admitted. "Do you know what it means?"

"Not a clue," she said.

And then the sound she lived for bubbled up between them, louder than the water running under the frozen blanket on the river.

Their laughter. And then somehow, they were rolling around on that blanket, and he was on top of her, pushing her hair back from her face and covering her with kisses. Her ears, her lips, her neck, her eyelids.

Homecoming.

An hour later, they were heading for home, nearly frozen on the outside, a fire so deep burning on the inside that Amy felt as if she would never be cold again.

And so the courtship began.

Ty amazed her with his deeply romantic nature. True to his word, he wined and dined her at some of the finest restaurants in Calgary. He brought her flowers. They went to movies and for long walks and horseback rides.

He began to include her in community activities. He brought her to fund-raisers and dances and pancake breakfasts where she met his neighbors and his friends. He brought her out to Beth and his dad's. They did things with Jamey—the indoor swimming pool, sleigh riding, quiet evenings at home playing on the floor with his toys and reading him stories.

The seasons were changing, winter giving way to the tender promise of spring, when Ty invited her to his place, asking her to drop off Jamey with his dad and Beth.

When she arrived, the two horses were saddled in the yard.

She mounted hers with confidence, a brand-new bravery in her.

That's what love had given her. The bravest of hearts. The most tender of hopes.

They followed a winding trail along Halliday Creek and then up and up and up the mountain.

Finally, they broke from the woods and crossed alpine meadows on fire with wildflowers, still going up.

The horses picked their way through rocks, and then Ty stopped and offered her his hand as she dismounted.

Hands intertwined, they climbed up yet some more, scrambling over rocks, his hand helping her, pulling her.

And finally they stood at the very crest.

Amy could barely breathe. She was standing on top of the world. She could see everything for a hundred miles. Ty's house and the old homestead were like dollhouses far down in the valley. Contented cattle grazed on new grass.

And he stood beside her, strong and sure. The strongest man she had ever met.

Only, when she pulled her eyes from the panorama of the view, that strong man was on one knee before her.

He had a ring box in his hand and was gazing up at her with a look in his eyes that dimmed the panorama of what she had just seen.

"Amy," he said softly, "you know I am not a religious man. But even so, I thank God as I know Him every single day for that wrong turn you took in the road.

"I thank Him for bringing me your smile and your laughter and your ability to listen and your ability to see things in me that I had never seen in myself.

"I thank Him for bringing your son into my world and for allowing me to know what it is to be a dad to that little boy."

To her amazement, the strongest man she had ever known suddenly looked shy.

And maybe even a little scared.

His gaze drifted from her to the view. "Do you remember when I read *The Iliad?*" he asked.

"Yes."

"Achilles had to choose between *nostos,* homecoming or *kleos,* glory. If I had that choice to make? I would choose homecoming. I would choose coming home to you.

"I cannot imagine my world without you. Amy Mitchell, I am asking if you would consider being my wife?"

She took his chin in her hand and drew his gaze back to her. In the sapphire of his eyes she saw her whole world and the future beyond.

She saw laughing babies and cattle and horses, she saw books and movies and heated discussions and quiet moments.

She saw what she had yearned for her entire life.

In the quiet strength in his eyes, she saw a place where neither of them ever had to be alone again.

She saw home.

She whispered yes, and he leaped to his feet and gathered her in his arms and then he lifted her and swung her around and shouted "yes" over and over and over again.

And his affirmation of love and of life, his shouted yes, reverberated off the mountains and the valleys, and echoed back to them and surrounded them.

In glory.

"Some of us don't have to make a choice at all," Amy told the man she loved. "Some of us are allowed homecoming and glory."

EPILOGUE

TY came out of the barn, leading the pony. It was saddled—that same saddle that he had given Jamey all those years ago. The pony had a red plaid Christmas ribbon woven into his mane and was tossing his head because of the red bow attached to his thick forelock.

His father disliked ponies, and had argued that for Christmas they should give Jamey a horse, just as he had given Ty a horse when he turned five.

But Ty had liked this pony. It had a soft eye and a willing way, and it was pretty with its lush black mane and the big brown spots all over it.

He sniffed the air as he moved toward the homestead place. Snow. It was going to snow very soon.

He hoped not too much.

A man, he thought wryly, should be careful what he wished for.

Because, really, he did not want to get snowed in right now.

The old homestead place had been his and Amy's for just over a year. After Amy and Ty's twin girls, Millie and Becky, had been born, his dad and Beth had suggested the trade. The new house was more practical for the older Hallidays, with its one floor and two bedrooms. It had been easy to make it one hundred per cent wheelchair accessible.

And the old homestead place had the four bedrooms upstairs that had been closed up for years.

Amy had taken that on as if she was on an episode of *Save This Old House*. The old homestead house was refurbished to shining. Every nook and cranny had her stamp on it, her love sewn into drapes and cushions and pot holders…and little pink baby blankets.

Now, on Christmas Eve, it was filled to the rafters. Her parents were here. And Jamey's grandparents.

For a long time, Ty hadn't known quite how to forgive his mother for her abandonment and indifference. But then, at Amy's suggestion, they had found out every single thing they could about her.

And they had discovered he had a grandmother, and an aunt and uncle, and a passel of cousins.

His grandmother, Elizabeth, had been shocked that she had a grandson. Since her daughter had been in her teens she had disappeared for long lengths of time and would eventually resurface with no explanation about where she'd been.

Elizabeth was desperate to meet Ty. When they had first met, she had kept touching his face and weeping. They had connected almost instantly, and through stories and pictures and shared letters, unraveled the mystery of his mother.

If the mystery of mental illness could ever really be solved.

Millicent Williams had always bounced between two extremes. On one side, his grandmother told him, her beautiful daughter had been high energy, on fire, talk-

ative, charming, brilliant, sensitive, creative, passionate, charismatic. On the other side she had been needy,
manipulative, darkly sensual, secretive, jealous, selfish,
conniving, and capable of unbelievable cruelty in her
ability to use people and discard them.

Ty had learned his mother had suffered a disease of
extreme self-centeredness where everything and everybody in the world were perceived only through the
filter of how they could benefit her.

And because of that, she alienated everyone she had
ever touched, had ended up alone, increasingly desperate, highly dependent on the alcohol and prescription
drugs that had led to her demise.

It was a tragic tale of undiagnosed illness.

When Ty looked at pictures of her, he felt a strange
and gentle tenderness for the woman he had never
known. He knew that he looked at his own life differently because of her.

Jamey, as far as he could tell, came from generations
of solid, pragmatic ambitious people. But as he watched
his own girls, the twins, just turning one, he sometimes found himself wondering how early you would
see signs of it.

His father had told him, even though he had never
defined it as mental illness, he had watched him the
same way.

Nowadays, at least, there was more chance of it being
caught. Treated. Not ignored or mislabeled.

His mother had just been considered wild. And unpredictable. Untamable. A lot of people had given up on
her way before his dad entered the picture.

When he thought of her now, he felt his heart soften

with sympathy. There was no anger left for the woman who had abandoned him with hardly a look back. He felt he loved her, despite it all.

And maybe that's what forgiveness finally was.

The ability to see it all in a larger way.

The lights from the windows of his house poured out over the snow, golden and warm. He could smell the wreath on the door. Amy had insisted on Christmas lights, and the whole place was lit up in traditional red and green. It had taken him about three weeks to get all those lights up tracing the lines of the roof, and every time he'd wanted to just forget it, he'd look down at Amy, tumbling around in the snow beneath him with the twins and Jamey, their happiness echoing on the air.

So hanging a few Christmas lights was a small price to pay.

The front door opened, and the noise from inside spilled out. Laughter, conversation. His family.

And wasn't it what he had always wanted?

Be careful what you wish for, he told himself again wryly. He and Amy would sleep on a mattress on the floor of the back porch tonight, snuggled together to keep warm because they had given up their bed to Amy's parents, Dolores and Adam, who were recovering from jet lag.

Cynthia and John had the guest room. Before she was done, Cynthia would refold every single towel in the house and arrange the tinned goods in order of their size, labels to the front. She would tut disapprovingly over baby clothes put in drawers without being pressed.

Amy's parents would bring out flowcharts and trap him into a discussion about a business plan for the ranch, and all their great ideas to make Baby Bytes the most visited website on the planet. They didn't understand that Ty was working at nights online to get a university degree for the simple love of learning, not so that he could turn the ranch into the most viable business enterprise ever.

Cynthia, John, Dolores, Adam, none of them got the concept of *enough*. That you could have enough and be enough. That you could quit trying so hard and just enjoy the plentiful gifts life had given you.

He saw Amy standing on the porch, hugging herself, watching his approach.

She was rounder than she had been, her curves full and womanly. Her hair had inexplicably lost its curl after the twins were born, and it hung in a soft, lush wave to her shoulder.

But her eyes remained the same, and the curve of her mouth.

A long time ago, without knowing, he had ridden through the dark to a light she had put on, without knowing it was for him.

At the beginning of all of this, he would have said that he and Amy were about as different as two people could be. She was city. He was country. She was small. He was big. He was rugged. She was refined. She knew all about computers and cell phones, and he used technology only reluctantly, as a means to an end. He liked nothing better than a good book. She liked nothing better than a good movie.

But underneath all those superficial differences, Ty knew he and Amy had the most important things in common.

They had both wished for that place called home.

And at one time, they had both given up on that wish.

It almost seemed the universe was offended by this refusal of its greatest gift, the refusal to love.

It almost seemed as if the universe had conspired to bring them together, had put Amy on the wrong road, that led them both to the right place. The only place.

She flew down off the steps and snugged under his arm, petting the pony.

"Hello, Sampson," she crooned to their newest family member.

One small, perfect moment, just the two of them, and then the door flew open and Jamey came flying down the steps, screaming the word Ty never ever got tired of hearing.

"Papa!"

Behind him, Cynthia appeared, one of the twins, Becky, in her arms, freshly washed and a new bow in her hair. "A pony? What are you thinking? Jamey is just a baby! Surely, he'll be killed."

And Amy's mother, Dolores, had the other baby, Millie, who was clinging to her early gift of a Baby Einstein calculator.

Dolores nodded her agreement with Cynthia, and added, "I can't imagine what it costs to feed one of those for ten years or so."

Ty didn't even bother telling her a pony, if you were lucky, could live for thirty-five years.

John and Amy's father spilled out onto the porch, too, arguing about stock prices, not even aware there was a pony in the yard. Or three grandchildren nearby.

His father wheeled out and scowled across the yard

at them. "A pony! Sheesh. I told you to get a horse. I've never met a pony I liked."

Be careful what you wish for, Ty told himself, remembering that long-ago wish to be part of a family.

He showed Jamey how to use the stirrup, refused to help him, even when his grandmother Elizabeth called out, "Ty, lift him up, for Pete's sake. It's too hard for him to get on by himself."

Beth called from in the house, "I've nearly got dinner ready. Don't be out there too long. Jamey doesn't have a coat on!"

Yes, be careful what you wish for.

Jamey, with a hoot of pure satisfaction, managed to heave himself into the saddle. Ty passed him the reins.

"You are not going to let him ride by himself!" Cynthia cried.

But he was going to let him ride by himself. As he watched the boy who was the son of his heart, Amy, who had once been afraid of everything, breathed her fearlessness after Jamey. She snuggled deeper under Ty's arm and sighed her contentment.

The pony stopped partway across the yard and Jamey flailed away, to no avail, trying to get the pony moving with his heels.

"I told you," Hunter said grumpily, "you should have got him a real horse."

The smile pulled harder on Ty's mouth.

He had wished for this thing called family.

And he would not change a thing.

* * * * *

LET'S TALK
Romance

For exclusive extracts, competitions
and special offers, find us online:

Or get in touch on 0844 844 1351*

For all the latest titles coming soon, visit
millsandboon.co.uk/nextmonth